Metal Mermaid

Book one
In the Storyteller series

By

Kez Wickham St George

Copyright © 2025 by **Kez Wickham St George**

Kez Wickham St George / Kez Publishing
Western Australia, Australia
Kezwickhamstgeorge.com

Book Layout © 2025 womensbizglobal.com
Book Cover design @Andy Burns
Proofreader @DStGeorge

Metal Mermaid / Kez Wickham St George—2nd edition.

ISBN 978-1-7638692-1-9

CONTENTS

A LETTER TO MY READERS

First of all, thank you for supporting me in my endeavours to take you all on an adventure with me. This 2nd edition has been brought into a version of a more personal nature. Not so much chat, but more action and exploring The Pinjarra of WA, Australia and New Zealand.

This story represents how our emotions can lead us into a new discovery of ourselves, including the good, bad, beautiful and ugly. I have always felt a story contains a large part of the author and Metal Mermaid certainly does that, trying to express the beauty, the richness of each country and its customs. There is no right or wrong way to tell a story; however, when I describe a scene of beauty or devastation, I wish that you feel the power of my words.

All through my travels I have hopefully shown the generosity of many. Along with the strength and camaraderie I have been shown. The human race is in fact a wonderful creation, the majority of us are doing the best we can, with what we have.

I sincerely wish you all

Enough.

ACKNOWLEDGEMENTS

To my family and extended family in New Zealand and Australia, thank you for the inspiration. To my friends and family, thank you for the encouragement, kind words, and willingness to read through my drafts, always with positive advice.

To my husband Lou, where would I be without that sense of humour you possess? Thank you for believing in me. And to all of you who add a spicy richness to my life, I consider myself blessed to be part of your lives, whether it be through blood or friendship.

Thank you also to my parents, Dick and Hilda Wickham now long gone, I would like to honour them both by thanking them for the childhood I had, they enriched it in ways they will never know, giving me an Irish, English, Māori ancestry, the Tuhoi Iwi known as the (People of the Mist) from the Waikato in North Island.

I hope you enjoy reading it as much as I did writing it. I also hope that it will encourage you, the reader, to travel in whatever Metal Mermaid of your choice.

SYNOPSIS

The name Mermaid embodies the freedom of spirit, a curious heart, and a life dedicated to adventure, all the traits a true caravanner yearns to experience. Tara sees herself as a Domestic Goddess, openly acknowledging her love for life in Perth. If she ever daydreamed about becoming a Grey Nomad, it was only for a moment. Her comfy lifestyle, family, and community consistently pull her back to what truly matters most. When her husband Russ returns from the Pilbara mines with a minor health issue, it sparks an unexpected conversation about one last road trip. Russ is keen on it, and reluctantly, Tara agrees, but only for six months. No one knew it would be Russ's final journey or the start of Tara's. On the road, Russ's illness worsens. Tara, reeling with grief and fear, is held together by strangers who have now turned friends, people she had only heard about through Russ. Among them is Gilly, a fellow traveller who offers comfort during Tara's darkest moments.

When one of these friends suggests a tour in New Zealand, soon it becomes something more profound: a make-or-break journey of self-discovery. As she travels across New Zealand, embraced by its landscapes and people, Tara learns to live in the moment, let go of control, and listen to the stories of others, each one offering wisdom, healing, and sometimes even laughter. The road teaches her what it means to be a true Grey Nomad: that adventure can start at any age, that magic exists in new friendships and fresh starts, and that, above all, she is more vigorous and freer than she ever knew.

Eventually, it's time to go home. But Tara is no longer the same woman who left Australia, as she has discovered a new world of adventure. I hope you enjoy reading Metal Mermaid as much as

I loved writing it. May it inspire you to embark on your own adventure, wherever your version of a Metal Mermaid may lead you, because life is meant to be lived. Our journeys and stories, no matter how unexpected, are worth sharing.

CHAPTER ONE

A ripple of excitement travelled through the expectant crowd, waiting for the sunset to deepen. Pinking of skies had started to creep through the blue summer sky, tinging it with orange and yellows. Fifty or more of us from the Happy Valley Camping Ground in Albany, Western Australia, all sitting in a natural amphitheatre of bushland cocooned by large gum trees. The most prominent tree was an old silver gum, its bark resembling an old unwanted overcoat now being shrugged off in large pieces, with its soft pink insides displayed like toothless gums. Any spare logs or ground below were now covered in bodies of all descriptions, race, creed, and religion and had no part in the spectacular show we were about to witness. A hum of settling down then - quiet, dusk almost here; the children hushed, a slight clearing of throats and a few coughs. Then he appeared - the Conductor.

By 'he' I mean a large blue heron gliding majestically onto a branch way up high. He makes his presence known, stepping very stately from one leg to the other, his wings fluffing up and then settling down to showcase his sleek lines. He preens himself, muttering into his chest about today's annoying issues he's had to deal with.

Then, in a wild, squawking swoop, the pink and grey Galahs landed, the dusky pink of the sunset highlighting their chests in a coral rose hue. Their greetings to one another involved a harsh screeching cacophony as they pecked and fought for the best spot. The noise gradually fades as the majestic Heron taps its beak against a branch.

With the experience of a professional, this large bird holds us all enthralled; the Galahs are now hushed in respect, as are the many other birds now perched for the night. This one majestic tree is full of bird life. This is the moment we have gathered for; as the sky gives off one last flame of deep pink, the conductor lifts his wings, his long beak pointing up to the sky. He then unfolds his large, majestic wings, opening as if in a wounded surrender that welcomes the dusk. The big gum tree now bursts with life as various mixes and breeds of Australian birdlife give one final salute to the day; it swells in a monumental crescendo, each small chest puffed out with effort, each beak wide open. The sound is thrilling; it winds around you, under you, inside you. As one or two smaller birds stop to gasp for breath, the others carry on. Then, slowly, silence falls, not a sound or peep from a human or bird.

That one moment in time is magical, not a sound for a microsecond, then it's gone, lost forever as the day changes to night. As always, one grumpy Gala fusses about finding another comfier spot on his branch. The night sky now puts on a dazzling display; a moody mauve that turns deep blue, with tiny pinpricks of light flickering as the stars begin their show. Then the dark, deep blue creeps in, with brilliant stars like scattered sequins on black velvet, showing off the Milky Way, too far away for the naked eye, its presence known as a splash of white in the night sky; the crescent moon shimmers in a ghostly light of pale lemon. Our nighttime show is over.

We now pack up our assortment of chairs, rugs, and baskets, with sleepy kids carried away in their parents' arms into tents that glow with gentle lamp light, offering a safe haven from the dark night. Those of us in caravans and cabins now shut the doors against the night, safely tucked up inside tubes of wood, steel, and plastic. At dawn, those of us who are up early enough head off once more to the bush amphitheatre to watch the Galahs leave their tree in a rush of hundreds. Their salmon-pink breasts flashing in the early light, while the branches that almost sagged under their weight, now stand tall and straight. Vast flocks of budgies land in the reddish dust beneath the tree, tiny bright jewels in green, blue, and yellow, flitting their wings. Once they complete their daily ablutions, they sip from the dew-laden grass and shallow puddles, creating large lakes of colour all over the ground; on cue, the tourists' cameras start snapping and clicking.

Next, the locusts begin, the native birds have already arrived for breakfast, with displays of their excellent aeronautics recorded on many phones. Magpies trill in the day, their song flirting with the sun as it breathes life into our day. The sky becomes a brilliant clear blue, and clean air, filling your lungs, urging you to take the deepest breath of intoxicating life.

The Black Cockatoos fly off in disgust at the competition of song and plumage, the white tuxedo of the Magpie shining bright against the solemn black of the native cockatoo. As the Magpies puff up their chests to herald the dawn, the musical chorus makes your heart want to join your voice with theirs. A brief interval of silence occurs, and that's when the Kookaburras take over, their intimate giggles between them erupting into full-throated gales of laughter.

Our first instinct is to wonder who the comedian was among them, then to see the expressions of those of us listening and laugh openly at this daily ritual of happy hour for these amazing birds. They sit in full view of us, chatting, sharing a secret known only to themselves. There is no other bird in the world like the Kookaburra. Its plain plumage is a cover for the delightful laughter that can draw together a small crowd of humans to join in; laughter from us both, bird and human, rises into the air to meet the sun. A lone jade-green fruit parrot stares at me, its little black beady eye glancing as if to say, 'Hey! I'm gorgeous too, what about me?' I must admit that its lime green coat with a navy-blue band around its neck is striking. With a sharp whistle, it flies off to find others to admire it. The small brown creek that bubbles through the grounds closely guards its little bunched families of brown ducks that search for scraps and weeds to fill their tummies. A soft, muted quacking now fills the air. The ducklings have been warned not to stray too far; I notice one stays close, hitching a ride on Mum's back.

My stomach pleads it's case, to be fed, the day's show is over. It's been a magical experience for us all, it's time to move on to another place. Our little bus is ready to take us on our adventure. This is our gap year, and we' re finally on our way, touring around Western Australia. Now, in our mid-sixties and following a minor health scare, we have decided to hit pause button on our lives: family, work, home and friend, while we embrace the Grey Nomad lifestyle. To be honest it was more than that; this trip was the culmination of many factors, mainly that we were now in our mid-sixties, and it was time for a sea change together. I had pushed for this for so long. I felt an urgent intuition in my chest that it would not happen if this tour didn't get crossed off my bucket list soon. We had been busy with our careers until five months ago, but now we were footloose. And again, I must admit, the first two weeks were bloody awful. We both felt hemmed in by being together twenty-four-seven, with nowhere to look at except put our heads into a book, a roadmap or each other. just the two of us in our tiny house, tripping over each other every ten minutes or so.

You see, in the past fifteen years, my husband Russ has worked away as a water driller at the many mine sites across the Pilbara; his busy roster defining his time with me at home in Perth. In the world of a mining wife, you create your own universe; mine was my passion for the Abstract Arts. As a writer, I had a few close friends and maintained a very independent lifestyle. I had learned to enjoy this way of life.

CHAPTER TWO

There's a sad but true saying among miners' wives, "Love to see them home, but happy to see them return." Russ's life and friends were up north at the mine sites. I knew some of his friends, just as he knew a few of mine. When he first went away, I had heard that this lifestyle could cause problems in a marriage, but I dismissed it. I thought we were okay. We were fortunate to have six weeks of holidays together each year and travel we did to many exotic destinations. Fun and laughter were always present between us, plus Russ was home every fourth week of the month. I did not recognise the barrage of emotions that would happen when he first went away, when he first went up north. Mainly, I felt abandoned and alone.

I soon came to realise it was a common enough feeling for those of us left behind to keep the home fires burning. After a while, independence set in. I had my life, and Russ had his. Those of us who weren't in the mining world didn't understand how much hard work it took from both of us to maintain a normal family lifestyle, especially when Dad was needed at home. So, when the health scare for Russ arrived, that might mean the end of his working life, this thought poleaxed him, never before had he was told to slow down or take medication; this was new, it was not life-threatening but enough of a scare for us to gather the troops and say we are off before we cannot do this at all.

A caravan or Mobile home was the question; we opted for a small purpose-built bus that suited both of us, it proudly presenting itself to us. I had to hide a smile when the salesman laid it on thick with the sales pitch about the dear old lady being the previous owner. It was second-hand which I had not been too keen on, but this was in excellent condition, clean, and tidy, with all the modern conveniences except for what I considered a bathroom. I was not too keen on going off-road or having to dig a hole in the ground for toilet purposes, so it would be camping grounds for us.

Shopping had proved to be fun, outfitting the little home on wheels, a new mattress was top of our list; it felt like I was shopping for a hobbit house; we both found it is more challenging when you were shopping for a larger home and family; we now had to consider the weight and size of what we purchased. The excitement of the unknown grew on you, and soon the tales of the Great Outback began to flow in. Friends, mates, and family all had stories of joy and woe, and it was up to us to decipher and sift through what we wanted to do or should avoid. There comes a time in everyone's life when you have to take a deep breath and take the plunge. Four weeks into our travels, we were both unsure of what we had done.

The day arrived when we were to say our farewells, we had planned a fabulous barbecue for one night before we were to leave, much later both of us wishing we had kept it very low-key. The champagne cocktails were still affecting us both, or maybe it was the one prawn too many. I was more than happy we were still at home with a bathroom nearby.

As we travelled down the Perth coast, I encountered the most fantastic scenery I have ever experienced. The exotic places we once visited throughout Europe, including Bali, Lombok, the Pacific islands, New Zealand, and Singapore, including a luxurious cruise through the Middle East, paled in comparison to the majestic turquoise, cobalt, light green, and opaque blue waves rolling onto the white sand.

The dark blue Indian Ocean is truly breathtaking; my new camera barely had a chance to cool off. We had stopped to watch dolphins glide by; sleek and carefree, now and again leaping up then diving deeply on their return to the ocean. We observed large white pelicans with their facial tribal markings as they swam past, creating an elegant ballet of white and black in the turquoise waters. Food was certainly abundant here in this beautiful ocean.

I loved it all, but deep down, there was a strange feeling of sadness; it sat just below my belly button, and I dismissed it as silly. One morning while having a cuppa outside our new home, I realised I was feeling homesick, which caught me by surprise, as I was not the one who became homesick; I was the sensible one.

Admitting this to Russ, he also agreed as he was missing his mates and work. We both sat outside our bus, watching the blue Indian Ocean shift from deep Indian ink blue to pale green with the tide and wind. Lost in thoughts of a life we once had, we finally confided in each other about what we missed. I went first: 'Well, I miss our family, our grandson Jess our daughter Raewyn, who at six years old decided to be called Miss Rae and should have been crowned Miss Independence.

I missed the closeness between us that blossomed after she became a solo parent; she turned to me for advice and support and, in doing so, we had formed a strong bond within our family. I also missed the community life that I had built while Russ had worked away. Then there were the gardens, for years I had battled the scorching summer heat to keep them alive, I had left a thriving veggie patch, and a flower garden, I even missed the chickens, my voice wobbling with my unshed tears.

Russ went next, but he missed the guys; you could see the distant look in his eyes when he spoke about the Pilbara, the red dirt, the camaraderie and mateship among them all. I felt a bit left out of his life, just as I suppose he thought about mine when I talked about my life in Perth. We both agreed we missed family, especially Jess, who dashed in and out of our lives. He was our twelve-year-old mini whirlwind, and we loved him dearly, just as we knew he loved us. Slowly, the little squirmy feeling in my stomach eased up; it must have shown because we both burst out laughing. 'I guess we're both homesick.' As we talked, the day rolled on; dinner was baked beans on toast, cooked and eaten outside, served on paper plates. It was just the ticket to feeling so much relaxed.

Russ wrapped his arms around me, both of us realising this was be much harder than what we had imagined. However, the power of tears and a good blow of the nose is incredible, Russ also admitting to a few tearful gulps. But, as we held onto each other, we knew that our life together was precious, not to be wasted or stored for another day; it was here and now, to be lived with a smile every day. This was our time to rediscover the magic that first brought us together, and it didn't matter what people called it or what label they gave it. This was our time; the hard work of keeping our home and hearts together was over, it was time for us to reignite our love and friendship with each other.

The next day we drove to Bunbury, a quiet little country town. The smaller towns had to advertise extra hard to ensure travellers wouldn't bypass them. We discovered a pretty home-based winery near a main road, choosing a bottle of crisp, fruity white wine for myself, Russ chose a bold red claret. However, since we weren't big drinkers and our tums still remembered our farewell party, we placed them in the wine rack for another time, spending the night in the serene comfort of a well-maintained campsite. What amazed both of us was how other campers casually popped into one another's vans. It felt a bit too laid-back for me, so I kept my distance.

The next day marked our big trip to Albany. I smile now when I recall our belief that a big day involved just a four-hour drive. The advertisements of whale-watching trips, wineries accessible by boat, and horse-drawn wagon tours, along with art stores, bookstores, and charming little side roads that meander into various shops. The main town was fashionable, blending Couture clothing shops with an element of old hippie culture. We discovered a camping ground called Happy Family Camping and Cabins; we chose to stay and explore; our spot was on a small rise overlooking a long valley filled with tent and caravan sites.

CHAPTER THREE

The new owners were friendly and helpful; they had just experienced one of their busiest Christmas seasons ever. However, our arrival was in late February and the park had almost emptied. They had been the ones to inform us of the dawn and dusk bird parade, and it was everything they claimed it would be. Their description was pure magic. We did all the touristy things in Albany. My favourite was a real gem: a small bookstore by a quiet wharf, with cobbled streets reminiscent of a Dickinson story. They served hot, delicious coffee, fragrant English breakfast tea, fresh croissants, and a muffin.

The biggest plus was that you could choose any book and sit down to read while enjoying a hot drink, relaxing and savoring a couple of hours. Russ loved to stroll along the sand dunes, hoping to spot the elusive flip of a whale fluke. So, we did both. Once Russ was engrossed in the day's paper his takeaway order of a black coffee and a blueberry muffin, while I flipped through an anthology, once my takeaway order of hot English tea with a lemon curd muffin had arrived; we took a walk along the beach, which was always windy and invigorating, hundreds of seagulls screeching with delight, squawking and fighting over the fishy bits left by last night's high tide. The wind whipped through our hair, our faces becoming ruddy as the sea air infused us with energy down to the very core of our beings.

Three days in Albany were charming, and the people were incredibly welcoming, but it was time to move on. As we drove back to the campsite to retrieve our van, the skies had turned grey; heavy raindrops splattered against the windscreen. A cloudburst occurred during the thirty-minute drive from Albany Township to the camping ground. Our little bus looked so forlorn, seeming to hunch down in the cold rain; we dashed into the office eager to pay for our three-night stay and leave, but they looked very stern as they warned us, "Don't go anywhere, as there are warnings of a torrential storm on its way." The camp manager advised us "To let him show us a safer, sheltered place." He drove a large blue Fergie tractor, showing us the way to a secure and sheltered spot. "You'll be safe here" the owner shouted above the howling wind; "Best to sit this one out." And sit it out, so we did, for four days.

If we dashed to the bathroom, it was flip-flops, a raincoat, and a dash over to the shower blocks, and by the time you got back, the freezing wind and rain had soaked you through. Our bus became a beacon of light, a tiny lighthouse you headed toward. I had never been so glad to be settled inside our wee home. There was no beautiful sunset or sunrise, just grey turning dark and the howling wind that shook our home as the cold, windy fingers searched for an opening or two. Thankfully, no gaps were found; we were snug as bugs in a rug. On day four, I had enough of being cooped up; I was about to make a dash to the toilet blocks wet weather or not. I opened the door to race over to the toilets, but the wind whipped it out of my hand with a huge bang.

The gust roared inside, snatching the air from my mouth as I struggled to keep my balance, with Russ clinging to me and the door to steady himself. His failed attempts were obvious as I toppled into the biggest lake of icy water I'd ever seen. It was muddy, oozy, freezing water, my undies now filled with mud, stones, sand, and little sharp stones. I felt like a small child as I wailed, "I want to go home now." Russ doubled over with laughter at the sight of me sitting in a large, shallow lake that surrounded us while I cried like a two-year-old full of misery. He giggled all the way to the showers after he'd hauled me out, the mud making a nasty sucking sound as my lower half pulled free from the muck and water that surrounded the bus, my pink flip-flops bobbing merrily in the shallow wake around me.

Between fits of snorting laughter, he ensured I hadn't broken or sprained anything then helped me over to the toilet block. As he held the door open for me, I caught a glimpse of my pathetic self in the mirror. My hair and face were splattered with gooey mud, and I was covered in it from head to toe; it was hard not to join in the laughter that kept shaking through Russ. Although my dignity was severely dented, I had to admit that I did look a sight.

When the day dawned with a bright sun, the birds once more began to cheerfully sing once more; the sun a golden ball in the azure, blue sky: the day had begun to warm up. It was time to move on. Our first problem was that our bus was firmly stuck in the mud.

Once again, the trusty Fergie was pressed into action. We had to wait for about half an hour while it assisted another camper, and then it was our turn. We were right in the middle of the big brown lake, with the wheels of our home sunk into the mud. To me, it looked a little dangerous; the water had crept up to our doorstep. Russ, being a bloke and having experienced all kinds of weather on the drill rigs, wasn't too concerned. "Looks like a small, beached whale," he commented. As the Fergie pulled out one small, bedraggled bus, I was glad to hear that I wasn't the only one making a sad, sucky noise when dragged out of the mud.

The camp bill was settled, farewells were exchanged, and the staff offered the customary, "Come again, love to see you," as we drove off. That's when I decided to paint the name of our bus across the rear. That night, after drying off in the quaint seaside village of Esperance, I revealed my hidden pot of black paint and a small paintbrush. I boldly painted the name of our new home right across her now clean backside. I called her the Metal Mermaid. Once I finished, I stepped back to admire my handiwork. Russ nudged me; handing over a cold beer, saying, 'We now proclaim the Metal Mermaid our home for the next few months. Did I detect a slight catch in his voice? Was he also feeling homesick?

CHAPTER FOUR

May she glide us safely to wherever we steer her. He then poured a bit of beer over the back bumper. The name sparked many conversation starters as we travelled from Esperance upwards, making new mates at the various campsites. Tonight, as we both snuggled down in our bed, the sea breeze whispered of the adventures yet to come. I truly felt this was to be the adventure of our lives, and I was not wrong.

A day that dawns with the golden sun awakening life all around is a good omen for us all. Breakfast was had swiftly as Esperance awaited discovery. However, the public toilets in Salmon Bay were another story; we had to wait for them to open and be cleaned. Thank God for understanding café owners! He offered us his private toilet, and we both dashed for it. The cafe had fresh cinnamon rolls and hot coffee on offer, so we bought our morning tea, grateful for his generosity. Russ and I stood outside the Metal Mermaid, sipping hot coffee and reading the discovery maps along the roadside.

We had parked in a small camp spot that overlooked the ocean, and below us lay a small cove with white sand and turquoise sea. I daydreamed, with Russ's voice, a pleasant hum in the background as he read about what to do and see in Esperance. I watched four senior ladies walk down toward the beach; they stood there dipping their toes in the water. I could hear their windblown words, "Ohh god, it's cold", another adding, "Bit chilly." They bravely stripped down to their bathers.

By the looks of it, these ladies were serious about going for a swim. All four of them walked into the water in a line until they were waist deep. They were all dressed in black bathers, with the array of bright-colored swimming caps on their heads, which made them look like a row of pretty flowers bobbing around in the sea. These ladies swam from one end of the bay to the other with powerful strokes that propelled them through the water. "I had to nudge Russ "Come and have a look at this, love." No sooner had I said it than two more dark, sleek heads joined them. Speechless isn't the word I'd use as two small seals joined these ladies in the water, diving and leaping, rolling and weaving in and out, while these four women just carried on as if it were a daily occurrence. It went on for a good half-hour; then the ladies left the water, the seals nowhere to be seen, all of them laughing and happy as they went their separate ways.

As I went to put our paper coffee cups in the bin, my mind still trying to process what we had just witnessed, when one of the swimmers walked into the café. I approached her and asked, 'Did you know?' She smiled and replied, "Every day, dear, for the last two years; we consider them to be our mascots, or at least, that's what we call them. We have no idea why; we just ignore them; they play around us until we leave." I inquired why this wasn't known to others. She looked at me and said, "Why? Life isn't about looking at me; it's about looking at life with me." That struck a chord as I knew she was right; it was about sharing and caring for one another, even if the other was a seal. That surprising scene set the mood for the week, and as we travelled along the motorway, the Metal Mermaid hummed along happily; the two of us finally felt the stress begin to lift a little from our shoulders.

The other oddity we had found in Esperance was the way the kangaroos would happily head for the beach for a swim or a snack; the locals thought it was perfectly natural. I was taken aback as we strolled along a quiet stretch of coast to get some fresh air; two skippies hopped past, these two young ones completely unbothered by our presence, foraging amongst the seaweed; before hopping down into the water, completely at ease with their surrounds; and as usual, I had left my camera in our bus.

We had been on the road for nearly three weeks; the time we had given ourselves to enjoy was nearly over. I made a home-cooked meal of pasta and fresh salad, and over dinner, we discussed whether we liked this way of living together all day, every day. Most of the campers we had met were couples who raved about the scenery, the people they met, and the places they had been. I also noticed that some of them didn't enjoy each other's company, while others had a far-off look in their eyes, as if travel and adventure were calling them. Some folks had turned their trip into a working holiday.

One senior couple I met made and sold soy candles at markets all around this vast country. While we were talking, her mobile phone was ringing off the hook with orders for candles and requests to sell at festivals, some as far away as Queensland. Her partner was experienced with council roadworks; he found work with different councils wherever they went. They were both very much in love with each other and their lifestyle. Another couple we met sold old forks bent into various shapes and marketed them as wind chimes. They haunted auctions and second-hand shops for these treasures, both absolutely mad about their passion. They followed wherever the Internet suggested there was an auction; otherwise, they lived in Bridgetown, where they made their creations, or forged more of the items they sold at the markets.

One woman we met travelled on her own; she really fascinated me, a hippy straight out of a seventies time warp. Her van was covered in brightly painted fluorescent stars, barely twelve feet long, and inside, charms and beads hung from every nook and cranny. She smelled of incense and sandalwood. She read palms, cards, or even the bumps on your head! Another specialty was that she was a professional belly dancer. Not that I'm knocking it. I've given the dance a go myself and loved it! This lovely lady was seventy or older, with an attitude of embracing life. She owned an old four-door station wagon, which also served as home for her two greyhound dogs, Butch and Cassidy. Nothing went near her home without a warning growl erupting from either underneath or inside. She gracefully shrugged her shoulders; when I asked, "Next stop? She shrugged her slim shoulders "Who cares? I go with the wind, my dear," was her reply.

As Russ and I sat there with our homemade hot cheese toasties, we couldn't help but smile at how these folks had affected us. Russ stopped eating, asking me. "Okay love, what's our story going to be to continue our travels?" Or are we heading home? We had met many people coming and going, obviously enjoying themselves and the freedom of this lifestyle. Our question to each other was whether we wanted to live this Nomad life ourselves or if occasional small trips were the best approach for us. I knew this was Russ's way of offering me a way out, to return to my life as I knew it or to keep going.

In one breath, I replied, "Onward bound, please! "I wanted to taste, experience, see, and do all I could, while I could, and to share this with my Russ. Apart from family and two best mates, there was no other draw card. I knew within a week my positions in many different groups and on councils would have been snapped up by now. I now waited for his answer; my eyebrows raised with anticipation. What would be his answer? Russ was a slow eater and tended to deliberate when and whether to swallow: When he finally gave me his answer, I could almost feel the seconds ticking away. "I think we should carry on; let's see this wide, bountiful country and what the fuss is all about."

CHAPTER FIVE

Now it would be unsettling for both of us at times, but the decision was made to carry on. If only I had a crystal ball to foresee what the future held, I would have said, "Let's go home now." Still, I did not. The adventure before us was exciting, a new learning curve for us both. Being naturally inquisitive, here was our chance to explore and play in our own backyard. Staying in touch with family and friends was always a must; but traveling like this meant living, seeing, meeting, and doing whatever we wanted whenever we wanted, no tours, no guides, no timelines, and no boats, trains, or planes to catch. We both agreed to give one year on the road as Nomads a go. I could not have been happier.

We opened my bottle of white wine toasting our new life, ready to accept what came our way. Then out came the maps of all the places we'd missed on our way to Esperance. "If we're going to see Ozzy, let's do it right," Russ said, and I agreed; we could take the road to Kalgoorlie or backtrack to check out what we missed. This was exciting; the maps and pamphlets showed us what to do and see, but we both knew it wouldn't be exactly as written since we had a knack for finding the unusual. That night, as we went to bed, our next destination, Denmark, was now written on a sticky note and attached to the dashboard. Morning dawned, and the camp we had stayed at was full of bustle, people going about their day, some leaving, some staying, and others were permanent residents who lived there.

As Russ cooked up his Sunday special the full English breakfast for a good start to our day, I decided to go for a walk around the camping ground; I found it amazing how people seemed to fit into this world of tiny homes and caravans. Some had made grand attempts; others were happy to live in a van with nothing around them but sand or grass. One side of this camp had permanent mobile homes; their gardens were nice, the owners of some gardens were expressions of the most vivid imaginations, a riot of plants, carvings, sculptures, art of all sorts was alive and well on this side.

As I walked around this well-kept side of the park, with clean spacious, even footpaths and lighting it led back to where we had parked for the night, it was quite an eye opener for me, as on the side we were camped had permanent caravan homes, nothing as splendid as the other side I had just walked past, but the odd place was well kept, small gardens, mostly a caravan awning or a hard annex of sorts. One place caught my eye, it was surrounded by large pot plants with healthy palms in them, the pots had all been mosaiced, colours of all sorts blending in with the surroundings. The caravan was a large one, with a small porch where large hanging plants grew. The entrance was through big double glass doors that lead into a hard annex, soft white net curtains hung in all the windows, it looked loved and cared for.

The owner, a tall, attractive, slim woman in her sixties, wandered out. She bade me a cheerful good morning as I passed by, her broom making a short shift of any sand or leaves. I stopped to admire her art on the terracotta pots, asking her if she had created them. My chat with her revealed that she, too, was an artist in abstract, also a prolific writer, had a family in New Zealand, and had a husband working up North in the mines.

This was her home now, she loved the simplicity of the lifestyle, she had met so many people that had travelled worldwide. She looked forward to one day, "You should see, or have you been to?" For now, she was content to be where she was. I mentioned my own large garden and home in Perth, sadness flitted across the woman's face as she explained that once she too had such a place in Armadale in Perth, but she had been the recipient of a savage burglary, the police had been involved and had warned her if there was a next time, her life may be in danger. Fear of this happening again while she lived alone was the drive behind here living here.

Her words were 'Here I feel safe; it's where my creativity has blossomed. Her optimism about where her life would lead her was just what I needed to hear as she said, "Why not give it a go, see if you like it, if you don't, go and explore, then you will never know." Now, I know a message when I receive one, how many times had I heard *give it a go* in the past weeks, too many times not to take note. I could smell our breakfast cooking as I walked towards our bus, Russ calling out to hurry it up, while we ate our fried eggs and crunchy bacon, I informed Russ of my walk and talk, to the residents of this park; he too had met an older Gent in the abolition block that had told Russ his story.

It was a story of sadness and rejection, heartache and fear, this man was on his own, did not welcome family around and did not want any nosy neighbours around. I knew exactly who he was describing, as his little caravan stood stark and bare, a tiny, deserted island he claimed as his own. This caravan park sounded just like any ordinary community that lived day to day with all the problems we as house owners had. And there are times when you know any sort of assistance would not be welcome. The coat of freedom had now settled quite comfortably on both our shoulders. Dishes were done, packed away, the bus tidied up, and the Metal Mermaid was on her way again, this time back the way she had come. We drove past the lady who I had just talked to; she waved us off, "Bye, safe travels", she called out.

Our last port of call in Esperance was the Mermaid leather shop, how amazing to see all sorts of products made from the skins of fish, sharks, and stingrays, the shop owner was very informative about all his products telling us of the preparation time it took for some of the hides to cure. The shire of Denmark called; we were on our way.

Taking the South coast road then turning off to Mt Barker; we stopped to take photos, both noticing that locusts were everywhere: we wound our way through the Porongurup's, a windy road that advertised the most amazing Authentic Windmill restaurant, we had to stop at this place to take photos, the picturesque scene of dry sunburnt fields and the tall brown windmill was a creative photo shoot. The windmill sails creaked and groaned lightly, as they turned so very slowly.

Inside, they served true Dutch coffee and homemade apple strudel; we just had to try it all. The extremely hot summer had literally baked the fields dry; only stalks of plants and skeletons of trees remained in the paddocks. As we suspected, locusts had also been a real problem this summer. There had been two huge swarms of them, one just recently and the other, as we had noticed while in Mt Barker not two hours ago.

While the restaurant owner Leo talked about the summer and his windmill I noticed our bus's front bumper was covered in what looked like a yellow paste, looking closer we, both saw the yellow paste had wings and long red legs mashed into it, Locusts, our radiator was full of them, no wonder the temperature gauge kept going too hot, we had put it down to the stinking hot day and having the air con on most of the trip. Leo offered his sage advice which was to get some sunshade cloth and tie it over your radiator in front of the bus, 'that stops the little suckers from getting in.' We did just that, sweeping and hosing away the hundreds of dead locusts from the radiator. Once we had attached the netting to the front of the radiator, we took off again. We decided that the sooner we reached Denmark, the better as both of us were uncomfortable in the desiccated countryside.

Denmark has always been a favourite of mine for one reason: it has a massive warehouse of dried flowers. As an avid floral artist, I have always placed orders through the Internet for these products, especially the gorgeous pods and seeds.

CHAPTER SIX

Searching for the actual source, we found it late that afternoon. My imagination ran riot at the colours of dried Australian flowers in this one place. All I could do was turn in circles, whispering, 'Oh my God,' it smelt divine. Huge sacks of Potpourri, made on the premises, lay everywhere, giving off a heavenly perfume. I wanted to bury myself in the delightful smell of Lavender and Rose. This place dried anything and everything.

Frustration was the overriding emotion here; I was on a bus, where do you put huge bouquets of dried flowers when you're away for a year? You don't; was the look on Russ's face, but potpourri was always handy, purchasing a very small amount to help the Metal Mermaid smell nice and very proud of my ability not to buy too much, off we went to the tree top walk, nearly forty meters above the forest floor amongst towering giants of tree. How exhilarating to walk through trees that were thousands of years old, you could imagine what a giant would feel like.

The next stop was Whale Rock, huge boulders of grey rock, from afar looking like a herd of grey mammoths from the past. To put my hand against one and feel the sun's warmth on it was like touching the warm side of the animal itself; you only had to close your eyes, and you could imagine the heartbeat. The folk here were so very friendly and helpful, used to people like us touring through; asking questions of what and where, all answered with passion about their quaint little village. I was also informed an international writer now resided here and many well-known artists and artisans were in residence. Many wineries were begging for a visit, offering chocolates, wine, art; this place we would revisit, for now we had a date with the road, to keep exploring.

The late sun was turning the sky into an orange kaleidoscope. A camping spot was to be found, and soon, off-road parking was easily missed if one was not on the lookout or 'in the know.' Suddenly, there it was, with two other vans that had stopped there for the night. Our little Metal Mermaid bumped her way into a spare space. Russ stopped, and out we stepped. As always, the other campers welcomed us with a 'Gidday and how ya goin,' the typical Ozzie greeting. While Russ set up the portable barbeque, I made the salad. Russ cooked pork chops that sizzled and crackled; the aroma was superb. While eating our dinner and discussing the day and what to see and do next, one of the campers strolled over to ask where we were from.

The conversation turned into a lively discussion on the pros and cons of bus versus caravan. His wife added her opinion, bringing along a large tray of freshly baked scones to the discussion. Not to be outdone, I contributed some of the produce I had made at home. Thus, we spent a delightful three hours in friendship, engaging in an interesting debate, while the other couple in their caravan, went inside, shut their windows and doors, their lights were switched off, obviously choosing not to join in. And that's okay; we all have choices, and obviously, a hearty conversation was not the choice they wanted. The couple we had a friendly conversation with were leaving for Esperance the next day and asked us for any information, so we added our story of the seals and swimming seniors.

The feeling of belonging was beginning to take place for us; we could now inform others of our discoveries. Both agreeing it was fun, wondering who would we meet next? The answer was there the following morning. As I said previously, we had no bathroom, so a bucket had to do. A big red plastic one had been installed for emergencies only, and today was an emergency, as no public toilets in a caravan rest area off the main road. You can't very well knock on another person's caravan door asking, 'can I use your toilet?' even out here I believes it's not the done thing.

I was happy enough to be sitting there on the red bucket, Russ still asleep, the kettle simmering ready for our hot drinks when there was a knock on our door. Who! What! I grabbed the roll of paper and go to stand up and again that weird suction thing happens to me again, one red bucket seriously stuck to my bum, 'Russ wake up' I whispered as the door rattled again, this time it sounded like it's trying to be opened, I grabbed for the door handle, trying to hang on while hanging on to my sitting position on the bucket. Russ remained in dreamland, so I struggled to shift over towards our bed to shake him, but the green carpet and the big red bucket didn't get on. I felt myself tipping over, one mad scramble to sit upright again, help, I'm literally stuck.

I ask loudly who it is, and the reply is we are off now, the other campers want to know if you going to stay on a bit, I replied "We don't know yet, enjoy," silently begging them to disappear, and wondering why they would jiggle the door handle. Still trying to struggle off the dammed bucket, I scoot over to the bench my hand searching for a weapon to stab the big this red brute who has a huge grasp on my bum, anything to let the suction go, a teaspoon is all I can find so I push the end of it between the bucket and my bum, once again that haunting sucky sound slurped through the bus and I was free, thank you, God.

Russ staggered with laughter as I retold my dilemma as he had slept on completely unaware of my fight with the bucket. "Only you sweetheart, why didn't you wake me? He managed to say before he collapsed into laughter one more time. I was not impressed. The day and our decision to drive to Walpole was about to begin, we also recognised what had suddenly become a tradition of ours; over dinner we would discuss the day and where to from here, the sticky note written with destination and popped onto the dashboard, then a check-in phone call to Rae and Jess, slowly we were evolving; becoming seasoned travelers thankfully with a smidge of cynical humour.

Russ pulled out the road maps, pointing out that so far, our journey was a zigzag around the southern part of WA. He was happy enough but wanted to explore this wide state of ours. Before I could answer him, there was once again insistent knocking on the door. Our remaining female neighbour obviously not happy with our answer one hour before, was now demanding to know "What time we were moving on and if we intended to come back that night." Russ and I were both speechless at their weird, demanding behaviour. It was a definite "No, from us we would not be back "We hurriedly packed our gear away, started the motor and left. In the rear vision mirror, we watched as the male side of this couple literally hauled her back into the caravan, while she screamed abuse like a wounded banshee.

It felt like they were waiting for us to leave so they could have a domestic; looking around us, they were in the outback if they were had to have one big argument this was the place for it. The amazing thing about it was they were our age. I guess we are going to meet all types on our travels hopefully not too many like those we had just left behind. Walpole was great, full of wonderful, happy, helpful locals who were only too willing to tell us the history of their village. Then it was onto Pemberton for brunch and onward arriving in Bridgetown. This small village was a delight so English; it was late afternoon the chill of the night setting in, the fug from chimney smoke, it lifted softly into a dusky pink sky, some of the homes had seen better days and some were quite grand. 'How pretty' I remarked especially when I spied two huge rose bushes climbing over a trellis in a front yard, the pink and white roses looking spectacular in the dusk, both roses giving off a heady perfume. And I must admit a small, tiny corner of my heart whispered, 'you have the same roses in your own front yard.'

Russ must have seen the wistful look in my eyes as that night we left our Metal Mermaid safely locked up in a motel's parking lot while we dined on roast lamb at the local hotel, then a warm relaxing spa in our motel room. Russ's excuse was "We can't forget the luxury of having a break every now and again." I could not say no to that now, could I? As we settled down in a huge king-size bed, Russ produced wine, chocolates, and the road map and sticky note for our next day. It was advertised Bridgetown was to have its annual Art and Flag fair.

CHAPTER SEVEN

Russ knew I would love to stay and have a wander through stalls and shops of art and produce, see the Brierly Jigsaw gallery; and wander I did the next day, drinking in all the sights and smells of a country fair, there is nothing on earth to take its place. The fruit and veggies on sale were heavenly, so we stocked up. The homemade chutneys, sauces, and jams I also purchased to stock our tiny larder. The gallery was superb as was the English breakfast tea we had at a small café in the village. Then it was time to go find ourselves a camping ground for the night and off to another destination. Busselton by the sea or further inland, driving through to Dumbleyung and Lake Grace to reach Hyden, a coin was tossed as both places sounded interesting; I called tails as the silver coin turned in the air, it landed on the ground tails up, my choice so Hyden was our next destination. This was fun, I was now the driver, and the open road was pure tonic in my blood.

Off we drove, our next stop, Diana Krall sang, while Russ gently snored in the passenger seat, the Metal Mermaid lulling him to sleep as we sped along. Stopping off at Dumbleyung to find a free overnight park was not too hard, they had a community ground there that you could park in for one night, so I carefully maneuvered the Mermaid to her grassy bed for one night, the slight bumping and rocking waking Russ up.

We busied ourselves with getting a meal ready, Russ now full of energy, me? I was really tired; I curled up on the bed and grabbed a half hours snooze. The sun was just about to set, and its last rays shone through the back window onto my spine warming my body, I felt cocooned in a bubble of content, happy that we had decided to give this adventure a go, only waking up when Russ called me for dinner. Over a hot fettuccini courtesy of Chef Russ, we discussed the pros and cons of our next stop, which was Hyden, including what we would find there and the search for a caravan park where we could enjoy a hot, soapy shower.

While quick washes in warm water were fine for a freshen-up, we always felt revived by a good scrub in a shower. We also realised that choosing the bus as our home without a small ensuite was proving to be a drawback; for others, it was all part of the caravanning experience. Lesson number one had been learned. Nevertheless, we enjoyed a great night's sleep, and the sticky note with Hyden written on it now held a place of pride on the dashboard. Waking early to the sounds of the countryside and the sunrise simply fills me with joy. Galahs strutted across the dew-laden grass, puffing out their chests in a display of ownership, while searching for their breakfast. Large crows cawed as their blue-black bodies flitted between ghost gum trees. The freshness of the air felt like no one had ever breathed it before; it was brand new and ours to enjoy.

With Russ now at the wheel, it was my turn to take happy snaps with the camera and admire the passing scenery, stopping for coffee in Lake Grace. I read the traveller's billboard on what to do and see before hitting the road again toward our destination. Hyden caravan park and hot showers; ahh, heaven sent! I hadn't realised just how much a body could ache from simply sitting or driving, but we both ached.

The hot shower and a walk around the campsite were a welcome and necessary respite. Wave Rock is a famous landmark just outside Hyden. Believe me, it's enormous! A monolithic superstructure of natural wonder, it's astounding to think that I was standing under the huge lip of rock, now known as Wave Rock, which is over 60,000 years old. Here I am, standing on it, inside it, beside it, making me feel a tad small, just a grain of sand within this great cosmos. Leaving something as wonderful as Wave Rock, I wanted to ensure I had it all recorded as it may change in some subtle way. Its colours and structure, worn and torn through the centuries, are awe-inspiring.

Close by is another natural wonder, Humpydo Rock. Its gaping mouth invites you to peer in; those brave enough may walk into this cave where strong native superstition prevails, sending shivers down my spine. It feels uncanny, or perhaps spooky. I tend to respect that feeling in my gut. Russ dived in, adventure written all over his face, while I stayed outside, snapping pictures of the incredible flora around me, very aware of the quietness. Tiny, delicate white rock flowers clung precariously to the little soil, so pale but pretty against the overcast sky. A photo opportunity not to be missed; I was getting good at close-ups of the bush. and my hands were itching to paint what I saw.

Back at the Hyden camp, our Metal Mermaid needed a clean. Those who don't travel may think cleaning happens by magic, but no, it takes good old-fashioned elbow grease to spruce up your home. Russ reappeared, bristling with brooms and brushes tucked under his arms. He tackled the outside while I took on the inside. The only way I could clean was to move everything outside and start from go to whoa. Russ was now busy running between washing the bus and giving me orders on what to do and where to put his gear. The poor man was exhausted from worrying about where I placed his 'stuff,' and cleaning the bus.

I couldn't help but smile as I watched his dilemma. I literally pulled everything out and went to work, soaking steamy hot water and disinfectant in that specific red bucket. Then I tackled the laundry that accumulates in any family. Dust gets into every crack and crevice, so drawers were brushed out, cleaned, and packed again. By six p.m., we were both tired, the good kind of tired that says "Well done, good job." Our home was spick and span, twinkling its thanks with shining clean windows; its silver body was now sleek and stain-free.

The insides smelled heavenly, with clean sheets, everything was clean from roof to floor. A job well done was to be rewarded with fish and chips from the local shop and a glass of white wine served in paper cups to celebrate our day, as I refused to do any dishes in my shiny, clean sink. Russ cleaned up the equipment we had borrowed from the camp owners. Plus our own cleaning gear, it looked like a small war zone had exploded around us. It was a ten-minute walk to the shop to buy our dinner. While I was there, I met another lady with the same idea of fish and chips for dinner.

Her name was Maggie, a South African woman who had lived here for over thirty years. We started talking, her story was amazing. This woman was in love with prospecting for gold in the outback. She admitted they had been somewhat successful, finding a few grams occasionally, not anything huge. Then quietly telling me about her big find, which was among the rocks by the shore in Bunbury. She had decided to take their metal detector with them on a weekend trip away. One day, she was simply having fun wandering by the rocks when her metal detector started to beep and to her delight, at her feet lay two or three small objects that resembled silver buttons. She took them home and washed them off to find they were ancient coins by the dates minted on them.

The next day, she saw a coin collector in Bunbury, only to find out she had found some high-content silver and very valuable Eighteenth Century Florins. Maggie returned to the same rocks the next day, finding more coins the same as before. She did not say how much they were worth, but by the glint in her eye, it was no small amount. The story fascinated me. The details were very sketchy, and I don't blame her.

Who knows what else she was going to find around these rocks? What did amaze me was that this brave lady had severe Osteoarthritis, her toes and hands so swollen and disfigured it must have been painful every step she took; but her smile told another story saying this is an exciting life, and I want to live every minute of it. Maggie was an inspiration to all forms of arthritis sufferers, me being one of them; but nothing as severe as this brave woman had.

I invited Maggie and her husband, Emanuel, to share our meal. The smell of fish, chips, and open fresh air always made me hungry; we were all ravenous. The conversation broached more adventures, calling us onwards. To do this, we would need a gold detector and equipment; I was busy adding sums in my head as Emanuel told us the value of the good equipment and the signs you would recognise when looking for gold. Emanuel was a school counsellor, lucky to find work wherever he went. We all agreed it is sad to think that today's children need so much emotional help. They were returning to Perth the next day for a grandchild's birthday.

It reminded me that I had to call family to check in for the night, and Russ and I needed to discuss where to go next. As we said our goodbyes to this lovely couple, I called our Ray while Russ searched for the sticky notepad and pen, grumbling about his rules on how to tidy up; he couldn't find anything as men often do. The news from Perth was good, nothing new, and everyone was well and healthy. I told her the news about where we had been and who we had met. Then Russ spoke to them, and our grandson Jess wheedling a promise from Russ that he could travel with us one day soon.

While the jug was boiling, we got out the maps, deciding where to next. We could take the coast road or head inland to Kalgoorlie. Once tucked up in our freshly made bed that night, I glanced over at the dashboard; there glowed in the moonlight one sticky note with Kalgoorlie written on it.

CHAPTER EIGHT

It took a while to reach Kalgoorlie/Boulder, as it's written on the map. The back road was quite empty of life in many ways, with Alison Moyet singing in her luscious throaty voice, Russ and I joining in with the verses we knew, laughing at each other's attempts to remember the correct words. Salmon Gums, with its small roadside house, was an excellent opportunity to stop, stretch, have a cup of tea, and buy a sandwich. The store owners were so full of information about Kalgoorlie, which is known worldwide for having one of the biggest open gold mines in the southern hemisphere.

Once back on the road, I rang a caravan park; yes, there were vacancies, so we booked in. The managers were named Barbie and Ken. These two, although obviously sprightly, were in their late seventies- both small, wiry, and full of cheek. They were so lovely. Ken walked us to our choice of parking for our short stay there, and he informed us, "You could have one under the trees, one by the pool, or another alongside the communal kitchen." We both asked, "What do you think? He replied, "I'd go for the one under the willow tree- a quite shady place that invites you to relax, there a rarity up this way, it's always too hot, but it's for that very reason we love it."

Russ backed into the Metal Mermaid and paid for the three days we had booked. The first thing we did was shower; the hot water was such a reviver for aching muscles. We both decided to cruise for the day, leaving our cares behind and doing the tourist thing. We caught a bus that showed us all the top spots, including Lily's old-time whorehouse, which is now proudly featured in tourism pamphlets but was once a symbol of shame. A blot on respectful society, today seen one of the city's famous icons. All the stables, as they were called, encouraged tourists to walk into a stable, sit and experience. An outside billboard advertised an English morning tea with the owner and a guided tour. There is always a jokester, and it had to be the one lone male on the bus, asking "If they served jam with their tarts." The guide gave him that look as if to say Is there an idiot born every day? Then walked away.

Then, it was on an afternoon tour of a mine shaft and a nighttime look at the mine working, the lights placed on; in, and around the enormous gaping pit, it looked like a scene from the movie Mad Max. At any moment, we expected Tina Turner or Mel Gibson to come tearing out of the enormous gates and start shooting at us. By the time we got back to our tiny home on wheels, it was about seven pm. Although there were very few of us in the caravan park for the night, it seemed to hum with a communal life of its own; as I was peeling spuds for our dinner, Barbie popped her head around the door. "Hey, Darl," she said in her raspy voice. "There's a small get together over in the camp kitchen, why don't you join us? Bring your dinner and add to what we have on the table. I raised my eyebrows at Russ meaning it was time to go. The spuds were cooked and mashed with butter and, my specialty, a dash of paprika, with a grating of cheese, over we went.

Entering a large camp kitchen, there would have been about thirty of us; 'hello's and gidday's' ringing out to greet us; the smell of cooked meat and veggies was delicious. We met so many people that night, all with stories to tell. The one that stayed in my mind was of the camp manager Barbie. She was a survivor of cancer; she blamed smoking for thirty years for her illness and was brave enough to admit no one had forced her to smoke; her condition was her problem.

The pencil-thin white scar across her throat was a testament to her struggle; woe betide anyone who lit up around her or anywhere near her. I agreed, 'Good for you, Barbie, you stick to your guns, it's a nasty habit." Barbie sat next to me at the long camp table. Her story of the shock of having throat cancer, the near loss of her larynx, and the near-death experience she had; had me thanking god we did not smoke nor did my family.

So, their decision to sell up in Queensland and take this job offered in Kalgoorlie was uplifting to any one of us listening to her story. The food laden table was soon emptied, when Barbie stood and announced, "Okay you rowdy lot today is my birthday, I am now in remission, free of cancer for the past nine years" we all cheered and clapped; her beaming smile spoke for itself, Ken then appeared carrying a substantial birthday cake, ablaze with candles, the tears slipping down his face as he warbled a happy birthday to his bride of over forty years, Russ and I stood up and joined in as did everyone that night in the camp kitchen.

Russ's hand squeezed mine so tightly, this was our niggling worry, recently a health scare of a mole on his back being cut out. The Doctor saying he felt he had caught in time. A few years in the past, Russ had had cancer scare with the bowel, it was also caught in time, we had been warned that remission is just a word, perhaps in five years or even nine years' time, it may return. Was this recent mole the prediction the specialist had forecast? Constant monitoring and health checks had been all part of his health care.

My eyes stung with unshed tears for my husband and the life we had been given back to love and enjoy each other, warts and all. Within minutes all sorts of party pastries, cakes, and biscuits appeared from vans, and tents. Ice cream, cream cakes, a jelly, bowls of chippies and lollies; once again the table groaned with food, a party began to take place, someone found a stereo, music good old rock and roll belted out, a celebration of life took place, and we were honoured to be part of it. As Russ and I danced he repeated the exact words he had told the day we married: "I want to dance with you together forever," tears stung my eyes.

I was truly blessed by the company we had found along the way and my marriage. We all took turns dancing with Barbie, whose smile never faltered; she glowed with gratitude for her reprieve.

The camp party puttering to a quite stop at midnight; once tucked up in our bed: Russ and I knew just how lucky we were to be together tonight, as who knows what the wind will blow into your life tomorrow. Kal, as the locals call it, had many attractions and we saw most of them. The nights were always warm, so a dip in the camp pool after dinner was always welcome, then a walk around the sizeable tidy camp greeting others that were also enjoying a relaxing twilight. The night before we were to leave, I saw the small yellow sticky pad on the table as Russ cooked our dinner, 'Go through the maps love, find somewhere where you want to go next.' There had been talk of a place called Gwalia, should we go there? I was told it was an experience.

If we were to drive the Golden West discovery trail; our first stop from Kal was Menzies, then Lenora and just out of that little town was Gwalia. I wrote the name Gwalia on the sticky note and placed it on the dashboard. Russ served dinner one of his famous garlic-filled spaghetti Bolognaise with fresh crusty bread. It was so delicious you could smell it a mile away, and so could those damned desert flies; without a fly net on your face, they crawled into every orifice available, I hated them with a vengeance. Russ was used to them, relatively calm and accepting this was how it was; me? Just the opposite.

As we drove out early the next day, Ken and Barbie waved us off. This time, a genuine "Come back and see us soon" was offered; our reply was, "One day in the near future, promise." The sky was a golden promise of another warm, fantastic day on the road, full of freedom and the adventures that only we could share; only we could see, as everyone perceives it differently. An emu with a large, silly feather duster tail ran beside us as we reached the outskirts of Menzies, with Russ cursing them. These huge birds often decided that running alongside the vehicle isn't good enough, so they would veer in front of the moving car, causing trouble for all concerned. We had been made aware of the danger these birds can pose to travellers; finally, the emus disappeared into the distance.

Leonora shocked me; Russ had seen it before. The hopeless look in the Aboriginal people's eyes seemed haunted and lost. On a boiling hot day of over fifty degrees, they stood in the sun, just staring at the cars passing by. One young girl truly captured my artist's eye - young, pretty, and lost, dressed in a long, floral dress with a woolen beanie and cardigan.

However, it was her striking beauty that caught my attention, with her large dark eyes seeming huge on her small heart-shaped face. She moved away before I could take her photo. Leonora boasted a golf course; but all we saw was dust and more red dust. Everything was closed. What a shame, as I had intended to inquire about the Aboriginal art of making a material dyed from local plant life, how they weaved it together without a loom, fascinated me. Then it was off to Gwalia for a lunch date at Hoover House. The history books said this was the home of Herbert Hoover, the 31st president of the USA; apparently, he was the mine manager. The house felt lonely to me, Russ saying, "Well, it is a museum, not a home," but to me it felt like someone's home into which I was intruding.

CHAPTER NINE

Our lunch, a picnic provided by the Metal Mermaid, was on the homestead's cool, spacious, shady veranda. I could not help but think here we are, just Tara and Russ, sitting where the 31st president of the USA would have sat himself, overlooking his small kingdom. Once again, that strange feeling of loneliness settled within me. Museums always evoke that feeling in me; the remnants of ghosts, their belongings on display, their lives long gone- just words to remember them by. I must admit, the house was superb in every way, fully furnished as Mr. Hoover had once lived.

Russ informed me that we had reached our destination by noon, so where to now? It was time to find a spot for the night; nothing was advertised or in sight, so it would have to be off-road. It was almost dusk when we saw a large caravan driving into a small layby just off the main road, so we followed. Surrounded by nothing but scrubby plants, we pulled up and opened the door, only to be met with a blast of hot wind blowing off the desert wind currents. A thick blanket of flies buzzed towards us as if to say, 'Oh, fresh meat.'

The other caravanner's had more common sense, as they wandered over to us, they looked like Aliens. Long dark brown trousers, on their long-sleeved light blue shirts, which were now crawling with tiny black desert flies, were matching monogrammed R&R, both wore Akubra hats covered in fly nets, greeting us with hearty handshakes. Rex & Raewyn invited us into their very plush caravan, with all the mod cons available, an ice-cold beer was offered to Russ, and a chilled white wine to me. I kept comparing our little home with this one. As I watched Mrs. R (which she preferred to be called) put together a small plate of snacks. Wow: the gourmet food that Mrs. R produced from her double door fridge freezer was amazing, a large platter of different cheeses, breads, crackers, jams, sauces and dips appeared.

The soft white leather cushions were heaven to the aches and pains in our bodies. I spied Russ removing the sequin-spangled designer cushion to another chair, I felt overwhelmed by the opulence of this caravan, it was like something out of Aladdin's cave, it held every mod con available.

Sheer curtains surrounding the round double bed, everywhere I looked there was another object of creative art. They even had antique framed pictures of their family on the wall. I do not think my mouth closed except to sip my wine. I was over awed by all the opulence in this huge fifth-wheeler caravan and our hospitable host's well annunciated words, every vowel crisp and clear with the English accents.

After an hour or two of debate on which road to take the Outback way or the Goldfields Highway, we said our goodbyes to this lovely couple. Once back to our little home, I could not wait to ring Rae and tell her what we had just seen. Russ called it gossip; I called it telling her all about what I had seen, the snack plate they offered had been very filling, so we decided on no dinner that night. The laughter from Rae over the phone as I described this couple's caravan also made me smile. She had a knack of bringing me back to ground zero "Mum don't be silly" she would often say with one of my more tactless comments.

This time it was "Mum you don't need all that stuff to have a great time do you? She was right I had the *I want a bigger van syndrome,* how come she was so wise in some ways and could be so immature in others I wondered, but very grateful for her grounding comments, good old common-sense won over. Russ produced a hot drink of Milo along with the sticky note pad, our road maps spread over table for our next date with a destination, however a more important date had been set for two weeks' time,

Russ was due for his check-up at the Geraldton hospital, this had been prearranged from Perth.

We decided to follow the road to Leinster on the Goldfields road; driving through Leinster, Meekatharra, at Mt Magnet we choose as an overnight stay, booking a cabin and a much looked forward to hot shower. To say it was hot when we arrived there, there was an understatement, the tar on the road had melted, it was literally steaming and bubbling. Then to find our room was a tin shed out the back of the pub, it was a bit of a shock. It was a furnace inside, the air con had not been turned on for our arrival, the carpet from lounge to toilet was wet, it stunk of stale urine, the teeny bathroom had seen better days but was serviceable.

We did not need to turn on the hot tap, I stood in a matchbox size shower with the cold water tap trickling hot water over me. We ordered our dinner, Russ was told to pick it up from the pub servery. I had expected a fresh salad, instead I received a limp lettuce and marmite sandwich was served in a plastic wrapping, a hot soft drink for me and a very cold beer for Russ. I watched with envy as the droplets of cold water slid down his glass. Sleep? was one of heat exhaustion. Russ constantly told me to stop moaning, so I told him a few home truths. His response was "Stop complaining Tara, this is a holiday." That is, until he got up in the night and trod on some sort of large bug slithering on the mouldy carpet. Then it was "What sort of shitty hell hole is the dump?" I could not wait for first light; I was up and had the Mermaid running by the time Russ appeared at the door. He grinned at me, "Welcome to Paradise."

One more night free camping, then Geraldton, where we had pre-booked a campsite, deciding to stay for three nights. Russ had his hospital appointment, I had decided once we were there I would restock our provisions and wipe down the inside of the van, while Russ would check over the motor, oiling up, checking brakes, tyres; in fact, anything connected to the motor, so we had no mishaps on our way, so far she hummed along like a bird; not one beat was missed. However, keeping our minds and bodies busy was paramount. Dawn in the desert is a stunning experience; any promotions you read are not accurate at all, it's breathtaking. For each of us, the experience is different. For me, I would call it profound. As the sun rises and its long golden fingers creep over Spinifex and native grasses, the long dark shadows of lone trees disappear as the sun climbs higher and hotter.

Plus, there is always a new story with a brand-new day. This morning, Russ came back inside while I was cooking porridge for our breakfast. He looked very angry as I inquired, "What's wrong, love? "We have two flat tyres" he announced, flopping down on the unmade bed. "How the hell do we get them fixed? He moaned. Then, as if on cue, Mrs. R from the R& R couple stood at our door with a cheery, "Good morning folks, how are you both? My mouth fell open. How the hell did they do that? Last night, when I went to bed, we were the only ones here. Seeing our distress at our situation, she immediately asked Rex to drive Russ into Mt Magnet to find a repair place for our tyres.

Rex was on the ball, "Of course," he said, "One's got to help out when one can." Off the two men went, leaving Mrs. R and I to become better acquainted. Two bowls of congealed porridge sat on our bench, accompanied by two cups of cold tea. Distaste showed on her face. Being polite, she invited me to "Pop on over for a cup of tea, dear, whenever you feel like it." I have no idea if I was being contrary or not, but I preferred to stay in my van with the fans on to catch up on some reading and writing, occasionally peeping out the window to see Mrs. R washing windows and sweeping around their van. She began banging mats with a wire brush, then pulling out a small folding clothesline, arranging their blankets and bed linen over it.

It looked like a mini-Aladdin's Cave market in Morocco. All the while, my brain was saying, what the hell is she doing? It's over 40 deg out there! But Mrs. R kept working, her hair in a French knot, a large diamante clip attached twinkled in the sunlight. Her makeup was perfectly in place, she looked perfect; not one wisp of hair escaped in the hot air and sun that pummeled us.

Not a single rivulet or glob of sweat was evident on her immaculate light blue monogrammed shirt. Her face beamed with joy as she cleaned; then repacked.

Half an hour later, she was hanging out freshly laundered clothes, I could not believe what I was seeing. Next to her I felt frumpy, old, and lazy as she bustled about humming. My sense of humour was certainly flagging as I continued with my writing, adding photos to the computer from my camera. Russ and Rex arrived back many hours later with two new tyres. Apparently, the old ones had been fixed, but they were advised to buy two extras just in case. I had tidied inside as best as possible; my competitive side had taken a beating, with Mrs. R being so industrious. In my mind I saw Rex having a cool shower and a fluffy white towel handed to him, a tumbler of ice water with ice cubes was his reward for being a concerned camper. Upon Russ's return, I had cooled water waiting for him to wash in, then chilled boiled water for him to drink.

He looked upset about having purchase new tyres plus the two mended ones, which he declared were downright theft. We decided to stay another night for safety's sake, as driving at night was not our forte these days, mentioning he had talked to Rex about it, and they also had decided to stay an extra night.

When Mrs. R tapped on our door, Russ had just finished his all over wash, so he was shirtless when he opened the door. She looked him up and down, then blushed as she gave him a handwritten invitation to join them for dinner that night, the look on his face was priceless. I had mentioned that I thought she was little overboard with her cleaning, we were camping not glamping.

His had been 'each to his own' however I do know flirtation when I see it, for some reason Mrs. R had taken a real shine to Russ, I also read the invite, it was made out *to Russ & Wife. My* first thought was how rude, my second thought was to get over myself; it was too hot to cook, as for her flirting with Russ? He had no idea what was going on, Russ had never looked sideways at another. So, at seven pm, on the hour we made the two-minute walk to the camp of R & R.

CHAPTER TEN

What greeted us there was a miracle; surrounding their camp were dozens of fairy lights twinkling away, lighting up the space that had been prepared for our dinner, a long table with pristine white table cloth, a large silver candelabra its long white candles flickered in the soft evening breeze, silver cutlery, with pale lemon coloured starched napkins lay in place, at the end of the table was a small bain-marie, little puffs of steam escaping from under the lids, the center piece of the table under a large domed silver meat dish a golden brown roast turkey, a silver gravy boat filled with steaming brown gravy sat beside it, under the table was a large cream soft carpet. The plastic picnic chairs were covered with a pale lemon calico, with large white bows tied to their backs.

My brain could not take it all in; Russ gripped my hand and muttered, 'Is this for real?" I offered my small, slightly warm, limp salad to go with dinner. They looked like amazing adverts for the Happy Glamper Magazine; in front of me there was a Silver Service Dinner for four in the desert, once again the cold crisp white wine was offered then a bold red wine for Russ. I know the look of surprise never left my face as side dishes were offered; pink curls of salmon on avocado slices and silver finger cups with thin slices of lemon were passed around before the main meal was served. Watching the roast turkey being carved made my mouth water; the roasted veggies were crisp, the beans and peas so sweet. Then desert; again, I was floored as a small silver dish was placed before me, a Caramel Creme Broulee. I could not believe my eyes or ears, all senses on high; a husky, smoky voice crooned to beautiful guitar music from a small speaker on the outside of their van; their story was told as we ate.

No health emergencies pushing them to travel Australia like us, and nothing to do with Grey Nomads. The reason being they were here was on an antique buying trip from the United Kingdom. Once they had reached a quota they would return and sell the collection for a small fortune, the older homesteads over here were riddled with such bargains; both their faces alight with what they had acquired and what was soon to be acquired. They were open and honest about their living; they advertised in all the local papers during their journey. It seems that in this day and age, modern folks did not want their ancestors' silver, gold, or jewellery; so these two offered to buy at bargain prices. The second-hand shops they visited had no idea of the value of what they possessed, so again, they bought at bargain prices. The conversation concluded with Rex announcing that what we ate and used was a little bit of the treasure they had found while travelling.

My first question was, Where do you store all of your things? Where is your storage space? He smiled and replied that their caravan was fitted with many drawers that slid under the van. Additionally, they had installed a false floor in the tow vehicle. It really was an Aladdin's cave. Russ and I were still speechless as they recounted their trips around the world as antique dealers. To top it off, we had movies- yes, movies! They projected a film on the side of the van, showcasing some of their experiences worldwide.

This was living; a calm wind in the desert, complemented by a beautiful meal, and now the movies-heaven. It was very late that night as we walked back to our small home on wheels; my offer to help clean up being gently shushed by our very generous and gracious hosts. Tumbling into bed, we both let out a big sigh, wondering what on earth had just happened. Then sleep claimed us, too tired to leave a sticky note.

Waking up at seven a.m. the next day, we saw the little spot where we had sat and dined, empty; their van gone. A small, embossed, thick cream envelope was stuck to our door." To Russ & Wife, lovely to have met you both. Keep well and safe." Regards, Rex and Raewyn. A small cream and gold business card with R & R engraved on it provided all their details if we were ever to visit London. Was I dreaming? Did that really happen? All sorts of questions battled through both our heads.

Our conclusion was whatever it was; we had a fabulous time with wonderful people. The only way I could tell it was all very real was the tyre tracks in the red earth leading onto the highway. Making a mental note, if I ever saw her again, I would ask her how they stayed so immaculate, so clean and unrumpled. It truly bugged me that by the time we pulled up anywhere, you could certainly tell we had been travelling, with our baggy shorts and wrinkled tops, our faces travel-weary, our bodies not used to all the sitting down we were doing. Russ agreed they did look a bit weird, as he delicately put it.

Who on earth travels thousands of miles on red dirt roads and comes away super clean? 'Maybe they have a super clean huge wardrobe in one of those hidden drawers they showed me,' I quipped, and to this day I still have no idea how or where they stored it all away? Where do you store crystal chandeliers, silver dinner cutlery sets still in the original wooden boxes, and China dinner sets? It really was a forgotten treasure that was once shipped to these harsh conditions by the colonists to remind them of life they once lived on the soft green shores of England. Now it was being returned, in a way never dreamed of by the original owners; by air, rucked up in crates, flying thousands of miles back to their original home. Soon it was our turn to take off onto the wide blue yonder. Losing a day with tyre problems was not the end of the world; we still had a day to reach Geraldton and could do it comfortably.

Russ had taken over driving; I had drifted into a light sleep when Russ shook my arm "Look at this," he had stopped; his camera snapping shots of what I would call a macabre scene, on a tall burnt-out tree was four large branches, on each branch was a large Black Wedge Tail Eagle, watching us as we watched them. It was the perfect setting for a horror movie.

Ever since we met; Russ and I had a code word Andiamo; it means *Let's Go* in Italian; if ever we wanted to leave any situation we would whisper that one word to each other. The scene that was before us had both of us saying "Andiamo." Russ gunned the Metal Mermaid down the road; shivers of superstition went down my spine. We seemed to hurry our once leisurely pace; now, grim determination had taken its place.

We rushed through small, quaint villages, finally reaching the outskirts of Geraldton; soon finding the caravan park that would accommodate us for three days. Russ then called the hospital and put the call on speaker. He made sure his times were right and confirmed where he was to check in. Any calmness and quietness had disappeared from my husband's face; a haunted look resided in his eyes. It replaced anything to do with fun, laughter, or the wealth of experiences we had just enjoyed. To top off the day, the hospital receptionist rang us back, informing Russ that his Perth surgeon was not happy with the last test results and now wanted a colonoscopy procedure. Russ glowered at me over the phone.

'A what?' he asked her. His voice was angry; I knew it was not directed at me, but at his body for letting him down, despite his efforts to stay healthy and fit. The surgeon in Perth had already had his little half-hour talk with both of us, providing information about various cancers and suggesting that in Russ's case, it might be hereditary. The cause was not always known. Leaving Russ to his own thoughts, I arranged with the camp office to stay a full week on site in Geraldton; my intuition was saying, *stay a while.*

That night, there was no sticky notepad glowing on the dashboard. A meal was prepared and consumed, the conversation felt forced. Sleep came in snatches; both of us restless; morning dawned, and our small clearing shimmered with the remnants of frost that seemed to shiver in the air with its cold energy. Waking birds preened, fluffing their feathers in the tall gum trees surrounding us. Blowing my warm breath onto my chilled fingertips as I began preparing a hot breakfast of porridge and honey. It suddenly occurred to me that there was no solid food for Russ today, so I tossed it all in the garbage bin, my appetite had vanished as well. Russ had risen before me, assuming he slept at all, his face drawn from lack of sleep and anxiety. What does one say to a man who has always been a strong and loving partner and supported me through any problems? There wasn't much I could do or say except hug him tightly, trying to push my love and courage into his chest.

CHAPTER ELEVEN

My heart ached, my mind insisting; 'Nothing has been proven that any cancer remains, so stop this nonsense right now.' I sounded just like my mother. We caught the bus into town; Russ checked in for his overnight stay, and the efficient staff relieved us of his small bag and showed us to his room for the night. Russ is not one to prolong goodbyes; I felt dismissed, yet this was his way-no fuss or bother just get on with it. I wandered down to the Harbour - seagulls, boats, people walking, talking, laughing - all busy with their lives. I sent up a prayer of gratitude for the time we had shared, asking the good Lord to give us more time together. The bus back to the park where our van was parked stopped beside me with a soft sigh; as if to say, "Can't wait for this day to finish."

There were five or six campers on the bus, all rather tipsy. I was greeted with, 'Hello, Mrs., come and join us.' Again, felt at odds with the world, so I politely declined their offer. Their dinner takeaways made my stomach turn. As we bumped along, they started singing a song called Whoopsie-Doodle. It was a funny ditty. I had to smile as they roared out the words. I had never heard of this song before; although a bit crude in places, it was very funny. My first smile of the day among strangers felt like a sudden ray of sunshine to my heart. I felt full of hope and love for my life, my husband, my family; and all I had been and done with them. It was late afternoon when I reached home. Settling into our little place with a much-longed-for cup of tea, I dialled the hospital number; Russ was in the theatre as we spoke. My heart did a small bump; my prayers now mixed with tears.

Deep down, my world was a huge part of that man; being without him by my side was not an option. Miracles do happen. As I prayed in earnest, a small 'Coeee' floated through my closed door. There stood a woman who had been one of the people on the bus. Her opening words were "My name's Gilly. You looked worried when you came back. Is there anything I can do?" It's funny what a kind word can do. This simple question undid me, my sobs escaped, her arms went around me, "Tell me hon, a worry shared and all that stuff."

Gilly was wonderful, making cups of fresh tea and almost force-feeding me biscuits for energy. A kind, plump young woman held my hand as the tears came, which ended in hiccups. She said, "Something tells me he's going to be just fine; you wait and see tomorrow he will be home, and then you will know you both have time together." Normally, I would ask, "Okay, how do you know this? This time, I let go of all my fears and thought maybe this was the answer to my prayers, perhaps this was the message I had asked for. Gilly invited me for dinner at her place, a small, blue caravan, three sites down. I accepted, feeling safe in her company. She shared her life story: its ups and downs, about her family, and about her husband, who had recently passed away.

Her story was one of significant emotional challenges. She told me about her two precious children: her daughter, who had been a successful personal trainer for a global insurance firm in Sydney, and her son, who was once an aspiring musician. She described her husband, Ron, a silent but caring man who had passed away along with both of their children in a tragic car accident; in just five minutes, her life had completely changed. She admitted quietly that they all had their sore points with each other, as all healthy families do; but the love they shared always shone true and bright. "Family first," she said. Her large, round, pale blue eyes stared at me, and her voice, now as wobbly as mine, said, "Thank God your man cares enough about you to do what he has to do, so he can be with you and yours." She was right; Russ was a healthy man in every way.

We had both encouraged each other to do the right thing by our physical bodies and emotional selves. "Healthy mind, healthy body" had been my Mum's mantra, which I carried with me. As Gilly's story continued, she made scrambled eggs on toast. Her story was about abuse and struggle; her husband's family had literally itemised everything that the two of them had owned.

During the reading of the will, cries of "Unfair, he promised, or he owed us" were yelled out. The shock of all that had happened still left her numb. If her best friend hadn't stood up for her during that time, Gilly would have ended up with nothing. Her grief took over; she shut down, feeling numb, fearful, and afraid. Her lawyer took two months to bring it to the Supreme Court, which then dismissed all other claims to the will. It was now Gilly's to do with as she pleased. Gilly had moved in with Wendy, it took what seemed like forever until the sun shone again in her life, but once it did peek over to brighten her day, it was time for a decision. She sold the family home, parting with everything she owned.

She gave the large sedan car to her late husband's parents, who grumbled that they wanted the washing machine instead. Now, I have no idea why this statement tickled me, but great hoots of laughter erupted from us both. Tears ran down my face; as a result of the joy, sadness, and fear that were all mixed together. Gilly felt the same; we just sat there, giggling on and off about the absurdity of some people and how the death of a loved one brings out the worst in others. Greed and mischief-making were their missions. Gilly decided that a caravan and travel was the life for her. Together with her friend Wendy, they went shopping all over Sydney. The expression on the salesman's face as two young women approached was hilarious; Gilly joked that she could see him licking his lips for a sale. Ultimately, she chose a small blue fourteen-foot caravan with a jeep to tow it, naming her van Dusty after the singer. I asked the obvious "No; Gilly laughed; it's named for *Eat My Dust*' as I travel Ozzie.

The hardest thing she had to do before setting off was to send the ashes out to the universe. This ceremony was kept very private, with four close friends invited to drive up to the Blue

Mountains to let the wind carry away her beloved family. The only request made of those who attended was a promise to meet here in five years for a memorial. Now, it was to hit the road, embarking on a journey filled with hope, discovery, and adventure.

I called the hospital once I was back in our own home, Russ was well and asleep. My own dreams came quickly, and thank God it did because, without this amazing lady's story, I would have done nothing but fret and fussed about Russ all night. It's remarkable that a problem shared is a problem halved. I slept like a baby all night, waking to a bright, warm day; the sea breeze gentle; as I stretched away the night's kinks in my body, the mobile phone rang. It was Russ, ready and eager to come home again. Within an hour, I was on the bus to collect Russ who was waiting, his arms encircling me as I entered the ward. "Let's get out of here," Russ growled.

He looked pale and thin, and my motherly instincts took over. I had always been, and always will be a mother hen, so it was no use trying to stop me. As we made our way back to the bus stop, a small blue Jeep pulled up. 'Want a ride, Darl?' Gilly called out. 'God, you were quick off the mark this morning,' she quipped." I pulled up to see if you wanted a ride into town without hauling that bus of yours here, but you had gone.' Gilly deposited us at the Metal Mermaid with a toot and a wave. I watched her hitch her van to her Jeep, waving farewell as she drove by to continue her journey. Russ and I both knew it was our Andiamo time as well; he now had a clean bill of health, and the fresh, clean air beckoned us to continue our trip. We called our daughter in Perth to tell her what we had decided.

Although I had kept in touch with her regularly about her dad's health, giving her the latest updates every night along with who I had met and my day-to-day experiences, I could hear the relief in her voice that all was well. Her news was that her Jess and a friend were off to Bali for two weeks, how exciting for them all! For Rus and I, it was delving into maps of the unexplored; we both wanted

to venture far and wide, feeling we had explored the south of
WA. The excitement of travel fluttered in my chest. We could
take the coast road up to Monkey Mia or go inland to Tom Price,
where Russ had many friends from his years of working there.
Why not? His friends had been there through thick and thin; the
sticky note was placed on the dash Tom Price in red across it.
Although I love the ocean with its deep ink blue fading to the
shallows of iridescent foamy white-I also loved how the colour
of the desert changed in hue and shape as we drove along. Our
next stop was Nantarra Roadhouse for a stretch; we indulged
ourselves, Russ ordered a large cream filled Apple turn over; with
a strong black coffee, I ordered a blueberry muffin with cream
and a hot chocolate. The continuous internal argument that sugar
causes cancer had gone quiet, Tom Price, here we come.

There was one place I really wanted to see before we went too
far inland; the seaside town of Kalbarri, which according to the
GPS was four hours away; driving at a leisurely pace from
Geraldton; followed by driving inland then crossing over to
Paraburdoo; hopefully reaching Tom Price in two days. We both
agreed that since we had four days in Geraldton, it was best to
take our time, as anesthetics in the bloodstream could take a while
to clear. I couldn't stop hugging my Russ; I was so glad to have
him beside me.

CHAPTER TWELVE

The information I received from a shop in Geraldton inspired me to visit Kalbarri; her tale of the fascinating underwater stromatolites, dated many billions of years ago, captivated me; long with her story of the pink lakes. It piqued my spiritual side when she added, 'it's so very special to anyone that's that way inclined.' According to the write-up I read from the internet, these living sea creatures marked the very beginning of Earth. Meanwhile, we toured Geraldton; and I loved everything about it- from the statue of a woman overlooking the harbour, eternally searching for the sight of her one true love; her soldier who went overseas, to fight for us and our country in WW2. This statue gave me goosebumps; I found myself searching the horizon as she did. Above us; seagulls wheeled, sculpted into a globe of silver, creating another wonderful piece of art. The shops were delightful; and the people were so welcoming. Soon, the four days were up; Russ was feeling well again, only once complaining of feeling tired and having a slight headache. The hospital was rung; they said, "If it gets worse, bring him in, "Russ mumbling 'he was fine.' Kalbarri, here we come! The Metal Mermaid sang along nicely, and we were happy to be on the road once again, with the sea wind, and sun on our faces.

What an amazing place, with the ocean booming over the reefs. The surfers seemed to be living dangerously, as the waves would either hurl them out, or suck them in; their boards and bodies cartwheeling in the bright green water. A dark, small blob appeared in the rolling, cresting wave; it was a person swimming out to catch the next one or, with any luck; riding the wave back to shore. The bellows of delight from other surfers on the shore encouraged them to ride it as much as possible. Russ, an ex-surfer, said, 'Not on your life, mate,' to which I added, "Amen."

We watched and bellowed with the other onlookers, my camera capturing the sea. The blue waves had grown into a growling tower of green power, the top cresting with foam that speckled like shattered glass before crashing down. 'Awesome' was Russ's term; mine was 'Magic.' The changing display of colour was truly amazing. I then took snaps of the young boys on the beach- strapping Ozzie lads? No, the majority of them were from the UK.

We started a conversation with two of them, waiting for their turn to jump off a small cliff to catch their wave. They smiled when I said, 'Does your Mum know what you're going to do right now?' His strong Irish accent in his reply, "No Mam, if she knew, she would skin me alive." It was time for our afternoon cuppa, so we headed off to find a camping ground. Russ was tired, as most people are after any hospital stay; a snooze and hot shower were in order, while I made the tea and coffee. The nearest camp for us was the Tudor Holiday Park, where we booked a site with electrical output and settled in for the night.

Russ slept while I read up on Paraburdoo, excitement building in my chest at the thought of seeing Tom Price and meeting Russ's friends. The morning dawned with a small finger of sun landing directly on the sticky note on the dashboard. We cleaned up any clutter we had made, our camp table and cups were now stored away, when we noticed our neighbours; two very senior citizens emerging from what was a one-man tent. I greeted them with, "Hello, how are we? and was instantly drawn into their life story or rather enfolded into it. Both were talking so fast that I became dizzy looking from one to the other.

Just then, Russ popped his head out and said, 'Ready to go,' they immediately turned to him with their story. From what I gathered, they were both in their seventies, originally from England, now touring Australia. It appears the wife had coaxed him into biking around New Zealand, thoroughly researching both islands before biking up and down the length and breadth of the country. I had lived in New Zealand myself, so I was familiar with some of the mountainous ranges there. I must have looked impressed, as she then mentioned that now; at seventy-four, he simply refused to bike anywhere, stating, "I feel like I have been biking half of my life; I just want to sit down and enjoy the view."

Russ and I tried hard to understand their dilemma, so I asked, 'Why don't you hire a camper van? she snapped back 'because biking is healthy; in such a bolshy way that Russ and I stood up, saying, "Time for us to go." He, on the other hand, was almost in tears as we left. I looked at their little tent and scant belongings, asking, "How long have you been on the road? "Close to fifteen years" he announced, I just want to go back home." To say I was taken aback was an understatement. 'You've been biking and living in a tent for how long?' I asked again.

This poor man's face was so crumpled and sad when he said, 'too long lady; I want to go home to our house in the Cotswold's." I wanted to wrap him up and send him back immediately; the only thing stopping me from offering any sort of advice or help was the ferocious scowl on her face. I could see the problem, but what can you say to a couple who had spent their lives bickering about which direction to go and how to get there? Russ squeezed my hand. As I looked back at this odd couple, he was bent over, as she continued her verbal tirade of how disappointed in him she was. He looked as if she had sucked all the joy out of him. This odd couple seemed determined to make each other's lives hell. As we drove off, another couple had been drawn into the heated discussion of bike or car; as for us, new adventures were calling.

The pink lakes and Stombolites were our next stop. The silence; apart from the sea and seagulls; made us realise that at our feet lay the very beginning of life here in Australia. It was a moment of reflection for both of us. If spirituality means contemplation, then yes; I would agree. It's a lot to take in during half an hour of photo-taking, as at my feet there were millions of years of history. Then there were the Pink Lakes, they are exactly that a deep coral pink. The brochures inform us that this is caused by bacteria trapped in the salt crystals. An unusual sight; even more so at sundown; it was said, but this was mid-morning, even now; it was impressive.

As for the Stombolites, they are these amazing coral barnacle-covered rocks in the ocean shallows that are said to be millions of years old; it's a shame they cannot talk, as the stories of man's evolutionary adventure would have been incredible. Of course, they are protected, as they should be. Just to view these amazing living creatures knowing these strange bumps contain our Earth's past, is almost like meditation-an experience I would not have missed for anything. So yes, I agree that a spiritual experience was had, one of an internal discovery, more than anything.

The next roadhouse signpost loomed ahead. We had been on the road for quite some time that day, so I was grateful for the opportunity to stretch my legs and take a brief walk around. There wasn't much to see, although there appeared to be a worn-out camel in the old tin shed, which isn't unusual for this part of the country. There was a discussion about whether we should eat the old heated greasies (chips and pies) from the shop for a quick snack or have a cold drink and healthy snacks made by me. We opted for the latter, so cheese, crackers, and cold cordial were served up. We sat in the van with the door closed, as the flies were horrendous. It's funny how you forget about the flies when you spend much of your time in the city or suburbs. Plus, the heat was now in the mid-30s.

Our next stop was to be Paraburdoo when Russ said if we continued, we could reach Dampier by tomorrow morning. He wanted to see his friends in Karratha, Point Samson, plus Port Hedland. I asked what happened to Tom Price; and his reply was, "We are on a holiday; what's the rush? To this, I had to agree-there was no time limit on us. That was the beauty of our home, the Metal Mermaid; with no commitments to anyone. 'I'm game if you are," I replied.

We camped in what is known as a free camping area that night, a small turn-off on the side of the road halfway between Nanutarra and Fortescue. The star-filled desert sky is truly awe-inspiring for anyone who takes the time to simply sit and watch. No campfires are allowed, but we were happy to just sit; eat our salad and cold meat dinner; rap warm rugs around us; and gaze at the stars. What an amazing blanket of quietness settles around you, filling your ears and eyes, resting from the noisy day-to-day buzz of modern life - motors, phones, etc. You can feel your body relaxing to the rhythm of the desert: quiet, relaxed; a deep pulse of quietness blends into your heartbeat.

We rose with the sun, had a quick wash, and enjoyed our hot drinks with toast and honey before getting back on the road. This time I was driving since Russ still felt tired from his hospital stay; he still attributed it to the anesthetics still in his system, plus the fact that he was a smidgen older than the last time he had been in the hospital; my instincts telling me otherwise. Dampier - what a thriving large township! The last time I was here, it was a workingman's town; rough, edgy, wild and simple. Now, it is very cosmopolitan. The once small harbour is now huge, filled with massive ships sorting and bustling themselves into some sort of order. The tiny little shopping mall has transformed into a sprawling shopping centre with blinking, winking signs, traffic lights, sirens, horns, and so many people, all coming and going about their business, all in a hurry to get somewhere.

I looked at Russ in horror, "What had happened in the past twenty years"? I asked. Russ shrugged his shoulders. "It's called progress, I think," he said. 'Do you want to stay here"? I asked, or do we move on"? I knew I wanted to move on, away from what we called progress, to somewhere I could actually pull over and think: at least sort out a road map or two.

CHAPTER THIRTEEN

"Over there!" Russ yelled above the din of this noisy city. He pointed at a sign saying Caravan Park vacancies. A red light blinking on and off 'Welcome to the Dampier Caravan Park."

In we drove; they had one small space left right beside the camp pool. 'It gets a bit noisy around six at dinner time but quiets down around nine,' said the manager. I thought fifty dollars for one night was a bit steep; however, it was obvious that it was filled to capacity. The manager informed us that this little caravan park usually had no vacancies at all; and we were lucky to get this one. As for the charges, he claimed to be the cheapest in town; Russ and I walked around our little bus; checking for anything that might be amiss; it all looked fine. I decided that when we got to Karratha, I would take the insides apart and give it a good clean, Russ agreed to do the bloke thing; check over the motor and brakes as today, we would enjoy Dampier, visiting places we once knew.

We had once toured the Archipelago Islands, the wharf that we had departed from many years ago had been replaced by a large floating dock that was home to four very smart fishing boats; shiny, bright, and modern. In my mind, I pictured the old Lugger that we lived on thirty-odd years ago. We hunted for the cafe where we once shared a bottle of red with the owner of what we then thought of as a dream escape. It had disappeared, in its place was a superstore for Asian foodstuffs.

Russ and I felt disappointed that progress sometimes strips away the past, leaving only black-and-white memories of the wonderful adventure we shared. Russ looked pale, and his breathing was quite heavy, so we took a taxi back to our little home and settled in for the night. I became concerned about Russ; his pallor was not good. Should we visit the hospital? I asked him to tell me immediately if he felt worse. He nodded; took the two painkillers I offered then settled back on the bed to sleep. Not even the foretold noisy six-to-nine pool party woke him. I settled myself outside in the shade with my book, the afternoon sun warm on my legs.

The teenagers who arrived at their pool party weren't all that bad, their chatter and music was quite next to some pool parties we had witnessed. I felt quite comfortable staying where I was, reading up on Karratha. Intending that when Russ woke up, I would prepare our dinner. As dusk settled into night, the vans, tents, and buses all seemed to become peaceful havens. Soft lights glowed, the hum of a TV or radio filled the air, and the smell of cooking made me hungry. I could have killed for a bacon and egg butty right then; what a good idea, I thought. So, into the Mermaid I went, bustling about. 'Come on, love, time to wake up and have some dinner." Russ opened one eye. "I'm starving," he announced; exactly the words I wanted to hear.

He looked great; relaxed, smiling and hungry, offering to make the drinks, while I sorted our dinner. There is one thing about living in such a small space: you have to allocate what you do, or you end up falling all over each other. For younger couples, that's fine, but for us? Well; I presume for other couples, who have led predominantly separate lives; you become impatient with each other; trying to untangle from each other's arms, feet, or legs; and the constant in each other's face 24/7. At first it had been fun, but after a month or two on the road it had become tedious.

I desperately needed some privacy; and no doubt although unsaid so did Russ. I made some egg and bacon bread butties, and Russ poured us a glass of cold light ale to go with them. For dessert I made a fruit salad. The warm, soft night wind encouraged us to sit outside and eat our dinner. Russ wanted to play game called *I remember when thing,* his humour and storytelling always made me smile, so we talked about our trip to the Archipelago islands on the Lugger.

We laughed about how young we both were, no planning, we simply accepted the cheapest fare offered. We had no idea we would have to work our way to our destination, nor did we question it. Not once did we complain that a leaky air bed on deck was our bed for four nights. I was the nominated cook, learning new tricks to liven up the stodgy mess in packets in the cupboard, tomato sauce became my new best friend. Russ catching the fish to go with our meals of rice or mashed spuds.

Memories of how we happily dove overboard in well-known shark-infested waters had not bothered us. Or snorkelling over pure white sand, where clam shells sat, ready to be picked for our dinner. We took delight in what we saw when we snorkelled over and around an old boat wreck, sighting a placid dugong, huge green turtles, plus many beautiful and graceful sea horses that rode the tide, their tails wound around and clinging to seaweed. We welcomed each and every dawn, our days busy. At dusk, Russ and I would sit on the deck, a blanket wrapped around us, and watch the sun dip into the azure ocean, its bronze tainting the small waves lapping the hull.

Today, we collapsed in laughter at the memories as they unfolded; when inflating the airbed every night with an old pair of bellows, it made the most sensuous, passionate groans ever imagined. Of course, the captain ribbed us about our love lives; if only he knew we were the innocent ones. The sea air, swimming, and all the deck work and cooking put anything sexual on hold; a deep, refreshing sleep was had every night. What did the captain do? He steered his true love; the lugger round the archipelago reefs; ate whatever I put in front of him as long as it had a good spurt of tomato sauce on it and served in a bowl. He ate with a fork that he kept in the band of his straw hat and drank copious amounts of red wine from dawn till dusk. On the deck was a crate of red wine in thick green glass bottles with straw around their bases.

Russ would often crawl into bed in the wee hours; worse for wear and slightly hungover in the mornings, while the captain did not move from his chair since we boarded. In our innocence not once did we question our surrounds or our safety; we thought it was fantastic to have this sort of adventure, and I guess in our younger days it was.

Now, we would be horrified; both of us agreeing that age and social and political conventions had brought change. It struck me just how simple our lives were then and how happy we had been. So, what had changed? Why were we not that content couple now? However, by ten that night, both of us were content with good food and wonderful memories; I took out a sticky note and wrote Karratha on it. By seven the next morning, we had pulled out and were on our way with Russ driving and Dean Martin crooning, "When the moon hits the sky." It was another gorgeous day, the sun already warm. I felt any stress leave my body in the excitement of another adventure.

Finally arriving in Karratha, the red dust tinted the bus pink with fine red dirt. Our first stop was a caravan park for a hot shower, where we booked a two-night stay to find Russ's mate Tim. My main concern was cleaning our home, the weather was scorching, there was no doubt in my mind we were heading in the wrong direction for this season; the sensible Grey Nomads were travelling towards Perth or back to the southern parts of Western Australia. But here we were wilting, sweltering, sticky, sweaty, my husband? he felt quite at home in this steaming fly- ridden town.

Russ rang Tino, his colleague of over ten years, receiving a warm welcome. Within half an hour, Tino, his partner Daisy arrived with their six kids, Daisy had the biggest smile I had ever seen. *Tino's Mob;* as he called them all shared that trait with their Mum; bright smiles and large brown happy eyes. Suddenly, I became the honorary Auntie, invitations to stay with them offered. Anything would be better than where we were, in the open with no shade; we gratefully accepted. Tino's mob squeezed back into an old station wagon, the kids arms, heads, and legs poking out in all directions. I had to smile; as this was not something you saw every day; their childish laughter flowing into the cab of the Metal Mermaid as we followed them to their home.

So much laughter, a feeling of welcome filled the air. Daisy shooed everyone outside except for the two eldest, who were ordered to 'make Auntie and mum a cuppa. To the two middle kids, Daisy ordered, "Get your dad and uncle a cold beer." I was given the best chair in the house by an open window since there was no air conditioning. A large plate of chocolate biscuits was produced; the heat making them soft and gooey, the flies making a beeline for the sugary treat.

A small chuckle escaped when I spied a small brown hand snake through the window, grab a handful of biscuits; Daisy smirked and whispered, "Watch this." When the hand crept through again; Daisy grabbed hold of the hand; yelling "Gotcha." The child screamed with fright, the kids encouraging him took off in all directions. The little rascal was rounded up, given a good telling off then received a big hug from his Mum. Daisy shoved the biscuit thief at me; "Say sorry to Auntie; then go and play." he did as he was told, leaving his chocolate fingerprints on my skin. This family was loud, raucous and obviously loved each other.

The two eldest girls carried in a large, blackened steel kettle. They filled the China tea pot. One pretty China teacup was placed in front of me, and the saucer was placed before their mum. Daisy sipped her tea from the saucer, the pleasure of this treat written all over her face. Dinner? Fish and chips from the local takeaway shop. Our plates? The newspaper the meal had been wrapped in.

A massive bottle of tomato sauce was offered around, plus a large plate filled with slices of buttered bread. Once all the busy hands had settled; grace was given. I expected noise, mess, hands going everywhere; instead, I saw manners being used; in fact, a few of my friends with grandchildren could learn a lesson or two from this family. Tino nudged me, "Come on, Duck's, fill up or go without." My hand coming away with a handful of delicious brown, crispy chips. When dinner was finished, the youngest child cleared the table.

Once the newspaper was in the rubbish tin, I was invited to clean up in their bathroom, which was a tin shack outside, a bare lightbulb shone; a tin bath hung from the wall. A rubber tube was attached to a water tap; the long drop toilet was closed off by a curtain; everything was spotless. I was happy to rinse off the grease, the eldest a pretty teenage girl, appeared with a clean hand towel. The outside bathroom was not what I had expected; however, I was privileged to be shown the start of a new bathroom that was indoors. It gleamed white and silver, with tiles adorned with lovely motifs of bush flowers around the walls. The only setback was that they were waiting for a sewer connection, which was due to happen any day now.

Her pride in the home and family was obvious; the love flowing from this large family was heartwarming. What a privilege it was to be involved, even for a day. It was dark when we left for our own home; parked in their backyard; nothing grew out here but scrub. The night wind was cold; however, the welcoming we had received had warmed our hearts.

CHAPTER FOURTEEN

Home has never looked so good. I was so tired that once inside, I literally melted onto our comfy bed, kicked off my shoes, and went to sleep. Russ didn't even wake me when he put a quilt over me and made himself a coffee, going outside to drink it and relax in the quiet of the night. Our next day was all about cleaning our home; the fine red dust had gotten into every nook and cranny, and the day's temperatures promised to be in the high thirties. While I cleaned inside Russ cleaned the bus's windows with a hose.

By three in the afternoon, I had everything back to where it was supposed to be. Bedding, dishes, cutlery, and mats were all in their places. I had borrowed Daisy's vacuum cleaner and washing machine. Try as I might, nothing could stop this family from helping. If I glanced sideways, there they were with offers of assistance. This family was amazing, carrying and lifting items to help their Uncle Russ. When we finally finished, feeling exhausted, a big ice-cold pitcher of lemon water appeared, gratefully accepted by us both. Russ had once again checked the tyres and motor stuff I had no idea about. By five in the afternoon, the heat had proved too much for me, I was asleep on our bed. I truly felt tired; my muscles were sore, my eyes felt gritty, a migraine was forming.

These blasted migraines had been the bane of my life from my thirties onward, at times lasting for four days. Along with them came nausea, blurred vision, occasional facial tics, and fatigue. The specialist I had seen offered little advice, saying more or less to learn to recognise the symptoms and take painkillers or whatever worked for me. He had written me a prescription for anti-nausea medications and paracetamol, then asked to see me in three months' time; the bill was worse than the headache. I had learnt by now to recognise the signs of the oncoming pain. Self-medication is never advised, but what do you do when you're in the outback? Two painkillers were needed immediately. I had also discovered that standing under a hot shower helped or lying in a dark room with a hot water bottle on the painful area. This approach helped me more than being doped up for days. Today, I felt the cause was the intense heat; it usually triggered one of these blasted headaches. Russ, muttering "We know it's stress, dear, learn to relax a little," it sounded "Like it's just a headache" and it was met with me firmly closing the door behind me, boiling the kettle for the hot water bottle, two painkillers, and headed back to bed.

Meanwhile, Russ played on the iPad, emailing his friends in Dampier and Port Sampson to tell them we were on our way, hopefully arriving within two or three days. It fascinated me how he relished this heat, how he worked in over 50deg at times, while it destroyed me. I could not figure out if he was just bloody-minded or I was not normal, but honestly even the birds took to the shade 45+ deg day. The next thing I remember is waking up to Daisy. She had popped over for a visit, Russ told her I was asleep with a nasty headache, so she had gone back to their home and boiled me up some sort of herbal mix. At first, I was against swallowing this mixture; the smell of boiled desert herbs was awful, and my tummy reacted with a wrench.

"Come on, Aunty, just try it,' as she cradled my head. I swallowed a little, then sat up and sipped it slowly. It tasted like old mushrooms and wood, with a bit of gritty sand mixed in. Daisy sat beside me; her long brown fingers curled around my hand. "Gotta getcha beta," she said. I have no idea what was in that drink, and I don't care. Within an hour, I was "Beta," as Daisy would say. I was up, feeling full of energy, and my eyesight, which normally suffered, was great. Both Russ and I asked for the remedy. Daisy grinned. In the dim interior of the bus, she resembled the Cheshire Cat from the Alice in Wonderland story. "It's blackfella's stuff, can't pass it on, belongs to my Mum."

What I do know is that when I went to bed I slept like baby; nothing ached or hurt; felt out of place or bruised. Daisy, Tino, and their mob all came over to the bus the next morning. I felt a tug of sadness at leaving them, their farewells lasting till they were out of sight. We had made wonderful friends, they called us their white fella's family. Usually, I felt washed out after a migraine; today was so different. Russ also noticed my energy levels and the spark had vastly improved from past experiences. He had made the traditional sticky note with "Point Sampson" written on it. After one stop to boil the Billy, then use that infernal bucket, empty the bucket, then disinfect the bloody bucket. I noticed how the red dirt showed many different colours, from baby pink to deep ochre, and the wildlife moved at its own sweet pace. The endless blue sky was amazing; it seemed there was no one else but us, the sky, and the endless ribbon of red, not another person in sight for miles. If you're not used to silence, and I mean silence, where you can hear the blood pump through your veins, then this is no place for you.

Stopping off in Roebourne for a stretch of our limbs, or so I claimed as I had suddenly noticed the dark smudges under Russ's eyes; his eyes were bloodshot, and when he reached for his camera, I also noticed a slight tremor in his hand. I enquired if he was in pain. I got a sharp rebuff, "Nothing's the matter." However, when offered to drive, he quickly agreed, which was unusual as he liked to be behind the wheel. He claimed he wanted to take some photos of the oncoming sunset; as we moved on I saw him rub his hands over his face; then he quickly fell asleep. I reached over to feel his pulse; he flicked my hand away. I was happy to see the sign that announced Port Sampson was an hour away. Our friends Kelly and Alison were there at their gate to meet us, these friends we had known for what seemed like a lifetime; they were our age. They had moved here after the mining life had nearly destroyed their marriage. Point Sampson, a small seaside village, was their savior.

They literally went fishing for a year, starting with a tent and then a caravan for the winter months- no TV, no radio, nothing that would let the outside world in. They had both agreed to focus on each other for a year. Now, three years later, they had their own home and had built a life with and for each other once more. They were now very much part of this small community with an extended family. Kelly was over the moon about having a new fishing buddy for two or three days. We girls loved the idea of taking time out to chat about women's stuff or just simply hanging out together. Russ and I intended to sleep in our bus on their lawn, but they had a different idea.

No sooner had we parked and enjoyed a welcome beer than Russ was told to pack up; they were off fishing and camping; a bloke's weekend had been planned. He raised his eyebrows at me as if to ask permission. My reply was "Go and enjoy, I'm quite happy here with Alison." I opted to sleep in our bus, as I felt more comfortable in my own bed than in a strangers. Quickly my days were filled with meeting her friends; she had arranged a sewing bee, plus a book group; obviously, my time here would not be boring.

The sewing bee made things for the Salvation Army; mainly for the homeless; once a project was completed, it was bundled up and taken to their church in Karatha. I watched and took notes. If it worked for this outback group, why would it not work for my friends and me when I returned? I did not have a specific job to do; however, many cups of tea or fresh scones and jam were called for, plus washing dishes or sweeping floors. I was on hand to help. It was fun, and I really enjoyed being part of it. The book club was my niche of knowledge; they wanted to write an anthology. I was happy to guide but pointed out that there were two communities here. The Aboriginal people, who have already drawn centuries of art as part of their story. As for the Europeans? Well, I had seen many old manuscripts in the Karratha library, so what did they want to achieve: a more up to date modern?

When one senior held up her hand, "I would like us as a group to write; but I would also like us to look after our ancestors' manuscripts you just spoke about; they are not in good condition and in time we will lose them." I wanted to applaud, "My thoughts exactly, and you can do this by going online and learning the basics of book repairs." It was settled they had ladies in this group who had computer knowledge, in no time at all, without my assistance, they had formed the Outback Heritage Book Club.

At night, Alison would cook dinner while I caught up on emails and family, they were still in Bali, so we messaged and sent photos. One night, she said, "Tara, I just have to show you this special place." It was a small café right on the beach called Mojo's. We ate the freshest fish I've ever eaten, big chunky chips, and ice-cold beer. However, the specialty of the night was not on the menu, as we watched the sunset from a bright golden day turn to the softest blue/grey lavender, then turning into a deep mauve before my eyes. It's gentle softness creeping onto the sand, touching my bare feet, then covering my arms, resting for a minute or two on my face, seeping into the backs of my eyes. Heaven. I had seen God's paintbrush work its wonders before, but tonight I felt the magic encircle me, enfold me, my one description of this experience would be that I felt I had been anointed; tears had pooled in my eyes; as the ocean, sky and sand became one in unified colour, it was endless.

CHAPTER FIFTEEN

On the third day we were expecting the two men home, we received a phone call from Kelly late afternoon asking if we girls minded if they stayed for the week while the fish were biting and the beer was still cold. We answered in unison, "You, go for it." After all, they were not the only ones enjoying time out. Two nights later; two bright headlights turned into the driveway; the men arrived home. My heart plunged, as Russ was helped inside by Kelly. "That's it, mate, take a big breath; just lean on me. Russ sat down heavily, gasping for breath, his skin a grey/ blue, trying to be calm. I sat beside him, taking his hand in mine, I asked, "What's going on?

He gasped, "Don't know, love; went to stand up and just lost it. Russ looked beaten; certainly not the man I started this adventure with. Kelly's forehead was creased with worry, repeating what Russ had just said. Everything had been fine until yesterday. Russ said he felt a little tired. Kelly went and put a long line out to catch bait fish; when he got back, Russ could not stand up, felt nauseous, fainted, and had problems breathing. Kelly insisted, they left the gear where it was and headed home immediately. I asked our hosts to ring for an ambulance; Russ argued, "He was alright, nothing to fuss over" he lost consciousness for a minute, his eyes glazed over; his facial muscles went slack; Kelly said, "Mate, we're calling an ambulance." I dialed emergency being told all emergency services were busy; however, a list of instructions were left, but Russ needed urgent attention now.

Russ slept poorly; I had given him two painkillers that the Geraldton hospital had provided. I also woke at every grumble or snore. Once Russ was up although groggy, he was most apologetic about his 'funny turn' blaming post-surgery shock plus the heat, excuses tripping off his tongue one after another. I was literally rushed by Russ through a hasty goodbye to both our friends, with Russ saying he felt fine. I had time to express my gratitude; we were back on the road.

Russ had completely ignored my wishes to stay a little longer and ask a local doctor to examine him. Did he need more medical help? He was focused solely on driving to Tom Price. In his no-nonsense voice for children, he snapped, 'Stop being melodramatic and relax.' So, to appease the situation, I did as he asked. Normally, I would say let's consider the consequences; this time, I remained silent and let him take the lead. Whatever demons were chasing him was obviously his lesson, not mine.

I did feel for Kelly and Alison; they were also concerned asking us repeatedly to stay over until Russ could get some medical help. While Russ and Kelly were on their fishing trip, I visited the local information centre. I knew we had to gain permission to cross the Millstream Road, as it was a private road belonging to the Hamersley Mines Company; permission and payment had been accepted by the time we left. The turnoff to Millstream Road was not well marked; the road was not sealed, and Russ began to drive he was in some sort of car rally; the poor Metal Mermaid began to bump, swerve and grind over the rough terrain. I yelled, "Russ, slow down, please. He braked then bolted from the driver's seat, throwing up on the side of the road until he was on his knees, dry retching. He began to complain of blurred vision and a splitting headache. From where I was sitting, it looked like he was experiencing a migraine. But why? That was my next question.

I once again sat behind the wheel, taking my time, Russ laying on the bed with an icepack on his forehead. It took the entire day to cross Mill Stream; the long, snaking trains full of iron ore from the mines seemed to be the only life around as they idled past. The most beautiful flower, the rare Stewart Desert Pea, was out in abundance, the rust red dirt road and bright red flowers broken by occasional pale greenery of a salt bush.

Halfway across was an oasis of silent beauty, tall white ghost gum trees surrounded a billabong. It was now mid-afternoon when we reached this little haven of shade. Russ was still in pain, so I turned off as close to the trees as possible for the shade and suggested he stay on the bed; with little complaint, he did as I asked. I made us both ham sandwiches with a cold drink, and his face blanched at the thought of eating. I gave him two more painkillers, keeping close by in case he needed me. My Russ was in a lot of pain; and there was not much I could do; it was not much use ringing Ray, to discuss as she would be in midair returning from Bali.

I heard Russ moving around, so I went inside to see if he was okay. His eyelids fluttered open, 'How about a cuppa?' was croaked through his dry lips. That was a good sign; hopefully, he was on the mend. A cuppa was soon produced; he ate the dry toast I offered, as it was my staple when I was headachy. finally, colour began to return to his pale face. The time for explanations had arrived. But Russ was as bewildered as I was, saying, "I suddenly felt super tired just like I did in Geraldton, but this time my chest hurt. But I will admit, when the headache arrived, I panicked, thinking just getting on the road and concentrating on something else would help it all go away." I insisted he see a doctor or visit the hospital in Tom Price. To this, he agreed.

I had no idea if it was illegal to camp here for the night? Too bad I was willing to take on the government itself if necessary; as we both needed to sleep and relax. Night gently closed over, after a light dinner, we were tucked up in our cosy home, Russ peacefully asleep beside me, the last thing I did was write Tom Price on our sticky note, then attach it to the dashboard, then gratefully close my eyes. When dawn cast its golden glow over the Mermaid and Billabong, we were up, washed, had breakfast, and were on the road. This time, Bette Midler sang 'The Wind Beneath My Wings' as we pulled onto the main road; both eager and keen to reach our destination. Russ still had a mild headache, but his stomach had settled down with two painkillers.

I drove again, my mind mulling over the why of his headaches; I had googled his symptoms on my laptop; what a rabbit hole that had proved to be. At least I still had the internet and phone coverage, for which I was grateful. An upset tum and headache I can handle, an emergency? How on earth did the pioneers cope when faced with an illness? I was still struggling to come to terms with Russ's erratic behaviour and driving, so I opted to drive, whispering to myself, 'today is going to be a good day,' wishing Tom Price would suddenly appear.

I drove carefully, aware that Russ was not in a good way; our situation felt anything but comfortable. I no longer wanted to be out in the desert; I no longer wanted to be a nomad without a care in the world. I would not have cared if dinosaurs had appeared in the distance; all I wanted was the safety I felt amongst a community of people I trusted. The Metal Mermaid was chugging along in time with my internal mantra: 'Please keep us safe.' Brian and Winn's house at Tom Price was our goal, and once we were there, solid arms surrounded us both. Thankfully, Alison had rung ahead and informed them of our dilemma.

I felt like I was ten years old again. Tears once stopped were now escaping as I sank down onto a comfy couch and told Winn and Brian all about Russ's health scare, the hospital visit, and what happened at Kelly and Alison's house. The loving care we both received here was amazing. Brian took charge; he made me sit and talk to Winn while he drove Russ immediately to the hospital, and we were to follow him as soon as I had calmed down. A hot shower and a change of clothes worked miracles. As I walked into the small medical room, Russ was ushered into the doctor's office to be examined again, receiving help as his legs could no longer support him. He was in real trouble health-wise, and we both knew it.

CHAPTER SIXTEEN

My heart sounded like a big drum in my ears as I sat there with Russ's hand in mine, ready to hear the news of why he could not physically operate properly. His tired, dizzy spells, nausea, painful headaches, and trouble getting lungfuls of air were baffling to us both, and now he was saying his right leg was painful. Two days had passed in the hospital; they had asked him to stay in for another night so that more tests could be done the next day. All tests were being examined by his specialists in Perth.

Russ was still very weak, his legs giving out, and his breathing became gasps with any exertion; his lips now had a tinge of blue to them. Doctor Benson came in, his face serious. My heart sank; "Okay, folks, we have found something a little more serious than expected and may explain why you're feeling unwell." Russ gripped my hand so hard it hurt. The scans were put to the light, Dr Benson pointing out a grey mass. They had found a large blood clot in the aortic vein in his right groin, suspecting that tiny fragments had been breaking off and travelling through the bloodstream to the brain and heart. Dr Benson said, "Luckily for you, we can deal with it through medication and a small keyhole operation." However, my heart tipped over as I waited for the only hospital that has availability for immediate surgery is in Perth.

We both sat there looking stunned; the Doctor continued "If the entire clot moves it could then it could go to his heart, causing a fatal heart attack or it could possibly pass through the heart valves causing major damage and or straight to the brain causing a major stroke." My next question was "Why has this happened?" he answered, "Who knows, hemorrhaging or hematomas could be hereditary, or it could be any recent surgery; there are a million reasons, but the point is he needs to have this seen to immediately; I will arrange to have him flown out this afternoon." Russ's eyes were huge; he had found it hard to take it all in. This healthy, strapping, strong male had met his match health-wise. There was nothing to do but sign the necessary papers. Hopefully, our insurance would cover any costs. All I could do was pack a bathroom bag for him and wait for the plane to arrive.

Russ was again placed back in the ward to await the *Flying Doctors; this* medical team flew across the outback, saving lives from infants to seniors. They are renowned around the world for their brave acts of courage. This organisation was always in need of financial support; it was only the many generous gifts from charitable people and caring philanthropists that truly kept them afloat. At this moment, I would have given everything I owned to keep Russ safe. Like most women faced with major decisions, a calmness crept in, giving Russ a hug, "I will be back within the hour."

I had some arrangements to make about the Metal Mermaid, which included putting our life as Grey Nomads on hold for a while. The news had spread about Russ; thanks to Brian his satellite radio plus the network of people we had met along the way. My phone was full of messages of support; just when I was feeling my most vulnerable and overwhelmed, a message from Russ's employer came through, "Hey Tara, sorry to hear about the old man, don't worry about the *flying doctor's* fee, it's been covered. My body sagged with relief; I was so very grateful for them all. The staff informed me that the medics would be here by one pm; it gave me two hours to organise calls to Perth. My first call was to our daughter Ray; she would have been back home from Bali for a day or two now. I explained our situation, asking if she would be there for her dad; until I arrived.

Then it was back to Brian and Winn's home to tell them the news and arrange somewhere to put our little home until we could bring her back to Perth. Winn offered her help in any way; and Brian offered us the use of the old lean-to in their backyard "For security mainly; a deserted bus was fair game for some folks." I gratefully accepted his offer, backing our little home onto their once grassy backyard, the scorching summer heat had desiccated what was once a pretty green patch, leaving nothing but dry red earth. Little pink Willie Willies (whirlwinds) kicked up the red earth as they wound their way across their backyard.

Winn's comment, " At least you will be home for Christmas, " was a shock; I had forgotten about Christmas. Booking my fare home online, as I had been informed, I was unable to fly with Russ. Rae had agreed to be there to greet her dad at the hospital; my calmness remained until packing my case and one for Russ, then locking up the Metal Mermaid. I almost wanted to hug her; she had been my safe cocoon for so long. Tears escaped, then quickly wiped away; time enough for tears once Russ was safe. It felt strange how everything was panning out, how unforeseen circumstances were hugely affecting us; from a small general check-up at our local doctor's six months ago to this major health problem. Meeting so many amazing friends, who had opened their homes and arms to help us get to where I was heading now: home. Winn and Brian, their kind faces worried, drove me to the hospital to say goodbye to Russ. He had been sedated, his sandy eyelashes laying peacefully on pale grey cheeks.

We then watched as they wheeled him onto the plane, soon the plane headed down the runway; I felt bereft as the plane lifted off into the blue cloud free sky as my tears blurred it transformed into a kaleidoscope of silver blue's. Being strong in front of the people who want to support you is fine; or a while, Winn had the sense to walk away, as I lay my head on the steering wheel of Metal Mermaid; the grief, sudden change of plans. The life we had imagined as Grey Nomads now on hold; the urgency and seeing Russ so ill. The inner child wanted to be held and told it would all be okay; the female adult acknowledged the responsibility of freeing those blocked tears. I let them flow. Then it was time for me to board my plane, I was then enveloped in a huge, firm hug from them both. "Take good care of yerself Tara; give Russ a good kick up the arse for me." It was said with concern and love for his friend; his goodbye brought a shaky smile to my face.

Paraburdoo Airport hummed with the miners heading home. My plane was ready to board; the miners showing concern for me. Russ was a popular figure in this world, having worked with and trained many young men as drillers or drillers' offsiders. He was also known as a prankster, his way of induction for the new guys. This was once a tough world, once a man's world that was changing. Among the men now stood women who drove massive dump trucks carrying the iron ore. To see a woman standing there with the men, drinking a cold beer and discussing work with the blokes before take-off; for me, it was unusual; however, they all treated me with respect, considering I only knew two or three of the folk in the room. Russ was considered one of them, and since I was known as Russ's Mrs.; as they put it, offers of rides to the hospital once we landed in Perth were offered; messages of "Get well soon" were genuinely given for Russ.

Three hours later, we landed, and I saw Rae and Jess waiting at the baggage carousel; we just hung on to each other, Jess squirming in between us; demanding a hug; suddenly, I realised just how much I had missed this little man and my daughter, the tiny niggly hole that had been there in the corner of my heart suddenly closed up. My family was with me; we were going to be fine. My arms were now full of the people I loved, and although I had been shown so much love and consideration from friends; we had met some wonderful folk on the way, there is nothing like the familiar touch of your family, children and grandchildren. The Royal Perth Hospital was where Russ had been admitted. Rae had already assisted with some of the details. I was told the blood clot had moved. An emergency was repeated while Russ was being prepared for surgery. I sat beside him; talking to him in a calm voice that belied how I felt.

I wanted to sob and cry out, "It's not fair." As they wheeled him away, I promised we would be there for him when he was out of theatre. I felt numb, whispering to the heavens, "Bring him through this safely." Thank heavens for the hospital coffee shop, as that's where I spent the next three hours. Rae had taken Jess home to prepare a meal and tidy up the spare room. I was staying for a night with them before returning to my own home. Finally, Russ was out of the theatre, the surgeon saying, "Everything had gone well; he felt he had caught it in time. We inserted a stent into his Aortic valve. There was also damage to the vein in his right leg, it's been replaced with a vein from his arm.

He will be confused and very sore; I will call in later and explain the procedure to him." He put his hand on my arm "It's a lot to take in Tara, and he will be out to it for a while, why not go home and get some rest: the staff will ring you when he's out of ICU. I rang Rae with the news while I sat holding my husband's hand; all the tubes and beeps from the machines made me feel very inadequate. These machines were for now his lifeline. I then called our friends Brian, Kelly, Alice, and Winn to share the news: Russ was going to take some time to recover at home, one day we would definitely come back for a visit.

CHAPTER SEVENTEEN

These friends had been invaluable in their support for both of us. Next, I called Tino and Daisy to tell them what had happened. Although shocked by the news, they also offered their support, "Anything you need, love, just let us know; you know that your family is to us. Russ came around; his blue eyes shadowed in pain. "What the hell happened? " he mumbled; I told him what I knew about the blood clot, not mentioning the operation on the arm, as I felt the surgeon could explain that much better than I could. After a while, Russ nodded off again. I kissed his brow, smoothed his hair; it was so hard to leave his bedside. Catching a bus home. I called Rae, saying, "I'm on my way now." Jess is meeting me at the bus stop, his hand reaching out to hold mine, his brown eyes filled with concern "Hello Nana, come home with me."

Suddenly, a faded memory returned, one of when I had been the one who had greeted my grandma when my Pa had passed; I was five years old, and the duty given to me had been very serious. I was told not to smile or play, as Grandma was very sad. I had held out my hand to her, "Come home with me, Grandma." I had never forgotten the lost look in her hazel eyes. I gripped Jess's hand my body almost sagging with relief "Yes, please, let's go home."

I felt so safe moving back into the familiarity of a life I had left behind. I literally sank down in my chair: not wanting to move a muscle. I felt so tired; my heart ached for my husband, that I missed incredibly. This was not the homecoming I had dreamed of. Rae had kindly provided all the necessary groceries I would need for a day or two and had made me a meat pie for dinner that night; I had no need to go out until tomorrow. My home felt enormous compared to our little bus that we had called home for the past few months.

My home had an old-world charm that made us feel we belonged here, surrounded by huge rose bushes of all colours, blue and white agapanthus, native grasses, palm trees, large agaves, and wide bricked paths that led around the large bull-nose veranda. The backyard featured a wooden swing beneath the shade of old gum trees; a fish or frog pond had been unearthed, cleaned, and maintained. Over time, whatever needed a watery home would reside in this much-discussed backyard oddity since no one knew exactly what lived there. Come summer night, the frogs sang in unison; the birds bathed there every day; it had a settled feeling to it.

There had been an old aviary that Russ had converted into a nursery for his prized orchids. Russ also had a passion for delicate native ferns, which were now thriving joyfully without his regular trimming. Today, I felt lacklustre, so I just sat down and remembered the old days when life was busy with family, friends, and projects. Inside the wide, cool rooms that were very modern for such an old home, the one thing I adored about this house was the French doors that opened from the kitchen to the veranda. When it opened, they created one huge open room. The many barbeques, parties, and family get-togethers brought such fond memories. Plus, our two children were conceived and born here.

First, a boy, a treasured son, Ross, who lived for six hours before he broke our hearts by passing away. A hole in his heart went undetected until he was born; his wee soul fought to breathe; he fought to live. His tiny baby fingers clutched mine as he battled for life, then with a tiny shudder and sigh, he gave in and drifted away in my arms, his Daddy's arm around us both, as we said our heartbroken goodbyes to our baby boy. A year later, a baby girl was born; we called her Raewyn, a request from her ailing grandma. She was perfect in every way; our friends called her sunshine. I had been blessed in many ways. Yes, this was our home.

I woke up from a deep slumber as the sun was setting. The lounge basked in its golden glow; dust motes floated in the air. To me sleep is the most healing thing the body can do. The fear had gone, so when I rang the ward nurse, she advised me that Russ was resting and comfortable; it would be best if he was left to sleep. I rang Rae; she agreed to let her dad rest, we would go see him tomorrow. I slept well considering; once I had woken to a bright new day; I felt Russ was on the mend; I knew our family would be together for xmas. The phone started ringing, friends, family, and extended family repeating the same message, "Just heard Tara; how can we help?" or asking if they could call in to see him. The days passed quickly with Russ mending well; any signs of blood clots were now gone, and there was no indication of any other health scares. In between my visits to the hospital, I spent a lot of time in the garden pruning wayward roses and plants that had decided to wander off. I decorated the house with Christmas decorations, even ordering a tree so the smell of pine would drift through the house.

Jess decorated it with the gusto of a preteenager; once finished, it resembled an exploded party popper, with very little tree showing under the tinsel, streamers, and baubles of all colours; his superb art piece had pride of place in the lounge. The day came for Russ to return home. Rae was picking him up once the doctor gave him clearance. On his arrival Russ looked pale, with thick bandages on one arm and leg. He hobbled into the house, and seemed to deflate into his chair, putting his feet up and closing his eyes; he fell asleep. Welcome home, Russ" I whispered, placing a light throw rug to cover him. Rae and I sat in the kitchen, having a cup of coffee and discussing what to cook for Christmas dinner and what to buy for Christmas gifts. Both of us excited; we were home for Christmas. I knew it was all going to work out; Russ would soon be on the mend, hopefully even continuing our travels perhaps in the New Year. My gift to him would be road maps and a new GPS.

What he needed now was encouragement to feel confident to resume our trip; while he healed, and this time, we could plan it much better than before. I felt we both now had the experience to Nomad properly. When Russ woke, he looked so much better. His one sentence was, "It's good to be home" I did the nurse thing- plumping pillows, making coffee and afternoon tea, asking what would interest him for dinner, and dishing out medications and painkillers. While he was feeling pain-free and comfortable, I explained the situation about our bus, that it was safe; Brian had offered to guard it with his life.

I suggested that once he was feeling better, we could fly up to collect her, drive her back down here; or perhaps continue onto Broome and then around the top of Australia. Russ smiled; he knew that this had been a passion of mine for years. We had both travelled the world, yet Australia's top end was still a mystery to us both. "Whatever you want, sweetheart," his voice sounded joyless. This was the part that always scared me most; when loved ones sound like they have given up on the joy of being alive. My job was to make sure he took an interest again. Russ stayed in bed most days, refusing to walk around the property because he hurt; he also refused to be part of the family.

We had to go to him if we wanted to discuss anything; there was an endless stream of family and friends wearing a path in the carpet to the bedroom. It annoyed me, as that was our private domain, so I had to be the bad cop again and move a rather grumpy Russ into the conservatory, making up a daybed for him. At night, I would support him to our room, but then I wised up and bought him a walking stick. His improvement was slow and steady; he began smiling at our private jokes, our trip memories, and the folks we had met. The blue/ back circles under his eyes stayed; his constant fatigue seemed to suck the life out of him.

By midday nearly every day, he was back in our bed. I checked with our doctor to confirm that the medication was not the reason. Our appointment the surgeon arrived; Russ had trouble getting into the car, snapping at me to leave him alone, pushing my hands away as I tried to tuck his sore leg into the car and once more; we quarreled. Tempers boiled over his with anger, mine at his situation, mine with frustration. Russ began to call me names when he yelled into my face, "Don't be so fucking stupid", his spittle speckling my face; I slapped him, hard. It stopped the abuse mid-scream. There was nothing more I could do or say, we drove to the hospital in silence. The surgeon examined his wounds and discussed his symptoms carefully and clearly with him. He then advised us to give it another month of rest, and if there was no improvement, he would consider changing the medication. My suggestion of an antidepressant was met with raised eyebrows from Russ and the surgeon. I was very grateful when the surgeon offered to send the Silver Chain ladies to help with bathing and re-bandaging the wounds, which I gratefully accepted. Robin, the Silver Chain nurse, arrived in two days. She was very professional, kind, and no-nonsense. She was allocated two hours to help Russ every second day. Shooing me out of the house with remarks like, "Go out, have a coffee, or meet a mate." She assured me, "He is going to be just fine; I 'm here now."

Russ and Robin hit it off immediately, he had no choice, as she told him. "Just do as you're told, young man, and we will get on just fine." So, I went out for coffee and met my mate Jo, enjoying it immensely. Her tactful humour always made me laugh. I also managed to get a lot of Christmas shopping done, I bought road maps, a proper diary for daily comments and destinations, etc. The new GPS was a beauty; I knew Russ would love it. Inside this little package, I added a bright yellow sticky note pad with a huge smiley face on it.

I have always enjoyed the preparation for Christmas- the baking, the smell of Christmas that wafted through our home as I mixed spices then added a little rum to the Christmas cake. Slowly, the Christmas gifts started piling up under the tree. We had agreed on three for Jess and one for each of us. Well, that was what Rae, and I decided, but since we were home for Christmas, why not spoil him a little? Russ nodded in agreement; he adored his grandson, and Jess was a good tonic for his granddad as well. 'Let's get the Grasshopper (his nickname for Jess) a mobile phone for his gift.' I was delighted with the idea. We read many pamphlets, and Russ finally chose the one he wanted to buy. He called and ordered it, ensuring it was the correct one and confirming the delivery date.

Russ improved very slowly. Some days were great; he shuffled from our bed to the daybed or armchair, demanding a coffee and the newspaper and as per normal, I would tell him where the paper was; could he fetch it, while I made the coffee. On other days not too good at all, his breathing shallow, his face pale, the arm wound causing the most pain. Russ would whine and want my attention nonstop when he was unwell, there were times I had to bite back a hasty reply.

CHAPTER EIGHTEEN

Deep down, I was concerned. It left me wondering why this health setback caused him to become so needy. My Dad had been the same as he had aged, badly. If not for me taking over at times Mum would have been worn out long before her time to go to God.

On the positive side, it was so close to Christmas, Russ was getting better every day, I was well, the visitors had slowed down, thank heavens; I could pamper this good man as much as he needed, so he would become active and well part of our family once more. Christmas day arrived; Jess and Rae staying overnight, as we both knew it would be an early morning start, and we were not wrong; Jess came hurtling out of his room at 5 am yelling, "It's Christmas" Normally, Russ would appear very grumpy and take his time; first a strong coffee and a hot mince pie was to be had, often family and friends from previous years would yell at him to 'get a move on.'

I intercepted our grandson in the hallway, saying, "Wake your Mum up first." For the first time since we were married, Russ was not in our bed beside me on Christmas day as a strange feeling. I made his coffee and hot chocolates for Rae, Jess and myself, heated the fruit mince pies, thinking he would be in his chair or asleep on the daybed. Recently, Russ would wake, hobble to the daybed so he wouldn't wake me. He had explained that the pain in his leg made him restless; admitting he had found the peace in the early morning, it had given him time to think. We had made peace over the temper display the previous week; we had gone to bed that night at peace with our world. While everything was brewing, I peeked in on Russ then quickly washed and dressed; the Christmas tree twinkled in semi-darkness.

Russ had not moved, asleep in his armchair; the leg troubling him, propped up on a footstool, his head laid back in the chair, and his soft grey curls still ruffled from a bad night's sleep. Jess was so excited; his hands reaching for a parcel; Rae and I both trying to calm him down, saying, "Come on, Jess, you know better than this, it's Granddad's job to give out the gifts." I filled a plate with Christmas goodies, saying, "Come on, sleepy, time to be Santa." Shaking him lightly, there was no response, I gave his arm another shake. This time, his head rolled forward. I looked at Rae, her eyes mirroring mine.

No! Walking over to her Dad, she gave him another shake, saying crossly, "Come on Dad, it's not the day to kid around." I knelt beside him, my fingers on his neck, feeling for a pulse. Nothing. I felt my body begin to shake as I placed my head on his chest, listening for the comforting bump I had heard for the last forty-odd years. Nothing. My Russ was dead. I have no idea what happened next; all I could think of was this was a joke, any moment now he would get up and yell 'fooled ya' Russ was famous for his silly practical jokes. This was surely one of them.

I have no idea how, why or even who came that day, all I know was I wanted to hold onto him and never let go, I wanted to scream 'No!' but it remained bottled up inside me, I don't remember much at all but having to accept my husband had passed away. A man I had never met before gently pulled my arms away from Russ's body, helping me into a nearby chair, my legs buckling under me as I tried to stand up; his voice and hands guiding me to sit down. When I looked up, they had put Russ on a gurney, wheeling him out to the waiting hearse. Watching the hearse door open, its cavernous mouth taking Russ away.

It was too soon; the cry I had kept bottled up inside me erupted into a moan that came from so deep inside it hurt. I don't recall much of that day at all, I said stupid things, I did stupid things.

I don't recall wandering in the garden weeping his name, my neighbour Perry hearing me and coming over to help, taking the secateurs out of my hand, this kind man understood my grief having lost his wife Nancy, a few years back. Russ and I had both been there for Perry. He just sat with me and let me cry it all out; I did not have to be brave for anyone with him, he wiped my nose and rubbed my back crooning to me 'let it go, just let it go.'

Rae was inside. I could hear her sobbing as she informed her friends. Jess was nowhere to be seen. What had happened to this bright and beautiful day? Why had this happened to us? There were no answers. Perry saying, 'it was his time; thank God he went peacefully' Then my brain kicked in, did he? What if he cried for help and I did not hear him because I agreed to him sleeping in a different room? What if he were in pain and through my grumpy behaviour, he felt he could not ask for assistance? The guilt set in. I held Rae in my arms; now it was my turn to be the comforter. We searched the house for Jess, he was found under the bed, in a foetal position; he had cried himself to sleep.

It was such a hazy time for us all; the hospital wanted an autopsy to prove there had been no medical mistake. Finally, his body was released; the day for his funeral arrived, the day we said goodbye forever; the small local church was packed to overflowing, folks standing outside; Russ in his will had requested no flowers, any money offered was to go to a charity of my choice; on his coffin was a simple posy of his home-grown Orchids. Our twelve-year-old grandson handled the situation like a mature teenager, his chin trembling with the need to sob his grief out. He took pride of place, leading the pallbearers as the coffin left the church. Russ would have been so very proud of Jess in his sombre black suit, no doubt teasing him, then hugging him, telling him what a good-looking guy he was.

Rae, pale with fatigue and grief, God only knows what I looked like, I only know how I felt apart from our son's death, this felt like a void so deep and dark, and I was sinking into it.

Jess was now the man of our family, not having a dad himself; Russ had taken over that empty spot. Over the years they had done so much together. His eyes had shimmered with tears at the funeral, his little chin stubborn, not one tear escaped, but once home, I heard him crying; I knew for him the healing had begun. I don't believe in an afterlife, but I swear I felt the soft touch of a hand on my shoulder as I held our grandson close. The funeral director rang to say that the death certificate had been released. Would I like to pick it up personally, or would I prefer it delivered to me? I chose the latter. Once it was handed over, I did not open it; I left it on the table by the phone. I did not need a piece of paper telling me that my right arm was missing.

Rae insisted we open it together. She said, "They say here embolism; that's not right Mum; they took the blood clot out" Rae was ready to ring the hospital; her anger simmering on her face "Someone has to pay for dads' death" I gently took her hand away from the certificate. "Rae; he's gone; that's all I can deal with right now." It took nearly a year for me to embrace the logical side of life and move on without my husband to encourage me. I constantly found myself thinking, "Oh, I must tell Russ about this," whenever something funny happened or our combined opinions on the news on telly, family debates, or simply saying 'goodnight, love you' to each other. I ached physically and emotionally every single day; however, they say time is your healer, and I still felt hollow. The following year, as Christmas arrived, all three of us dreaded the celebration, aware of the painful memories it would bring back.

A week before Christmas, I still hadn't done anything about gifts or a tree; it felt overwhelming. I knew that Jess had become disappointed with me; I had no enthusiasm at all. He, however, had bounced back, full of life as young ones do, and Rae? She had met a young man, her face full of happiness, for her love was in the air. How do you express that for you it's too soon for change? We had all changed, yes, time is healer; however, my heart was still raw with the memories of a life we had once shared. One afternoon as I was daydreaming, watching the bees busy in the garden, the late afternoon sun warming my body, when I heard a knock at the door.

I called out, 'Coming.' To my surprise, there stood Gilly, the woman I had met in Geraldton. She hesitated before saying, 'Hi, remember me?' she laughed, as I swung the door open in amazement, she held out her arms. 'I only heard about Russ last week. I'm so sorry.' 'Come in, come in, please! I'm so glad to see you!'

Gilly had entered our lives, she made us all laugh, her bubbly personality lifting the curtain of gloom that had settled over me. I woke up with something to look forward to; she brightened my day. The lonely days that dragged on were now filled with 'female stuff,' as Russ would have put it. I felt like Gilly was the catalyst I needed. We all got on so well, so I insisted she stay for the xmas week. When she made her version of a Xmas pudding, that would blow your mind with the amount of rum and brandy mixed into it. I made sure that Jess was under strict instructions to eat Nana's Xmas pudding only, he was encouraged by Gilly to decorate the Xmas tree that they had both sourced and dragged home.

Once again, the tree exploded with every garish ornament they could find, beg, borrow, or steal. Gilly helped make our Xmas wonderful; I loved having her around the house, her little caravan now tucked up in the driveway. I even hosted a New Year's Eve party, the first one in years, as Russ hated them with a vengeance. I invited all the neighbours and friends who could attend. Rae brought her new man Tim with her; she looked stunning and so very happy. Her man was tall, dark, handsome, and Greek; together they made a beautiful couple.

CHAPTER NINETEEN

Our house bulged at the seams with everyone turning up. We had such a fun time dancing, laughing, eating, and singing in the New Year with Auld Lang Syne. By one o'clock the next morning, all that was left of the party were streamers, dirty plates, and glasses, and as I wearily- cleaned up, it hit home. I had been a widow for a year, and I also knew there were many ways to remember a loved one without falling into a deep pit of grief. The problem was, did I still have enough life in me to live life to the fullest, while I was healthy enough to do so. Rae had opted to stay the night with me, asking if 'Tim was welcome to stay as well.' Jess had opted to stay at a mate's place overnight. Gilly was out on the daybed. The night was so silent after the music, the loud chatter, laughter, and clinking of glasses; sleep took a while to come as many thoughts ran through my head.

I began to remember the arguments we had about having parties, Russ preferred small intimate dinner gatherings where he could shine as the host and disliked and discouraged any sort of large gathering in our home with more than six people, but he would willingly accept invites to large gatherings in other folk's homes, why was that? He picked Ozzy blokes only for his girl Rae, so she rarely brought home boyfriends of any other nationality but a true-blue Ozzy.

One memory that came back was the embarrassment Russ caused when Rae brought home a young Indonesian student she had befriended. I planned to invite him for dinner when Russ intervened with his opinion, leaving both Rae and me in an awful situation. Luckily, the young man sensed the animosity and left with an excuse of needing to get home on time. Rae was furious; Russ's smug answer was, "My home, my table." We had had many arguments, Russ believed he was the man of the house, or should I say any decision made about the family had to go through him. Yet, if I decided to buy something new for the home it was "You're the lady of the house, I leave it with you."

If I agreed to go out with one of my social groups, and he was home, he would sulk or interrogate me with the whereabouts and with whom. He knew it would make me angry, and yes, I did let it get to me; I was not a child. Russ liked me to himself and had a jealous streak. However, I was also at fault, as I had given in; anything for a peaceful life had been my motto.

Rae, however, saw it differently, and they would argue day was night. She was her own boss and told him so in no uncertain terms: "I will date whoever I like, whenever I like, I'm not a child." Any arguments or opinions from myself or her dad were shut down immediately.

This past year, I had had a small taste of freedom. It felt wonderful to have my head out of the gloomy bin and to realise that Russ had had a very big say in my life, and I had let him; I had built my own independent life when he was working away, but once he was home, we had all catered to his needs and wants. But the days we enjoyed as a family far outweighed any unpleasant times. His memory would always be a strong reminder of our combined values and boundaries within our family. Most of all; the deep love we had for one another.

"Good morning, sleepy" Gilly called as she moved from the sunroom to the kitchen. Rae called out, "Morning Mum, your cuppa is on the table." Looking at these two new lovebirds made me smile, especially since Russ would be furious if he knew I had permitted our unmarried daughter to sleep with a man under our roof. When the two of them saw me smiling, they both blushed, they had no idea what I was smiling about. Gilly was busy packing her caravan; she intended to leave within the next day or two to go south to visit some friends before heading back to Melbourne to catch up with her sister. I was dreading her leaving as it meant an empty house again.

Rae and Tim said their goodbyes; they were off to find Jess and enjoy their day together. I decided to clean up the house, take down the Christmas tree. Winding so many coloured streamers around my arms, I suddenly realised how freeing it was to act like a child when no one is watching.

Taking down a Christmas tree full of Christmas cheer is no mean feat for any adult; so, I played, like a kid, aiming the Christmas ornaments into their box. Suddenly, grief took me by the hand, a Christmas ball from our engagement days, and stood directly in my vision. Russ's handwritten message, 'together forever.' I sank to the floor, my thumb going over the words; knowing that a love like ours was rare to find. We had annoyed the hell out of each other, we had bickered, demanded, argued, and as we grew up together, we both became opinionated. However, I knew that Russ was my soul mate, we had loved each other through it all, and we had shared a lifetime of forty-plus years together. Play time was over.

Gilly had joined me for a quick coffee before she left 'What's up?' she asked. How do you say, "I'm going to miss you", to a woman you do not know all that well? I'm not one for silly excuses either, so I dived in the deep end saying, "You're leaving too soon." Her smile was worth a thousand words. By dinner time we had figured out what we could do together. She would head to her sisters, then return in a fortnight; then I was going to show her my beautiful city, Perth. I loved the idea of being a tourist in my own hometown, then we would fly up to Tom Price taking Russ's ashes with me, bringing the Metal Mermaid home.

By the time we had finished making plans, Rae, Tim, and Jess arrived. Leftovers with chicken pie were on the menu. Rae then told us her news: Tim had asked Jess and her to move in with him. She was ecstatic, but Jess appeared unsure, and it showed. Maybe it was time for a Nana and grandson talk, I thought. Excusing us from the table, we went into his room a discussion about what the new year would mean for him. This little man was a huge part of my life, so any decisions we made as a family would naturally involve him. I told him about my planned trip to Tom Price, and he immediately brightened. 'Can I come, Nana? You promised me, last time you went away that I could take a trip with you."

That was true. 'Let me see what Mum thinks, and then we can discuss it properly.' Rae was all for it, as was Tim, both agreeing it would make things easier for them communication wise if Jess was occupied. Gilly, true to her word, returned eight days later; Perth shone its best for my new friend, our first visit so close to home was Penguin Island at Safety Bay; we took Jess with us delighted in these small seabirds; then a boat cruise around Penguin Island to watch the seals, ice creams on Rockingham foreshore. Jess invited Gilly and I to the movies, he had saved his Christmas money so 'The *Warhorse* Movie by Stephen King' was chosen; and I must say I thoroughly enjoyed it

Returning a very tired young man to his Mum, Gilly and I went home; I also headed to my bed as it had been big day. The following day our Perth tour continued. I must admit I was now seeing this tour through Gilly's eyes. First stop the Royal Mint, we rode the double-decker bus around Kings Park. It had its best summer hat on, picture perfect. The Swan River Cruise, watching the dolphins play, is always a tourist's delight. Catching the train home-another new experience for me. Once home, all I wanted to do was collapse on the couch, bliss.

In that one week we went to the zoo; we visited Government House and the Perth Museum. We walked along St George Terrace, taking snapshots of all the wonderful bronze statues, we encountered, and explored St George's Mall, where Ye Olde World curiosity shops still thrived in the older part of town. Fremantle was exciting; we took a sailing trip on the tall ship The *Llewellyn,* waves splashed into our faces while seagulls screeched at us; clearly amused by how wet the tourists were getting.

The next day, we explored Subiaco markets to meet my friends; an Argentine couple, Carlos and Margarita, who owned a food stall there serving us a Greek dish a spinach, soft cheese, and pancake specialty. We spent three days exploring the city by train and bus; enjoying each other's company and getting to know one another better. On the weekend, we drove to the Kalamunda markets-where golden jams, homemade candles, jewellery and fresh fruit awaited.

There had been a minor setback when Gilly admitted her bank account was low, she would apply to her superannuation for more cash, would I be happy in loaning her $500.00 to see her through, "Happy to write you an IOU babe." Her enthusiasm for life had me hooked. I was happy to loan her the money, and to be paid back within the month. On our last day at home, with an early 4 am start, we soon found ourselves on the outskirts of a small shire called York, where a hot air balloon ride took us high above the beautiful sunlit treetops. It was breathtaking; our cameras were working nonstop. Once we landed, the champagne that flowed at the barbeque breakfast was a gourmet delight. Once home it was down to earth; as we made chutneys and jams from the fruit and vegetables we had bought, stocking up the home pantry plus packing some of this produce into a small box for the trip north.

That night I sorted out the banking and bill paying, transferring Gilly's loan request of $500.00 to her account. The time had sped by so fast; suddenly, it was time to drive to Perth airport to Paraburdoo. The small wooden box with Russ's ashes in it was now packed alongside my clothes. In a way I was looking forward to lifting his ashes to mix in with the pink tinged winds; watching them swirl into the red desert Russ had adored; bringing some closure.

Jess was beside himself; he was finally going on a trip with his Nana and his new best mate Gilly, who obviously adored my grandson. Rae and Tim drove Jess to my home, wishing us all a safe trip. They both looked smitten with each other, "Take care

Mum, Jess be good for Nana please." She then looked at Gilly, a look I had not seen before, it was calculating, but why? Rae floated off hand in hand with her man, was I ever that in love? Did my parents ever see that kind of glow about me when I introduced them to Russ? I was genuinely happy for our daughter; at last, at last she knew love.

Up and away, we went into that endless blue sky that Australia is known for, Jess sitting at the window with a running commentary on whatever took his fancy - this being his very first flight. Everything, including the toilet, was an amusement, his comment on the huge *whoosh* the toilet flush gave, plus how much he liked the blanket and the kids' colouring-in pack they gave him as he boarded, soon Gilly and Jess were chatting away like old mates. My quietness caused by memories of Russ coming up here as a young man so keen and eager to conquer it all; very much like his grandson. I felt sad that I was going to greet all our friends this time without him by my side, this would be our last *Andiamo* together.

I had always loathed the name widow, it just seemed demeaning to me, some ladies I had known in the past gloried in widowhood, they wore it like a mantle, sad, lonely and like attracts like or so they say. Me? I was anything but that; for me learning to be truly independent hurt like hell; however, this was the beginning of a new life for me.

CHAPTER TWENTY

The plane glided to a halt. Jess unbuckled himself from the seat, standing in the aisle before the motors were switched off; placing my hand on his shoulder, murmuring, "Calm down, Jess." I needed to stay focused, as his excitement I found a tad disconcerting; thank heavens for Gilly who squeezed my hand then began talking to my Grandson. Brian was there waiting for us, the withdrawn pale face told me how he felt; I could feel him tremble as we hugged, "It's okay, Brian", I whispered, our eyes shining with the unshed tears.

He had been Russ's right-hand man in every mine they had worked in together; I truly felt for him; he knew Russ as well as I did. The only difference between us was that I knew Russ as my husband, one who could take the reins when I could not, Brian knew him as a man of his word, trusting each other in making quick decisions in their mining world. Our ride into Tom Price had been a silent one; Brian and I had some time out together; where he told me of the memorial that the Tom Price mine management had put on for Russ in the mess hall. I had different plans, which I now divulged to Brian, no fanfare or salutes, just Russ's last wish that his ashes be thrown to the wind at the top of Mt Nameless or Jarndunmuha, which is the Aboriginal name for this Mountain.

A spectacle of dawning light highlighted its crags, peaks and valleys. Just Brian, Jess and I made the trip, a silence settled around us as Brian drove us to a stop point, from there a 10-minute walk to a flat plateau. We stood together as Brian offered a prayer; "Safe travels, old man, god willing, we will meet again." I asked Jess if he wanted to say a few words; I could see he was struggling, his boy body shaking with his sobs. Jess's hand shook as he placed it on the small wooden box that contained his beloved grandfather's ashes. 'Love you Ranrad you were the best." Together, we lifted the lid, tipping the grey, white ashes into the wind; a pink willy willy claimed the ashes, they swirled high into the sky; my words followed them, "Andiamo Russ," Jess' arm went around my waist, I hugged him to me.

That night was spent in our friend's home with smiles, tears, and the 'I remember when Russ said or did;' it was a glimpse into the past to understand what a strong friendship these two had formed. I slept in the Metal Mermaid for the first time in fourteen months. Gilly and Jess bedded down in the house. I sobbed myself to sleep, no more twosome, no more squabbles about who stood where so we could dress, eat or drink. The Metal Mermaid was made for travel and adventure, but where would I go on my own? Would I revisit the old haunts we visited together, rehash old memories? Or new ones? Another thought entered my head; could I sell this little home on wheels?

We had had so much fun with her; or would I keep her to treasure our last days together? My eyes closed with exhaustion pondering this question. Morning arrived with Jess banging on my door. "Wake up, sleepy. Here's your mug of tea." Once Jess had entered, his eyes became enormous; everywhere he looked were reminders of his Grandad. The shaving mug and razor Jess had given him for a birthday present one year, a large, framed photo of all our family above the bed, Russ's aftershave and his fishing hat. I knew at that moment I would sell her; if I was going to make a new life for myself, including my family, we did not need Russ's footsteps following us wherever we went. I asked Gilly what she thought, and she agreed with me. Stopping outside a Vinnie's secondhand shop, I cleared out all of Russ's clothes and removed anything we did not need. Jess claimed the photo of the four of us together, which was fine by me.

Gilly offered to drive. Once we reached the main highway, the Metal Mermaid was once more on the road, and hopefully, happy adventures were ahead. I rang and left messages for our friends,

I knew the bush telegraph would have spread far and wide, Russ's Mrs. had returned. So, I felt the best option for me was to say we will be back later in the year, it was hard enough as it was without memories of when and why being regurgitated time and time again. Which way to go? Well, I had never been farther than Port Sampson and Gilly admitted she had never been to Broome, so Broome it was. Metal Mermaid chugged along; quite content to be back on the road again.

I'm quite certain that this bus could ferret out an adventure. On the outskirts of Broome, with a heart-stopping bang, one flat tyre, which meant stopping just on the outskirts of Broome, those bloody little flies swarming us everywhere. Thanks to Russ, who belongs to the RAC, national breakdown service. One phone call and one hour later, the yellow and black truck showed up. One tyre now fixed, now a caravan park was to be sourced, and it was almost time for dinner. Jess claimed he was ravenous. There are many, as it is a Tourist's mecca. Jess asked for a camp with a pool, which I also preferred, as the Northern Territory Ocean is known for its (Salties) saltwater crocodiles and sharks. Gilly had complained of a headache, all she wanted was a hot cup of tea and painkillers, the sleep.

Me? I just wanted to find a caravan park to stop driving; call my daughter Rae and have a chat with her. I spotted the sign advertising the Beach Cove Holiday Resort, with the all-important pool, big shady trees to park under and close to the beach, where I would have an hour just to wander by myself. I booked for five nights; paid the bill, and even though Jess swam like a fish in water; I made sure there was a lifeguard was in attendance. Jess was off like a rocket, the green pools his sanctuary. I checked on Gilly; she was out cold.

I almost ran to the sand hills, finding a spot where hopefully no one would find me, and lay a blanket down in the warm sand. I wandered in the shallows, picked tiny shells off the beach, and literally caught my breath. Time to breathe, time to exhale, then slowly breathe in the ocean air. Time to ask my heart; how are you feeling today? Time to watch the beginning of a burnt orange sunset; some needed time out. I felt the wind become brisk, the small waves rippling the sand and sea. This was my time- and I needed it. No tears or emptiness as I wrapped my arms around my body, the orange sunset on my face and a huge sigh that said it's over, it's done. Exhale, and asked the sky that glowed around me, "What now?"

I have no idea how other women handled a loved one's death; I dealt with it in my own way. I called Rae and informed her about what we had done regarding her dad's ashes and his belongings, where we had been for five days, and that we would hopefully be back home in eight days; she reminded me that Jess began school in two weeks. Her news was also exciting: Tim had proposed. There was a pregnant pause for a microsecond; my reply was "Rae, sweetheart, you were made with love, and you deserve to have it in your life to.

"Oh Mum, I love being in love" she replied: she had no idea how surprised I was. Still, this was her life, and she must live it the way she sees fit. Once back at the caravan park, I was pleasantly surprised to find Jess there in his pyjamas, showered and ready for bed. Dinner was almost cooked, and a glass of cold white wine awaited me on the table, which had been set up on the outside of the van. A gorgeous, crisp green salad and a fillet of fish sizzled on the barbeque, creating a heavenly aroma. Gilly laughed at my expression, Okay, let's enjoy this meal, then sort out this city called Broome." I raised my glass "You have a deal." All three of us had a list as long as your arm of what we wanted to see and do in Broome.

Over dinner, we all put forward our ideas and came up with a mixed bag of what would be fun if it all worked out. I, for one, wanted to visit all the art galleries and knew that Gilly and Jess would not enjoy it, so it was compromise time. We all agreed that once we were back at the Metal Mermaid after sightseeing for the day, we could do our own things: Gilly with her photography, Jess at his beloved pool. Me? I would focus on writing again.

Once settled on the sand dunes, with the ocean and sky my inspiration; I could feel the stirrings of excitement about what I could now do with my life. Maybe even a novel would one day appear; a skill I had loved to play with in the past, the words were there just waiting to spill out onto paper.

Gilly clicked her way through the day with pictures of the public of people whose faces told a story to add to her yearly calendar; her hopes were that the Tourist Bureaus throughout Australia would be interested and purchase. Her main theme was the older population. I found her photos tasteful; a large amount of her time was spent editing. Jess? Well, he had found his nirvana in the large pool, meeting two other teens, the camp manager's sons. The manager kindly agreed to keep a close eye on the energy being released by these teen boys. During the five days we spent in Broome, we discovered Chinatown I was agog at the Pearl shops, art galleries galore, cafes and the amazing culture. We also loved the museum where we learnt about the divers that had given Broome its fascinating name.

The diverse cultures of Indonesian, Asian, and Aboriginal people working side by side; if there was any racism, we did not see it. We went on the bus tour to visit the home of the 130-million-year-old fossils and booked a camel ride. Gilly and I hung on for dear life even though we were only at walking pace, while Jess wanted his Camel to go as fast as possible.

Thankfully, the camels were tethered together; otherwise, I think he would have ridden it back to Perth city by himself. We wandered through the markets, in the day and at night, watched in awe as the firewalkers, magicians, and jugglers entertained us, the juice of fresh mangos running down our chins. We tasted the many dishes available; some hot and fiery, others so delicious that you wanted more. I arranged a surprise for us all; we went whale watching in the morning, and in the afternoon, Jess was dropped off at a kids' fun parlour.

His one obsession was electronic games, and this place had them all. For two hours, while he played, Gilly and I enjoyed some pampering just five doors down from the games shop, the phone number of said shop emblazoned Jess's mobile phone. Oh bliss! As the oils seeped into my dry skin, her hands began on my feet. I woke when she called my name and said, "All done, dear." I felt sleepy, free from the pressure of having to do or say anything; it was pure bliss. Gilly looked like a sleepy gecko as she floated out of her little room. A lukewarm shower was offered, and then our hands and feet were all buffed. Our toenails were painted; what luxury! Then it was time to pick up Jess and head home, our stay in Broome was nearly over. The next morning, I woke up very early.

Our sleeping arrangement wasn't the best but would suffice for a holiday. Gilly had the spare bed, composed of a table fitting into the surrounding seating arrangement, an airbed, and a sheet with a throw blanket over it. Jess and I slept top and tail, with a small bolster dividing the bed so he had his side, and I had mine. Broome in the summer is scorching, with temperatures in the 40s on even a cool day, the humidity is awful. Thank goodness for the fan, as it certainly worked overtime with all three of us inside.

CHAPTER TWENTY-ONE

However, this particular morning, I tiptoed out, not wanting to wake anyone. Now I know the warnings and had read the danger signs of what lived in these waters but the ocean with its calm azure beauty called out to me for a shallow paddle. There was no one around; the beach was empty. I wadded in, feeling a wee bit risqué. Dare I? All I had on was knickers and a sarong.

My heart urged me to be a child once again. 'Go on, have a swim; it won't hurt anyone.' Before I knew it, I was up to my waist, then feeling a tad scared, I headed back to my sandy spot to sit and meditate. As I slowly waded back to shore, I felt my back sprayed with water. I screamed, bolting onto the beach, positive a salty was on the attack; the shore had never seemed so distant. Panting, my clothes stuck to my body, my face covered in stringy wet hair, my voice whimpering. When a Botticelli song rang out as a senior citizen trawled past, his backstroke was strong and clean, his voice so clear. While I stood in ankle-deep water, whimpering and no doubt looking like a scared drowned rat, he shouted 'Morning, Ma'am' and off he swam, while my heart hammered with fear in my chest.

Back amongst the sandhills, I sat down, trying to quiet my pulse. The senior had also come ashore stark naked; he casually walked over to his clothing, towelled himself off, dressed, then strode off along the beach singing at the top of his voice. I felt like a voyeur watching this old gent dress; on the other hand, not once did he check to see if anyone was about. I had to agree, what a wonderful way to greet the day; maybe one day I would shed my fears and do as he did, embrace the day.

Walking back to the bus, my smile erupted into laughter as I told Gilly about it. 'You should have woken me! 'she cried. ' I could have photographed him.' I silently disagreed. Why would you ruin another's day by interrupting their solitude? We visited the Crocodile Park, watching these ancient predators fighting for food, raising the hair on my neck, I would not be foolish with a morning paddle again. Jess asked me if he could have another camel ride?' I knew my limited budget was being squeezed until Russ's insurance came through, but I hated to say no. Once he was into the saddle and settled, he took off for an hour-long ride along Cable Bay.

As Gilly and I waited for his return, we wandered along the sand. We spotted two people sitting on a rug, with a small instrument in their hands. She was winding furiously on a small machine while he parted coloured threads, feeding them into the machine. I just had to stop and ask what they were doing. Reta and Steve from Switzerland introduced themselves as they shook our hands, saying they were on a trip around Australia. The machine they were using looked like an old-fashioned eggbeater. I crouched down beside them to get a closer look. Sure enough, they had modified the 1940s eggbeater; what they were doing with it was pure magic. Somehow, they inserted a large steel ring and clamped it tight.

Then, by hand, Steve fed the coloured string into the beater while Reta turned the handle slowly at first, then faster. Steve picked colours at random, inserting them while she wound. The finished product was amazing, a multicoloured ring like a tiny dream catcher. Reta snipped and tied the threads, then pulled out a small pair of pliers to attach a silver ear hook to the top of the ring. I held out my hand to hold it, and there lay the most perfect, bright, multicoloured earring. Pure magic. We invited them to the bus for dinner that night so we could learn more about their travels; we both found them interesting.

Racing back to the camel pickup point we found Jess, then went food shopping, much to Jess's disappointment, his face sulky because his afternoon swim was cancelled. My response was, "Tough, sort it out; either join in or go to bed." Jess knew I was getting a little annoyed by his attitude; thankfully, he chose to join in. His task was dessert: choosing some creamy cheeses with crackers and mint chocolates for after's. 'Good choice!' Gilly and I chorused. We had bought food to make a spaghetti Bolognese, with Gilly crowing that "Her recipe was to die for."

Greta and Steven arrived at six that night. Jess and I had set the outside table; a blue and white check tablecloth completed the look. Gilly proudly dished up her meal, and I must admit it tasted wonderful. Then Jess brought out his dish, all perfectly displayed on a small plastic tray, a nice complement to the meal. Of course, he was praised as all enjoyed his efforts. The night air was cool, but we had good food and company; or so we thought. Steven told us all about his adventures, particularly how he met Reta, who sat there demurely blushing at Steve's recounting of their meeting. It went something like this: 'He saw, he liked, I chased her, then she was mine.' Wow, what a love story, I thought. What about the courting, the cuddles, and the build-up to a life together? I queried, Greta, who was so shy she hardly spoke; Steven always seemed ready to take control of the conversation.

His long, dark, braided hair contrasted with her platinum blond hair, which was swept up into a top knot, tiny white shells nestling in the coils. Tattoos covered his hands and muscular arms. Reta had a tattoo of a butterfly on the back of her neck and wore a pair of her own earring creations that sparkled with metallic thread. Both of them looked healthy and tanned, their lifestyle obviously agreeing with them.

A thought crept into my head, who would have thought I would ever be having a nice, relaxed dinner in far north Queensland, with a lesbian, two hippies and my grandson, surrounded by signs of "*Be aware of snakes, and crocodiles.*"

I wonder what Russ would have said. Steve began to tell us that only yesterday they had made a necklace to match the earrings, he said, 'they had found many small objects to add to their jewellery, some of them were old and valuable, so he sold them to an antique dealer, adding to their own coffers.' I had to ask, "Do you not hand them to the police in case they're lost and valuable? "No, finders keepers' he said, snarling. Reta went to say something, but he barked "Enough" in her direction; she cringed away from him; the subject was closed. His anger at my question was palpable, but his bullying of his partner I would/could not accept. I immediately stood up, my words spilling, "This conversation is over, good night."

Steven challenged me, standing so close I could feel his breath; Reta was in tears as he roughly took her arm and shoved her in front of him. "Put the fuckin' torch on!" he screamed at her, giving her a push. Reta stumbled; he slapped her hard and then marched ahead; leaving her behind, softly crying out for him to stop. Jess had just witnessed a nasty side of life; tomorrow I had some explaining to do. Gilly looked at me and then burst out laughing. "What?" I asked. "Hmm, look who's growing a pair," I must admit, I felt good to choose who I shared my company with. The next morning, I explained to Jess why I had asked Steve and Reta to leave, saying finders' keepers was not a responsible thing to do; it may be a family keepsake, plus his anger was not appropriate. However, all Jess wanted to know is what Gilly had meant when she said I was growing a pair. I was in no mood to explain. Gilly's voice reminded me that it was time we headed home.

As I prepared to begin the drive home, Gilly slipped a slipped postcard in front of me; "Ever thought of doing this" written across the front was Travel New Zealand the picture of Mount Cook, dazzling top bright with snow. I knew a little of her New Zealand heritage; she had always said she had a ton of family back there. She explained her idea, to sell her caravan, then invest in another van in New Zealand. A worm of interest began in my chest as I had always wanted to tour New Zealand. I looked at her face it was one huge smile; "Come on Pet, I'll sell mine if you sell yours." I spluttered, "I'm not sure if I can", she roared, laughing "It's not the holy grail, pet, and you yourself told me that this had been on your bucket list when the big guy was alive, so why not now? Let's do something fun, we sell it all and buy something over there, motorhome or caravan, who cares? "Let's go on a real adventure."

CHAPTER TWENTY-TWO

Could I do this? Could I leave it all behind, just pack up and leave? What about Jess and Rae? What about my home? And my life in Perth? It all seemed too much, I was fresh from a graveside so to speak and now I was being invited to tour around another country. My brain said No! Impossible, while my gut said maybe? Her question, "Would I mind if she stayed for a while? Her superannuation has not come through yet," caused my intuition to spark, but me being me, I pushed it away. My reply was "Of course you're welcome."

Something niggled in my mind about her finances. She still owed me money. However, we were due to leave the campground by 9 a.m., so I got busy packing camp gear away. Deciding to have breakfast on the road, about two hours out of Broome, we saw two hitchhikers, their thumbs out, trying to get a ride. It was Greta and Steven. Gilly looked at me; I shook my head. No! I was not becoming involved with them again; we drove past.

I could feel the nausea building before the headache clamped itself around my skull. I asked Gilly to take over, it was a good while before the next roadhouse. For the first time, I saw a side to Gilly I was not prepared for, her voice had become loud and intimidating. "For Christ's sake woman, it's just a headache, keep driving, you're not bloody dying." It felt like she had slapped me. Jess whispered into my ear, "Pull over, Nana, I'll make you a cup of tea." Gilly lost it, "It's a friggin headache, and no! She won't pull over, and you, young man, should mind your own friggin business.

Excuse me!! I swerved into a layby, the migraine forgotten. I walked to the passenger side, pulled the door open, "Let's get this straight, this mobile home is mine, and you are a guest. I grabbed Jess by the shoulder. This is my grandson, and I find your bullying attitude obnoxious. Do you understand what I am saying, Gilly? Now you can apologise to us both, or at the next roadhouse, we part company, you can find your own way back to Perth. Now, whether you like it or not, we are camping here for the night and yes, please Jess, I would love that cup of tea. Tomorrow, we will find a roadhouse for breakfast. And Gilly, if your attitude has not changed, then I suggest you find other transport. Surprisingly, I slept well, we left our overnight camp just as the sun rose. Gilly had apologised to us both, remaining silent for the rest of the night.

The roadhouse appeared. I knew it would be pure greasy finger food, but I did not care. I just wanted to get home and feel safe within my own four walls. We had reached the outskirts of Barradale, another dusty red, hot, two-shop town. I stopped here to buy all of us some breakfast.

The store owner still very sleepy as it was still early, all he had was ice cream "No deliveries till next week" he said, so the three of us sat in an old net enclosed lean-to; the small pedestal fan; ticking away, unsuccessfully trying to create a cooling stream of air; while we ate our breakfast; which was three tier ice creams, chocolate strawberry and banana, I'm not an ice cream fan, but believe me, they tasted delicious.

I started a game of I Spy; as we ate, which began to turn argumentative between Gilly and Jess; I wondered who the child was? It was time to leave, a cold flannel was passed around to wipe off sticky ice cream from hands and faces, Jess being the worst affected - I swear he had dived into his ice cream headfirst. We decided on reaching Carnarvon by nightfall, "I'll drive for two hours, then you take over Gilly offered. That was all right by me. The day was a hum of motor, red dirt with scraggly trees; the termite mounds were huge. Stopping off at Minalya roadhouse for gas and a much-needed toilet break. I once again bought the cold drinks and sandwiches for a quick lunch. Gilly and Jess were outside, beside this roadhouse was a menagerie of native birds including an emu, Jess had ever been this close to a bird of this size before, he was mesmerised. Carnarvon here we come.

Finally, I saw a peep of the sea, then the sea wind blew in through my window. Carnarvon, it was a busy township. My main concern was the number of trucks on the road. When Jess spied a pool of blue water, he excitedly cried, "There's a park, Nana." It was a small caravan park that was close to empty. Where is everybody? I queried the manager, he said in the slowest Ozzy twang, 'Gone south, lady, too damn hot here in the summer.' I had to agree this had been the hottest day so far. We all headed for the pool. Once in the water, you could hear pure bliss escaping from all three of us. I had half his energy. Gilly sat on the other side of the pool under the waterfall, her head back, eyes closed, relaxing as the water cascaded over her.

I allowed myself to study this woman who claimed to be my friend, who was she? What was the catalyst for her to be lesbian? Or had she always felt an attraction for her own sex? Why did she choose me for a travel companion? When surely there were women of her own age she could travel with. Gilly was in her late fifties a small woman in stature, a little plump, short curly once blond hair now glinting with silver threads, blue eyes that had a fine mesh of lines around them.

I was the opposite: tall, slim, short, spiky silver hair, hazel eyes, and a web of life's lines around my eyes, a twin furrow between my black eyebrows. My interests were in the Arts, my community and my family. I knew of Gilly's family and their dislike of her, I felt sad for her, but her interests apart from photography and travel, I had no idea. She caught me studying at her and smiled at me, "Why that look on your face, Tara?" There was a pause between us, I felt something was being hidden from me, but what? "Nothing, I replied, just pondering life." To break the tension, I began telling her the story of the Antique collectors who initialised everything with R & R, it seemed to relax the situation, or was I once again ignoring my intuition?

Jess and I headed back to the Metal Mermaid, Gilly stayed chatting to another young woman covered in Tattoos. I rang Rae, she reminded me to have Jess home in time for school. Jess had also found mates that had bikes. I journaled for a while, had an uninterrupted Nana Nap. Feeling refreshed, I prepared a pizza and salad for dinner. Jess arrived back, I sent him off to shower, we had our dinner, Gilly? She never showed up till the next morning, looking a little embarrassed, then shrugged her shoulders, "So I had some fun, sue me."

She obviously felt that I was judging her, so I apologised for surmising what was none of my business, she gladly accepted my sincere apology. "We'll sort it, Tara, when you're not used to another's lifestyle; well, it takes time to understand that my sexual needs are very different to yours. And may I add, don't knock it till you've tried it." I knew the look on my face spoke a thousand words.

I had booked us in for two nights, today I intended to go grocery shopping, Jess begged to be left with his mates at the camp and Gilly wandered off munching on cold Pizza with "See you when you get back." I queried what they wanted, both of them crying out in unison "Fish & chips." The camp offered a buggy ride into the township, why not? It proved to be just what I needed, on my own for a while. First, a little bit of window shopping, then buying the groceries. The hairdressers offered me a trim and blow dry, again why not? It felt so good to be pampered, and by the time I returned, it was 4 pm. Two very hungry people met me at the camp gates. It was perhaps a ten-minute walk to the chippies. Once we had our dinner, we sat on the harbour rocks that faced the ocean.

The Sealife was abundant, there never seemed to be a dull moment, as pelicans, seals and seagulls flashed past picking up any tit bits we tossed into the water, little windblown splashes of the cool sea wetting our feet, it felt good to be here relaxing, talking to Jess about his new school year that was about to start. I asked if he had enjoyed the trip with Nana and Gilly? What were his favourite places? And his experiences. His answers were not what I expected. He talked about Pilbara with such passion - my heart sunk, had I lost another to the Pilbara desert? I felt I did not have the right to contradict him, so I just nodded in what seemed the right places, after all this was his adventure as well.

CHAPTER TWENTY-THREE

Nighttime fell quickly, I did not want to sit outside and wonder over 'who did what today.' I wanted my bed, by eight pm it was a quick wash, then a good night to all, the three of us settling down with books and soon all fast asleep, our next destination was Monkey Mia, I wanted to show Jess the Dolphins; this time the tourist advertising came in very handy, it was not a long drive, plus I had prebooked a camp site over a week ago. This caravan park was super busy, international tourists everywhere, not all of them English speaking so translators were hard at work with their groups. Gilly also wanted to feed the Dolphins; it was not cheap by any means, as I handed my card over to pay for myself and Jess, Gilly walked outside, and I was asked, "Is she with your party? I nodded and immediately charged for three. This was beginning to be annoying.

Feed them by hand at the water's edge, said the advert - not to mention fighting for space between the tourists, who pushed, shoved, yelled, some slapping the water trying to attract them their way. One tired looking ranger was so busy trying to keep one lively Asian family at bay, as they bombed the water with huge chunks of bread. She did not have time to notice that one very small dolphin was not too far behind her, nibbling the fish bits that floated out of her container. I saw an opportunity, taking Jess by the hand, we left the large group, walking farther up the beach and together we waited, hoping for a dolphin to swim past. My prayers were answered, one Dolphin swam past then swiveled over on its side and looked me straight in the eye, an experience everyone should have, because in that eye was pure beauty.

I have no idea of the time we spent being with this incredible creature. I just knew this experience had touched my soul deeply.

I could not believe what had just happened; Jess saying, "That was really cool, Nana." I repeated a story I had heard "That a Dolphin knows when you're very sad or lonely, how it would swim up to you to make sure you smile again." I had to admit, amongst all my adventures, this is one I would not forget. One more day on the road, then home to Perth to Rae and Tim. Our holiday adventure was nearly over. The meal that night was full of what we had seen and done, the folks we had met and one day we would do it again.

Dongara was our next port of call; another small seaside town, with quite a bustling community around it; time to shop for tonight's dinner as tomorrow night we will be in Perth. Gilly looked tired; we pulled into a free overnight camp park. This time there was no pool, and no takeaways for dinner, It was scrambled eggs on toast, a hot wash, read books, then sleep; for an early take off the next morning.

I love the silhouette of Perth city, you can see the tallest of buildings from afar, but to me the silhouette of the Bell tower is perfect, the streets are wide and clean, most of them lined with bright green Elm trees. The excitement was building inside my chest, Jess was also becoming animated, soon he would be with his Mum and Tim. I felt content and safe, although I loved being on the road; but I knew I also loved being in my own home. I imagined driving down the Farmer's highway, onto the Tonkin freeway, a main artery to South Perth, one hour away from the city was my home in Rockingham. I was so excited about it all, I could not wait to plonk my bum onto a non-moving seat; put my feet up and relax, no added responsibilities to a twelve-year-old. I felt, emotionally drained, I had done what I intended and what Russ would have wanted. Now, this was my life and how I intended to live it.

Finally, I was driving along the Rockingham foreshore drinking in the sights and smells of where I lived, turned into my driveway; turned off the motor and almost ran to the front door. Standing there with her arms held out to me was Rae - her smile wide, her face glowing with health and happiness. Jess bounded out of the bus, almost knocking her over with joy. He wrapped his arms around her; his adventures already pouring out of him. Four weeks on a bus with Nana, scattering Granddad's ashes, Kangaroos, Eagles, giant Lizards, Camels, Emus and Dolphins. The people he had met; he loved the red earth of the Pilbara.

Rae gently put her hand over his mouth, "Shush, honey." Wait till we have helped Nana unpack the bus; once we are home, we can go over every little detail. Plus, I have some news for you. She winked at me. Everything okay, Mum? "Yes, I'm tired honey that's all." However, when Gilly walked inside, she greeted Rae with "Hey, babe", then put her case in the guest room. Rae looked at me, raising her eyebrows. I offered no explanation, only 'talk to you later." I watched her and Jess walk down the driveway, Jess patting the side of Metal Mermaid, "Bye Mermaid, see you soon, I hope."

They had no sooner left when I sank down into Russ's favorite chair, it looked out towards the garden that we both loved so much. As the sun sank, I smiled as I thought how much I love the sunrise; I adore getting up, breathing the clean fresh air; the early wide-awake birdsong, everything fresh and new. Russ was the opposite he would sit in this chair enjoying the sunset, telling me every five minutes of the coloured change in the sky as the sun went down. The way wildlife settled onto branches and into the garden's nooks and crannies ready to greet another day, the way the world quieted down. I wondered if he knew how much I missed him, or if he missed being with me. "Love you Russ" I whispered into the dusk.

Gilly's voice interrupting my daydreaming, Cocoa? Or Cuppa my Pet,' for some reason it grated. And I knew why, I needed some time out to decide on our next conversation. Up to the moment I had pulled into my driveway I had financed the entire trip. Maybe, when I invited her along that's what she thought I had meant, she did not have to pay her way. But then why would she borrow money off me then not offer to contribute? I would sort it tomorrow, flagging any drink I opted for my bed, a hot shower than a relaxing sleep in my own bed was bliss, when the sun peeped through my curtains at five am the next morning I was up, did my yoga stretches then as quietly as possible opened my home up to the early morning sea breeze.

Today was the start of a new day and I was full of energy, now feeling able to have that much needed discussion with Gilly. Going over my accounts, she owed me a fair amount, including the $500 loan. So, before I flung my lot in with hers and waved my home and Perth goodbye for a year, it needed to be discussed I had to make it clear that I was not the bank of Tara. Gilly was always a late riser. I made myself herbal tea and peeled a gorgeous, fresh Mango, compliments of Rae. I wandered outside, finding a sunny spot on my garden swing. Then I began to write down all the things I wanted to discuss with Gilly, plus noting all the jobs there was to do around the house.

I was still unsure about her invite to travel New Zealand, and most important, who would look after my home? Did I leave it empty or rent it out? The thought of that idea sent shivers along my spine, some stranger in my bed! I don't think so. Today was the last day of January. Where had the past year gone? What had I done in the last year? The wind ruffled all the bright yellow stickers that stuck out of my Diary, as if saying Look what you've done, look how much you have grown. I opened my small book on our life and travels. It was full of small road maps, small sketches of roadhouses we had been into; stunning bare trees that fires had tried to disintegrate. They stood defiant against all odds stood their ground. Reading through the scribblings of each day's accomplishments, I also noticed two entries from Gilly which annoyed me greatly, as my diary was off limits: full stop.

No one reads my thoughts or feelings except me. I was uncomfortable with her opening my diary and decided to say something once she was up. Time out for me to ponder; meander amongst my plants, think of a few things I would like to do to improve this overgrown garden, pick a few roses put them in vase of water, perhaps scribble a few lines of poetry. Today, all I wanted to do was saunter down the café strip and eat a Gelato ice cream. Perhaps dusk would be a good time to sit on the boardwalk watching dolphins and or pelicans swim by.

The sky changing into navy blue night: how the stars here seemed reachable, the sky so clear. Or perhaps I could drive to Safety Bay to watch the windsurfers fly across the water, the aeronautics of these folk who braved the choppy waters always amazed me-or admire the learners who wobbled their way through the shallows till they took off. And in the back of my mind was how to approach Gilly on the subject of paying her own was. A memory of Russ and I popped up, how we would get out of the car and cheer them on as they floated over the small white-top waves, their faces a mixture of excitement. I wanted to show Gilly why I loved this place so much; the people were always friendly- even the local chippie welcomed me like an old lost friend "Geez girl, I haven't seen you for Yonks", would yell out to me, I guess 'Yonks' meant ages." I wanted to show off places I loved, including Dwellingup, Pinjarra and Mandurah.

Dwellingup had a B&B that Russ and I loved, the master bedroom upstairs had a trapeze bed, we soon discovered that with every movement we made - we swayed, laughing made it worse. The grounds of this beautiful place were amazing, full of bushes, trees, and a very tiny marsupial that was almost extinct, a Black Glove Wallaby. They had the dinner train that wound its way through the bush, and a degustation meal with wine was served. Once you returned to the station the B&B car was there to take you back. Russ and I had such a fun time. The question was? Could I repeat the joy of the past if I replayed it with my family? My intuition said no, that was your time, so leave it be. My main decision was New Zealand with Gilly for another adventure.

First, some breakfast, and a morning read of the newspaper,
I knew I was putting off the inevitable, looking back I'm very glad
I took this time out just for me. I had no sooner gone inside to

put slices of bread into the toaster when the phone rang and that was it. An Avalanche of rolling emotions was now in motion.
The phone call was from Rae; between gulps of distress her news was not good. She had spoken with Jess about Tim's proposal and of living together, if it worked out and everyone agreed then they would marry. Jess's reaction had been the biggest tantrum she had ever witnessed; he had screamed NO! In her face then began to tear his room apart until she had to physically calmed him down. Tim had been disgusted by Jess's behaviour, calling him derogatory names, which only inflamed the fury. Tim had then left. I had no answers to help her. I suggested she leave it alone for a while until the drama had calmed down."

Once Gilly was up, I was ready with toast and coffee in hand to discuss our trip; she's definitely not a morning person, to be fair she had warned me more than once, however she was more than happy to suggest ideas as we sat together writing down the pros and cons of New Zealand; leaving Perth and family and away for year. She had no commitment but was certainly helpful in her suggestions as she had been where I was right now and not so very long ago - or that was the impression I was under. It seemed silly that such a small answer of 'Yes or No' could put into action the consequences; I was about to face.

The day turning to noon, I admired Gilly's patience as I was impatient with myself- why could I not throw my hands in the air "I'm off." Gilly's voice was calming me, "Because you care, because you have spent forty years building up this life and because you are who you are. It's okay to say no, you're not hurting anyone." She walked inside saying 'I'm going away for a while, I need to attend to some issues over East. Let me know what you're going to do. I'm selling my van and intend to leave for New Zealand in one month; you know my phone number.

CHAPTER TWENTY-FOUR

"Thanks for the wonderful trip up North to the Pilbara." It dawned on me that Gilly had been quietly packing while I was on the phone to my family, which irked me. Why not say something? I could only stare when she threw her kitbag into her Jeep, hitched on her caravan, gave me a wave, and drove off. It all happened so quickly that all my questions about what she owed me and when she would pay me back were silenced by her actions.

What did affect me was the stillness of my home; It was just me, and the Metal Mermaid. I was all alone, and once that had hit home, I almost panicked, fumbling on my phone for Gilly's number; why did I feel like crying? When she had obviously used me. Or had I encouraged her to do so, by not confronting her earlier, crying just seemed easier than phoning and ranting at another who had another life that I knew nothing about. Gilly had a life waiting for her and my job was to rebuild mine. My heart was tired of feeling torn about what I felt was right and what I wanted to do, plus what was expected of me. Sleep evaded me, it was one am in the morning exactly when I knew what I could do and what I could not do, somehow the answers all fell into place. I knew with such clarity what I was going to do.

I woke up at nine am, leapt out of bed and rang my daughter, Can you meet me at the library café in an hour? 'I can, she" said, "What's up? "You'll know soon enough, see you soon." I rang Gilly, her sleepy voice answered, 'Hello, pet,' she said, 'Did I forget something?' my overnight decision was blurted out, "Yes, you did, Me." "Well, that's bloody brilliant. Welcome aboard. I will be in Brisbane next month. I let you know when I'm on my way back.

Once I had made that decision, my plans to travel to New Zealand blossomed into reality so fast, it took my breath away. Rae arrived at the café in the library, and now that she and Tim had sorted Jess out, she seemed nicely settled. I told her of Gilly's offer, a year of travel through New Zealand, and how I had agreed to do so.

I inhaled deeply, then told her of my idea, "Why don't you and Tim rent my home of me?" I hate the thought of strangers renting it and it's also part of your history and who you are,' her smile said it all "Mum that's brilliant, as you know we have been searching for just the right place for us; we have only just signed an agreement to an apartment." My great idea deflated-my words felt empty saying "That's good Rae, I'm sure Jess will be okay with you all being together, it will take a while before he feels he is on familiar ground." She could see my disappointment "Mum, if anything changes, I'll let you know."

My next chore for the day was to go to a caravan dealer to see if he was interested in selling Metal Mermaid for me. His answer was "He could be interested, things were slow and there was a backlog of caravans he had on his lot, but he did not have a mobile home, so why not? He offered to drive out the next day and give me a price. The idea to sell Russ's Jeep? I did not drive it; I considered it a relic with too many breakdowns. Russ had been in his nirvana every time he lifted the hood; he almost crooned to it.

I rang the local newspaper placing an advert in the car sales for one Jeep. Then it was outside with mop and buckets, lather up the Metal Mermaid on the outside and spruce up the inside, till everything shone. Everything I did bought back memories of when we did this or we did that, so many memories. Whoever bought this lovely lady would be getting a prize, all the priceless memories were stored in my heart.

Rae, Tim and Jess arrived at six pm for dinner; it had been a spontaneous invite on my behalf. I had already prepared a salad, asking Tim to barbecue the steaks; Rae was asked to pour us all cold crisp wine. Rae had already shared my news of travelling, Jess's brown eyes pleading with me as he asked, "Please Nana, can I come with you?" "No sweetheart not this time, perhaps another trip in the future." Tim and Rae where beaming from ear to ear, "Will I tell her, or do you want to said Rae" my heart did a little thump as Rae took my hand. "Mum, when you come back from your trip; there was a deafening pause. "Mum, would you escort me up the isle? I was humbled and sad at the same time. This should have been an invitation for her dad. "Yes, of course I will, I raised a glass of wine, "From your dad and I, congratulations." Rae's humour always offbeat said, "You'll soon be departed as well, Mum."

Tim nudged his bride- to- be as if to say enough, Jess did not take it lightly. The blue light of telly in the lounge flickered on, he was not impressed with any of our decisions. His Nana was off on another adventure and his Mum? That was what seemed to offend him the most, was it because he was no longer the number 1 man in her life. I had a broken sleep that night, my mind wondering if I had done the right thing? The front doorbell rang at 8 am, my neighbour Perry, who had comforted me the day Russ passed away, stood there, it had been months since we had seen each other.

"Hey Perry, come on in, shall I put the jug on? Perry had been a godsend when Russ had been away, saving my bacon so many times, with home, kids, transport. I appreciated him as my neighbour.

Our kids grew up together, going to the same schools- we had the occasional morning tea together, Irene, his wife, had passed away two years ago. I will always remember at her memorial when Perry had stood raised his glass to her photo and serenaded her memory with a song. "Irene Good night, Irene, I'll see you in my dreams" I had felt the hair on my arms prickle.

Today, Perry had arrived on my doorstep with news; he was moving on, selling up his four-bedroom home, it was too big and lonely for him now. He and his companion Francine were going to do some traveling. He offered me some of the plants he did not want to sell with his home. I felt sad that he was leaving the neighbourhood. Perry was a true gentleman. As he was leaving, my brain then mouth kicked in, "Perry, do you want to buy a caravan or a motorhome? Mine is for sale, he stopped and pondered. "That's an interesting situation. Let me ask Francine. I'll get back to you." Late that afternoon Perry and Francine both came over to take a good look at the Metal Mermaid, Francine was so tiny and petite like an ancient doll with curly white hair, deep brown eyes that held a naughty sense of humour; I could see that Perry was smitten, as he gently helped her into the Metal Mermaid. Good for him, everyone deserves someone to love.

I showed them through, telling them about her quirks and how much I had enjoyed driving her. Next, came the asking price, without having to pay the sales commission, they thought it was a bargain; the agreed price was five thousand, much less than Russ and I had paid it. The ownership papers were signed over a glass of port, I looked at the time was 5.55pm, triple numbers means good luck, don't they? They asked why the name *Metal Mermaid* I retold my memories of the mud puddle experience in Albany.

Suddenly, it struck me that they might change her name. I wanted to cry again, my eyes saying what I could not, for fear of sounding like a two-year-old. Francis saw my face, "Metal Mermaid it is" she said. I offered them afternoon tea not wanting this very comfortable scenario to finish, it felt like old times. Good, trusted friends enjoying each other's company. I broke the news of Rae becoming engaged, Perry saying, "I guess you'll be having the wedding in the backyard? I had not thought of that, a range of possibilities ran through my head. Yes, we could, and if Rae and Tim were keen; the wedding could be held before I left for New Zealand,

Metal Mermaid now sat next door, I could hear her new owners rummaging about inside, they seemed delighted I had left the majority of the gear in her. I sat down feeling like I had run a marathon. Relaxing for me was not on the agenda, as no sooner had I sat down than the Caravan salesman arrived, and I had forgotten all about him. He seemed a little peeved, however as he walked away, he spied the *For Sale* sign on the jeep; how much, he enquired? I told him what I had advertised it for, however if he paid cash, I would take $500 off the price. He stood back rocking on his heels, his forefinger and thumb rubbing his chin. "I'll be back tomorrow, I would like to take it for a test drive, and to see it in the daylight" fine with me I thought, at the moment I just wanted to lie down. Twenty minutes later he was back, don't worry about the test drive, I'm happy to buy it for what we agreed on. I watched as he tapped a few numbers, my phone dinged and as if by magic I was looking at a very large amount in my bank account, I signed the ownership papers, gave him all the paper, "I'll be back tomorrow to pick her up" I said it's him, it's called Jack. He gave me a strange look, "Really? That's unusual; but it suits Jack it is."

My meal of poached eggs on toast settled nicely, slipping into my pajamas, once I had made a cup of tea, it was time to ring my closest of friends, first was Rae's engagement then I was going away for approximately a year, I was surprised that they were not questioning my decision; Jo and Robin asking 'what has happened to the careful, steady Tara we all know and love? "Well, it is time for a change" I answered. They both agreed, "You are so right, enjoy, keep in touch, send lots of photos, see you when you're home again."

Why could I not sleep? In just two days I was thousands of dollars better off. I wanted to dance and sing, "It's midnight, you silly women I chided myself; no one's awake at this hour, go to sleep." I'm sure the clock smirked at two am when all I could do was lie there and listen to its ticking; thinking to myself this is not happening, I'm going to wake up and realise it's all been a dream.

Then it clicked Rae, wedding, the backyard, and if we timed it right, I would be here to walk beside her to be married. I felt the excitement build. Pointless trying to sleep, I looked at my phone on messages her green light was on, do I tell her now?

I messaged her, "You awake?" Her answer was "What's wrong, Mum? UOK? Was I? I was about to explode. I rang, her voice sleepy "What up, sugar lump?" Knowing that I was 100% on track, this was the reason everything had sold so quickly. As I explained my thoughts, I also said, "Rae, this is from your dad and me. I know this is what he would have wanted." Rae began crying, waking Tim, she told him my suggestion. "Come over tomorrow and we can begin to make plans, that's if it's what the two of you want."

CHAPTER TWENTY-FIVE

I hardly slept at all, so when Gilly rang at 7am to tell me she was flying back into Perth that afternoon, her girlfriend Wendy had found another. In the space of a half hour, Clark turned up to take the jeep away, and Francine and Perry came over to ask about water storage and how it all worked. Rae and Tim arrived. I literally gave them carte blanche about any wedding plans with one request, it was to be formal and exclusive. I looked at the time, cripes time to pick Gilly up. I borrowed Perrys car, I had opted to take Jess with me, not telling him who was arriving, I decided to keep it a secret, his questions answered when he saw Gilly his first adult mate, he yelled "Its Gilly" rushing over hugging her' she pushed him away saying "Come on mate, I've not been gone that long." Jess looked hurt at the rebuff; I also thought it was a strange action from one who claimed she was his friend.

She looked drawn, her eyes had dark snudges under them, I knew she was grieving for a lost love and even though I would never understand her passion for the same sex; I certainly knew what grief felt like; my heart went out to her. The drive home was silent except for my warning, "It's nuts at my house today, Gilly." Jess began to describe his school and "Mums was getting married", until Gilly snapped "Alright, Jess, enough, I get the picture" Again, I saw the rebuff had hurt him. I was becoming concerned; this was not the calm happy soulmate that had left Perth recently; she seemed to be on guard. Gilly asked, "Are you sure there is room for me? You seem to be extremely busy." What a strange question to ask "Of course" I answered, my smile felt tight, I had this feeling like there was a storm brewing.

The plans were made, one small private wedding was to be held in the backyard in four weeks' time, what a whirlwind, first marriage license, then when the family church banners were read, Minister Baret was to perform the ceremony. I found a gardener who repainted the gazebo and planted white hydrangeas in large terracotta pots all around it. Rae decided on an oyster Champagne Juliette-style wedding gown. As mother of the bride, I wore a deep turquoise cocktail pant suit. Tim had bought a grey morning suit and Jess as his best man was dressed in a matching outfit. A team of women bounced into the house on the wedding day, a beautician, a hairdresser and make-up artist plus a nail technician and florist that wound baby breath flowers into Rae's hair.

It was a beautiful sunny day, neighbours and close friends attended, a group of fifty people. When Rae and Tim stood together; they looked stunning, Rae had declined a bouquet of flowers, instead choosing a small bible, tucked inside was a photo of Russ her beloved dad. The buffet wedding breakfast was superb; the caterers were amazing, the wedding cake was two tiers, one for the wedding, the smaller one was to be kept aside until the christening of their 1st child. I looked at the two of them together, hoping our daughter had found that one special love.

Gilly, who had done nothing but scowl through all the happy busy days of our wedding preparations, had opted out of attending the wedding, choosing to go to the movies for the day. For which I was grateful, as Rae was vehement when she said "She was not invited." And I will admit that Gilly had changed, her attitude plus her language had become rough. She now did not like Jess, which she made obvious and at times she barely contained her dislike towards Rae and Tim. Two days after the wedding, Gilly demanded we make plans for our trip to New Zealand. I tried to be amicable and make jokes, no sooner waving the married couple off on their honeymoon, than her demands became insistent.

It seemed Gilly craved attention. One night, as Jess and I relaxed in front of the telly, she stormed into the lounge. "Right, it's now or never, time to make up your mind, you're either coming with me or staying here." I took a big breath, "Gilly, can I just have some time to breathe. Her wail of despair alarmed me, "You're always too busy for me these days. To be fair, she had waited till all the excitement was over, so our plans began. 1ˢᵗ step to fly into Auckland, stay with her family while we found a mobile home. Tomorrow we would arrange for our flights, I would buy my travel insurance at the same time. Gilly suggested we open a combined bank account; I would have to think carefully about that idea. I knew from my past experience money and Gilly was not a good mix.

The honeymoon was over, Rae rang to say they were home, when could they begin to move in. As far as I could see, there was nothing stopping them from an immediate start. My tickets were booked; my case was packed. All I had to do was attend an afternoon tea, hosted by Jo to say goodbye to my friends, then I was free to leave. There were many moments shared between my friends that afternoon, the main one was I should be leaving for so long. My fears laid to rest by Gilly who had accompanied me, she promised my friends hand on heart she would look after me and so would her family. We left Jo's home late in the afternoon, only to find my family moving in, to my home.

The garage was in a mess, clothes and boxes strewn everywhere, as was the lounge floor. I asked Rae what was going on? pointing to the jumble of her dad's clothing, her answer rocked me, 'he's not here, is he?" He's not wearing them, is he? So why the bloody fuss? Her face reddened with anger. I had not seen this side of her for a while, but I knew what it meant; she wanted what she wanted-and to hell with everyone else. She flounced out muttering about "Over sensitive people." Tim also surly; his retort of "Thought I was welcome." That got to me; Tim was still a stranger to me; how dare he dump my husband's belongings on the floor? Rae began to scream at Jess to "Get in the car," he was slumped in his Grandad's chair. "I hate them both" he yelled at me "Why can't I stay here.?"

"Happy families Gilly" I said, deciding if anyone was going to have a tantrum it was me. Their tempers brought to an abrupt stop as I yelled back, "Shut up the bloody lot of you; this is still my home, until Gilly and I leave, Rae interrupting me with ", Oh, it's Gilly and you now, is it? The implications shocked me. 'How dare you be so rude?' I asked. "Oh, come on, Mum, since you two met, it's been Gilly said this and Gilly that; we all know what's been going on, you're all over each other nonstop." I could not believe what she had just said, "Get out, now", I yelled, pointing to the front door. "Until you apologise, we have nothing more to say to each other."

I had never spoken to my daughter like this before, it even shocked me as the words spilled out. Gilly was now sitting in the conservatory "I'll find a motel she offered; would you drop me off?" I refused "You will not, this is my home, I say who goes and who stays." she smiled patted the seat next to her: "It's a good thing to remind your kids about respect and boundaries." Later that day Gilly helped me re-pack Russ's clothing: both of us were very quiet. I waited till mid-afternoon, my heart squeezing tight with disappointment in Rae. The silence from Jess and Rae was awful, usually we rang each other every 2nd day sometimes more, just to say "Hi, how's your day going, love you." I left a message on her phone, "Leaving for New Zealand tomorrow, love you."

With no news from Rae, I decided I was just going to lock up everything and leave, this was my time. Gilly and I had talked through the night about the family blow-up, Gilly saying very little; her main concern was whether I was sure about going on a holiday with her.

It infuriated me that my daughter felt she could meddle with my belongings and my life, accusing me in no uncertain terms that I was gay, and her husband was just as ignorant, both carrying on like spoilt children. So, when Gilly informed me that her caravan had been sold, the moment was lost on me because of the silent argument I was mentally having with my daughter.

Tomorrow we were leaving, I checked everything off my to do list. Making sure the alarm company knew I was going away for the year; we spread dust sheets over the lounge and dining room furniture. This was my last night in Rockingham for a year. I wandered outside, touching the roses, my hands trailing over ferns, feeling the warmth the sun had left on the bricks. Earlier on my neighbours had driven away, I had watched as the taillights of the Metal Mermaid disappeared around the corner. My heart creaked with sorrow as the dream of Russ and I adventuring together was gone, forever.

Still no apology was offered, not even a phone call just to say, 'hi Mum how are you?' so I gave in and rang Jess on his Mobile, 'Hello Nana?' he whispered, "Hello Jess, how are you?" then his voice became muffled, the phone went to dial tone, the beeping of the disconnection, cut into me deeply. Obviously, Jess was not allowed to talk to me either. I felt guilty; I was the adult, and it should have been me apologising, self-blame, repeating, "You should have tried to contact her; been more understanding."

What saved me from acting on this train of thought was when Francine arrived. They were ready to hitch the Metal Mermaid up. She saw my distress and asked why. I told her about my family's behaviour and accusations. Her advice was, 'Why should *you* apologise?' You opened your home and heart to them. My reasoning was purely emotional: "Because she's my daughter, and Jess is my only grandson."

"Makes no difference she advised, if you accept this abusive behaviour, it's condoning it." First and foremost, she added "You have a right to be who you want to be, if you choose to be Gay, then so be it," she was right. Between her and Gilly, I was feeling like I had made the right choice in setting boundaries. It was an early 4 am start to the Airport, I had ordered an Uber to drive us there. No sooner had we checked in; our seat numbers allocated- we were on the escalator going up to the departure lounge with three hours to wait before we boarded, I thought breakfast at the airport was for best. I was overwhelmingly tired, and it showed I had dark circles under my eyes, it hurt not to say goodbye with love or a 'see you in a year,' then my anger would storm in and say 'Tara, if your friends and acquaintance can wish you well, safe journey, what the hell is wrong with your daughter?

There were too many confusing emotions to think straight; so, when Gilly said "Guess what? The money from my van is in the bank, I can go back to New Zealand without stressing now." Her erratic mood swings made sense. "Do you mean you have been relying on the sale of your van to get by on?" I almost choked on the words, What has happened to your super? Gilly has a way of looking at you like there was a secret locked behind her eyes. "Gotta have faith sister", she replied. What sort of answer was that? Her actions at times concerning, was Gilly bipolar? If so, I wish she had confided in me. My thoughts of doom and gloom about my family were now replaced with what if she had not sold her caravan. Was she going to rely on me to finance this trip? She knew the financial costs, as we had planned together.

Gilly said, "I'll pay you back for my fare once we arrive in Auckland and I'm on the internet." At first, I was amused that she thought I was that naive. I asked, "Why not now, Gilly? The airport has internet. She stopped, digested what I had just said, then exploded 'Tara are you calling me dishonest? 'No Gilly, I'm not, but I would appreciate it if you would clear the $3000.00 debt you owe me. Then, I can also relax and enjoy this adventure." Her answer caught me off guard, "You have more than enough, and you know it, you're being selfish." What? Enough of her nonsense. I was well and truly over being told what, who and when to obey or else.

I walked up to her, so close I could feel her breath, speaking slowly, clearly and quietly making sure my words were not misunderstood in any way or form. "Gilly, stop and think, do not abuse our friendship, now pay me what you owe me then let's put it behind us, shall we? She stomped off, her fingers stabbing at her phone, then holding the phone up in my direction yelling out "There's not much left now." I looked at this woman who seemed to thrive on a negative response. Thinking Gilly, it's not my problem-please be an adult, it's what I need right now.

CHAPTER TWENTY-SIX

Too late, our boarding number was being called, you are now strapped into an airtight metal tube, and your adventure is about to begin. I concentrated on the people wandering in, finding their allocated seats, putting their luggage away. I knew I could not leave Australia without telling my family I loved them, I grabbed my phone and texted 'I love you, hopefully we will speak soon. The plane began to taxi down the runway. Gilly saying Here we come, New Zealand, land of the long White Cloud." She nudged me when the male host, leant over me asking if I could place my cabin bag under the seat in front of me." My face flaming at what her nudging and eye rolling suggested. I was old enough to be his mother, I pulled my eye mask down, hopefully Gilly would get the message.

Five hours being stuck between two other people is never comfortable. Gilly was quiet at home, she had the aisle seat, getting up and down like a fiddler's elbow. If I found her annoying, heavens knows what others thought. I tried to doze, watch TV or read; finally, I gave up on sleep; I wandered off to the bathroom, I spied an empty row of seats right at the very back, I wondered if I could sit there and work on some poetry or simply relax without the constant games about who Gilly fancied, or who she thought was sexy, informing me and the other person in the row, she was keen to join the mile high club.

There is never any harm in making an enquiry, so I asked one of the crew members if changing seats was possible. The crew members in the Galley looked at where I had been sitting, then looked at Gilly, then looked back at me, and in unison said, "Of course you can." As fortune would have it Gilly was in the bathroom, I fetched my small on-board bag, settled into my new seat, just enjoying the peace and quiet. Whatever Gilly said or did to upset the senior staff member, I have no idea, I only heard her being told "Mam, please return to your seat." There was a distinct no-nonsense tone to her voice; Gilly complied, but the way she stormed off then jammed her body back into her seat, well let's just say for middle aged woman who was trying to join the mile high club? It was certainly not attractive.

It was what I needed; the words flowed like music on paper like never before; I did not even notice the plane crew preparing to land till I was asked to move back to my delegated seat and buckle up. We had a stopover in Brisbane for two hours; I went and did some duty-free, purchasing my favorite perfume and body cream at the L'Occitane body shop, what heaven, you can feel the body relax as the heady perfumes invade your nostrils, like butter on hot toast, you just want to breathe it into your lungs.

Once I had made my purchase I ambled back to where I had last seen Gilly. She had been fairly optimistic about a new friend on the plane. All I saw was a scowl that always preceded her bad temper, not knowing what had happened, do I dare ask? I wanted to comfort her, but another emotion kicked in; warning that this was Gilly, any sort of rebuttal, refusal, or if it did not go her way, her life was crap with a capital C.

I seemed to be constantly on my guard; appeasing her or patting better, yes-she had helped me in the caravan park when Russ was in hospital, yes, I was grateful for her kindness, but kindness and love is something you give, no one can force it from you. I was getting tired of the posturing and brain games she played. I had packed a book in my carry-on case, I now put my nose firmly into it, waiting for our departure to New Zealand to be called; Gilly could sort her own mess. At long last we were boarding, I noticed we had the same crew as our flight to Brisbane, the crew member who had allowed me to sit at the back smiled at me, as she did with everyone boarding, it was not flirtatious it was more like a hello again. Gilly saw it and fumed, her wise crack as we sat was nasty "What's the deal between you two" she nodded towards the crew member.

Now was the time to speak my mind while she was buckled in. "Gilly please, I've been through so much this last year, let's give the innuendos and the hormones a rest." Her mouth gaped open, "I mean it Gilly, you're acting like teenager." I spoke quietly but firmly, just as I would to my grandson. Her reaction was to turn her head away from me, I may not have been able to see her face however her body language spoke volumes, she was angry, again.

As we flew out of Brisbane the pilot called our attention to an unusual cloud formation, there in the sky three huge tornado shaped columns, the pilot giving us all the run down on what sort of weather caused these formations, saying "They were harmless and quite rare to see this late in the day," my camera capturing these truly beautiful formations. Then as dusk deepened: as we flew over the Pacific Ocean, another announcement came over the intercom. "Ladies and gentlemen, if you look to your right." There-staining the night sky a deep crimson blood red, it was the reflection of the fires in Victoria, it was a scary thought that folks were losing their homes.

The hostesses began handing out envelopes to put cash into, in aid of the destruction of bush fires. Most envelopes were bulging before they reached my seat. Then time for walk and a stretch around the plane, we had one hour before we landed, I touched Gilly's shoulder as I passed her, she flinched, tossed her head away from me almost turning her whole body in the opposite direction. I walked around the plane once more, the staff asking me to return to my original seat. Excitement coiled inside of me, we were here. Once we had landed, passed through immigration, I followed Gilly to collect our luggage off the carousel.

She grabbed her case then walked past me. I hurried after her, calling her name, my case banging against my legs "Hey, come on silly, I'm on your side, remember." She turned and looked at me, I will never forget the anger on her face and her words. "Fuck off Grandma, find your own way." What?

She walked towards the exit doors calling out and waving to people that were obviously family or friends.

And I was left standing there; alone, the fear I felt cramping my breathing. I was a stranger in a country I knew nothing about and knew no one but Gilly, who had just flicked me off without a backward glance. I was literally on my own. My first reaction was terror, my world tilted for one second; I quickly sat down, common-sense and logic skittered around my head, I took a deep breath, then checked the time, it was right on midnight. Then began mentally ticking off the questions that were racing into my head, shelter was the 1st question. I walked to the taxi rank and asked the driver if she knew of decent motel, if so, would she drive me there. She was an older Māori woman. "Sure, can love" she said "Hop in."

We sped off merging into the traffic on the Auckland motorway heading for the city I guessed; stopping at traffic lights, all was blurred, the tears sitting so close I just wanted to sit in a quiet room and cry; the driver kept looking at me in the rear vision mirror, asking "anything I can help with love" I told her I had arrived with a friend; she had left me stranded at the airport; she looked shocked, "why not join me in a cuppa love" she said, "let's see if I can help you." I agreed to stopping off, which we did in a city called Mangere Bridge, the driver pulling into a park outside at quiet coffee shop although they were taking in their open signs, they were kind to make us a cup of tea. We sat in her taxi with paper cups full of sweet hot tea, and I told her my story.

I had agreed to travel around New Zealand with a friend for one year; tears were now slipping down my cheeks unashamedly that we had had a fight on the plane when we had landed, she told me to "F off" while leaving the airport.

All the driver did was listen, sip on her tea, then said "Well that makes a change; I expected a man somewhere in the tale, let's get you into a room for the night, then tomorrow is another day. I'm Margi - what's your label." In no time a hotel was found, cheap but clean, Margi gave me her card "Call me if you need a ride" and off she drove, she was right- tomorrow is another day. The hot water in the shower poured over my aching body.

My last waking thought was what on earth do I do now.? Is it wrong for a sixty plus year old women to burst into sobs crying "I just want to go home" well if it is, I'm guilty as that's exactly what I did when I woke up from a bad sleep and freaked. I wanted to catch the plane back to Perth as soon as possible. I rang the airport from the hotel's reception desk, as I had no service; I had forgotten to change my phone company once off the plane. I could feel the anxiety building up I wanted to throw up. The hotel reception were kind enough to let me use their phone. Dialing the reservations desk at the airport; it took time to connect me to the cancelations department where I was informed 'all cancellations and re bookings are done via the Internet."

My thinking becoming clearer, it was best to keep safe, so I re-booked my room for another four days. Next, find an internet café or mall where I can book my flight home. I felt a little brighter doing something proactive; next step, ring the taxi driver from last night-Margi, who was more than happy to taxi me to an internet café. Her smile was so wide and welcoming "Hello there, you look a little better." Little did she know, I still felt like I had been side swiped. As she drove, Margi told me about the previous night. "I thought about that rotten friend of yours. I made a few enquiries as this is not the welcome that we, as Māori, give to our tourists.

I know where she lives, I know her whanau and I know if they knew what she had done, they would be giving her a bloody good whack." Now, that brought a smile to my face; I had not heard of a whacking for a long time; however, I could not condone hitting another, because of my anger. "Margi that's not necessary, she owes me nothing, I naively expected an adult friendship. I'm more than happy to explore Auckland, then return to my home."

Margi had a determined look to her face, "You're better off without trash like her leaching off you, you don't need her, why don't you just go and do what you came here to do, have look around New Zealand, you may never have this time again." It was a light bulb time for me "You're right I said, it's not the end of the world; I guess I was in shock that she would do that to me." Margi stopped her car, leaning over the front seat she said, "Well girl, what's it to be, ya wanna have some fun first or you wanna go back home to Ozzy." If I had known, then what I know now?

Would I have been so keen and eager to proceed? Would I have been so naïve to think it will just work out? All I can say is the adventure I was about to go on: re-shaped and re-modelled how I saw the world, then and in the future. As I can honestly say; my adventures and the people I met in New Zealand changed my life.

CHAPTER TWENTY-SEVEN

I chose the first option. "Fun, please, I've had enough of tears" "righto, mate let's sort you out" was her reply. Margi was worth her weight in gold, we decided that for a reasonable fare. I would be driven to many of the major tourist spots in Auckland "It's cheaper than a hire car she said." It was actually nice to be treated as a tourist, no waiting in queues or catching buses or trains, the hop on hop off bus seemed continuously jammed packed. I was grateful for her chatter, plus her knowledge of Auckland city.

Auckland was very busy, we had visited so many places, some I got out and took photos, some I told Margi to drop me off and pick me up later, and some we bypassed with her sage advice "You don't want to go their love." Margi arrived at the hotel at eight am every morning, and I was dropped off by five pm as she had to feed the whanau on time. I learnt she had eight kids and the old bugger Tom, her old man. Margi was simple, honest, looked at life without blinkers on and called a spade a spade.

Day four and Margi's cab was waiting for me as I left the hotel on an overcast Thursday morning. I had a skip in my step as I was leaving New Zealand tomorrow. My flight had been booked; I was on a red eye flight. Margi's voice calling out "Come on girl, pull your finger out; I have something to show you."

Her eyes alight with excitement. Driving over the Auckland harbour bridge, heading north, she refused to tell me what she was excited about. "You'll know when we get there" she replied. We stopped at a caravan sales yard and there in the yard was the smallest caravan I have ever seen "Perfect for you" she cried. Margi was determined I was going to see her country. I stumbled and stuttered, "Gee, I don't know Margi." Her hand grabbed mine as she dragged me forward 'Ah, come on", she said, "Be a daredevil."

Oh boy, a dare devil is not what I am, in fact I was discovering I had a fear of failing. I looked at it carefully inside and out, all the time trying to channel Russ's sage advice about buying a lemon. I could also hear the advice from my mate Jo, "If it's a lemon then make lemonade." It was down to business with the dealer Mark, if I was worried, I was going to be cheated, there was no need: I had Margi, my watchdog, with me. I knew by now she would stand up to a cyclone to get the best deal for her 'bestest customer' as she called me. Mark was thorough as he pointed out it was a Teardrop van made popular in the 1940's / 50's. This little gem was one of the last ones in New Zealand that came from that era-it had been fully upholstered and refurbished. I must admit it smelt and looked clean and new; there was nothing to mend, nothing to fix.

Inside there was basics only-a large single bed, a small light above the bed, in the roof was a large ceiling vent that could wind open. A very small table beside the bed, small windows each side, in a tiny cupboard there was space for a basin, toaster or cleaning gear, the choice was mine. Mark lifted the bed up where a small storage unit had been built into it. It was basically a bedroom on wheels. He then showed me the quirks of the outside of the Teardrop, a miniature water container and tap where a hose could be attached to for whatever purpose. Plus, a little pull-out kitchen hidden inside the smallest cupboard I had ever seen. All my cooking was to be done outside. The more he showed me how it all worked; the more positive I became that this could work. Yet, the inner critic 'who are you to do this on your own?' kept creeping in, warping my judgment. Could I manage this all by myself? It was so light weight; I asked as many pertinent questions about the van as possible, trying hard to remember what Russ would have asked.

Margi made me smile, apart from her following me, opening and closing compartments, she began asking for his personal pedigree. Now came the difficult part, I found myself agreeing to buy it, however it was Mark who showed me how to get Wi-Fi in New Zealand. Then advised me to go online and inform my bank I was travelling overseas. That way any transactions, especially large ones, would not be queried. 'I can't do this, ran through my mind.' Logically I knew I could, I was healthy, mentally fit and strong, so what was the problem? My old nemesis fear of failure was hard at work, sitting in my chest, whispering negatives. Taking a big breath, I did as he suggested.

Opening the bank app, putting in my password, Mark showing me where to tick to inform them I was travelling overseas. I began transferring the asking price. Mark looked like a proud Mumma duck, as I added his bank details, then transferred the asking price. My hands shook; Margi put her hands on my shoulders-I felt a calmness settle around my heart. "Well done, Tara, you have my *Whakaute*" Mark adding "She means respect. Lord, I felt so damned proud of myself, as we high-fived each other, I agreed to pick it up the next day. How? I had no idea. I will be forever grateful to Margi as we trawled car market after car market; she bullied, harassed, told off, and argued till I stepped in-stopping the haranguing, by saying "Margi I really like this little Suzuki."

A bright red, two-seater, automatic, was perfect. As I went to sign the papers, the salesman asked to see my license. "We have a problem he said, you need a New Zealand current license to purchase." Margi stepped in "No worries, come on Tara we just have time to go to the licensing department." We raced there, made out the papers, I now gave him all the paperwork to prove I was the owner of a kiwi license. Time to buy Suzuki. The deal was done, the money transferred, I had the keys, I was now a proud Suzuki owner. As we left, Margi said to the salesman "Give my love to you Nan." The salesman waved, "Will do, Auntie" I had to ask, "Is everyone related in Auckland? Margi grinned 'You could say that."

Mark was very kind; knowing this was my 1st attempt at caravanning on my own, he went over Suzuki; once satisfied it would tow the Teardrop. He showed me (twice) how to hook up my little van. He had filled the gas bottle and the water tank for me. Margi asked, "Where to now?" I had no idea, my fear stepped in 'Told you, stupid is as stupid does.' No, I was not having it. $50 grand lighter in my bank, and an entire country waiting for me to explore, I was going to make this happen. Margi pointed to the right, "That's Northland, it's beautiful country where my tribe, the Ngāpuhi people, are from. She then pointed to her left, that's South- keep going and you will arrive in Wellington from there it's the South Island. Enjoy my country, Haeremai (welcome) to Aotearoa" she touched my nose with hers, the Māori hongi is their greeting, then Haererai' Tara, (farewell) keep well and safe, keep in touch, please." Driving out onto the highway heading right, I was excited as I had been on my wedding day-all nervy and twitchy; I was on the road, on my own and I was going to see New Zealand from the Cape in Northland to the Bluff in the South Island. My very first stop-a camping store at a seaside village called Orewa.

This store owner must have thought all his Christmas's had arrived at once, I bought way too much, I know I did-I was making sure I was warm and fed, including maps of Northland. The store manager advised me to join the AA the car and caravan insurance place like the RAC in Australia, they also pointed out it was nearly seven pm, if I was not used to the roads why not stay overnight in a local campground. Finding out all the pros and cons of caravanning in New Zealand was exhausting. The camping ground was found, one night booked, learning to reverse my little van into the space? Five attempts later, I was sort of straight. I will get better at this-I vowed as I heated up a tin of soup, buttered a slice of bread and listened to the sea crash onto the shore, I felt flat; tired, and a wee bit homesick, so far this had not been enjoyable.

CHAPTER TWENTY-EIGHT

When my phone rang, Rae's name came up on the screen, my heart skipped more than a beat-it trembled, I was going to answer in a friendly manner. Her outburst beat me to it "Mum, I'm sorry" she said, "Jess and I want you to come home, we miss you." My heart gladdened "I miss you too, but I'm not coming home, not for a while honey," my face and heart smiling, I was in touch with my family again.

We chatted about my pending adventure, Rae was worried for me, I told her about Gilly, she became furious; Someone needs a lesson. I told her about Margi, how this complete stranger had wrapped me up with love. We talked about my recent purchases, the Teardrop and the Suzuki "I would love to be there with you Mum" my reply was "I need to do this on my own for now." 'Why? she asked, "You were so secure and safe in Rockingham." It was true, "I have no idea Rae I just know I'm not ready for the retirement home," I chuckled when she said, "I doubt you ever will be mum; goodnight, sleep tight." I had noticed that Tim was not mentioned, I was relieved we were talking again-but there was something else there; my intuition was picking up - or was I tired. I curled up inside my little home; tucked up on my new bed under a feather doona. I woke to birds singing, no cawing or muttering or spluttering like our crows and parrots, but singing, cheeping and peeping, how very different.

As I showered in the camp bathrooms, changed into clean clothes, my phone rang again, this time *number unknown* came up. I bet it's either Mark or Margi I thought, "Hello, Tara speaking" was met with silence, so I switched off, boiled eggs and a big mug of hot tea was today's breakfast. This Kiwi fresh sea air certainly made me super hungry, the phone rang again, I answered "Hello Tara speaking."

"Tara," came a small girly voice "it's me Gilly, can we talk?" I went silent, so did the other end, then a thought came to me, stuff it, I do not need her unbalanced rude bad-tempered behavior in my life. So, I said in a bright happy voice "No Gilly, fuck off" then did something I rarely do, I blocked her. Childish? Maybe, however, bubbles of laughing erupted from my chest till I was bent over; I laughed and spluttered till my face ached, I chuckled right through my breakfast. I felt liberated, at long last no hangers on whining "Pat me better, now." I was going to see New Zealand and from there on who knew where the wind would blow me. Packing up my little home, I drove, heading north, who knows where and when I would stop. Waiwera-another seaside township with a huge water fun park and thermal pools. It looked packed to the top with people, I decided not to stop, continuing to Warkworth, now this was more like it.

I loved it, quaint olde world looking, it also had a cute camping ground. I enquired if there was a vacancy for two nights; Yes, there was, the manager walking me to my site under tall willow trees by the river- it looked and felt welcoming. Opening a tin of stew, it simmered on the little gas stove at the back of my van, that with a slice of buttered bread, I felt replete. I turned to packing everything I had purchased the night before into the right places, the little cupboard soon filled. I then packed all tins and packets into a large plastic box and put them under the bed; I was relaxed as I could be. Boiling the kettle, I settled down to a cup of sweet coffee, I read my book outside till the light would no longer let me read.

I locked the Suzuki up, had a hot shower in the camp bathrooms, sleep claiming this very tired traveller. I certainly enjoyed this pretty little place with all its little art shops, the riverside café and the million ducks all vying for that one last crumb you just might toss in the water to them. Just out of Warkworth is a place called Goat Island Reserve, a little out of my way, but I'm so glad I drove there before I left the area, Goat Island is a natural marine reef.

I drove through small country towns, surrounding me all the way were green hills; Goat Island was serene, its waters calm the surrounding bush grew in greens of all shades. I waded into the cold Pacific Ocean, and the most amazing small school of turquoise coloured fish called Blue Mou Mou nibbled at my toes. I paid for a ride in the advertised glass-bottom boat; it was amazing. That's the only word I know to explain what I saw, fish of all types and genders, huge, fat, healthy and as inquisitive of us as we were of them.

The beach was almost deserted except for two ladies that sat on the beach under a large striped beach umbrella, reading magazines and chatting, and two people snorkeling. And as people do, the two women and I got talking, the older of the two said where are you from I said, 'I'm an Ozzie from Perth 'me to' she cried I'm from Gosnell's." they invited me to join them, I had not much else planned so why not? As we chatted and I ate the wonderful fresh sandwiches they offered, feeling a wee bit cheeky as I had bought nothing with me. When the two people who had been in the water joined us, the woman introduced me to their menfolk.

One was short, chubby, bright blue eyes, and sporting a bright red beard. The other male tall, skinny, a black beard. What made me stare was the tall skinny one who had on a wet suit that was obviously a women's wet suit, too small and much too tight. He saw me look more than once, then explained he had borrowed it off his mate's wife so he could dive at the reserve. The shorter one of the two had masking tape wrapped around his wrists and ankles of the wetsuit, he explained the dive suit was old and leaked.

They both looked like the poor relations of Jacques Cousteau, but if they were happy puttering about for the day in the ocean, who am I to judge. We all chatted about Perth and touring New

Zealand; how small and close all the little townships were and how wide and distant the shires were in Australia. They began to pack away their picnic, it was time for me to go. Thanking them for their hospitality, I was on my way, the cares and woes of my world that once felt like a log across my shoulders had gone, I was really and truly foot loose and fancy free. What a wonderful feeling, driving back to Warkworth, it was time to hitch up my home and onto the next township-Wellsford.

I drove through slowly, finding it a place of loneliness-it reminded me of Mt Magnet in Australia. Maungaturoa township was next, it had approximately one shop and a gas station, I kept going. After an hour arriving at a turn off to Ruakaka. I had been warned about the Ruakaka stretch by the two men on the beach; they were not wrong as they described the winding road. I was not used to the small roads and the winding curves, but the scenery was breathtaking. Waterfalls spilt off mountainsides, cascading off the black rocks and green ferns, the views from up here was amazing. The off-road parking giving me the opportunity to pull my small convoy over. I began taking as many photos as I could in every direction. One day I would be showing my family and friends where I had traveled to, I wanted them to see the beauty as well as the adventure.

I drove past Marsden Point turn off as I had been warned by a lady in Warkworth 'this was not a place for tourists.' I was driving to the seaside town of Whangarei, a three-hour drive and by the time I had found the way to the Whangarei falls Caravan Park I was more than tired.

I had an immediate reaction to the waterfalls; they had a weird sound to them or was that my imagination? I enquired about parking my van, yes, there was availability for three nights. I was still a bit wobbly with reverse parking, but I did it. Unhitching the Teardrop, putting chocks under her wheels, winding down the jockey wheel, pulling on the van brakes. I could have sworn I heard a voice say, "Look at you Tara, you're doing alright." Whangarei city here I come. Clapham's clocks were still open, so

I visited there, an interesting museum, some clocks dating back to the 1800's. which made me think of meeting the R&R's, the antique dealers in the Pilbara. A finger of loneliness tugged at a heart string.

I walked along the wharves, watching the fishermen unload their catch, ribbing each other about the days catch. Across the street there was a market, many different fruit and veggies were on sale. I wandered through, purchasing a bag of Feijoas-a local fruit. On the opposite side of the fisherman's wharf was a small café, it reminded me of our holiday in Paris, walking along the Seine sitting at a sidewalk café watching the French live their everyday life. While I sipped a hot chocolate drink, I sketched the sights and sounds around me. Tomorrow, I intended to drive further North. The brochures raved about a city called Russell, I added that to my bucket list. The blurb on Keri Keri and surrounding districts was interesting. The Café was putting out its dinner menu boards, why not' I thought? Ordering myself a child's portion of Reef and Beef. I asked what entertainment was like around here; the manager said pubs, clubs and movies, I opted for my van and bed, as tomorrow was another day. I'm not the club or pub type so why bother?

Once back at the park everything was in darkness, pale lights blinked as the huge green and brown bush moths crowded around them. I walked to the waterfall, it was pretty in all its moonlight splendor; frogs croaked their greetings to each other, a native Morpork owl calling out in its eerie lonely sound. This place had a ghostly feel about it; I knew I was not welcome here. The only friendly sound was the click of my light switch once I had found my way inside my van.

"Lonely yet Tara?" Came that internal whisper, I wrapped myself into my bedding, warm and cosy, reading my book trying to ignore the fact that yes, I was lonely, I missed everyone, tears formed and fell. Being a Sagittarius I was the gregarious type, I loved company, I loved entertaining and having my friends and family around me, so what on earth am I doing here in a small caravan alone in a strange country? I'm also known for my tenaciousness so I'm giving this trip all I've got. For some reason I felt edgy, I put it down to the weather, hot and very humid. I woke at dawn feeling very unwell.

CHAPTER TWENTY-NINE

That morning was a blur as my temperature had shot up, I went out to the back of my Teardrop to boil water but ended up dry retching; having to lie down on the wet grass, the world was tilting too much to stand upright. "Can I help" a woman asked I was about to say, "I don't know, I can't stand up" when a putrid stream of vomit erupted. When I came to, I was in the local hospital, being poked and prodded, a doctor asking, "Can you answer some questions," my head was exploding, there was no way I could answer anything.

"You have gastroenteritis" (food poisoning). If I tried to sit up a wave of nausea would hit me hard. If I tried to open my eyes for more than five minutes the pain in my skull was unbearable, I just laid there, incoherent with confusion and pain as they pushed catheters into my arms for pain relief and liquids.

The staff nurse asked if she could search my phone to contact an emergency number, all that came out was a groan, "Is there anyone you want us to phone in particular?" My tongue felt swollen, stuck to the roof of my mouth as I croaked "Rae." I could hear my daughters voice on the phone 'Tara? My Mum? in Hospital?' Why? What's happened? Rae was told the circumstances of my hospital stay, Rae requested regular updates on my condition.' Three days later when I was able to sit up and ring her, she said "Jess and I are really worried, Mum, I'm happy to come over and help you" I had to smile, I could just see both of us tucked up in the teardrop caravan. I declined her offer saying, "I was well." She was disgruntled, I told her I appreciated her offer, but this was my adventure, and I had to do it my way.

Discharge now complete, I flagged a taxi back to the caravan park. I was on medication for the headache that edged around my eyesight, the doctor advising 'no driving for a day or two until it had settled.' A taxi was ordered to drive me back to the campground where I asked management if I could stay an extra night or two. "Yes, by all means, did they find out the cause of your turn? I was surprised, then explained "Turn? No, I had food poisoning." I don't think they were convinced, once I looked in the mirror, I knew why, I looked like a ghoul. Blue black rings around my eyes, my face a grey white, my dry lips were peeling, my hair was an oily mess, and my clothes stunk of vomit. Hopefully, a long hot shower would help.

I had one more night, the ablution block my only walk for the day. It irked me that to have a cuppa I had to go outside and boil the kettle on the tiny pull-out stove, then go back inside for milk. I lay on my bed, the warmth of my feather doona spreading through me. When I spied the electrical outlet for the toaster. I groaned at my stupidity, knowing my next purchase would be an electric jug. As nighttime arrived, I had eaten a few plain biscuits and enjoyed a cup of tea and thank heavens, I was feeling so much better, the air was cold, I knew a short walk just may put some much needed fresh air in my lungs.

Wrapping myself up, I headed for the path to the waterfall, not a wide public pathway more like a woodland trail, the bush smelt wonderful, the waterfall was pretty, the moon casting a soft glow around me. Finding a large flat stone, it jutted out over a deep pool, I sat there breathing in deeply, listening to the frogs and other night insects. This cold was different, this felt like I was invading a space where I was not welcome. The next day I was ready to move on, to Hikurangi, where the countryside was amazing. Huge slabs of volcanic rock lay strewn in the fields; they had been noted as thousands of years old. Sadley there was nowhere to stay, not even for a tiny teardrop on my GPS. It stated Kawakawa would be my next stopover.

Once again, the scenery was beautiful, white sheep, deep green hills and deep valleys filled with deep pools of water, the most gorgeous tall flax plants, this part of the country was filled with green rolling hills that lead to boulder filled craggy mountains, waterfalls fell from amazing heights, it reminding me of our holiday in Ireland. The signpost for Kawakawa came up, time to pull over and find out more about this little township and if there was a place to stay overnight. It was here that I found one of the biggest tourism spots- the Hundertwasser designed public toilets, tall columns of mosaicked pots of all different sizes, were stacked on top of each other they were the support system for the verandah. I waited for my turn in a long queue of tourists to take photos.

Well done Kawakawa for preserving this monument to Hundertwasser the artist, how it had not been vandalised I have no idea. My camera worked overtime, Kawakawa advertised a ride on the original steam train *Gabriel*, but once at the train station it was out of order, I had been told this was a common problem, through lack of government finances most of the cute little places are virtually closed, to have any fun you had to be or know a local. I went to visit the glow worm caves-Kawiti Caves, the narrative was given with a bored attitude! I left early, feeling very disappointed in what I had expected be a lesson in nature. So, onwards I went, driving though Morewa, once more anything interesting to stop and look at or tour, closed.

Maybe they relied on the scenery as it was the most glorious scenery, it was everywhere I drove, mountainsides and valleys full of abundance, native fernery and massive trees, waterfalls gushing onto roads or slowly meandered amongst the hills. Pretty little beaches fringed by the famous Pohutukawa trees, a bright red bottle brush flower, New Zealanders call their Christmas tree. I would often park on the side of the road just to take it all in, the silence that greeted you, at first was unnerving then calming.

Occasionally I would see a family of Māori in dinghies with lines or nets out, but nothing like the bustling sandy beaches we have in Australia. These were peaceful inlets, why this gave me such a strange sensation of freedom? I have no idea. I was really on my own here and I was 'doin it' as Margi would say. Signposts to different little townships popped into view I was tempted to find a spot to rest, but Pahia was only a short distance away, I could not believe the short distances between each village or township, if you were touring my country you would spend hours on the road to reach your destination, to those touring on their own they should understand that Australia is wide and vast, warning signs were highlighted on every highway to take water with you.

Paihia what a pretty little township, curio's plus every sort of beach trinket on offer-they advertised a camping ground. I drove up and down searching for the advertised campground. Nothing, fed up, I stopped off at the local pub to make enquiries. It seemed that a biker's get together was happening, these people have always scared me, their reputation of violence throughout both countries was not pleasant, however, they seemed to be just having a friendly chat and a beer. Once inside the dim interior, the stale smell of hops slid into my throat, not a pleasant sensation. I placed my order, a big bowl of fat, salty, crispy wedges, plus a mug of ice cubes with a bottle of lemonade. Everywhere I looked were remnants of a year, old pit saws, old axes, bottles, jugs, pots etc. I felt the headache behind my eyes begin to niggle its way into another migraine.

The publican was not that helpful with any information, but the Bikies had overheard, I was soon being giving advice, that any fear of these tough looking men and women soon went. They asked me where I was from. This was new, it was usually me asking that question, the painkillers had begun to work as I began to tell them about my life in Perth, when the publican yelled 'closing time.' I looked at my watch and I had been there for three hours. Now it was important I find somewhere to stay and park the Teardrop for the night. I was about to leave, when the group suggested I follow them, a hot dinner was promised, so why not? I was in no hurry. I thought of Rae, she would have been horrified her Mum with a gang of Bikies, but these folk weren't drunk or rowdy, I saw no drugs being taken, although I was pretty sketchy about what to look for in that department.

I followed them onto a deserted road, then a kilometer or two they turned off into an ancient farmyard, a lone relic of a chimney jutted up, silhouetted against a night sky. The bikes formed into a circle; this was obviously their spot. My teardrop followed till one of the bikies stopped me and yelled, "Park it here, mate." he pushed his hand through the jeep window, "Hi, I'm Jeri." His American accent strong. He looked tough, a definite swagger to his stride, his arms and neck covered in tattoos. His hand on my elbow leading me to the circle of people that had formed around a huge bonfire. Then, like children waiting for a bedtime story, they asked me to continue my story about my travels.

I told them about Russ, our life together in the bus travelling the Pilbara, as I talked, I was handed a plastic plate of hot spicy baked beans, balanced on the side a thick slice of bread with yellow creamy butter slathered on it, I ate with a plastic spoon, using the bread to slop up the gravy on my plate. A 2nd bottle of whiskey was opened and passed around; I declined, pleading exhaustion. I was asleep before my head hit the pillow. If anyone had tried to enter, I would not have known, I was out to it. Where they slept? I had no idea. When I woke, it was to Jeri tapping on my door, telling me they heading back to Auckland.

The bikes roared past me, like a hive of black hornets, each one rumbling with hunger to get back on the road. I was happy enough, by now I had learnt to enjoy my own company. I took my time warming up a large pan of water and having a wash outside the van enjoying the privacy, the quietness. Magpies and their wonderful song, the smell of pine trees, the only noisy sound was me splashing in the bucket of warm sudsy water.

CHAPTER THIRTY

Stripping down to my underwear, lathering myself with the warm soapy water, it felt wonderful. As I towelled off, with the fresh air on my body and scalp, I tingled; this was the medicine I needed. The buzz of a motorbike broke the peace around me, panic rose in my chest. My first thought was here comes trouble, tripping over, then reaching the safety of my van, I locked the door, fumbling around in the semi dark for clean clothes, and of course when you panic, nothing goes right.

The bike roared into the yard and stopped opposite the van, heavy boots crunched over to the door, it shook a little under the heavy knock it received. Oh God, I'm going to be raped and killed, no one knows where I am. Terror ran like wildfire though my body, my clothes now scrunched up in a tight ball in my hands, my actions becoming clumsy. 'It's Jeri here Tara, saw you were still parked up, is everything alright? "I've got a coffee and muffin, you wanna share?" I could have hugged him, I was starving. I quickly dressed, he had pulled up and old log to sit on and re started the fire from last night. He carefully halved his blueberry muffin; while I made myself a mug of hot instant coffee.

When Jeri started talking about himself, I soon discovered my intuition was right. Jeri was an educated man who had fled his normal life, stumbling into this nomad bikie gang halfway around the world. It was easier to be tough and free, than let his heart twist with hurt over losing his family in the Twin Towers disaster in America. His breath ragged as he told me about his two children and wife that were never found in the rubble. How he and the volunteers had searched for days. The worst part was trying to sleep, yet he could hear their voices calling him. A memorial was held, their combined families attending, all day he heard the word condolences. He booked his ticket to Australia the next day, locking up his life till he felt he could return.

Between the stops and starts of his story, I placed my hand over his. Jeri, I recently lost my husband, although nothing as horrific as your story. This trip is my way of working through it; it's okay to grieve. I felt the change of emotion as his arm went around my shoulders. I quickly stood up, saying "Let's find that famous Pacific Ocean and go for a swim." Grabbing my swimsuit and towels, locking the Suzuki and the teardrop up, Jeri doused the fire.

For the 1st time in many years, I rode pillion on a Harley, we stopped for snacks at gas station, then found our way to a beach, where we swam and sunbathed. I built a sandcastle, Jeri collected seashells to decorate it, a calm pleasant afternoon, but as all good things, it was soon time to head home. Once back at the van, Jeri suggested the local pub for a meal, locally known as pub grub. Throughout dinner I pretended not to notice the invitation in Jeri's eyes, his hand giving mine a gentle squeeze as we both reached for the saltshaker. No! I was not becoming involved, we were both carefree, he was in his forties I'm in my sixties. When he dropped me off at my van, we held each other for a microsecond, I will admit a small part of me desired him, the commonsense side said *no baggage*. The keep in touch promises were made, phone numbers exchanged.

Today, I was driving to Waitangi, a beach township that looked promising. As I drove, I thought of Rae and Jess, this was a Tara they did not know, one that was learning to roll with the punches, in fact I hardly knew the new me that was evolving. And I was enjoying watching her grow. I would ring them as soon as I reached Waitangi. The tourism pamphlet promised a clean well - run camping ground, however not realising it was school holidays, I had not booked ahead, valuable lesson learnt. I was really disappointed to be told "Sorry love, nothing available" until the camp owner saw how small my van was. The manager asking "On your own then love? This was not the first time my status as a single woman had been pointed out. It was definitely food for thought, was this how all single women on the road felt, slightly ostracised? Definitely something to write about.

I think he could see my frustration as he offered me a small space just behind their woodshed, the manager connecting my electric plug to the outlet, as I attended to settling the van in for the night. I was all set. I had commented that for such a small town it was teaming with a large international mix of tourists, the owner nodded "Used to be such a nice pretty seaside village, I guess this is progress" his attitude was one of disappointment. I turned towards the ocean there in the distance, I could see what looked like boat full of Māori warriors coming to shore, I pointed it out to him, he sighed, don't get to excited love, it's just a plastic version of a *Waka* a Māori canoe, its bringing in one lot of them, he thumbed the crowd and taking the next lot of them out.

The Māori song that went with the dipping of the paddles was hypnotic. I wanted to be in that Waka, the manager giving me the phone number. I tapped the numbers in; it was answered with 'Kia Ora' the Māori welcome. I booked my seat, the asking price making me gasp, but I was now booked on the next Waka leaving. I headed back to my van, dousing myself in suntan cream, jamming on a sunhat and sunglasses. Excitement was rippling through me I had never ever done anything like this before. Soon enough, I was helped into this magnificent Waka. Hone-the owner gave the order in Māori to cast off. I was now part of a team; instructions were how to sweep your oar in the water. As we each dipped our paddles into the ocean they began to sing a melodious chant.

It was pure magic you could almost imagine being part of a tribe coming home from a day of discovery; I loved it, every minute detail of the Waka stuck in my mind so I could relay it all to Jess tonight. Being so close to the water; the sea spray in your face, its coolness sprayed onto my hot skin, my arm muscles bulged. I could feel my core muscles working, what an experience. I did not want it to end. I walked back to the camp feeling very different, looking in the rear vision mirror, the tanned face and mile wide grin was a tell-tale sign that Tara was having fun. What struck me most; there was no makeup, the hair do I once sported, had long gone. In its place was a soft white curly head of hair that was unruly and windblown. I was looking healthy and tanned, when I changed into a long skirt and singlet, they were both loose on me.

For once I was totally natural - it felt wonderful. I remembered all the fussing and fluffing when I was with Russ, applying makeup and gel through my hair, making sure he was pleased with the way I looked. Tara had changed dramatically, and I liked her, I was responsible for me and me alone. I pleased no one else but me. I wanted to keep it like that.

Dinner that night was a can of Tuna and a light salad, my thoughts a thousand miles away. Dusk here was a little different to dusk in the Pilbara, it became damp, cold with the ocean wind coming straight into the campgrounds. At home, the cold settled like blanket at night. But the stars are still wonderful no matter what country I was in. As I ate my dinner and leaned back in my camp chair the peace and solitude was soothing, the other campers obviously gone out somewhere, there was no one around, not even the tinny sound of a TV or radio, the camp was dark. All I could hear was the lapping of the ocean, the occasional sea bird settling for the night.

Now was the time to ring my daughter and I also thought I would ring Margi in Auckland. Rae was still unenthusiastic about my tour of New Zealand, we exchanged pleasantries and what I had done till now, I do admit to whitewashing my story about Jeri somewhat, no need for her to know the exact details. I told her of where I had been and done, then it was Jess's turn on the phone, he demanded 'I return home as soon as possible.' "Excuse me? He was showing all the signs of being a rude stroppy young man. Rae took over the conversation saying, "He really misses you Mum, we both do." I felt like yelling at them both "You had your chance, and you threw it away." My thoughts were to keep it peaceful, what they did not know was the more they argued, blamed and contorted the truth to suit them, the less I wanted to go back there, life on my own was becoming comfortable.

I asked about her Fiancé Tim, there was a silence Rae then said, "Mum because of your opinions he is having second thoughts about us being a couple." That gobsmacked me, "I beg your pardon, you're blaming me?' "Well, who else is there to blame?' she said; because of your recent actions and not letting us live in your home, it all fell apart.' Apparently, every time she reacted to any problem Tim would say "Look at the mother see the daughter. How original I thought, perhaps a trip away on her own would help her grow up and stop seeing the world as her enemy. Rae's words became bitter, "This is all your fault Mum, maybe once you're home and act like a responsible parent, we can work on our relationships, especially between you and Tim."

What? Did she honestly think that I would hand over the keys to my life and my home and be a good, quiet, obedient Mum and Nana. They had no idea of who I was or who I was becoming. I ended the phone call sooner than I had expected by saying "Better go I have places to go and people to see." I seethed at her rudeness and the fact she was teaching my grandson to be just as rude and demanding, where had my daughter gone. Margi was my next call, the phone answered by one of her many children, Margi yelling "To give her the bloody phone or else. Tara, she yelled at me, "Where are you? Been thinking of you" I told her all the goings on and about Whangarei- food poisoning, my hospital stay, meeting Jeri and going on the Waka trip.

She chuckled at my adventure saying "You don't do things by halves do you girl, hey, when you're in Kaitaia ring me, I have family there, you can stay with them" that sounded promising, I said I would, and we said our good nights to each other. I tidied up, showered then making a hot milo, journal about my day, tomorrow was my day on the tall ship R. Thomas Tucker.

I was up early waiting like an eager school kid for nine thirty to arrive. The sailing ship was moored to the wharf, the passengers were a mix of ages, mostly people of my age, instructions given through a loudhailer on what to do, and who to take our orders from. Our teams were chosen. I was on team B.

CHAPTER THIRTY-ONE

The 1ˢᵗ Mate introduced himself as Jackson - a tall, tanned, male who had a twinkle in his hazel eyes, he had worked on the *Tucker* for the past ten years. He gave us the spiel on this working ship. Then he gave us our orders of where we were to be stationed. His love for this ship showed in the way he demanded respect for her. He worked the two crew and passengers with style; his voice brooked no arguments "Do it my way or sit down and shut up."

Once I had my turn at the wheel plus learning the different seaman's knots that secured the lay lines, I made for the galley for a hot cup of tea with fresh scones, jam and butter, I was hungry. The brunch was part of the cruise deal they advertised. Apparently, I was too late, the two family's on board had made short work of anything presentable. The Galley was a mess, jam and doughy crumbs littered the Galley floor, butter and cream was smeared all over the table, empty orange juice paper cups littered on the bunk seats and half empty tea mugs were in the small sink. Jackson had descended into the galley just after me, he saw my face, and it must have shown the same disappointment as his. Jackson bounded back up the stairs, shouting about disrespect.

In no time it was cleaned up, apologies, tripping off the tourists tongues. However, while I had been waiting to make myself a cup of tea, I had found a dog eared journal, my interest taken as it was handwritten. There was deep cadence and rhythm to the words inside, they flowed from the soul. The name signed on each page was Jackson's. The story was about a small statue of a Mermaid, it had been a treasured landmark in Russel, made of bronze and forged with passion, a popular icon for all, her tail had been twisted like a 'koru' the heart of the New Zealand national silver fern plant.

Some folks believed she held the spirit of a Māori maiden, some believed she was good luck, and some believed the site she was on was haunted. The entire nation shocked to find she had been stolen. How can you steal a 12 ft bronze statue? In Jacksons story I could feel the love, outrage and the sorrow in his words. Once back at the caravan park, it was time to study the road maps. My goal was to reach Cape Reinga to see the famous lighthouse. The Māori belief, that the spirits of their dead leap from this point to fly to the heavens, I found fascinating. Waitangi was another pretty seaside township. Its history was a large part of New Zealand; I stood with the crowd as a speaker told us the story.

I found the story of the treaty flagpole being chopped down by a Māori warrior amusing, yet this treaty of Waitangi was now a recognised national holiday in recognition of European and Māori people living together as one. It seemed within some faction of the Māori, all was not well in that field. I was of the opinion that having a political point of view when it's not your country, a little unwise, but we all have different opinions. I was not prepared to argue my case with the orator as others were, this was turning out to be an uneducated slanging match.

It felt more comfortable to walk away, time to move on, I rang Margi, "Hello," barely out of my mouth, when I heard Margi's voice greet me with "Tara, gotta run love, have you got pen and paper handy? Here's the details of my cousins, they are expecting you." I scribbled the number and address down; the phone went dead. Her family lived in Kaitaia which the last big city on the map. After that, a village called Houhora which touted that it had the last pub in Northland. If I stayed on this highway, it would lead me to the Cape Reinga lighthouse.

My plans were after visiting Margi's family, on my return to Auckland, I would drive along the rugged West coast highway, I wanted to see life off the beaten track, to see a community living life, not the tourist trap, advertised as a true Kiwi experience, to tour New Zealand in three weeks, I wanted more. If it took me months to visit every nook and cranny, then that's what it would take. I was not time poor, for once I had no demands or regulations to fit into. I now wore a warm woolen jumper and jeans, finding Northland was not the subtropical paradise advertised. It felt more like Tasmania-basically on the cool side all year round. I packed the teardrop, excited to be meeting Margis' family. I had a long drive ahead. Tonight, I would try some free camping, maybe I could find a farm who would allow me to stay overnight?

How wrong was I, as I drove through deep country, there were no open paddocks or farms, just miles of thick bush or pine forests with one or two laybys for vans, but these spots were already taken. Finally, a layby that looked promising, the owners of the 4 wheel drive had parked, already pitched their camping gear. My heart dropped, the camp bristled with guns and traps; they were hunters. Although very polite and welcomed to share their Billy tea.

That night shots were fired and something crashed through the bush close by. The cries of a wounded animal, then the cries of victory. A sound sleep was impossible; in the morning I gagged as the smell of fresh blood flooded the air.

Two wild pigs had been slaughtered, the gutted carcass's hanging only meters from my door. I could not leave fast enough. I rang Margi's family twice, no answer, their address was in the GPS. I drove up to a faded blue cottage, it garden full of red and white Roses, flowering impatience plants spilled from hanging baskets. Their front door was wide open. The innocent "Hello, anyone home" was soon answered "Hello, we're out the back." The greeting was by Pania, the matriarch of this family, her grey hair in a bun; an apron tied around her frock, woolly slippers on her feet. I was immediately embraced by her smiling welcome. She introduced me to the many faces staring at me "Ok, you lot; stop lollygagging about, this is Margie's mate from Ozzy, she staying for bit, okay?'

This backyard was huge, filled with fruit trees, a large veggie garden, pots of all descriptions brimming with herbs, this place was overflowing with an abundance of fresh food and people. All of their faces alight with a welcome, their hands offered in friendship, names in English and Māori flew around in the air; my one thought was, how will I ever remember all of them. The first night after a more than welcome roast meal, Pania served a homemade Pavlova. The old rivalry question put to me, well Tara, who created the Pavlova first? The Kiwis or the Ozzie's?" I shrugged my shoulders "I have no idea, I just know this is delicious." It seems I gave the right answer as the person who had asked replied, "You'll do." From the very first night, the van and Suzuki parked in the back paddock.

Sons, daughters, cousins, nephews, aunties, uncles, 2nd and 3rd cousins. One rowdy happy family that showed the utmost respect for my hosts, the two elders of this family, Pania and Mathew. The days sped by each day I was involved with what they did, play or work I was part and parcel of this large happy family. There was no question of who was coming for tea, it was simply expected that all their family turn up. If there was any admonishing of her family it was quick, honest, to the point, and it worked; they had four rules to their house, no booze, no smoking, no swearing and respect each other. If you followed the rules, you were fine, if not then the family came down on you like a hornets' nest, when one particular teenager tried to be dishonest, I overheard a male adult say, "Don't test me son, or you won't sit for a week." This family was no nonsense; the men did the hunting, fishing, net mending, wood chopping, and running the small farms that surrounded the original homestead.

The women tended to the food preparation, home gardening, child rearing, the caretakers of the family health, hearth and home, to me an old fashioned way of life but as I watched and listened, it worked. They practiced the saying 'if it's not broken then don't try to fix it.' Each and every one of them healthy and happy. If not then Pania was the first to question, why not? She was really in tune with her family and fifteen grandchildren. I was included in their women's work, cooking, gathering seeds, gardening, the preserving of food, and the making of home remedies. I loved it, every day something new. I was involved and welcomed at any family celebrations of which there where many.

Mathew took time to converse with me, a shy man but well spoken, he told me of their history in the area, how after watching his parents struggle with the ownership of the land sold to the Pakeha, 'the Europeans.' Mathew had been wise, seeing the future as the two cultures having to live side by side, he worked hard, buying a huge acreage around him, he combined his Māori custom with modern education and machinery.

The majority of the land now farmed by his son's and their son's or Mokopuna as he called his grandchildren. Pania and her daughters taught me how to clean and cut the flax leaves, weaving them into flax containers known as Kitty kits, these were used for anything and everything. I was taught to dance with Pois; a small flax ball stuffed with lamb's wool. Laughter at my clumsy attempts where often hushed by Pania, however there was no escaping that night when I was encouraged to use my own Poi poi's.

The soft guitar music began, I stood in line with the women folk, at first everything went well, then one of my Poi's broke loose, flying off into the watching crowd. The other broke apart, hanging limply from my hand. There was no stopping the mirth that erupted. Not even Pania could stop the laughter as she herself was having trouble not to join them. I felt a little silly, but the family applauded my clumsy attempts at joining in. Believe me when I say when the Māori laugh, there is no way you cannot join in, it comes deep from the belly and can turn dark to light. I was once more encouraged to join in their song and dance, after my last attempt, I declined. I was more than happy to help in the kitchen.

When we were all sitting outside, Pania began to sing, Mathew accompanying her with guitar, soon her daughters took up the tune, their voice's hypnotic, their song entrancing. They sang many songs, in particular one song, Pokarikariana, it was truly beautiful, my heart willingly joined in its melody, deep inside my very core, where the Crone wisdom responded to the love I felt. Mathew and Pania opted to come with me to Cape Reinga, while I drove, they explained their beliefs and the sacred ground I was about to stand on.

Once we had parked, I was shocked at the amount of tourists tramping all over the place, rubbish littering the ground, overflowing rubbish bins. Family's screaming at each other, running amuck, there was no sanctity, yet this place to my hosts was holy ground. I felt embarrassed. Two bus drivers' stood leaning against their tour buses, both smoking cigarettes. When they finished, they stamped the butts out into the ground, Pania's face flinched, I put my arm around her, here was tourism at its worst. Mathew began to explain that when they die, their spirit leaves for the heavens by leaping off this majestic point of land where the waves of the Atlantic and the Pacific Oceans meet. "Pania and I will leave from here, when we are called."

CHAPTER THIRTY-TWO

To me-a stranger to this land, it looked very different. The two seas literally mashed up against each other, sprays of sea spray erupting into the air, booming out its discontent, as the ocean rushed over the rocks beneath us, then leaving with a deep sucking sigh. It felt terrifying, Mathew had only one thing to say about the scene at the lighthouse. "I wonder how they would like it if we emulated this behaviour in their countries." I had to agree, remembering the respect we were asked to show to the 1st nations people and their land. I too had experienced such disappointment at one particular celebration at the Swan River in Perth, a few young men urinating on the grass, calling out to each other in a foreign language. I empathised with Matthew and Pania's emotions.

That night I told them how the Orewa camp shop told me about a different road to get to Kaitaia to reach the lighthouse. Mathew grinned, "You could have done that, instead the spirits brought you to us and our home." I had to agree it had certainly proved a blessing for me. I shouted fish and chips for our dinner, Mathew drowning his in brown vinegar, "I like them sour and mushy." Pania adding more salt and tomato sauce to her packet. Each of us silent with our own thoughts. I was certainly looking forward to getting into my bed tonight. On our way home they showed me the Paua shell house in Kaitaia, a small home with its front and sides covered in huge Paua shells, an artist's dream, it glowed once I shone the headlights onto it, it really had the wow factor.

Pania told me the history of this house, it all started approximately fifty years ago as a small decoration by the front door, the local Iwi plus community had taken an interest, occasionally leaving sack's full of shells on the doorstep, that's how it grew to what it is now she explained. The first occupiers had long ago passed on, but the house was kept like this by all descendants. Now it was a tourist attraction. There is also a ghost story attached to that house she whispered like it was secret, "they say the very first owner often walks around the house at night, sometimes a Paua shell or two is missing." I was going to say maybe it's the local kids taking them, I looked at Matthew's face; he shook his head slightly, meaning let Pania have her ghost story. I felt beholden to these two wonderful people, how to say thank you for your generosity, to those whose hearts and lives were full.

One particular day I had been invited into Pania's cottage, at any other time I had been asked to sit outside in the enclosed veranda, or under the huge plum tree in their backyard, where an eclectic mix of chairs of all descriptions gathered, where sage advice was given out: where Mokopuna's were soothed and tears dried.

Where flirtations were discussed, this communal patch was the heart and soul of the farm, and it was here that some relationships were dissolved. To be invited inside the house was something else, the wooden floor was polished to within an inch of its life, giving off a golden sheen. Their home was sparse yet the driftwood furniture that was inside was a designers dream. A magazine rack, coffee table, two cleverly made armchairs, all made out of the local driftwood.

In Australia, we would pay huge amounts for furniture to look like this or import it from other countries, here the wood was washed up on the beaches to use as they saw fit. White net curtains hung at the windows, a well-used leather couch was covered with a black and white cow hide, knitted cushions and weaved rugs where everywhere. One sepia photo on the wall of this couple's wedding day, both standing there in the European wedding attire, Pania and Mathew married 1945-that was over sixty years ago, this couple had been committed to each other from the very beginning. This home and garden was Pania's kingdom; the farmland was Mathew's domain.

Two days previously, before this invite, I had been witness to Pania and one of her niece's talking about going to nurse's training college, I had overheard the request for assistance then Mathews immediate refusal. She wanted a career in nursing; the family budget could not do it. Since my stay with these people, I had observed how any big decisions were discussed within the elders first and I knew this could take hours of debate, so I was surprised at Mathews instant refusal. When Pania invited me to help her make sponge that afternoon, I soon found that her concerns about her niece were very real. So, as many women do around the world, we baked, we talked, and we shared. As a women close to Pania's age, over the weeks we had formed a kinship. Today, she wanted my advice on how my Pakeha world could help.

I spoke about the grants, loans, advocacy, perhaps addressing the local MP, for advice. Did the government have any dispensation or scholarship in place for this 1st nation? When I had worked with the local Citizens Advice Bureau in Australia, there were many avenues. Perhaps they had the same in New Zealand? Pania listened, mentally noting any advice I gave. The sponge looked magnificent, fresh cream slathered all over it, the home-made plum jam peeking out where the cream had not covered. Pania looking thoughtful as she cut into it, first serving it to the six elders. As she passed a slice to her niece, she patted her arm, saying, "Tomorrow we will visit the authorities; they may have answers." I could see concern on all the adults faces, as this was not about only one of their children leaving a home. It was about change. It was about preparing them all for scholastic world they were about to step into.

I was making plans to leave when I was asked to be present at a ceremony that night; A Powhiri to welcome me to their Marae. It was quite a shock when 1st Margi and then Pania appeared at my caravan door. They walked with me to the meeting house, the Marae, this was the one place that had been off limits to me until now, it was thrilling and scary all at once, the two women each had an arm about my waist, we was stopped at the gates where

Tikis with wide Paua shell eyes glared at me, both women patting my back for confidence, a hush fell as I approached the gates. A female elder challenged me in Māori, was I friend or foe, my two friends whispering what I should do, the elder walked towards me, slowly laying a silver fern leaf halfway between us, I was urged to pick it up, this was their way of greeting me, I was led in behind her.

The women then broke into song as I was led down a long line of relations the Hongi greeting given and returned. Speeches were given in Māori, words of greeting, words of welcome, this Marae and this Iwi was now my home and my family.

When it was time to celebrate the Māori do it in style, long tables groaned with food, the Hangi was ready, the men dividing up the cooked meat. It truly touched my heart when Margie placed a small Greenstone pendant around my neck, beautifully engraved with a Koru. The symbol of a silver fern bud uncurling, it meant protection and wisdom. I was told I was family; a daughter of this iwi and it would be forever so. It was midnight before I was in my bed, their love for me still flowing around my heart, as I went to sleep. I woke to a soft tapping on my door, Margi stood there smiling offering me a cup of tea and kai, her freshly made Māori bread. We sat under the orange trees; the bees humming over the pretty white buds forming on a new harvest, the day proving already to be a hot one. I could get used to feeling this relaxed when Margie asked me when I was moving on.

I was stunned it sounded like an order; my answer stuttered "In a few days' time, does that suit everyone? Should I be insulted? Was this my dismissal card? She patted my hand "Don't be so touchy, we are all going to our Matariki, to honor our ancestors, Pania and I wanted you to feel safe while we were gone, or you can join us. But, if you're leaving in a few days, we will stay with you to keep you company." Three days before I left a young teenager came to see me, he was painfully shy, a pink blush staining his dark skin, a sleeveless t-shirt, his denim shorts tattered, almost thread bare. Warike asked if he could paint the caravans name across her back. I was stopped short as I had never thought of that. I must have looked apprehensive, as he hung his head and shuffled his feet, till someone amongst the onlookers yelled "Show her ya art Warike."

An unkempt textbook with smudgy pencil sketches was shoved into my hands, before me I saw Art in all its wonder, as I turned page after page, asking questions and the meanings, sea creatures, Tikis, fish, crabs, mystical creatures from Māori fables, pictures of carvings all from this young man's imagination. Until one small scribble took my eye, a Mermaids tail with Māori motif surrounding it, I had found Metal Mermaid II.

It was love at first sight, my forefinger touching it lightly "This would be perfect" one huge smile split Warike's face, I asked "And the cost? He shrugged his shoulders, he mumbled. "Ask Auntie." I loved the respect these teenagers showed their elders. "Okay Warike when can you start? The next morning Warike started painting, his paint gear was from the ark, the tin of black paint that looked like treacle, his brushes were old house brushes.

However, true to his word, he worked early till late every day, he sat on an old wooden apple box, his aunties Margie and Pania regularly popping over to feed him. Warike's concentration, dedication and ability to transfer his sketching of a Mermaids tail was outstanding. Slowly, a Māori motif encircled the tail, it said Moana Ika. When I asked the meaning Pania explained. "Our people don't have a word for Metal Mermaid, so Warike has called it Ocean creature." Warike's face flamed when he realised I did not speak his language, he quickly cleaned his brushes packing them into an old tin can, his lean brown body flecked in black paint, he mumbled "There ya go." My heart ached, I wanted to hug him, he reminded me so much of our Jess, I did notice his stance had changed, one of pride and all because of this small motif of a Mermaids tail, it stood out like a true piece of art always does. I offered his aunties payment for the art, it was declined, "What you have given him is payment enough."

My day had arrived to leave; I was packed up and ready to go, sad? Yes, to leave these wonderful people. Pania and Margi and their families, both women patting my back, to comfort themselves more than me, Margi repeating over and over "Who would have thought aye love." This family was what I had dreamed that my family would be like, loving, kind and inclusive. When I had spoken to Rae or Jess, telling them what I had done and or seen in my day, it had gone down like a lead balloon, their only questions were 'when are you coming home? Or bet that cost a fortune?

What was wrong with them? Where was the "That sounds great Mum, how exciting, or can't wait to see the pics, Mum." Often thinking to myself, why aren't they happy for me? Instead, this large Māori family who I had only just met, could not do enough with or for me.

CHAPTER THIRTY-THREE

But my family of two in Perth? they oozed discontent and sarcasm, why was my family so bloody rude and demanding? Was it because we had tried to give them everything they could possibly want? Rae only had to look at something; Russ and I would try to get it for her, when it came to education nothing was too much trouble. It was the same with Jess, as his grandparents we had paid his way in education. Being a solo Mum seemed to have given Rae privileges, nothing was her fault, when she told us the news of her pregnancy "It's not my fault" she cried "Then who's' fault is it?" I asked. Russ telling me to "Leave it alone, it's happened, she needs our support" so I shut up. Rae never wanted or needed a thing; she had never struggled or budgeted her pension.

We paid- or should I say her doting father, had paid for anything extra she needed. Whenever she needed food, it was unspoken that she help herself to our pantry or freezer, I still remember her face filled with delight when Russ and I revamped our home. Yes, it was a relief to give it away and not have to throw it out, we were happy that she wanted it all, when we learnt she had sold her old belongings and replaced it with ours we did not blink- it seemed the logical thing to do. Now, I just saw an open maw of greed.

Recently Rae had asked about Russ's will and when would she be able to read it, I had asked why. It's all in the lawyer's hands' to which she grumped and hissed about unfair, she needed to know how much she had been left. When I had quietly said "That's my business" since then our conversations had been short and sweet, it was me that kept in touch, any communication from her had stopped. The concern she had shown when I was in the

Whangarei hospital, had been a real surprise. I knew if she even had a hint of what it was all worth, she would ask for a large portion of it, so kept I kept it between my lawyer and me. I certainly was not in need. Maybe if I had been stricter with her? Admitting to myself that we were partly to blame, as we had never denied her.

Now I was all packed to go, keen to do more adventures, on her tail the Moana Ika proudly displayed, I hitched up and drove out onto the roadway, behind me, I was leaving the most generous of families I had ever met and a heart full of memories. Unbeknown to others, I had left a small amount of cash in Panias care for Warike, as an incentive for him. Asking to be informed of his success that I knew would come his way. "Haere Ra", I called "Keep in touch, love you all." I drove past the little cottage, beeping my horn, waving, the young ones in the family running after me "Bye, Aunty." I was going to miss these people; I had to agree with Margi when she uttered "Who would have thought love." She was so right who would have even guessed that through one hurtful disaster at the Auckland Airport, then meeting Margi, it would have turned into this adventure. I could have sworn that my van wiggled her tail, just that little bit to show off her new Mermaid Motif.

Mathew had told me about the seaweed pickers at Awanui, it sparked an interest, I wanted to capture this on camera. The drive there was one long winding road, my spine was beginning to ache with the prolonged sitting. At last, the signpost saying I had reached Awanui the West Coast of New Zealand.

It then registered that I had recently driven to the end of this country where you could drive or walk no further. Now I was on the opposite side of the country looking at a different Ocean, one that seemed untamed, seaweed and huge amounts of driftwood lay strewn along the beach. Once again Tasmania came to mind where I had been witness to two oceans, the Atlantic and the Pacific, it was called the end of the world, they mashed together in an uproar. I had watched in awe as trees as big as trucks were simply tossed in the air, then plummeted back into the heaving seas.

Today as I drove looking for a place to park overnight, I came across a few small old shacks built from driftwood. I had to stop and capture some photos of this strange little settlement. The road was deserted; I pulled over. As I walked closer some of them were not so tiny, they had a telltale permanency about them, a pot of bright red geraniums on a windowsill, some had small verandas, some doors shielded with wooden porches, others with small fences around them, some pristine and tidy, others their back yards a bomb site, all sorts of paraphernalia had been collected, a hoarders paradise by the looks of it.

The one I was standing in front of sported glass windows of all shapes and sizes, an old rocking chair sat proudly on a small porch, the house looked like something out of a kids story book, or a hobbit house. Around it were large rocks painted white to mark their boundaries. From the roof sprouted a small chimney, even that looked like a scene from a Disney movie. I knocked on the door, a windchime of sorts hung from a porch rafter made from a chunk of driftwood and shells that clacked tonelessly in the wind. Nothing but silence, and yet it looked lived in. Walking back towards my jeep, I heard "Piss off." I turned to see an old woman running after me, her ancient face full anger. I literally sprinted off the beach, to the safety of my jeep. She also stopped, she began throwing stones at the Suzuki, time for me to leave.

I stopped a half hour away, flicking through the photos I had taken. The scenery was moody, the ocean backdrop of the pickers cottagers stunning, but that reception was not one I wanted to repeat.

Next port of call Maungatepere a very small farming town, first find a stop for a milkshake then onto Dargaville. Nothing much to offer here, obviously a mix of farming and fishing, but there was not a soul in sight to ask about what went on here. Okay, where next? Helensville was next, this place was again really pretty, after buying a milkshake at one of the local stores, I was told I could camp up at a local farmer's field. The store owner ringing the farmer to ask if it was all right if they gave me the directions. It sounded positive, then I was told the fee being charged, "Fifty dollars a night," if I stayed for three nights the fourth night free, "But it's just a paddock" I said, "What was there, for me to pay that amount? The shop owner blushed.

I declined, so where to from here? Well, to get anywhere that I wanted to go, it was a winding drive through Auckland city and suburbs. Or I could take a bypass through Auckland that would lead me to the Coromandel peninsula, I pulled over to put the directions into the GPS. Dry dust was swirling everywhere; old dry desiccated corn husks rattled in the soft dusty wind. An old wood mill on my left looked deserted, it seemed the perfect time and place to take photos. The atmosphere was silent, in fact a photographer's dream. My camera lens zoomed up into the upper hatch way of a rundown barn, a rusty winch and hook hung down from the opening, it creaked its rusty song as the soft wind played around the old links, the place smelt of decaying old wood, a forgotten era, this could be a classic country town photo.

 I clicked away, quite happy with the results checking on camera settings and the photo taken each time, I was quite comfortable and in my own little world. Perhaps, once I was home I would enter it into the local photo competitions.

Suddenly in the gate way not six meters away, stood three men, young, unkempt and beer bottles in their hands, 'hey bitch' one of them called "Want a bit of this" he gyrated with his hips, his hand starting to unzip his fly. My heart raced, I launched myself into Suzuki, locking systems on, putting my foot down I took off, the Mermaid swinging suddenly behind me, loud crashes followed me, I knew they were throwing bottles at me.

I could not go any faster to get the hell out of this town than I already was. An hours' drive away I stopped and checked for damage, there was a small dent high up on my van and a shard of brown glass on the Mermaids little bumper, I was still shaking from the crude malevolent behavior towards me, why? In fact, my last two experiences had not been pleasant at all, I had been chased off a public beach, threatened with rape by three drunks. Should I report this to the police or was I just another stupid tourist. I was certainly going to add it to my Facebook to warn anyone thinking of stopping along the country road to leave as fast as you can, I must admit the photos I had taken were charming, sadly the people left a bad taste with me.

Time to put my GPS into action, typing in my destination took maybe two minutes to reconfigure. A four hour drive awaited me through Auckland's highways and byways the GPS not failing or faulting me once, I was not stopping off at Margi's, I was on a mission to get further South. Names of Papakura and Papatoetoe whizzed by the making short work of the miles. By nine pm that night I was finally in the Coromandel. As I drove into the township I saw a caravan park sign, I headed straight there, praying that they had a vacancy for me. The blinking red sign said, 'No vacancies,' bugger. I drove up the road for half an hour. It took me maybe ten minutes to feel the road change from sealed to a dirt road. It became clear I was going to have to reverse down the narrow road in the dark, it was then I also realised there were no streetlights, my worst nightmare coming true.

The lurch I felt had me instantly slam on all brakes. The Mermaids back wheels had suddenly lost traction, she started tipping to one side, my foot and the brake pedal now glued to each other, I tried to go forward, the wheels just spun around, I went to get out of the Suzuki, finding nothing but air under my feet. It was pitch dark with no solid ground that I could actually see or feel to get back onto the road. Terror took hold, I wanted to scream with the suffocating fear that gripped my throat.
Fumbling around for my phone I found the number of the RAC; the office was on recording for the night. "Leave a message please" that was not much help. I searched for the torch remembering it was stored in the boot, without light I could not

find the road, or see where I was. Was I dangling over the road? Ready to crash down the bank into the sea, the words drowned or missing went through my mind. I had to fight the nausea that was started to roll over me. I had to stay in control, I had to, my imagination causing all sorts of horrors to erupt in my head. What if I crawled over to the passenger side? That would mean taking my foot off the brake, not a chance that I was willing to make.

The only option was to sit with my foot on the brake and the handbrake pulled up tight, I could hear the sea surging over rocks. I had no idea of how bad my situation was. Dawn was taking its time to creep up over the horizon, every time I dozed off, I would jerk awake, the fear I felt, was like no other I had ever experienced ever. Dawn started as a very faint line then a slight glow, I held my breath as sky brightened, hopefully in maybe ten minutes or so I would be able to see where I was and what had gone wrong.

CHAPTER THIRTY-FOUR

Morning had never felt so welcome in my whole life ever; to say it felt good is an understatement, I was ecstatic. I sat up to take in what and where I was, the situation was dire I just knew it, I was holding my breath expecting sudden death to swoop in and grab me. Knowing I was in the most perilous of situations and that my holiday was now over. Foolish is not the word I would use, when I discovered I was backed into a small ditch on the side of the road next to a paddock, the Suzuki and Metal Mermaid both on a slight tilt on the paddock side, not the sheer drop into the ocean I had imagined. If I had just reached out with my foot one extra centimeter or two, I would have found a foothold.

I got the giggles, my knees sagging with fatigue, my nightmare of driving off a mile high precipice firmly fixed in my head. My overactive imagination had overruled my common-sense. I then realised that the reason why I could not get out on the passenger side was the door was locked. How stupid am I? grabbing my phone again I rang the RAC number again and got a male voice saying it would take him an hour to get there, that was okay be me, "I'm was not going anywhere" A cow with huge brown eyes and long lashes had wandered over to see what all the fuss was about, she looked at me, then at the fence line that the Mermaid had clung to all night. Then wandered off - indifferent to my situation.

Finally, the RAC truck came barreling down the road to haul me out. The old man that was driving stood there, hands on hips and harrumphed at my stupidity of backing into a drain on the side of the road. He looked really peeved off and I had one sleepless scared night, so don't mess with me buddy.

He must have read my attitude, as no sooner than he towed me out of the overgrown grass ditch, made sure everything worked, revving hell out of the Suzuki's engine? I presumed it was blowing out anything struck up the exhaust pipe, and off he drove "Follow me", he grumped. What is it with some people? "Well, I would if I could, but I don't think I can," with a bellowing sigh, he said, "Get out, I'll do it" My mood was just as foul "That's your job, isn't it?

"I beg your pardon." He just stared at me "Look here lady, you want this thing of yours turned around or not." I have never wanted to slap another person so badly until now. With gritted teeth, I replied, "This is the aim of this exercise." Although his attitude stunk, he turned my little rig around. This man riled me, treating me like the village idiot. I felt that if I said something he did not agree with, he would walk off and leave me stuck. So, I decided to keep my mouth shut, just get the job done; then I was going to call into this person's workplace and have a word with his manager - or was I being small minded, tired and childish? Time to think about it once I had found a caravan park.

I signed papers, shoving them in his direction, he did not check my signature, just shoved them into his glovebox, slammed it shut and drove off without a word, fine, I've met many obnoxious people, I just added him to the list. I followed his taillights out, rounding a corner that just blew me away, the sea was grey, flat, calm, and terrifying, as between me and this side of the road there was a massive drop into the sea, no fence, no signs of danger, just huge rocks below that would have killed me outright, if I had driven over. Realising that late last night, I had driven past this death trap, too busy looking for that sign that said vacancy. My body shook with relief as I finally drove into the Coromandel town ship.

Two caravan parks later, I finally found one that had a vacancy, as I paid my fee for one week, I asked why there was so much activity? The receptionist shoved a pamphlet towards me; I gave it a cursory glance, tucking it into my bag, I went to find my patch of grass, back the Mermaid in, then sank onto my bed-the fear that had clogged my heart all night, escaped with the tears. A hot cup of tea worked wonders; I slept for three solid hours, waking with so much gratitude as I just may not have been here. I spied the pamphlet I had rammed into my bag advertising the Coromandel Art Trail; it looked like the tonic out of the doldrums, just what I needed. I found the Coromandel alive with energy, not all of them advertised. However, once you ask for more information, that's exactly what I got.

The Art trail was fabulous; I received the hands-on treatment with most of the artists. I visited wood-turning studios, abstract paintings, montage, collage, pale watercolours, there was always a different atmosphere. One particular artist painted amazing beach scenes; I succumbed and bought a miniature canvas to hang inside the Mermaid. The pottery, my hands loving the feel of river clay, in one jewellery studio I was invited to make myself a small pendant from a small trumpet shell, inserting into a small hole a tiny chip of Greenstone - the New Zealand Jade. I was elated by the outcome; it looked so natural and raw. I loved the feel of it on my skin. In another I watched glass blowing turn into a multi-coloured glass fish. A studio two doors down, formed wrought iron into amazing works of art. A small run-down building across the road made tri cornered canvas's, each side depicting the story of the subject, that was a first for me.

The days sped by, I asked if I could stay another week, I was having fun. The little tour bus that pulled up every morning in front of the caravan park drove me around the Art trail. Alby the driver had begun to call me by my name, 'Morning Tara, where are you off to today? Sometimes the bus was full, sometimes there was only one or two on board.

Alby gave me a timetable and an itinerary; I had arrived here at the right time it was the Coromandel Art Trail Festival. When he informed me about a tourist train that went to visit the renowned potter Barry Bicknell, who lived on a few hectares up in the hills.

I was interested, agreeing that he could arrange a ticket for me to go, to my delight the next day as the train station a three carriage steam train arrived, I was ushered on by a female conductor along with other tourists. I had not been on a steam train for a very long time; it felt as exciting as the first time I had ridden one with my parents. With a steam billowing hiss, we began the winding way through a magical Kauri Forest to a stop at the top of a mountain called the Eyefull tower, the view from this point was amazing. This potters art was sought and bought internationally. I was charmed by his studio, his ability to explain to me his passion of pottery, how he used different clays and what to mix and not mix; this man was a mine of information, an interesting three hours sped by.

The next day I visited the Nest a weaving studio, not the Māori weaving that Pania and family had tried to teach me, this women could weave concrete if she wanted to, the itinerary calling it a work of indigenous art, I felt the brochure did not use any descriptive words, I would have called it sublimely delicate, the only words to describe her exhibition, her hands flew over strings of colours so vibrant, on the wall was a multi textured wall hanging that took your breath away. I was invited by Alby to accompany him to the Coromandel fireworks exhibition, I was keen to go, who doesn't like fireworks? I had expected there would be other tourists from the camp on his bus, safety in numbers and all that. However, when Alby knocked on my van door, I was surprised, weren't we all meeting at the camp gates? He shoved a bunch of carnations at me, muttered "For you."
He commented "Gee, you scrub up well." I had not been complimented for a very long time.

Our transport was his car I felt like a child as I asked, "Where is the bus? He looked mildly surprised "At home, just you and me tonight." In the back seat was a picnic hamper, two Champagne bottles were tucked up in the ice bin. Placing his hand on my elbow, guiding me into the passenger's seat, leaning across me making sure my seat belt was secure. "Hmm, you smell nice too."

My thoughts racing, good heavens, he thinks we are on a date? Do I say something? Make an excuse? Or just sit it out?

Changing my mind was not an option, Alby took off at great speed, finally parking in the bus space at the communal grounds, where many others were sitting on picnic blankets, kids ran around screeching and playing tag with each other. I felt quite safe in a crowd, he greeted many as he sorted out the picnic gear, spread out a blanket for us to sit on then proceeded to open the Champagne "To us" he declare and literally threw the champaign down his throat, I watched as his prominent Adams apple bobbed up and down with eager appreciation. Prickles of apprehension went down my spine; I sipped mine thinking keep a clear head; there's something going on here.

My escort for the night chugged his way through the bottle, then opened another, "Come on, Babe" he slurred "Keep up", so I was Babe now, not Tara. "Sure, thing Alby" tipping mine out on the grass. The fireworks went off; we all oohed and aahed at the pretty lights blazing their way across the sky, as I looked over to where Alby was sitting, I received the thumbs up sign and a leering wink, "Time to snuggle up" he slurred. "Oh, dear God why me? he got to his feet, "Gotta Pee, Babe, back in a tick" Searching for the local taxi number on my phone, booking one immediately, wherever Alby had disappeared to? I was grateful.

CHAPTER THIRTY-FIVE

Tonight, I wanted to feel my husband's arms around me once more, I still missed him incredibly, I wanted to hear his chuckle and listen to his deep even breathing as he slept, I wanted to lay my head on his chest and listen to his heartbeat strongly and soundly, 'I miss you Russ' I whispered to the night sky. Would I ever feel for another as I did with you? Sleep arrived of happy dreams of a life with Russ and Rae as baby, I woke with an aching heart for times long gone, I woke feeling alone.

On the Itinerary I had seen an advert for a day spa in Whitianga, not too far from where I was camping. Just what the doctor ordered, some personal pampering, I rang them and yes, a booking was available the afternoon. I knew being busy was my way of pushing the loneliness away, soon I was off to do some grocery shopping and be pampered. Whitianga here I come, even the name of the Spa sounded mystical *The Lost Pools*. This treat was so worthwhile, I walked into a tree fringed, nature sculpted pool, with Geothermal clear crystal warm water. A Waterfall filtered down through fern covered rocks into the pool where I floated and let go of the tension.

My muscles twitched in relief, as I breathed in the clean smell of minerals. Hearing soft footsteps, I looked up to see a young Māori women entering, she held up a white robe, "Time for your massage, Tara." The massage was brilliant, hot stones melting the stress in my body. Falling asleep on the massage table, I woke up to the young girl softly shaking me, I felt wonderful, full of energy, today was worth every penny I spent, thank you Whitianga thermal pools. I was now ready to set forward on my journey. Relaxed and full of vigor, I headed back to the caravan park, I had still had two days to stay and intended to travel the district a little more, maybe I should take the Suzuki and steer clear of the camp bus.

The tourism shop informed me Thames and Paeroa were worth a visit, it was the right decision to drive myself; both townships were packed. If need be, I had all I needed and I would sleep in the Suzuki, not the most comfortable but it would do for one night. As I drove out of the caravan park there was a forlorn looking Alby sitting in his empty bus, I waved as I drove past, his face looked haggard. I hoped he understood, I was not looking for a companion now or in the near future.

Waihi the hot water beach was tempting, apparently you dig a hole in the sand, thermal hot water bubbles up, creating a sandy muddy bath, all along the beach you could see people laying there bathing. I take my hat off to those who say its therapeutic, I was not going to be one of them, not today. I was also warned about the Karangahapae gorge, apparently it was a tourist's nightmare, the corners tight and twisting, often slippery with black frost, to keep my speed down. They were not wrong, it was a nightmare of a twisting, turning, road that at times I almost squealed when I met oncoming traffic there was no way I was going to attempt this at night, memories flooded back of my introduction to the Coromandel.

There was one parking bay that looked like it was worth stopping at, the views amazing. The one stunning attraction in Waihi was a church - stopping to take a photo, I was invited inside by the one of the parishioners, the Māori motifs where incredible, what really took my eye was the huge stained-glass window the Virgin Mary and Christ both cloaked in Māori costume. Paeroa was amazing, driving around looking for some sort of tourism billboard, but it was Sunday, everything was closed, it was by sheer fluke I spied on some young teenagers walking along in the street dressed in Scots kilts, so like every good tourist I asked questions.

They were very helpful, inviting me to attend a practice of the highland Paeroa Highland games &Tattoo, it was so much fun, laughing, applauding and cheering all the teams on. I was thrilled that I had seen something few tourists got to see, this time I videoed it on my phone. It was a kaleidoscope of music and colour; the strictness of formations was amazing. How they remembered what foot to put where would have confused me, but these folk were smart, the steps were perfect, no one was being silly, it was all taken seriously. It became late and I was not brave enough to tackle the mist covered mountain range I had just driven over. I pushed the driver's seat back, if felt okay. Now dinner? Nothing was open except a corner shop that sold newspapers, cigarettes and lollies, a warming oven contained four meat pies, so a pie and a lemonade was my choice for dinner that night.

Time to find a public toilet, a signpost pointing the way, I quickly walked there and back, the cold water tap was a blessing. Once settled, I began to read up on Tauranga, my next city to visit, but first I had to tackle that horrendous gorge again and pick up the Mermaid. I was fast asleep having parked under a streetlight for safety when clunking on the window woke me, the local police asking me to move on, I explained my situation to the officer, they let me park in the police car park for the night with strong warnings that this area was not safe at night especially a women on her own. I thanked them for their kindness, admittedly feeling a lot more secure than I did parked on the roadside.

Waking up to a glorious day, I once again dashed off to the public toilets, time for a quick wash, brush teeth and hair which always made me feel so much more human. Once I was back at the Suzuki, I spied something weird about the side of it, a long deep scratch that had torn into the paint, I had been keyed.

I went into the police station and complained, they looked amused, the same policeman who had told me to stay there the night saying, "You were warned, imagine what would have happened if you had not parked here." He was right, his advice was "Ring your insurance firm they will sort it out for you" then adding "Mam, you're a senior woman travelling on your own. If you were my Mum? I'd be having a serious talk with you, it can be dangerous out there, not everyone likes or encourages tourism. With that he wished me a 'good day,' I had been told off and dismissed. Goodbye Paeroa, I was more than happy to leave.

Three hour's drive back to pick up my van, hitch her up and go where? I was tired and annoyed that some miserable sod could happily ruin another's vehicle like that. Once back at the caravan park, I requested an extra night. The answer was "No sorry" my space had been prebooked. They gave me an hour to move on. I wearily hitched the Mermaid up, pulling out onto the main free way, I decided to drive to Tauranga. It was a city and appeared to have many caravan parks, the warning from the Paeroa police still in my head, I rand a caravan park from the Google directory, I was booked in for a week. Now, with my gut in my shoes, I was to tackle the mountain gorge again, but not before I refueled my vehicle and more importantly own body. A café was my next stop, ordering a plate of scrambled eggs, hash browns, baked beans and toast with a large mug of strong coffee, it hit the spot.

Tauranga is a wonderful place, after finding my caravan park and settling in, as I set up my little camp, other campers came over and greeted me, an older couple, Conner and Bridie his partner, both Irish, they were touring New Zealand working their way around the New Zealand.

They seemed to be a delightful couple, their van was their home and had been so for the past two years, they had been in this caravan park for nearly a month, picking fruit around the countryside. Their life was simple, and I was delighted to have found like-minded people, Bridie loved to cook, often when I had come home from my touring, I would be called to pop over for a hot cuppa and a biscuit or two, I knew she really craved another woman to chat to, I wondered why no one else had bothered to friend her then realised that Bridie could talk the leg of an iron pot.

CHAPTER THIRTY-SIX

Tauranga was a tourist's mecca every little knickknack or Kiwiana was there in every shop I ventured into; I had to buy some new clothes as my own were now too big for me. I opted for a secondhand clothing. A hair salon two doors down was a walk in one, so walk in I did, having my hair washed and trimmed. I felt 50% lighter when I walked out. I had contacted the RAC who had made an appointment to have the Suzuki looked at, once I had arrived and the accessor had walked around, making notes on his clip board he wrote *vandalised* on his report papers, they would find a repair shop and be in contact.

Tauranga is a large bustling city in the Bay of Plenty. If you want to find something to do, there are many choices to choose from. I found a picture theatre where a re-run of Avatar was showing. What better way to spend three hours, immersed in an action movie eating a choc bomb. Once back at the caravan park I unpacked my shopping. Switched the jug on to make a cuppa, I set out my small picnic table, when Bridie appeared enquiring "What have you been up to all day and why the taxi? This was the one thing in a park I did not enjoy, everyone knew what each other was up to.

I felt mean as they had both been so welcoming, pulling out a chair I said, "Sit and I will tell all, would you like a cup of tea and a piece of chocolate cake? Before I could say would Con like to join us? she hollered "Oi, Con - cuppa at Taras place." His reply was "Good God woman, you wail like a demented Banshee," that made me smile, I had not heard sarcasm like that since my father died. The days rushed by, with no vehicle I was stuck in one place, so I offered to help Bridie make jams and chutneys to sell at the local farmer's market that weekend. Again, women working together brings forth many remedies as they say a problem halved is a problem solved.

Bridie told me of her sorrows in Ireland, her three children she had left behind; Con, her savior from a brutal marriage, although she was ten years older than him, he said he loved her. It was a flurry of enjoyable activity, by that weekend there were jars of onion jam, jars of lemon and persimmon jam. And jars of a courgett chutney. I offered to help with the Saturday morning markets, my Suzuki had been returned, she looked clean and bright, I had seen the sights and most of all had met lovely people. Sunday morning, I was on my way again. I was up early, the receptionist at the office had emailed me the invoice, which I had paid. She commented on the motif on the vans tail, I told her what I knew of the fable, that it was called Moana Ika.

"You're heading South, right? she asked, "Do you know the Māori folktale of a Mermaid." I had to confess I did not, she told me the tale of Pania the Māori Mermaid in a city called Napier, I was all ears, this I had to see for myself. And that name bought back memories. So, it looked like Napier was to be my next stop over. I reached Ohope beach after a three-hour drive, and I was ready to try a free campsite that was offered by the community for one night. It had a cold water tap, plus an ablution block. Once I had parked, I just sat and watched the world go by, journaled and wrote more on my laptop.

If there is one thing I have learnt on this adventure, it's that you don't have to be busy all the time; it's nice to simply watch and listen. By eight p.m., I had visited the ablution block, showered, and snuggled up into my bed for the night.

I slept peacefully, waking in the morning to birdsong. Again, I wandered over to the public toilets. Is it just me, or do others appreciate the smell of disinfectant? I met Marty, the janitor, she had seen the Mermaid art on my van. She told me the story of a dolphin that used to swim at Ohope Beach, "It became very famous, we had tourists visit from all over, then someone shot it, but that happened nearly forty years ago, since then the dolphins have not made themselves known to us again." I felt sad that just one human's actions could affect so many people.

Once back in my van, I could hear the sea washing up onto the sand, birds calling, wind in the treetops and then a distinct "Yoo-hoo, Tara where are you? Bridie and Conner's van soon pulling up next to mine. 'What the? I thought, surely not. "Missed you", they cried in unison, 'what? why?' I was a little fazed by it all. Why are you here? What are you doing? Conner's grin was so wide "Mind if we become neighbours again?" he asked. I was so confused. "I'm moving on, guys; I'm not staying here." Bridie, pointing at me "Your face is a picture." Their laughter annoyed me, what was going on? "Tara, we both thought, as we have another four months here in New Zealand, why don't you join us as a team and pick fruit, work our way around the North Island? Hey, what do you say?'

My first instinct was to say No! with a capital N. I had planned on doing it on my own; owing no one my time or money and must admit I had begun to enjoy my own company. I asked for some time to think it over.

This is not what I had planned or was this an opportunity to travel onto the unknown roads and meet the locals, not the touristy places on the picture-perfect brochures. Sure, the scenery was stunning wherever I went; but I wanted real stories about real people. My brain overriding my intuition why not it, surely It can't harm? I grabbed a packet of chocolate biscuits and yelled, "Put the jug on, I'm coming over." My decision was made; it was a "Yes to teamwork, but once in Napier, I was going on alone."

We planned our next stop at Taneatua to attend the country fair being held there the next weekend. Our next question was where was our next campsite? We also needed to source a farm where we could pick fruit and or veggies. I felt a lift of excitement, as anyone who knows me knows I love country markets. This was a first for me, I could feel my energy return. Who would have thought at this stage in life I would have a new career, entrepreneurial jam and chutney maker. However, any thoughts of staying here a little longer till we sorted out the finer details was dismissed by the tractor that chugged over and the caretaker who held out his hand for the ten dollars per night, his look deterring any requests to stay longer muttering 'Bloody Camp Gypsies' under his breath.

I looked up at Con, he shook his head. I could not help myself, "Excuse me", this awful person, with the name tag caretaker that looked like a dogs breakfast, was calling me names? I grabbed my phone; he stayed long enough to hear me speak with the manager. I reported him, suggesting they retrain their staff if they were to be known as caretakers. In unison, we pulled out of that place, heading off towards our destination and hoping to find a place to stay. Problem number one was that my van was so small I could park anywhere, almost; however, their van was over the campgrounds' limit, and so was their tow vehicle. Con and Bridie needed a lot of space; we needed a caravan park Genie to sort it.

Sure, enough as we pulled into this tiny little township that was fluttering with flags and posters and advertising the Bucking Bronco competitions with a country fair, I stopped at the local bakery to enquire about parking our vans. "Sure, thing love, round the back-you're the first to arrive." I could not believe our luck as round the back was a huge grass patch, an ablution block that was so clean and fresh with plastic flowers adorning the changing washrooms, the showers so clean they sparkled.

Rangi was the camp owner's name, the price, ten dollars a night with the use of all amenities. My next question was how long can we stay for Rangi? She was so laid back, "Long as you like sweetie, love the company." Bridie explained what we intended to do, make jams and pickles for the county fair. Rangi offering her advice on where to pick fruit. My last thought that night as I went to sleep was how safe I felt. As Bridie and I began sorting jars the next day a horse float was pulled in. I soon got to know the occupant, her name was Beauty, a tall, beautiful brunette, sporting a white muzzle and socks. I had been horse mad as a child and still favored them above most animals.

Later that same day Con arrived back to their van, a little worse for wear, he'd been down at the pub. My tum hit rock bottom, alcohol and I had never seen eye to eye. Over our combined dinner she whispered, "He's fine Tara, himself is celebrating his new job." Con was now employed to build the stalls for the country fair and was very proud of his new position in life. Bridie and I had been informed that a farm wanted fruit pickers, we joined the queue the next day, by lunch time I was sore by knock off time every joint ached.

All I wanted was a hot cup of anything and a lie down, the pickers had been allowed to keep any windblown or bruised fruit, Bridie and I both delighted at the boot full of promising jam, as for chutneys to make pickles there was nothing, although we searched high and low for the ingredients. Rangi tried to help, ringing her family and friends, nothing available was the answer. As Bridie rolled up her sleeves to dice, splice and cored all sorts of fruit, I washed the jars in a huge old copper supplied to us from our host.

I decided to ring Rae and Jess; lately I had become quite hesitant in the past, as all I got was snide comments or demands to come home. Today was no different as I said, "Hi hon, it's Mum, how are you both? I was told 'there are three of us here Mum." I could sense the mood immediately. "Just checking in to say hi, I'm fine staying at a place called Taneatua. Rae's voice became brittle "Mum, we need to talk. I can't discuss it right now. I'll ring you back in an hour, ok? It sounded serious, so I agreed "Chat soon, Rae, love to all." The phone went dead. It played on my mind how easily I let Rae pop my happy balloon; her unhappiness stayed with me as I joined the communal dinner that night. I let them talk, only answering when asked a question, excusing myself as soon as possible to go inside my little home and await the phone call from Rae.

The phone rang and her first words were "Mum, what you are doing with the house, it's an overgrown mess, Tim and I want to move in; someone has to act responsible. We want to start a life together, but you are holding us all back with your disappearing act. I was stunned, all I could say was "What are you talking about Rae, I have hired a gardener that regularly mows my lawns, trims gardens and hedges. As for money? Well, the trust you inherited will be released when your thirty-five, that's only a year away."

She interrupted "Yes, I know all that, however the three of us feel it's totally unfair. You and dads descion is stopping me from owning our own home." What a bloody cheek, then Tim joined in the conversation "We need answers Tara, or we are looking at having my lawyer involved with this mess that you have left us with." The line went dead, who were these people?

CHAPTER THIRTY-SEVEN

The light was still on in Rangie's kitchen; I badly needed someone to talk to, sitting at the kitchen table was Carole, Con, and Bridie, coring and peeling fruit, Rangi was making a pot of tea and buttering scones. The heartache must have shown, Con ushering me into a chair, eventually when I had calmed down, I told them about Russ, Rae and Jess, how once we were close as a family and now after Russ's death it was awful, I could not blame Rae's partner Tim, as she was a free agent and could make up her own mind.

I then told them about Gilly, Rae's accusations and how I was sucked in by this friendship, to be told to 'F off' at the airport, Bridie's face looked worn and sad, Carols looked indignant, Con was open mouthed, and Rangi tut tutted while she bustled about preparing our supper. I felt I was amongst good friends here as they wrangled with my problem and what I should say, and what to do, it was Carole who came up with "Do you have a friend that can take photos of your home and grounds, then email them to you. It was a light bulb moment for me, "I knew exactly who to message, I knew Jo or Robin would be happy to. Carole continued, "Now the big question is, can the will be contested by your daughter?" Can you release the trust or some of the trust?

Or do you wish to keep your husbands wishes, seems to me he knew something." I was sure everything was in order, but we agreed to ring my lawyers in the morning, just to make sure that I knew was informed and up to date. I went to bed very stressed, my night full of Rae's demands, the morning bringing no relief, I could not eat or drink till I had sorted this mess out. I rang my best mate Jo, she was very surprised to hear from me, our weekly emails to each other was our normal way of our catching up. Jo was shocked at my news about Rae's demands "Cheeky little bitch" she declared, she offered to do the photo thing and came up with a brilliant idea. "Tara, I have my cousin from the UK coming over here to visit for a while, why not rent to her and her husband for the next few months, I will vouch for her, in fact, let me know the rental you want, I'm happy to pay the deposit for them, I know they will love it."

Rent my home out, fully furnished? Why not. I felt my diaphragm release, I could breathe, "Okay if you vouch for them, let's do it." One problem solved, I agreed to email a rental agreement with a minimal amount for full upkeep of the house, in return she would email me photos of the grounds, front and back gardens and any comments of neglect, wear and tear that I needed to see. Next it was the lawyers, I told the receptionist it was urgent. His reply was "Do nothing, she has rung us and she's playing games, it's as you said, the house and all contents are yours, your shares? Of course she can contest, but in a court of law she better have a bloody good reason, I know we feel that the legal system has let us down at times, but they are not fools Tara."

The trust fund is for your grandsons education, if it's in Jess's best interest, and it will have to be proved in a court of law, then yes, we can consider it. Somehow, I was not surprised, suddenly I was over the whole dammed thing; let them have the money. "How do I go about releasing the trust to her?" I heard him chuckle, Russ made the trust to be inherited by Jess not Rae.

Legally, Jess does not come into his inheritance until he is eighteen. His next words where a warning; "Rae is making waves and from the sounds of it she intends to make you miserable" this was not my lawyer talking but a friend. "I don't know who she is being advised by, but it's not legal advice, rest easy Tara, where looking after you."

I was emotionally exhausted; this was too big for me to manage on my own. I had promised I would ring her, so I pushed in her number, she answered with a curt "Yes." I could hear her hold her breath as I told her "Rae, I've rented the house out to friends it will be looked after from now on. She exploded "You bloody nasty spiteful old cow, you want to see me fail don't you, you would be happy to see me single all of my life, you'll pay for this" the line went dead. I collapsed in a heap; I had done what I could and given her whatever, whenever and it had come down to the money not what we, Russ and I had tried to instill, family, love, loyalty.

The disappointment in our daughter broke my heart. Bridie heard me, then found me, sobbing into a pile of wet tissues, her arms going around me. "I wonder what her Da thinks of her, God rest his poor soul" she said crossing herself. "Come on now my colleen, don't waste your breath on that daughter of yours, you have a life to live and fruit to boil my lovely." Wiping my face with the edge of her pinny, her voice soothing me as a mother would, "I'll make some tea while you wash your face. We'll all look after each other, won't we just.

The next day I received the photos of my home and grounds. They were lovely, not overgrown at all, but neat and tidy. It made me a little homesick-I also received a large deposit for the rental on my home. I replied "Many thanks, all under control, have decided to keep gardener on while your family stay there. Thank you, love you, talk soon." Hopefully sooner than later the disappointment would lift from my heart.

Rangi's wisdom and kindness was what worked on my heart; her gentle approach to heartache was day by day. One day her arm went around my waist, "I have a challenge for you young lady." I was a year younger. "You come with me;" she led me out the back to her garden, "I hear you're still having trouble finding veggies for your pickles? "Yes, I am, there seems to be a shortage of zucchini that we want to make into relish." We walked around her veggie garden, it was not a huge one but enough to feed her, and the Whanau when they came back home or on occasions like this. She stood back arms open wide, "Well I have these, and there all yours." Growing on an old trellis was a bright green leafy vine, it covered the side of an old shed and trailed onto the ground, "This here is known as a Choko, it's a vegetable that you can cook, to me its tasteless; but some people stuff it full of chicken or meat then roast it, I prefer it as a filler for pickle's or jams."

There was also the last of the season's corn that was drying up, some parsley and spring onions, and half a dozen full grown over ripe tomatoes. I had never seen or heard of this veggie Choko before, it was shaped like a large egg or a pear almost the size of an ostrich egg, it had a light lime green skin with sharp prickles all over it, inside, once cut open the flesh was translucent, small seeds clung to a fibrous stem that was the core, it had no smell and very juicy, its taste was sour with a slight yellow tinge to the juice. What a strange looking plant, are you sure? Rangi guffawed "Tara I've eaten these for years, I don't actually like them, but a good filler for days when you think bugger, not enough to go round."

This was such a new idea for me - experimenting with a veggie pickle. I thought it may be of interest to you and Bridie, you can make so much stuff with it." She was right; I was intrigued, so while Bridie was humming away, busy over a large pan of some sort of jelly she was making; I set too with the Chokos.

Experimenting with different herbs and other small amounts of veggies from Rangi's Garden and what would complement this strange vegetable. Not having a kitchen to cut and dice the veggies, Rangi offered me a hot plate and a large wooden bench in her shed saying, "I could do as I wished," I must admit I would have stayed locked away for hours, I felt like a secret scientist writing down all the ingredients, cooking, dissecting all sorts of other veggies to make a tasty pickle.

I also made a few failures that were trashed when they proved inedible, once burning the bottom of my favorite pot-one of the two pots I had purchased for my own use. Rangi to the rescue once more providing me with a huge cooking urn, then back to the drawing board again, often Rangi or Carole popping in to make sure I had all I needed, by the end of the week, I had found a recipe that worked; made with corn, parsley and tomatoes, adding sultanas , sugar, spices, salt, black pepper corns and a few Chilli flakes plus the treasured Chokos. Time to have a taste test, Con took a small spoonful of my chutney with the roast pork that Rangi had cooked that night for our dinner, it was not so much his face that told me it was good. It was the fact after the first spoonful he took two more helpings one after another "Yum, he drooled, Tara, that's really good."

We all took a teaspoon of the chutney I had made, and yes it tasted like Zucchini in a butter sauce with a Chilli tang to it as it left the tongue, even if I did say so myself it was very nice. "I think you have a winner here" Carole said. Rangi smiled-her work was done, I was feeling so much happier than two weeks ago, I had let go in more ways than one with her encouragement and her ability to let me mull it over in peace, while I was busy creating.

Once again, I had proved that women together, solved problems as they worked together. But when I looked at Bridie for confirmation the pickle had created was good? What I saw disapproval, what the hell was going on?

Carole was an enigma, not adding a lot to the dinner time conversations in the communal kitchen, she loved horses that was obvious, she was a close friend of Rangi's, again that was obvious by the easy banter with each other. With the three of us she was guarded, but I would often see her staring at Con. When he spoke to her, she would beam at him, her smile transformed her face from pretty to attractive. Rangi took it upon herself to inform us that it was not a personal slight or dislike for us, she had been bullied and molested by a female member of her family. She had been eight years old when Rangi became her foster Mother. My heart went out to Carole, it made me sad to think of all we had given Rae in her life, while this poor woman still suffered from memories of her family's abuse. Meanwhile, Bridie had become distant where I was concerned, when I questioned her if I had slighted her in any way, she shrugged and walked away.

My chutneys were a success, ten jars of Tomato and Zucchini chutney sat all in a row. Bridie had made her specialty home-made onion jam, plus Jars of fruit salad jam, jars of mint and pear jelly. The first two hours at the festival dragged by, nobody passed us by, except to buy from the candy floss man three stalls down. My spirits flagged until Rangi introduced us to two older women insisting, they have a taste of our jams and pickles. Bridie produced wooden spatulas just for this purpose, giving a very professional spiel about the produce, ten minutes into their tasting, they bought two jars of my product. From that moment on we sold to anyone and everyone that passed by, by early afternoon, I sold out, Bridie? She had struggled to sell all she had made.

As Bridie and I drove home, she was still acting distant towards me. I asked again, "Had I done something wrong?" She pulled over, her blue eyes furious, "How would you like it if I took over like you did, making those pickles behind my back, then selling them under my brand name. I thought I knew you. You're a backstabbing bludger, I don't care to be in your company." I could have spoken my mind, as I found her recent behavior rude and ignorant, but why bother? Instead, I said what I had been thinking for while "I'll be moving on tomorrow."

My little van looked so inviting, the light inside glowed from the window, I just wanted to crawl inside and sleep. I wanted to be on my own tonight. My phone rang at two am the next morning. I croaked a "Hello" expecting it to be an emergency at home. I was wrong it was Rangi, I could hear crying in the background, my alert button immediately on go "Can you come over Tara, she whispered." Rangi was waiting for me on her front porch. "We are trying to sort something out Tara, I could do with your help." Sitting on the front porch was Rangi beside was Bridie, her face swollen with tears, it seemed that Con had been seeing Carole, and had been doing so for a week or two now, "What, just seeing her?" I asked, "Rangi tutted at me "Don't be naïve, Tara, they say they're in love and want to be together."

CHAPTER THIRTY-EIGHT

Bundled up against the cold air, Bridie told us of her misgiving's but had ignored them; "This was not the first time that friggin Irishman's eye has wandered" she cried, I looked up at Con, his face haggard, I thought he was about to apologise, when he floored us all by saying "Bridie, it's over, I want to stay here, settle down with Carole, if she'll have me, and become part of this community." Bridie howled like a hurt dog, Con was a spent man, he kneeled beside her, each word he used, cut into her heart, "Bridie, sweetheart, you want a different life to me, you don't want to settle anywhere, I do; you don't want to share our lives with my children, Carole and I do. I have found a real purpose here." He stood, his eyes so very sad, "I'll be back tomorrow to sort things out." I had learnt something tonight-love is never secure, and life never failed to amaze me, one moment love surrounds us, buoying us up, next it collapses like a lead balloon, dragging us down.

The morning signaled her arrival with a bright orange streak across the dark blue sky; we all went to bed in our own vans and homes. My brain sleepless, trying to understand what had just happened; my heart grateful to Russ for his faithfulness and belief in us as a couple. If he ever did or considered to stray, I had never known about it or even a hint of it. Then it struck me, where was Carole? What were her thoughts about all of this? The next morning Bridie was not to be seen; Rangi had made her a rich sweet coffee and toast with cheese, asking me to deliver it to their caravan, asking me to "Have a wee chat with her Tara, try to lift her day she's in sore need of a motherly shoulder.

Knocking lightly on her door, calling out "Bridie it's me Tara." Her van door swung open as I tried the handle, her hand lying on the carpet white and still was the giveaway, I screamed, Rangi came barreling out of the kitchen. I stood by the van door shaking, looking at Bridie's still form, it lay half on half off the bed, her face-tinged pale blue- her eyes open, glassy. I had seen this look before: I knew death when I saw it. Rangi was rooted to the spot. 'No!' she moaned; I went into auto mode my fingers tapping out emergency and then ringing Con-his voice cracking in horror at my news, the place became so busy with cars and officials coming and going, the most I could do was be there for Rangi or Con, the officials suicide. Rangi shook her head we both knew it was from a broken heart.

I had no idea what the consequences of Bridie's death would to Rangi's home and business, a suicide in the Māori culture is huge. Rangi's small campgrounds now *Tapu* to the public. Rangi closed down in nature and business. Her family surrounded her; then her sons ordered Con off their property immediately, in the same breath it was suggested that I do the same. Any friendship once offered was now replaced with a hard look to their eyes. Her son's watched on silently while I hitched the Mermaid, then turned their backs as I drove away.

I had seen this happen once when staying up North with Pania, a relative had upset then somehow, in unison they had turned their back until the relative had walked away. In other words, we don't know you, nor do we want to. I had decided to head off towards Rotorua. I pulled over to find a caravan park on the GPS one, that I could settle into while until I sorted myself out, then I was going to ring Margi. I needed to talk to someone soon, before it all got too much for me. My request for a caravan site was met with "Yes we have a vacancy." Time for Tara to do as she declared months ago-travel solo, people and their motions are too hard. I was not sorry I had met Bridie, Con, Rangi, even Carole, we had met and enjoyed each other's company, had many laughs and so much fun.

The women I had met had helped me over a huge hurdle with my own family-for that I was grateful, they would always be part of my life's tapestry. Once I was safe in the caravan park I emptied my van cupboard out, I emptied my small kitchen cupboard, anything I had that looked like it was Bridie's, a jar of her jam, pickle, knife, tea towel I threw out, the Māori were not the only superstitious people around, I had my own beliefs.

To be honest I felt disappointed in Bridie, as in my opinion the struggle comes when we choose to deal with the emotional hurts and may need help to start forgiving and healing within ourselves. But I was not here to judge.

Rotorua is a beautiful place, gorgeous gardens, mud pools, plus Māori culture everywhere you looked. I rang Margi, her advice was "Keep going Tara, keep seeing and doing what you came here for, you will know when you have had enough, you're here for a reason, you will know when it's time to go home." She was right, my gut instincts said just a little further; she had good news for me, her nephew Warike who had painted the Mermaid on the van he had been accepted into an Arts course at his college; my small sum I had left behind for him had provided him with a computer "First one of us to have one of those things."

I had booked for a week at the *Rainbow Trout Caravan Park*, it looked very pretty, and true to their adverts you could see the Rainbow trout swim downstream. I visited a farm demonstration of sheep shearing and watched well behaved Rams stand to attention. I attended a Māori dance concert, but all the fun of watching, seeing and doing had just gone for me, time to move on, I was restless. Although Rotorua offered a lot, after four days of tourism and many sad thoughts about Bridie and Con, I decided to move on. I drove away without a backward glance, my GPS had *Gisborne* typed into it. Happy I was on the road again, hopefully Gisborne would be better. It was going to be a long drive, so I was told-a good five hours. Be prepared to free camp, if possible, that was a loud mental no from me, not after the last time in Paeroa.

I arrived in *Gisborne* at dusk making only two stops, one to re fuel, one to eat and use the bathroom, while there I asked the café person if they knew of any caravan parks that I could book into. She gave me a phone number, as I drove away my phone on speaker, I booked my site.

I arrived to twinkling city lights, pretty foreshore, stunning trees silhouetted in the sun set, my little faithful Mermaid ducked into her resting place for a week, I curled up inside my tiny home, I felt exhausted, mainly because of Bridies death plus the anger, it had curdled my adventure, maybe I should just sell up and head back to Australia.

Once I showered in the morning; combing my hair in the mirror- I saw a new me. I looked haggard; I had lost too much weight, my hair now long in a straggling plait, even my eyes looked worn and sad. I felt old beyond my years, my head ached, I felt tired- generally rundown. I recognised the symptoms of stress. What I needed for myself was a good clean up physically and emotionally. My go to cure was to rest up; eat well, read, sleep walk and journal my feelings about Bridie. Time for some self-care, finding a hairdresser making an appointment with them for the next day. Then it was time to sort out any clothing to be washed, ironed and put away, tidy up the little pantry and fridge, then a sweep out. I ran a hose over the Suzuki washing the road dust away.

By two pm I was out to it; my body was tired, a migraine had begun it thumped behind my eyes, painkillers and a hot water bottle wrapped around my neck to relax the muscles, this was my personal remedy. I switched my phone off; the world could wait for a while. I lay there with no one knocking or calling, ringing, asking me to attend, or giving advice, no anger, weeping or noise, nothing but peace all I could hear was the wind in the trees. Sleep they say is the best healer and I tend to agree. Whenever I woke, I would drink a big glass of water, wander out to use the bathrooms, shower, make a hot tea, nibble on a biscuit then back to sleep, no one bothered me, not one little peep, it was wonderful.

CHAPTER THIRTY-NINE

On the third day I woke with a clear head, and so hungry, my energy had returned. Wandering the main street I found a hair salon, my unruly mop was washed, trimmed by Lucy the hairdresser: she informed me that having a soft body perm was so much easier than having to plait it every day, her huge blue eyes taking in all the split ends and general untidy hairdo. Going with her advice and at the end of two hours my hair looked stunning, soft curls pulled back by two large Tortoiseshell combs. Then it was off to find a secondhand shop for some clothing, the weight loss was now considerable.

Lucy had informed me of a Second's Boutique two roads away. She was right-it was an Aladdin's cave and not too bad on prices, taking a few items into the changing room, the shop assistant said I was buying the wrong size for me, what do you think I am, I asked, "Let's see", she whipped out her tape measure, 'I am going with a size twelve" she announced "No! I cried I'm a large fourteen to sixteen," we both looked at my image in the mirror. "Well not anymore" she quipped, "Good for you, here try these on."

She gave me at least six garments, ¾ pants, tops plus two pairs of light jeans; she was right, size twelve fitted beautifully. I was in shock I had not been a size twelve since I married Russ. My thoughts strayed to Bridie-how she was always trying to lose weight. I forced them away; I was not going there today. Walking back to the Suzuki with my arms full of parcels, I spied a coffee shop, it sold fresh baguettes with a savory smoked ham and cheese filling.

My mouth watered, to my delight it also sold books of every description, time to stop and refresh myself I mind and body. I was starved for some great novels; I was sick of quick reads like magazines and newspapers. I ordered a huge green salad with my fresh baguette. I left the little café with another fresh bread roll and three new books, bedtime reading here I come. I had seen a tourism shop, admitting to her I liked this city -it reminded me a little of Perth. The woman behind the counter offered me the opportunity to buy a tour packet, which included a wine tour for tomorrow, plus an East land Aquaculture tour then a Farman helicopter tour. She also thought I would enjoy a sunrise tour to Mount Hikurangi, the tour operator would confirm this one as sometimes the land was closed as it was on private land.

I was really excited about my plans; once back at my site I bundled my purchases through the door, retrieved my fresh laundry off the clothesline to make my bed up, it smelt divine full of fresh air and sunshine, even my bath towels were fluffy and looked brighter.

Once settled, I sorted out my new clothes into the drawers under the bed, deciding that my old clothes were too big to keep, so I bundled them up taking them over to the office, to ask if there was clothing bin close, she told me of a Vinnie's clothing bin a street away, the walk there and back feeling good, stretching my back and leg muscles. My trip to the wineries was great-I tippled, sipped, judged and lunched with other tourist; enjoying the repartee as none of us were professionals in the wine business. On the ride home I opted out of any conversation; I was a little fuzzy in the head not being used to the wine, but the apple cider definitely a favorite with me. I slept like a baby, not waking till midnight and slightly confused where the day had gone, the next day was going to be even more exciting. I was up early, showered and dressed warmly, the wind was quite chilly in these early mornings.

Eastland Aquaculture was amazing; once more I was picked up at the park's gate, then driven out to the Paua shell farm and showed the process of Paua shell farming, it was fascinating. I had seen the same sort of Oyster farming in Bali, almost the same technique except the pacific waters are cold; so, the system of growing these beautiful sea creatures is almost mathematical. I defy anyone to leave this place without buying something made from the most beautiful of shells the Paua or the Abalone as we in Australia call them. I succumbed to buying small drop earrings and a dainty heart shaped necklace; then it was time to go, the driver dropped me off at Farm Helicopters. I was so excited my stomach quivering in anticipation, first a short introduction to the pilot a young Asian chap called Cho, in his late thirty's; then we began the flight instructions; it was explained about the what to do and what not to do, put simply do not touch or fiddle with anything.

I was strapped in, Cho placed the earphones on my head, his tinny voice saying with this apparatus I could converse freely with the pilot, the rotary blades clattered to a start, up we went, lift off. Cho made conversation about our destination; he also gave me instructions of where the sick bag was, he did this with a smile. We followed the Motu River. It was so shallow in places white pebbles glowed up from the banks-where it was deep; it flowed strongly in deep green and browns. We flew over Lake Waikaremoana its colours changing from deep blue to deep turquoise, our shadow a small black dot on its surface.

My camera was busy clicking away, I was looking down not noticing the thick white clouds we were headed for, Cho's voice now changed from light to a more serious tone said, "This is White Island Tara, a live volatile volcano," my stomach did a huge flip as his words hit home "A live volcano? you're kidding me?" I had not read the brochure correctly, I know I would not have booked this tour. We flew around the perimeter of it, thick steam covering our vision, the lava glowed deep inside its bowl, my face and knuckles turning white as I clutched the seat under me, I was finding it hard to breathe. Cho took one look at me; we immediately flew back to Gisborne. I was obviously shaken, Cho offered to drive me home, which I gratefully accepted. To this day I cannot explain the feeling of terror that raced through me, but it felt like purgatory was leering at me.

My third and last day of the tour package had arrived. I was to watch the dawn come up on Mount Hikurangi apparently this is a photographer's dream and even if I do say so myself, I'm not too bad behind the lens. Before I took off for the Mount; I replayed the previous day's photo session in the helicopter.

It started off with Cho smiling and waving to me, shots of rivers and lakes, so beautiful in their vibrant colours, the White Island experience I deleted.

Mt Hikurangi was open-the tour was on, it was a good half hour hike to the summit then we witnessed an amazing sunrise, it left you in awe. When the smallest line of pink stretched across the sky, the Māori elder greeted the Sun with prayer, soon the thin line exploded into a glorious canvas of pinks and mauves only the heavens can make. Believe when I say it's not until you become part of it, when the glow covers your face, hands, and reaches into your heart in a molten orange glow, you can feel it seeping into your skin, this is when realise you are in the presence of a Super Nova.

The prayer of welcome ended with "There can be no doubt of a greater consciousness, a belief in the magic of this creation." I agreed whole heartedly, my heart was full of the immense pleasure that being part of this ritual was powerful and healing, reinstating your belief in the universe, that all was meant to be as it was, or as my Mum would often say "God is in his heaven, and all is well in your heart." Although I had captured it all on camera, nothing could match the experience of the power we had witnessed. There is actually no word I can use to describe the majesty for without that orb of life we would live in darkness.

The line of tourists descended silently down the slope into the tour bus, all of us touched by the glory we had just witnessed. To write, I took a few shots and continued my journey' would sound quite shallow, as I felt like I had just been on the journey of a lifetime. The sunrise I had witnessed was powerful, spiritual, a personal blessing, an experience-I for one would never forget.

Napier was a four hour drive away, so far it was enjoyable I had had my Suzuki checked over at a gas station, everything was as it should be. The radio played Red Sails in the Sunset, a personal favorite of mine. I hummed along as I drove, not a care in the world, a cool breeze blew through the windows, my new hairdo was tucked up in a scarf. My attire was minimum and relaxed a pair of old brown overalls, a sleeveless T-shirt, and no makeup. I felt really good, everything I was doing to restore the cheerful side of me was working, long walks, sleeping well, healthy food, journalling and de-stressing. I had deliberately kept my phone on silent, it all seemed to be working, was Tara on her way back? Almost. Until the Mobile phone beeped, it was a text message from Rae, "We have decided no more contact" I stared at the screen; my light heart sinking, why does this keep happening? Hopefully when they grew up or saw sense, we would again be a family, I prayed for the best outcome for us all.

The way things were going though, the chances looked slim. I sent up a prayer that Tim would be a good father figure for my grandson, and Rae would have a strong loving man in her life. Still, this was her life, and her descion, sadly one I had to learn to live with, warts and all.

I had heard the weather forecast proclaiming rain, and rain it did, the heavens opened up, after the initial deluge, it drizzled nonstop, I was getting to know this weather, a cardigan or wrap always close by. I wound my way through water burdened hills; muddy shallow water ran across them; in places a waterfall splattered onto the road. I was having to drive very carefully; bright red road signs were being erected up warning drivers of flash floods or rockslides.

CHAPTER FORTY

A rain sodden view of Napier with surf pounding its grey beaches came into view, the streetlights giving it a watery sad look. I seemed even though I was hundreds of miles away, Rae and Bridie's angry faces haunted me. "Stuff it" I shouted and slammed the wheel with my hand, I'm bloody sick and tired of that bloody woman ruining my life with her precious tantrums. Russ's voice in my head saying, 'Calm down Tara' my reaction was "And you can stuff off as well." God give me breath; I am so over other people's problems.

Yesterday, I had booked a caravan park and been given the site number as they might not be available. I followed her instructions and found my way there without too much trouble. The rain soaked me as I unhitched the Mermaid, grabbing a towel and bath bag from the van, then running to the shower block hot water and warmth was my aim, only to find you had to put two dollars in the meter to have a hot shower, I immediately felt anger build inside my chest as I had no cash with me. 'Breathe, you have let Rae rattle your cage again.' But she pressed every button I owned, what had happed to gratitude? The rain had eased a little as I walked back to my van, noticing there were many smaller type vans in the campground, some of them had bunting or colourful little flags all around, others had coloured lights glinting on and off as the rain and wind made them jump around. Making myself a steaming cup of beef broth, and a hot water bottle warmth spreading through me as I curled up on my bed with the Doona wrapped tight round me, opening the book I had begun to read last night. The rain continued, I had everything I needed, warmth, fed, dry and comfortable, the little bedside light cast an orange glow as I continued to read into the night.

Early morning I heard soft footsteps stop outside my van, voices were whispering. The door was tried; I immediately yelled "Clear off." Quickly dressing I stomped my way through large mucky puddles to the camp office. I heard my own voice screeching my complaint, the manager looked shocked, offering his apologies. Feeling slightly mollified, I made my way back to the Mermaid, only to find I had been burgled, the vans door swung open; fresh wet muddy footprints were on the floor, I saw that my iPad and printer had gone, along with the jug, toaster and my bedding, to add insult to injury they had nicked my book as well. What the hell is wrong with some people? Had no one had seen it happen? Surely, they would have stepped in and stopped it? My purse and camera had been locked in the Suzuki thank God; I had my phone on me as I had rushed over to the office to complain.

I dare not leave the van unprotected, I rang the office, Winnie the female side of management was soon at my door, her husband following, "He's phoning the police now dear," she suggested that I lock up the van, "You're coming back with us till the police arrive." The police duly arrived took my statement, then retired to the café across the road. The husband now introduced himself "I'm Trev, I'm really sorry" he said, "This is not the norm for us, I presume you have insurance?

How simple it all was-one phone call, later that day an inspection by the Napier RAC branch. The following day I had money in my account which meant I could purchase all I needed. In the meantime, Winnie and Trev were generous to me, not only including me in their meal that night, but I was also given the keys to one of their holiday chalets, free of charge till I had sorted myself out. The Chalets were cozy, the hot shower heaven, the double bed I could really stretch out in, and an indoor toilet, the simple pleasures of life. I slept like a baby knowing the next day I would buy what I needed for the Mermaid, I considered moving on or maybe finding another campground, however commonsense said if I stayed here my van would have an eagle eye kept on it.

Everywhere I looked were adverts and postcards for *Pania of the Reef* I had been told the Māori fable, story about a Wahine Maiden who fell in love with Karitoke, the handsome son of a Māori chief, he had asked her to become human; she became frightened running away to return to the sea people. So, it was a shock to be informed that Pania had been stolen, what! Stolen when? The tour guide saying, "Oh a year or so ago, the good news is it had been found, under someone's backyard under a manky old tarpaulin. She had been badly damaged; an ongoing investigation was being made." What is it with Metal Mermaids and thieves what's the draw card? Bloody, sticky fingered, plonkers, why can't they just leave the Mermaids alone? Once more, that ripple of anger shot through my chest.

The tour continued to the Sea Horse farm and that was brilliant so peaceful the way they cling and sway to whatever their tails curl around, completely harmless yet again an endangered species made so by us humans, "Can't leave a good thing alone" another tourist added, which did not make me feel any better. I was still feeling very disgruntled by all the thieving that was going on. The Insurance money had come through a nice little amount sat in my bank, I stopped at a shopping mall for what I needed, once back at my camp site I unloaded all of my new gear, good thing about it was the sales person had shown me the more modern digital equipment, I was impressed by most of it, purchasing what he advised. I would not call myself tech savvy, but he was. It felt like Christmas, wrapping paper and boxes were strewn over the floor.

The moon was so full, shining a deep yellow that night, sitting on the vans tiny step, I had a choice, I could stay in the Chalet if I felt unsafe or I could stay in my home. I pondered my life, the moon and I keeping each other company, the silence broken only by the wind. I pondered on the adventure I had chosen. Why do I keep getting involved with others? Had I made the wrong decision travelling on my own? And most importantly was I content to carry on? Why was Rae and Jess so upset with me? It seemed I attracted the emotionally helpless or the immature like bees to honey.

This adventure had begun on a sour note, yes, I admit I had needed help, I was still learning who I was? It had been the point of this journey-this was my journey, it was not about Mother, Nana, Wife, Friend or Lover, this was about discovering who I was! So why was I now having regrets about my choices in life? So many why's danced inside my head which was now heavy with lack of sleep. Wishing on the moon, as I had done as a child to keep me safe through the night, I locked up securely and slept the night away the feeling of being unsafe, invading my dreams. Two or three times jumping awake as I swore, I felt the Mermaid move.

I felt awful the next day; my sadness invading my eyes, I dragged myself through a guided tour of the Art deco that Napier was so proud of. The tour bus had picked me up at nine am, there was one other passenger and myself. It felt good to be bumping along with no one to talk to just me and my thoughts; Russ had once warned me "You spend too much time in your head Tara." Which I now knew as true, as I often was caught daydreaming, my mates referred to me as a deep thinker, got a problem? Just give it to Tara, she'll worry for both of you.

CHAPTER FORTY-ONE

The humidity was building up, the last two days of drizzle was steaming off the ground, the evergreen paddocks bright with moisture. Our first stop today was a frame repair studio where they showed us how they restored the old frames of yesteryear, all old, stained chipped woodwork stripped back to an original. Shaun the manager insisting we wore masks and aprons, I found it interesting watching them lower large frames into a chemical mix, the drying racks were already packed, it was interesting to see the finesse that went on when reproducing a clean frame.

Morning tea as at a riverside café, once again locals and their art pieces adorned every nook and cranny. The tour visited the art deco on and in buildings, the tour guide giving a running commentary. 1pm arrived it was time for the promised plowman's lunch at a local hotel; I loved the local cheese but not keen on the blood sausage offered. We visited four studios, all well worth seeing, I was a little disappointed in the fact I could not get my hands dirty with learning something new in the studios.

The Napier Art gallery was wonderful, the old Maestro's looking down in disdain at the newcomer's work on the opposite wall. A huge oil painting of the 1986 earthquake was impressive, as was the written description next to it. It was horrifying that this was no folktale, this volcano erupted with such force that the heat and sand made little glass bubbles that broke apart as they landed on the street. This painting showed the pink baths, they had been classed as one of the 18th century wonders of the world, many international tourist had made their way here to bath in the heated mineral water in them, but they too had exploded, the painting capturing this terrifying experience.

Then it was onto the strawberry farm for afternoon tea, strawberry jam, cream and two fresh scones, I could have choice of regular tea or strawberry tea, I decided to live a little ordering the latter, sighing with contentment, what an enjoyable day I had. Hot air ballooning was advertised in the café window; I pre-booked my seat on my phone as I was being driven back to the caravan park. I knew if I had stopped and scanned myself, I would have realised the sadness I was feeling had not shifted, I was pushing it down by touring, looking for a distraction. The tour bus chugged up to the camp gate; I waved it off, strolling into the campground and stopped still.

The camp was alive with people, it looked like someone had painted the camp with bright colours, it breathed, it moved, the once unsettling deadness of the camp now vibrant, there where people everywhere, lots of people doing all sorts of things, some sitting outside their vans, some talking to others, some busy sweeping windswept debris from their doors, others cleaning out annexes and windows, suddenly this caravan park had a life that pulsed, and I had no idea why.

Winne greeted me, I had to stop and ask, "What's going on? Who are they? Her reply was "Oh, just family paying a visit. Really? She stood beside me beaming with pride. "Well sort of, we are the last of a long line of performers with a circus troupe, some still do private work, like kids parties but most of us have retired and often end up here." It took a while to realise I was actually camping in a retiree's circus; this is where the old, injured, fed up and brassed off with circus life come to live out their lives. A song by the Eagles Welcome to the Hotel California went through my head; it felt like I had stepped back in a time warp, where had these folk been when I had arrived?

"We often go on trips to see shows in Wellington this time it was the opening of the Wellington Museum TePapa, plus we see our families." I must admit it felt really safe to be in camp that night with a lot of other folk around, the bathrooms steamy and hot through constant use, smelling of lavender talc and shampoo, it was a pleasure to go over there and be greeted by others. I sat in my van feeling a little lost for words this was surreal, my phone rang "It's Trev here Tara, why don't you join us for dinner we are having the gang over tonight." Why not? People were arriving by the minute to join in this Welcome Home Party. As I walked in a seat was pushed under me, a glass of warm beer pushed into my hand, they bombarded me with questions, how come I had been robbed?

Why was I travelling on my own? Was I enjoying myself? I was grilled for information until it was all too much. Pleading a headache, I left them to party on without me, it was time for my bed; in six hours I was booked on a Balloon Ride.

I woke with excitement, only to find out due to weather conditions it was canceled. It had rained once again, it was damp and cold, the ablution block a two minute run across the camp site. The mud stuck to everything, I sloshed my way back to the Mermaid once inside I yelled "I give up, I bloody give up, we will do it your way, I am over it; I agree, I'm selling up and going home. And surprisingly I actually felt really good, once I had made up my mind, I felt settled. I read or snoozed most of the day, the weather was not set to improve, the internet was on and off, I swore the moment this rain stopped, I was heading out.

Her laughter woke me, it was so joyful it had me smiling, I had to find out why and who? In a caravan not too far from me she - was stamping in the deep puddles around her van, her long dark hair whipping around her face as she jumped in and out of puddles with unbridled glee; she had tucked the bottom of her dress it into her knickers; she looked up and I saw the most attractive dark skinned women smiling at me, "Come on in, it's awful" she yelled. I shook my head "I hate cold muddy water" I called back. She threw back her head and laughed at my discomfort, "You either like it, or you let it get to you, come on have some fun" why I joined her, stomping in the freezing muddy water? I have no idea, perhaps I was drawn to her sheer defiance of this crappy weather.

When she spoke or should I say chanted it made complete sense "At the end of the day there is only you to make adult decisions about your life. At the end of the day there is no one to answer to but you and your maker. So, you can stamp and howl about life much as you want to, because no one gives a shit especially. when you're your dead.

CHAPTER FORTY-TWO

Lately my dreams had been of our son, who now wandered the spirit world, each time I dreamt of him, his tiny little face tucked up in white wool shawl, my heart would squeeze so tight I found it hard to breathe. So, when Venus had tapped on my door, inviting me over to her caravan, I accepted. When she took my hand, I felt her warmth "Your son is with his father, they both know your love for them will never wither. They ask you to accept the mantle of wise woman you are becoming. My legs felt like rubber. "How do you know this?" Venus offered me a chair, "You're so unsure of what awaits you, you must learn to trust that the universe has had this planned, for us to meet-for your past to unfold as it has." She placed a crystal in my hand, "When your heart is heavy, hold this to remember who you were and who you have become, Tara, your wisdom grows inside you with every dawn."

The RAC pulled the Suzuki and Mermaid out of the muck onto solid ground, then drove off to attend to the next cry for help. Once out of the gates feeling like I was a survivor from a very bad science fiction movie. A blanket of grey had lifted from my head and shoulders. Who knows why I was put on that path, life is no accident, this I knew; we are all here to experience life on this planet, maybe it was to meet Venus and have her test my faith in myself- for now I was on the road again, heading towards Taupo caravan park. After a four hour drive, I was parked up and spruced up as I was off to see the sights including the Waitomo caves famous for its glow worm caves.

Taupo was sunny and warm, very different from Napier, the caravan park was just that, a fair dinkum caravan park, concrete pads divided each caravan to its own little plot. To enter there was a security gate that needed a special card to swipe before the boom was raised before you could drive in, security roamed the grounds at night with dogs on leashes, this camp was policed tightly for their client's protection, I liked that idea, no noise after ten pm, the boom gate was locked off at one am.

My first trip out was to find a grocery store to re- stock my pantry, small it was, but if I was careful I could get three days of canned food in there, in the small cupboard inside, more like little upright box with a lid, I put all my drinks and powdered milk, I had discovered how to make Milo milkshake, if I put it all together before I started off on any trip then when I reached my destination I had one very frothy milkshake. I had also discovered that if I put warm water in a large bucket, put in the days washing with liquid soap, made sure the lid was tightly clipped on, I could pop it into the back of the Suzuki, by the time I pulled over for the day, my washing was done, all I had to do was rinse and hang up. I had learnt that if I shared my clothing with the underbed drawer, I could squeeze in a spare pot, glass and cutlery, which gave me a little more room in the pantry cupboard, I was getting very creative at living in small spaces.

This Taupo camp was what I was looking for, the receptionist took my details, printed me an invoice, I tapped my card. They produced an envelope that contained camp rules, a few brochures on tourist spots and things to do and see. Their attitude was pleasant, no nonsense quite the opposite from the last two camps I had stayed in. They warned me that showering was not advised any later than ten pm, I was given a code to both shower and the toilets, a polite thank you, a small map was printed that showed me site I was booked on. Perfect, no fuss.

Off to the shops a list of items made out, there is something healthy about bringing order into your life, and I liked this feeling. I shopped for my groceries buying only necessary items mainly fruit, in the mall I noticed a hot roast shop it smelt divine, ordering my lunch and sat down with a huge sigh, on the plate served to me was a mix of roasted veggies, umara the kiwi sweet potato, pumpkin, peas, corn, carrots and a large piece of roast beef smothered in thick brown gravy, for a hot drink I had a double shot cappuccino, my body sighed thank you as I ate and digested the first real meal in seven days.

As I walked slowly back to the Suzuki, my arms loaded with parcels-I saw a movie being advertised the *Lady and the Tramp* a kids cartoon; guess who took herself to the movies, relaxed, ate some popcorn and smiled all the way through. Driving back to the park I noticed a large white sign that said, 'Caravans wanted -good price for all interested.' Should I? Was this an opportunity being offered? My day had been perfect-my one question as I went to sleep was, do I continue to travel, or did I simply sell up and leave?

The day dawned, and I was up and off to the bathrooms early, washed, cleaned teeth, and back to my little home to put the day together, I rang a tour bus company that promised to show me Taupo, "You will not be disappointed" they said, I was picked up one hour later, the bus was half full of tourists like myself, finding my seat in the back of the bus, nice I was on my own. We were off to the Huka falls; the largest water falls in New Zealand; you could hear it, long before you saw it Once you got out of the bus, the ground shook under your feet, a fine mist was high in the air but still I could not see it, rounding a corner I was shocked into standing still-we all were.

Now I saw what all the fuss was about these falls were the epitome of maleficent, they thundered, roared, the water reared up in boiling demonic anger; falling hundreds of feet into turmoil filled pools of green and blue, the huge sharp boulders, formed over thousands of years resembled teeth that littered the bank declaring certain death, if you fell. The same feeling in my chest as when we flew over white island arose, a locked scream in my throat, except this time I was hemmed in by excited tourists all sussing out the perfect spot to snap a photo. I pushed and shoved my way back onto the bus, not caring about the comments of being rude, I needed to find a place to sit it out and wait for the tour of the lake Taupo.

Lake Taupo is reported to be the biggest natural lake in New Zealand, no one knows the depth in the middle, the bus driver was very adventurous in his description of how the NZ Navy had used today's modern technology to measure the bottom of this lake, it had proven impossible. It was on this rocky shore I was introduced to the pumice stone; this is a stone that when a volcano erupts it shatters enormous rocks into this white powdery sandy stone. We were warned before we excited the bus, it was not permitted to remove it from the shore as it was considered (Tapu) by the local Māori Iwi.

However we could pick it up and touch it, what a feeling to know I just may be holding a piece of stone centuries old. I watched as some tourists picked the Pumice up and threw it back into the lake, it floated back to shore. I watched as people went off the path provided, crushing this stone underfoot, and I watched an older couple replace the stone in exactly the place they had found it, that was respect.

We visited two studios one made Māori carving; the other studio sculptured in stone. Day two of my stay in this well controlled camp was a cleaning day for me washing, tidying, dusting, cleaning the van. By nighttime I was muscle sore and tired, enjoying a meaty broth for dinner, that night I slept deeply, feeling safe is always a good conducive to sleep. There had been a sudden change in energy, and I welcomed it. I felt stronger more in tune with what I wanted to achieve. Day three, time to plan another tour, I chose a trip to the Waitomo caves, booking my seat on line. My pickup time was seven am the following day.

Today I was touring on my own, following the maps instructions I visited the Taupo community gardens, the Taupo Māori Museum, the Taupo library that had many carvings in it, I took photos of an original Waka in the large communal garden, fond memories of my adventure in a Waka, made me smile. An English afternoon tea was advertised in the gardens tea kiosk, I had no sooner settled in a cane chair when a trolly was wheeled up to me, I chose the hot crumpets- the butter was melting into them, a big blob of raspberry jam on their tops and a pot of fresh lemon and ginger tea. This place was very 19th century English; I only had to look sideways when a waitress would appear "May I help madam? "If only" I thought as my decision to sell my rig was still niggling, it would be so easy to sell up, pack up and fly home.

I was enjoying my day so much the wind was light but breezy, playfully sticking its cold fingers down my neck, goosebumps broke out, so it was back to the Suzuki for a jacket, when the phone rang it shook me out of my reverie. "Mum, its Rae" it sounded urgent "What's wrong" I asked, she sounded desperate my heart sank for her as she sobbed "Mum, he's gone" "What are you saying" I asked, "Mum, Tim has taken all of the money, he's left me." My heart squeezed to hear the misery in her voice as she told me the plans of buying a home they had both chosen, their money along with the government money to help as a 1st home buyer was a big deposit; Tim had said he would take their papers over to the home builders office 24 hours ago- he had not returned.

She had waited for a day and contacted the police. Apparently, it was all quite legal, no charges of theft could be made as she was married to the cockroach and willingly given him the money so no extortion charges could be made either. I was speechless "Mum, I'm eight weeks pregnant." The joy that I was going to be a Nana again flooded through me. The feeling that something was not right stopped me "I'm going to ring our lawyer to see what I can do from here, I will ring you tomorrow" she hiccupped "Love you, Mum." Hmm, funny when my heart was breaking, and I wanted to hear those words more than anything else in the world, and she snatched it away from me. I shook of those thoughts, but they were determined to hang on in there, I could not figure out if I was being bloody minded and selfish or I was again being conned.

This time I'm not rushing into anything; I was going to let my lawyer sort this one out. I love this modern technology, one phone/video call, that's all it took. I rang Jo and asked her to visit Rae and Jess, just to make sure she was okay, she promised to go over the next day. As night fell and I was snug in my van, I rang my daughter to tell her the news I had received from the lawyer, "It's going to cost time and money to find your husband; he could be anywhere by now." She cried and made all sorts of promises- if I could just loan her another five thousand, just to see her through, please Mum, I have debts to pay."

That feeling in my gut grew, I could hear her waiting for my answer, I also felt that Tim was beside her, waiting for my answer. Breathing deeply, knowing I would be abused in some way or form, I replied, "No Rae, I can't help you." Usually, I would apologise that I was unable to help- but why should I apologise for a situation I had not created. Rae was going to have to grow up and be responsible for her actions.

CHAPTER FORTY-THREE

Today the Waitomo caves tour was happening, my body felt wonderful any aches and pains were absent, as I was walking to the gates for the tour bus a little early, and just as well as the bus was already there. I was greeted with "Kia Ora, good morning" by a charming female tour guide. It was worth every penny. They are truly beautiful-a fairy land of lights that actually twinkled, we were asked not to speak as they might go out, so none of us spoke except for 1 bloke who let rip the loudest sneeze I've ever heard. The pinpoint lights dimmed then flickered on again. Thankfully, they kept glowing as we settled into small inflatable boats called 'Rubber Ducks' once our group had settled, we glided into velvet black illuminated only by glowworms, how magical.

Ornate cave patterns were shown to us by torch light as we glided towards two hundred years of natural history now showing itself, limestone tapestries fanned out over rocks, stalactites, stalagmites were words that belonged in another world. Once back at the wharf it was lunch time, I must admit these Kiwi's certainly feed you, I had a brilliant day. Once I was back at camp and everything in order, I opened my emails to see what Jo had written, she had been to Rae's home, taken her a box of groceries as I had requested; and was happy to report all was calm and Jess, although busy with his Xbox game, seemed happy as well. "No drama's Tara, everything was very cordial. PS: was added, Tim was with Rae, I thought he had left? My intuition was correct I was being conned.

The next tourist attraction was the fixed wing fly-over the National Park. It was one day's drive away. I also wanted to visit New Plymouth, to do this I would have to drive to the National Park through Tauranga, see what I wanted to see there; then cut across to New Plymouth. The most popular flight was open seven days a week. For some reason on line booking was not available, once home from Waitomo, I rang the tour operators. My booking accepted, I asked if there was a caravan park nearby. He informed me that if I had a small rig, I could leave it at the airfields till I got back from the flight, it would be safe there. The road to Taupo the desert road was bare, brush and scrub dotted the plain bare sandy loam. I pulled over to make my breakfast, I wandered round the teardrop, giving the mermaid art a pat, thinking to myself this wee one has done so well.

An hour later I reached the airfield, they must have seen me coming, as I pulled up-a young man walked out and guided me to a parking bay, introducing himself as Daniel, he then ushered me to a small four seater fixed wing plane. A head set was offered to me; the usual formalities took place between pilot and air control. The plane climbed to 10,000 feet, flying over all three volcanoes, including Mt Ruapehu-the live volcano that steamed away in the distance; he explained this was where the Peter Jackson films 'Lord of the Rings' was filmed, this piqued my interest as Jess and I both loved those movies. We flew over lakes turquoise blue, the surrounding land filled with tussock, mountains ranges and desert, what an unusual place New Zealand was, formed around so much water, yet in the middle there were three were volcanoes, two topped with snow 'the sleeping ones'

The third volcano? As we flew over the crater, steam rose from the placid blue waters, Daniel saying it seems to be a quiet day for the three sisters. As the plane came in for landing, Daniel informed me there were herds of red deer, wild pigs and wild horse's roaming the desert: and to be aware of these animals as I continued my journey. Our descent was so smooth. As I drove off it was close to dusk and I needed to find a camp spot, I had been informed it was illegal to free camp on the desert road. Looks like my next stop was going to be Stratford, if the weather was fine, approximately a two hour drive was ahead of me. There was no internet here in the desert, so I would chance it.

Driving alone; knowing you have to be extra diligent, ready to slow down if an animal crossed the road, can be taxing, I was very happy to reach civilization once more. Close to 6pm when the lights of Stratford came in to view. Large elm trees with their hats of gold and red leaves grew each side of the main road. The housing looked small, almost ancient. I was informed later the they were the original railway houses, they had been beautifully restored, the detailed fret work on the gables I found fascinating. Stratford had the most amazing flower display, it seemed everyone grew something that blossomed, sweet peas ran riot over old stone fences, large broken rocks dotted fence lines. Everlasting daisies swayed in the breeze; the green grass lawns were smothered in white daises. Forget me knots, Tiger lilies, and naked lady Lilies, it was obvious the people took pride in their gardens, and the city rewarded them for their efforts as many signs of best tidy or clean street were added to the road signs.

What I needed right now was a campground to park in and lie down-the headache had returned, my stomach felt queasy. Google on my phone pinged into life, informing me 500 meters to your left and there was a caravan park. I must have looked drunk or hung over as there was a distinct pause when she welcomed me, her eyes measuring me up, a No! already placed on her lips. I informed her I had a migraine; her eyes changed again with empathy. "Site 30, love," she said. I drove in, found my number, parked, and unhitched my Mermaid. My head felt like a huge drum crashing inside my skull. I boiled the kettle, placing a hot water bottle around my neck, finding some painkillers, then fell asleep for the night. Sleep did not help; I woke five hours later to throw up. I needed to rehydrate as soon as possible; very slowly, the change in pain became significant.

The camp manager knocked on the van door the next morning, I hate to ask as I know you're not well but how long are you staying for?' she queried. Her name badge stated Madge, I looked at my Mermaid her insides musty and messy, my Doona and sheets wrinkled and sweaty. "Is it possible I can stay for a week"? She recognised my accent, her blue eyes smiling. "No worries,

Darl" she replied, I recognised her Ozzie twang, she held out her hand, introducing herself from "Silverton mate, Opal country. Her handshake more like a miner's grip, as she pumped my hand up and down.

Off Madge stomped; as bandy as a monkey on a barrel, rolling from side to side as she walked away. I was soon to appreciate that fact that Madge was strict, no nonsense and proved to be quite the character, living in a ramshackle caravan out the back of the office. The grounds around her home and office were kept immaculate, if a leaf or feather dare blow onto the pathway she was out there with her broom. Around her home and office grew dozens of bright coloured roses, geraniums of pink, white, red and orange climbed over fences, a fernery grew along one side, I wondered what my fernery in Perth looked like now.

I borrowed the camp vacuum, and as most females do, we had begun to chat. I asked why she had moved here. She shrugged her shoulders, "Why not Darl? I had a rotten marriage, three rotten kids that don't like me, and I don't like them. I also have five grandchildren, but they are not allowed to see me. My heart went out to her; I knew how that felt. My brother owned this, he died and left it to me. I had nowhere else to go, my family informing me, if I went into an old folks home, don't rely on them to visit or help with finance. To think I spent the majority of my life helping them" It was said without malice, but the hurt and defeat showed in her face. As she spoke, her hand stroked the mangiest cat I have ever seen; he lay on her lap, his fur was all tangled, one eye missing. On Madge's face was pure glowing love for this little moggy.

Her work-worn hands, blue-veined with wear and tear, carefully cleaned him down. Her voice, almost like his purring, offered endearments to him as she rubbed a soft cloth over his head and eyes. 'Poor old Tom, not wanted just like me, aye Tom? Never mind, old boy, I love you.' It brought tears to my eyes, as I felt the same way with my lot in Perth. Later in the day, housework completed, my washing on the line in the sunlight, I drove into town thinking over my list groceries, my first stop was a café for a hot coffee and something nice to eat, the chocolate lamingtons looked so fresh; I could not resist. Madge was a mine of information if she thought the tour advertised was crap, she would say so, if not she would beam, tap her finger on the advert and say, "This is for you Darl."

It was a quiet city, one for retirees, The Men's shed, and CWA were prominent on the main street, as was the RSA, a hospital and four hotels. I had this feeling that Stratford was were you went when the world became too harsh. And I must admit there had been some days on my adventure, when living here would have been a blessing. Marge was old school, cash was king, I paid in notes as requested, hitched the van on, I waved to Madge "Lovely to have met you take care" I called, she waved back "You to Darl, safe travels." New Plymouth was my next port of call; a caravan park had been prebooked two days ago. Victoria the voice of my GPS said in her very oxford English accent, "Take the first turn to your right. "I did, there was a sign board 'New Plymouth, alongside it a barometer 10 degrees and falling. It was nearing winter-the wind had now become bitter, chilling the bones. After a two hour drive with only one toilet stop, I reached the campgrounds, Victoria announcing "You have reached your destination."

CHAPTER FORTY-FOUR

My camp site number was 53, I was an expert on backing the Mermaid in by now: however, the manager Rick insisted he walk me to the site. He began to bellow orders at me, "Lady, turn right, a little to the left, stop, come forward a little." It was not until I was in line with his calculations, when he decided all was well in his world and strutted back to his office like he had won a war, stomping and bellowing at anyone who looked his way. This camp ground ran amok with seniors; they were everywhere. I was no sooner out of the Suzuki when many hands appeared to help me stabilize the Mermaid. I had a brochure tucked into my hands announcing a dinner-camp ground get together that night, BYO stated in big black letters. Why not? I was not exactly busy. I showered made myself look presentable and at five pm on the dot, I found the community hall in the campgrounds. I was greeted with wolf whistles and "You'll do love," not knowing anyone in the room I was a little embarrassed.

As I queued with two others, a warm plate was pushed into my hands, the Bain Marie was full of lovely hot food; I asked the male behind me where I paid. He introduced himself as Romeo. Really! He nodded towards a large bowl on a table, pop it in there, lovely. The problem was I did not have cash, so I said, "Be back in a tick, I'll just get my wallet" his answer was "Don't need your cash, babe, just your keys." I did not understand "What do you mean by my keys? His eyebrows wiggled up and down. I looked in the bowl, it was full of keys. What was going on? "Babe, (there was that word again) it's our Friday night get together."

Once again, the eyebrows wiggled, "Or you and me Babe, we can have go private, my place or yours?" Now I got it, this was a *key party,* I had heard about them when I was at university; but here?

With all the Zimmers and walking frames piled up by the front door? It's a wonder there was not a bowl for dentures as well. I put my plate aside, and left, hoping no one thought this was an open invite to join me. I shuddered at the thought of what was being insinuated. Ewww, I locked myself up tight that night.
The tourism shop was most helpful, giving me a big handful of brochures. Advertised was the fly over? Done that, River cruise? Done that, Kayaking? Done that, Tour buses to many Māori culture displays plus a Māori greeting with a lunch provided? No, had done that as well.

There was Bungy jumping, mini-golf, and movies; all I wanted to do was drive around, take snaps of what I considered interesting and upload my journal to my laptop, so that's exactly what I did. Grocery shopping was often as I could not buy a lot, once all was packed away, I opened another book, transported to another world for an hour. I made myself a light lunch, then snoozed, my neck still tender from the muscle spasm the previous week. I added the latest photos onto the laptop and entered my diary on my blog page. I considered a shower; hot water always relaxed the kinks.

My neighbour, who I now knew as Thelma must have seen my door open, because she was there greeting me and inviting me to a Bingo game that night at the camp. I claimed I was speaking with family about the same time; I really did not want to get mixed up with the camps nocturnal life. The shower or should I call it my saving grace, was hot and healing, I turned the water off, only to hear Thelmas voice describing me to another "She's an Ozzie you know, they're all big drinkers over there, I bet she's a boozer that's why she's on her own? Most likely her old man kicked her out, can't blame him, she's not friendly you know, told our Romeo to sod off." Well, she was right about one thing, I did dismiss Romeos advances. I had more respect for myself than becoming his camp paramour. And that was one of the reasons I enjoyed my own company, because of gossips like her. I made my way to my van, dressed in my cosy Pj's, made myself a cup of

Milo then called Margi, I needed to tell someone, just to see if it made sense or not.

There was a silence, then she said, 'Oh Tara'- I heard a giggle escape by the time I had finished the story. We were both giggling like two naughty schoolgirls. "Jeez you manage to meet them don't you" Margi said, I'll make a couple of calls, try to get some sleep; I will ring you in the morning." Sleep! You're joking? What I had witnessed and invited to partake in was not normal for one of a certain age, or was it? Is this what seniors call a hobby? I had no idea; and I was not going to enquire. But I was going to leave this camp once the sun was up, I was definitely not comfortable staying here.

The morning dawned, pearly blue, a perfect winters day, the air sweet and clean. I was about to enjoy a banana milk shake for breakfast, when Margi rang. "Okay here is the name and address of a good mate of mine. Her name is Petra, she lives at Opunake beach and has invited you to stay with her for a long as you like, I have given them your phone number. They will ring and give you the details of how to get there, text me when you are arrive, I worry about you." I took the comment as endearing not as the later-you're a concern.

When Petra rang me, it seems that Margi had informed her of my current situation. I could hear the mirth in her voice, her comment we are a working farmlet, but you're most welcome to stay. I decided then and there to leave, I would have to forfeit the three days, it did not matter, I did not feel safe here. I stored everything away, pushed my hair into a small ponytail, pulling on my favorite driving gear, shorts, T-shirt and sneakers. Once I began to pack things away, Romeo arrived. So, this was Thelmas husband, in daylight and sober he was not bad looking. "I know what she's been saying" he admitted as he helped me store my table and chair in the boot. "My apologies love, she's a right little bitch with a few in her."

Romeo hitched the Mermaid onto the tow bar for me, as we shook hands, we both spotted Thelma galloping down the road at great speed, her eyes bulging, her mouth already spitting abuse at her husband. So, before she could accost me with abuse I drove off. Stopping just once to hand in my gate pass and to inform them I was leaving. My thoughts about selling up had been quieted I would give it another go, if this next stop did not work out? Then I would leave. Opunake beach here I come, hopefully to stay a while as New Zealand still had more to offer.

Opunake is a very small community, the scenery of ocean and beaches leading to it, are inspiring to any creative. The sand looked black and course, driftwood built up in huge piles on the beach, while huge, fat, brown kelp lay bundled across the shore. The very air sang with salt and sea, with waves far out heaving and rolling, their weight proving too much as they approached the shore, changing to foaming tops that whispered of their journey from exotic lands to this quiet beach. Seagulls rode these rolling waves like experienced bronco riders; one lone seagull flew past me squawking what I thought was a welcome.

The hills and forestry had a wind- worn look yet were still lush. Native flax grew everywhere, with Tui birds and wood pigeons perched atop the long poles of flax flowers, their song a delight. I still felt stunned by the seniors' behavior, other than that, my pride and health were intact. Petra called again, and I pulled over, to answer. It was Petra offering to meet me at the shops so I can lead you to where we live.' I agreed, scribbling down her instructions. The scenery as I drove into Opunake was breathtaking. I must have stopped ten times to take photos. The West Coast of New Zealand is known for its wild weather and raw beauty, and I fell in love with it, gone was the tourist buzz, this was the raw New Zealand.

I spied Petra's Red Pajero as I drove beside her, she waved, backed out, and I followed her back to their piece of Paradise. Ronan her husband came out to meet us, saying "From what we've heard, you're very determined to do your own thing, but we would like to offer you the Bach to stay in, Petra saying "Just give life a rest."

Moving out of the Mermaid was not hard, I never thought it would happen while I toured; but here I was enjoying life in a beach Bach; when on calm, sunny days, I often sat and watched Ronan carve mythical creatures from driftwood. Petra was a jeweler, her works of art in antique silver jewelry and precious gemstones was simple, elegant and beautiful. On the days when strong sea winds buffeted my little home, hard cold rain pelting against the windows. I hunkered down inside; warm and cozy, a small pot-bellied stove in the corner would puff out the occasional puff of tea tree smoke, which smelled wonderful.

On those wet days, I spent my time reading books in from their small library, ranging from model shipbuilding to the history of dinosaurs. I also took great joy in writing again, expressing my thoughts, printing them off and collating them, as my intuition was saying one day there would be a book. Petra and Ronan were the hosts from heaven, I only had to sneeze, and one of them would be there to ask if I needed something or say, 'Are you okay, Tara?' These two lovely people were so naturally beautiful inside and out, which I happened to see quite a bit of, as they were both nudists. I knew it would take some getting used to; however, their one concession towards guests was they both wore a small flap of tanned hide. For that I was grateful after all it was their home. If Petra leant across me to gather her jewelry instruments, at times a soft firm breast would brush my arm, a soft 'sorry' was always given, I guess she would see the shock in my eyes.

Respect for one another was always shown. I ate their holistic food, enjoying the exotic the flavors. Petra was also a practitioner in bush and flower healing; I had seen this practiced in Northland with Pania's family. The careful steaming and extraction of the precious healing oils and herbs, then the oils added to ointment and candles, which were made from beeswax from their own bee hives.

As you entered her workshop, two massive poles served as the lintels, both carved with the Nordic gods that Petra grew up with: fish, crabs, shells, and mermaids. Across the top lintel was the king of the sea, his beard and tail curling around one pole. His trident was held proudly erect; I thought it was sensual. These poles had come from an old shipwreck that had run aground in the early 1900s. They were stained, gouged, and deeply scratched, with huge iron bolts still studding the wood, it seemed to fit in with their holistic beliefs.

Petra's jewelry was intricate designs, some of shells cast in silver, in the center a local periwinkle, or 'cat's eyes' as she called them. 'Where do you find all this stuff? 'I asked. She replied. "You wait and see; If we have a storm, once it has calmed down, we will show you how to fossick. Although I agreed I felt like my time here was coming to a close. Over dinner I shared my decision over dinner, "I wanted to move on, to see the rest of the country. Wellington was just a day's ride from here."

There was a silence "And then what?" Petra asked. "The South Island where it is snowing and cold?" Ronan agreed. "Just stay a little longer; tomorrow if you're willing and interested you can work with me-can't have you feeling lost." His sentence cut off as their landline rang. Ronan came to the table smiling. "The gods are in our favour, my darling; he kissed Petra's cheek. Looks like no one is going anywhere; that was the Met service warning me to buckle up for a day or two because there is a big storm on its way.

"Petra began to organise her home, "Tara it's not wise to leave now, but it's your descion, you're not our prisoner. Ronan closed down the sheds and workshop, "Tara if you're staying, shut the chook pen down, pop the Mermaid into the big shed, and park the Suzuki around the back of it." I shooed the chooks into their pen and closed off the aviary with steel shutters.

My Mermaid was pushed inside the big shed, closed the large steel shutter doors, and parked the jeep around the back of the shed under an open-sided shelter where firewood had once been stacked. I was so busy doing what I had been told that I had not noticed the swollen, dark purple bruised clouds forming over the ocean. The waves were now tall angry, no longer a gentle hush as they crept to shore, these waves were pounding, an ancient rhythm of anger as they hit the shore. Gone was the light foam playing with the soft wind that I had once seen upon my arrival. I saw destruction and anger as the sea hurled itself onto the shore and across the road.

CHAPTER FORTY-FIVE

The next thing I needed to tie down was the beach Bach, close all the windows, shut all doors, and pull down the shades. Petra was now instructing me to sleep in the house that night or until the storm was over. "I'd rather have you safe and sound with us," she instructed. Steel roller doors now adorned the front windows; the once cosy small fire was built up to crackling flames. I felt very safe and comfortable with these two people. We spent many hours talking about Paradise-their home, they had found this small block of land when they were on their honeymoon ten years ago, fell in love with it. Petra's story went, once meeting Ronan she had fallen deeply in love with him, she returned to homeland Scandinavia sold up her livelihood and home, soon after becoming a New Zealand citizen, "I'm a Scaniwi." It suited her.

The storm threw whatever it could at us, it was wild, terrifying, exhilarating and breathtaking. There would be a second of silence, then away it would scream again; it shook the house, rattled roller doors, and sucked out the smoke from the chimney. The fire roared its delight. Once when there was a lull in the wind I had stood in the shelter of the doorway, watching the waves grow, hurl, and charge the beach.

From far out, they would build up until there were mini green rolling mountains careening towards us, then dumping themselves onto the sand. The boom of thunder was a warning that Mother Nature was once again doing some housekeeping. Petra stood beside me, rubbing her hands together, "Great fossicking when nature has finished showing us her might." While huddled inside we discussed the many storms we had all encountered in our lifetime, the only one I had not experienced was a snowstorm. Living in Perth, I experienced tornadoes that tore bricks from buildings and sucked the very air out of your lungs. Once I had been so close to being struck by sheet lightning, making my skin and hair fizz when it jolted into the ground five meters from where I stood.

The Roof of our Donga had been partially torn away by a hurricane when I lived with Russ in Cloncurry, Northern Queensland. I encountered tremendous rainstorms with raindrops as big as light bulbs and immense flooding. On one occasion, a flood tore down a steel bridge and hurled it onto nearby boulders; Chinaman's Dam overflowed with deep chocolate coloured water, and huge trees were thrashed about in the turmoil. The floods had also delivered three large saltwater crocodiles (salty's) into the local swimming hole; it became a tourist spot; it gave me the creeps. Thunder shook the house, growling and prowling around the skies for ages. Lightning was terrifying, especially the forked variety, which announced its arrival with a boom as it delivered its electric punch into the earth.

Random, silver gum trees would burst into flames like tree sentries with torches. The very air became alive. This storm was nothing like before; it felt oily and greasy, almost like a sneer at humanity as Neptune's green waves surged into peaks, crashing onto the sand. Lightning flickered in shades of peach, violet, and yellow across the ocean, while thunder rolled and growled like a lion searching for its prey.

The wind screamed and hammered against doors and windows, sounding like hell had been unleashed, it was frightening, but we were as safe as bugs in a rug here in their Paradise. As we sat waiting for the fury to calm down, more stories unfolded: Ronan had built the house himself, and Petra worked at home to bring in the money. On her days off, she drove to the seaside town, running workshops in jewelry making and homeopathy remedies. Roping in anyone and everyone, especially tourists who wanted a nudist bush adventure, "That proved a popular event," she giggled; my imagination went for a wander.

Petra and Ronan had the community to thank for creating this paradise. An open invitation was issued for a meet & greet BarbyQ sausage on a stick was offered to everyone who showed up, the opportunity to trample straw into mud bricks was offered. At times, there could be up to twenty people there, all stomping, talking, and often singing as they made mud and straw bricks to build the walls of their house. Although there was some bad publicity from those who shunned them. Of course, name calling and bullying arrived, describing them as raving rude hippies, health nutter's, tree huggers the new favourite with Ronan was the title Liberated Inebriants, they ignored it and moved on.

Ronan would gather huge tree trunks from either the forest or the ocean to construct and carve door frames and lintels. He had a backlog of orders; their own home was built from recycled products.

Petra smiled at him. "He's a collector; you might call him a hoarder, but we utilise everything he brings home." Inside their home, a Koru and Tiki were carved into the doors. The massive kitchen bench was made from swamp Kauri; it filled one side of the kitchen. Within small pockets of this bench, Petra had placed seashells, various tiny fossils, a small nugget of gold, a garnet, and even a petrified bush Weta, a New Zealand insect that existed when dinosaurs roamed the earth.

Ronan had devoted many hours to varnishing the Kauri slab, and these little memory treasures were now embedded forever. The circular bathroom was a work of pure artistry, seven feet above was the massive shower head, forged by Ronan, its template an old steel bucket. It felt like standing under a tepid waterfall. The bath, with claw feet, had been professionally re-enameled inside. On the outside, Petra had painted an amazing scenery of the Swiss Alps as a tribute to her parents." The hand basin Ronan made was in wood. The taps were new; given to them by a friendly plumber who had run the pipes through floors and walls for them. The toilet was in another small room, almost separate from the house. It was what they called a green toilet, no flushing. You did what you had to do, then sprinkled a mix of sawdust and potash over it all, closed the lid, and off you went.

The door posts above the toilet door were a work of art; you could sit there for a day discovering the fable of Bacchus the mythical god of Wine, he was draped over many nude maidens that seemed to watch you as you contemplated you day. It amused me as there was only the lower half of a door, when I questioned why? they said, "Why not enjoy looking at the sky and trees while you contemplate?" I had to agree. Their home was one large room, a cosy bedroom that was curtained off. Scattered on the floor lay lambskin rugs of every hue and colour. The roof was domed, inserted were three large, mullioned window, as the sun rose the light splayed across the room.

The splendid intricacy of the lounge captured my attention, as inserted into the walls of the lounge were two six foot stained glass windows, the rainbow lights coming from these I found hypnotic. Ronan had found these two beauties at an auction in Auckland city. As we ate dinner the conversation meandered from one topic to another, touching on the things Petra and sales of her jewelry. She intended to visit local markets and even more distant places if necessary.

She had been busy booking stalls; an arts gallery had shown interest as well. It was Petra's lack of marketing skills that she saw as her downfall, so she hired a professional she would meet in three weeks in Wellington. Ronan was preparing his carving; he had been commissioned to create five totem poles for the local council. He designed each of them in three sections, so each section of the pole could slowly spin around, his goal was to engage the children as well. When Petra pulled out a road map of the South Island, it was crisscrossed with red lines, Ronan had cleared the table, replacing dishes with handwritten note pads and their laptops. In unison the asked "Would you care to be part an adventure we are about to embark on."

It was tempting not to rush in and say yes, however caution made me I wonder if this would fit with what I wanted to accomplish. While the storm raged outside, we calmly discussed all possibilities. What they suggested were two opportunities. First, Petra was going on a fossicking trip. Her goal was to find gemstones, her informant had told her that the far southern beaches abounded with tiger's eye, moonstones, and the occasional Coquina shell, these particular shells were rare. Once leaving Opunake she was to attend small country markets to sell her jewelry and mix and mingle with other artists, picking up ideas. A dinner was planned in Wanganui to meet other artists of the same creative expression that Petra followed.

Now Ronan took over the conversation; he was going to travel to Wellington with Petra, collecting a consignment of five to fifteen-foot tree trunks that had recently been milled in Fielding. His one fear was that this milling company was big on using preservatives to age the wood. He disliked preservatives in any form, acknowledging that, in this day and age, sometimes it was necessary, "Bloody stuff is a toxic danger to man and beast."

Then they both outlined what it was they were asking of me, "We both know you want to travel, and we both acknowledge that this is our path, not yours. What we are asking is that you accompany Petra to Wellington, there are so many small townships on the way she knows about, that you would never find, as they're not on the main route. Then once in Wellington accompany Petra to the South Island, where I will join you." "And option two? I asked." Well, if you choose not to accompany us, would you think about being the caretaker of Paradise while we are away about three months in all.

Questions started forming in my head, the two of them sitting quietly, waiting for my thoughts. "Let me sleep on it; I have other plans but nothing that cannot be sorted." Normally, sleep by the sea is instantaneous for me; tonight, my head was buzzing with questions. The storm was now strong breeze; it looks like Mother Nature had run out of puff for a while. I tossed and turned for an hour or so, then, as quietly as possible, I let myself out the back door, patting the face of an owl which was carved into it, this was Ronan's totem; it protected them and the household. I made my way to the shed where the Mermaid was kept, suddenly realising that if I thought they were quaint for having an owl as a totem, what would they think if they could see me now, patting my caravan's mermaid, smiling like an idiot, and murmuring endearments to it? An inanimate object, yet I felt it was part of my life in New Zealand.

CHAPTER FORTY-SIX

Okay, the scales had tipped with these two opportunities, I sat inside my caravan, fetched my notebook and pen, writing the pros and cons of these two opportunities. There are times when I have written a problem down and the answer becomes clear, while other times it just remains sinning in circles. Was I more concerned about the path that I personally wanted to follow? And if I did tour with them where I would end up at the conclusion of my trip to New Zealand? Did I enjoy their company? I finally feel asleep tucked up in my own bed, the universe could work this one out.

I woke to the soft sound of Ronan voice as he offered up a prayer of thankfulness for the carving he was about to commit to. I had had often joined in their prayers of gratitude for the opportunity to experience and share our life on earth. I always enjoyed our nighttime discussions and appreciating their intense passion of their beliefs. The debate around the evening fire was not about hierarchy or asserting dominance; no ego or attitude was welcomed. We discussed philosophy and the reasons for our existence, referencing scriptures from the Bible, verses from the Koran, the Catholic Douai version, and even texts from the Salvation Army. I soon learned that our values may change constantly, but your principles and boundaries remain for life.

One night Petra had sat there amused by my belief in a God she could not fathom, one of terror and anger, ready to destroy humanity with a flick of his finger. Loving only those who obeyed him unconditionally. Her opinion was "When I hear your man-made conclusions, it confuses me. What does this invisible God want? All I see is an pissed off money sucking image, who is judging me with fire and brimstone, yet on the flip side, there's undying love for all humanity-it smacks of hypocrisy." I was not impressed.

Petra tried another angle, "Don't you think your God might be a tad upset about the wars and the immense global meltdown we humans are causing? Maybe we come to this planet as teachers? Or perhaps we come to experience what the spirit cannot, the unfathomable nature of mankind?" She explained her lifelong theory that when we incarnate as spirits on earth, we come with a pre-signed contract, so to speak, to teach what we had promised to do in a higher realm. Ronan made it very clear my faith and what I practiced was my choice, I did not have to follow or believe; I had my own path, my own beliefs, and my own theories. I was aware my feelings were divided part of me wanted to stay in paradise were I was surrounded by harmony and peace.

The larger part of me desired more travel, I guess it all depended on who you chose to accompany. When Petra woke me, "Why are you sleeping out here? time you get up and earn your keep because" she clapped her hands together "We are off fossicking." First to harvest the seaweed, this was not a small job; bull kelp that is still full of water is very heavy, it took all three of us to lift the long fingers of brown kelp into the trailer. Ronan drove back to Paradise to begin unloading the trailer. Meanwhile, Petra had pulled out two large straw baskets, between the two of us, we went searching through piles of sand and stones for treasures the sea had given up just for us. We were not the only ones on the beach; this was the locals' favourite spot.

A carnival feeling permeated the area, and we were met with open arms- hellos, hugs, introductions; some treasures were swapped, others given, some were repayments for favors in the past. I loved it, the wind whipped through our hair, blowing brown sea foam onto us, our laughter mixed with the call of the seagulls. Both exhausted by the time we walked through the front door of paradise. Ronan had made me a pot of tea, he admitted to still enjoying a good aromatic black coffee.

Petra sipped from her juice in the flask, from a cupboard she produced a tin of Nestle's dark chocolates, we all sat contentedly slurping away on our chosen brew and eating dark, bitter, delicious nut filled chocolate. I had left the baskets we filled in Petra's work room, with cold water trickling over them to wash off the sand. Next, the trailer where Ronan was shoveling the kelp into two large old baths to cure, a small bung at the bottom to release the fertilizer onto his garden once it had all melted down. Both of them were now in their little skirts, their skin covered in salt and sticky bits of seaweed.

Seeing sense in this, I slipped off my jeans and T shirt, leaving my underwear on, they stopped what they were doing and applauded. "Good for you Tara" said Petra, "Never be ashamed of your body, it creates disharmony with your ego." Now, I was not sure I understood this comment, I would think about it later. By lunch time, I needed a shower; I stunk, I offered to sweep off the trailer, "You guys clean up first, I'll tidy up here" my two friends accepted my offer disappearing into their home. I washed everything off, sorted the spades and brooms out the entered the house, calling out to Petra. I wandered towards the shower, again this room had a half door, a woven screen that you simply pulled across. I could hear the water falling then stopped, recognising the sounds of two people making love.

Glimpsing two slim bodies entwined, Ronan's deep voice encouraging Petra, while she whispered her love for him. I fled straight to my van. I felt like a voyeur. Memories of Russ and I sharing a shower, being held against his body. Would this be part and parcel to travelling with these two? I had nothing against it- they were in love. My decision of happily travelling with Ronan and Petra on their journey now felt like broken glass, I sat in the Mermaid feeling sad, fearful, embarrassed. I must have sat there all afternoon. I dozed, read my books, or added many photos to my laptop.

I heard them both calling my name, locking the Mermaid's door when they knocked, I said I had a headache and would not be in for dinner. I felt childish and silly making these excuses, my embarrassment would not budge. I called Margi, asking her opinion of travelling with her friends. There was a sternness in her voice when she replied "I put you in their path because I know these two people, they are not only loving and generous, once they befriend you, they would do anything for you.

I think you're bloody lucky to have been welcomed by them, the choice is yours." I had to acknowledge she was telling me a few home truths. Thank you, Margi I appreciate your honesty." A moment of silence then "Remember Tara, they are also - my dear friends." It was some time since Jo and I had chatted, I rang her "I was wondering how you were? What up." We discussed about her family going back to England, within the next two weeks, how they loved my home and had appreciated it. Jo also pointed out that my home would now be empty until I returned. I knew what she was going to suggest before she spoke. "Why not let Rae and Jess live there till the baby is born she said "At least it will be lived in."

My stomach did a flip "My main concern was her husband Tim, I had seen another side of him, one that encouraged dishonesty." Jo knew me well, I would not dismiss the idea, I would mull it over before I made a descion. "It's your home Tara, just a suggestion" she replied. I promised to send photos of where I was staying, it was now midnight, pin pricks of starlight in a blue back sky, the sea calm, the moon a misty orb. Petra's finger tapped on my window, "Thought I would find you here." I invited her inside; we sat on my bed, I told her about my family, Petra made a little moue with her mouth, I cannot see why you're beating yourself up? Could you have changed anything? She did what she wanted to, and so did you.
This life is all about give and take, in love and war. Choosing to love and protect yourself is far more important than winning any war." I then told her about Bridie, and her death, once more Petra shared her wisdom, so you're blaming yourself for an affair you

did not cause or instigate? That's a harsh judgment for anyone." The spilling of one's intimate self is hard, I told her of the letdown with Gilly, the anger towards family, and how I still grieved for my husband. It was dawn when I finished sharing my problems. "And you can't see the side of this that says this is one big lesson?" Petra queried "Well, no, I can't. It can't all be about me and my lessons."

As we walked back to their house, Petra turned to me, put her arms around me, and said, "Tara, when you learn that all love comes easily when you first love and respect yourself, once that happens, everything else that affects you, is secondary." She held my face between her hands and softly kissed my lips, I did not react or pull away, Petra patted my cheeks, "In my country when there was a grief or a loss, my close friends held and kissed each other, we were taught as young ones that those two emotions need support and guidance to a brighter future" I stood in the silence of the morning as night faded into day within the circle of her embrace, "You are loved Tara, you were lost, that's all.

Once breakfast was over and since it was Sunday, we decided a day off was in order. Everything could wait; it would be there tomorrow. We all drove into the small township of Opunake because Sunday was their chocolate muffin day at a local café. After settling ourselves in the beach, we chatted for a while about how the storm had changed the landscape. Tall trees had come down, leaving oddly shaped spaces in a clean blue skyline. Ronan rubbed his hands together and said, 'All the more poles for me to carve.' Petra snoozed on the sand, wriggling her body into a small hollow, I mimicked her actions, the sea a musical cradle to our dreams.

I had found the West Coast winter a little daunting, it was cold all day, the wind could whip up in a frenzy with a snap of your fingers. The ground had become permanently soggy, like a lime green sponge; the only dry places were where my van was parked, their workrooms, and inside the house. This afternoon I was quite content working to my own rhythm. In the background, music played; Petra was in her workshop, I could also faintly hear the comforting sound of wood being carved by Ronan, dinner time arrived, Ronan calling me in to eat with them. Informing me that in a week, they would be leaving, had I made my descion? I had a choice, housekeeper for Paradise or travel companion for Petra. "We need to know Tara." Everything here looked so comfortable, I admitted this was hard, "I can't decide, I want to do all of it."

I really liked these two wonderful simple living people, whose ethics and morals were pure, a glow of happiness they lived what they termed as their truth. "Can I help with your decision Tara?" Ronan decided to tell me his story, his past and present, he had a deep musical voice that held me captive as he outlined how he came to live here. "He was a Vietnam Vet, the killing on both sides had shocked him, the results of Napalm horrified him, again both sides affected badly, even today the screeching of a skill saw bought back memories, hence the reason no electrical equipment when carving, the fear, the crumping sound of bomb's falling fire, panic, terror, the smell of fear and despair would never leave him.

A psychiatrist pushing pills his way, they numbed him, booze plus smoking pot blanking out the painful memories till the next day. He became depressed and hit out at anyone who suggested he needed mental care, so they locked him up for a year, the memory a blur. When he accepted an invite from a medical schoolmate to his class gathering. He had arrived at the party stoned; they parted in dismay and disgust at his appearance and smell. He lost it screaming abuse into the faces of those who had never seen war, nor did they understand. When he came too in his own apartment, sitting beside him was this goddess," he pointed at Petra. To cut a long story short we very slowly felt our way from best friends to lovers, I was nursed by Petra holistically, spiritually, and physically, I found this place on one of our many walking trips; it was for sale and overgrown and here we are today, living both our principles, values, love for our life, each other and our surroundings.

People are drawn to us because what we value defines how we live our lives. Yes, the land is part of it, but even if everything were taken away and we were left with nothing, we would still have faith and belief in each other. Now, we need your decision you are not the only one who has to make arrangements." I felt the weight lift from my shoulders, it had been my prayer to meet the people of New Zealand and here it was, being offered to me. I nodded, "Okay I will accompany you till we reach the South Island then we would take stock from there." Petra jumped up "Good for you," I was hoping you would say yes." The relief of making this decision made me feel lightheaded.

CHAPTER FORTY-SEVEN

My position was as Petra's offsider, cataloging managing business appointments, journaling her day, but mainly recording her fossicking finds. This was usually Ronan's job, but he now had deadlines for construction and delivery for his work. These two were great at their crafts but business-people. If not for spread sheets or Google I felt they would have been lost, however I now had a clearer picture of what was expected of me. Now for arrangements of my own. I had made the descion to offer Rae my home to live in until I returned.

The phone rang twice, her voice happy, "Hey Mum, I'm just having a cup of tea with Jo." Taking a big breath and feeling unsure I asked "Rae, I was wondering if you and Jess would live in my home, until I return." I waited for the angry retort. There was silence from her end, so I continued, "It would make me feel easier if the house was being lived in." If she refused, I would be okay with it. "You bloody beauty!" she yelled. "I've just shown Jo the letter from White's real estate; they want me to move in four weeks. I'm being shown other rental homes today. Oh Mum, that would be so great! When?" "Whenever you want, Rae, Jo has the keys; store your gear in the garage, we can sort out the details later. Just move in and be safe. "Mum, I'm due to have this little one in four months, and I'm huge now. What if I'm still there when I have the baby and you come home?" I could hear the wheels of concern ticking over. "Honey, it's a three-bedroom house with two bathrooms. I'm sure we can sort something out."

Petra arrived outside my door with a mug of hot tea and a fresh whole-meal scone topped with homemade lemon butter. My mouth watered; the smell was heavenly. They asked me to look at a proposal they had put together. As I understood it, I would be paying for myself; any camping fees they would cover. It was the accommodation I was wondering about. Was I to camp with them in their tent? That would be a no from me. Wandering into the kitchen I noticed they were both huddled over their computer, a map of the Zodiac and stars on the screen. I had no idea what they were on about, both scratching away at maps in front of them, aligning auspicious dates, so I wandered back outside to enjoy my day.

All around me seemed to be satisfied with their role in life, Ronan's budgies preened themselves in the hazy sunlight, they seemed happy enough, at the bottom of the cage were spotted quails and in competition with the budgies were Zebra finches, all fluffing up their feathers at the large bird staring at them from the outside, me.

All four nanny goats were doing their munching thing and one Billy goat who was chained up over the hill was complaining loudly that he was very ready to make baby goats and would someone please untie him so he could do so. Herod the rooster and his thirty Delilah's were happily pecking around Ronan's woodshed, Herod keeping an eye on me as twice now I had shooed him out of my van, so now I kept the door shut, he was a handsome bird, and his clucking lady loves all vied for his attention. The three new lambs all stood by the fence their long tails wobbling away in the air. Petra usually kept the bottled milk in the fridge in her laundry, so I warmed up a bottle, feeding them for her, while I fed one the other two butted me with their little heads demanding for a turn on the bottle.

Once I had finished I wandered back inside to see the outcome of all the auspicious and alignments, only to find that Petra had her angel cards out, "Choose one" she said. I asked, "Why? What's it going to do." She raised her eyebrows, "Oh, come on, relax and join in, let's plan our trip with blessings and bounty." The cards were old, their edges now frayed with use, I chose a card, reading it aloud. *"From the Angel Rachises.. We are all Inventors -each one of us sailing out on a voyage of discovery, guided by a private charter of which there is no duplicate, this world is the gateway to other realms and possibilities.* Petra leaned forward, want a reading? I declined, pointing to the road maps on the table, so when do we leave and what do we leave in?

I offered to light the urn; it was a samovar that hissed and squeaked in steamy displeasure at being woken up. I loved the ancient old thing; I guess it was the oldest item in the room next to me. For me it worked, producing fragrant black tea, Ronan preferred the steam kettle, saying the Samovar was too old and slow, Petra was scared of it. I patted its top "Then it's up to us to educate these two on the art of tea making." Ronan bustled in, his arms full of firewood. "In two days, my friend," he puffed, stacking it by the fireplace.

"Are you prepared to leave all this behind?" He waved his arms in the air. "I will be, when I know what the accommodation is like,' I replied, expressing my concern for my Mermaid, I wanted to know whether I was expected to drive my Suzuki and follow them. By now, there was a mini mountain of camping gear in the middle of the room; it had initially started as a small pile on the coffee table but had overflowed onto the floor.

"Okay, let's do this, let's figure out what is expected from each other, how we're going to travel, and who we're going with. I laid my thoughts out, parking any emotion aside. "If I'm going to help and be involved as you've suggested, here's what I need to be comfortable. I will not be a paid member of the correct? They nodded. "Ok, I want my own bed, I will not share a tent or expected to sleep in the Pajero. All my accommodation and meals will be paid for by your business. Anything I buy or consider essential is my own financial responsibility." Ronan asked me to follow him. "I hope this explains what we do when we're away on field trips or fossicking trips," he said as I followed him to the big wooden shed at the back of the section.

He pushed at the door, a dark, musty shed now alive with dust motes giving us sunny halos. There, to my surprise, was a big

Jeep, the Daddy of them all, and a massive caravan, at least twenty-five feet in length, I just stood amazed. "Did you really think we were going in the little Pajero and a pup tent?" That's for Ronan on his trip back, this is what we call home while we are touring" Petra tapped the side of the caravan. "And you're going to help us drive this baby around the country." I was gobsmacked. No words could come out; I'd never driven anything like this. I thought, 'bugger, what have I committed myself to.' They saw the look on my face "Come inside Tara."

Ushering me towards their caravan door, inside it was a home away from home, with chrome benches, a stovetop, a double bed down one end and a single bed at the other end, in the middle where there should have been table and chairs instead they had replaced it with small office, with desk and shelves for a laptop and filing drawers, tucked away where a wardrobe once was Ronan had built a mini bathroom. "It's all here, Tara you only need to pack your clothes, and we are off, your Mermaid and Jeep will be safe, it will be here waiting for you, when we return."

I felt a tad silly, Petra easing the situation "It's okay, Tara, we were not clear we aren't used to having others help us on our trips, and we didn't explain ourselves very well." I packed my clothes and personal gear in the drawer under the single bed, while Petra packed the pantry, and Ronan packed all he thought was necessary, I had found a cupboard above the single bed (this was obviously going to be where I slept) I stored my book work, journals, camera and laptop.

The night before we left, they asked me to attend a celebration and ceremony that Petra apparently held every time they departed from paradise. This woman loved her ceremonies, and who was I to scoff? After all, I once enjoyed going to church to hear the singing and be part of a ritual and celebration. Outside, a fire was lit, Petra offered a bowl of fruit from their property, Ronan maintained a steady beat on his hand drum. It was lovely, as they chanted together, thanking Gaia for bringing me into their lives, thanking me for my love for them, asking for protection for paradise and asking for our protection on the road as we travelled. I was surprised when Ronan asked me if I knew my what my totem was. I tried to be flippant "Nope, did not know I had one." Ronan's eyes were so serious, "Your totem is canine, which is one of love, trust, and empathy for others, man's best friend, I believe this is what the gods have shown me."

'Good morning, Tara today's the day!' I had slept in the lounge that night, my mermaid had been stripped bare. Ronan suggesting "I head for the shower first." I'm not silly, these two wanted time alone. By the time I had washed and dried myself off. They appeared with silly smiles on their faces, a blush of contentment lingered, their eyes soft with love for one another. At breakfast two men knocked on the door, they were introduced as the David and Kingston they were going to be the caretakers of paradise while they were away.

I had made a large fruit salad, stirring in creamy, fresh yogurt made from goat's milk, shaved almonds were sprinkled over the top, there was plenty for all to enjoy. I lit the samovar to make dandelion coffee, Ronan asking the two men to watch carefully, as Tara seemed to have mastered it. Everything on the breakfast bar was either homegrown or fresh produce from a local farm. Petra and Ronan weren't strict vegetarians, occasionally eating meat or fish, but mostly they lived off the produce grown in their garden. Petra would have been horrified to think she was eating one of her beloved pets. She depended on her animals as a weather barometer; if birds sought shelter or animals huddled under trees or tucked themselves inside their sheds, she would say, "Storm's on its way."

David and Kingstone were two strapping blokes in their thirties; they radiated health and vibrancy. Ronan guiding them out back, where I presume they discussed the ins and outs of keeping paradise in order. I heard the big shed's door give its sharp squeak as it opened, then the stutter of an engine starting, it spluttered into life.

Ronan drove the jeep out of the shed with their caravan attached, as dust swirled around while he parked the caravan next to the house. He locked up the shed where the Mermaid and the Jeep were stored, securing it with a padlock, which he gave to me. "Just in case you're back before we are."

My heart lurched; I was leaving my Mermaid behind. Petra saw the look on my face. "She's here whenever you want to come back; nothing is set in stone, Tara." I had to agree with her; no one was forcing me to do anything." I scrambled into the back of the jeep - buckling up my seat belt, when Ronan said, "No, you sit in the front; you're driving." Wait! What! "Don't be stupid" I replied, "I have no idea how drive this thing." "Well, you had better learn fast, because that's what you're doing today," there was an annoyance in his voice. Where had my charming sooth sayer gone?

We bunny-hopped in the damn thing for maybe two minutes, Ronan's voice became a notch higher "Tara, double clutch." What the hell is a double clutch? For the first time, I saw anger flash in his eyes. Maybe this together thing was a bad idea. I braked, slowly rolling to a stop, "Mate, if you want me to drive, then you had better show me how to drive this bloody thing, because I have no idea." Nothing like a bit of honesty to get the ball rolling. I could feel the weight of the caravan tugging at the back of the Jeep. Ronan patted my knee and said, "You see, when you're prepared to take responsibility for your actions, things become much easier for you." He often spoke in riddles, hopefully it meant when I no longer felt like driving, I could stop and say, "Your turn." In fact, it felt great to be behind the wheel again, the road beneath us humming away. Our destination was the country fair in Taihape, a small town in the Waikato region; it felt right.

CHAPTER FORTY-EIGHT

Taihape was quite lovely; it was a pretty well set-out town. At one end there was what used to be a small village, while the more modern housing and buildings seemed to surround it, blending both the past and present. We entered the caravan park and stopped to check in at the office. That's when I held up my hand and said, "Your turn now, Ronan; I can't park this thing on my own."

Once checked in and paid, it was dinner time. Petra offered to whip up something in the van. If I thought I was leaving a holistic lifestyle in paradise, think again. Petra produced a magnificent feast, a four-bean salad, hot homemade egg and feta pie, steamed pumpkin and broccolini, along with hot lime and mint tea. I was starving and cleaned my plate completely, asking for another helping. We sat outside the caravan, all rugged up against the weather, each wearing woolly beanie's, gloves, rugs around our bodies. And we all looked similar, thanks to a very generous neighbour back at paradise. Sue, who had black and white sheep, carded and wove, blending the two together and knitted her creations, and we were wearing the fruits of all her hard work. Our breath escaped in steamy puffs the air was icy cold and damp.

An early night was in order; we had to be at the county fair and set up our stall by five am. My job was to calculate the GST and tax, plus record sales. I drifted off that night grateful for all I had dreamt of Russ sitting beside me. He told me, "It's time for me leave; you're doing great, you're exactly where you're meant to be." I wondered if he had anything to do with where I was right now. Ten am precisely we arrived at Petras stall, Ronan had left early and set up the small tent she used for displays.

We passed a coffee vendor who also sold hot chocolate, it smelt amazing, buying three large paper cups filled with this amazing brew, so sure they would appreciate my gesture, however they put theirs aside. Petra saw my look "We don't drink commercial cocoa Tara it contains too much sugar and additives." I shook my head, they were missing out, and with my very first frothy slurp I felt my body relax.

"Excuse me, Miss." I had not been called Miss for years. I turned to find myself looking into deep brown eyes that sparkled with humour "Hello, how can I help?" I asked. "Michael's my name, and poetry's my game." He handed me a flyer advertising a poet's night at the town centre at the Blue Goose pub, a one-man show. He fascinated me, as I had not seen a male wear makeup before, his eyes were lined with eyeliner, accented by his mascaraed black eyelashes, which set of his rich brown eyes, he flashed a smile at me, "I'd love to see you at my show tonight." Petra and Ronan wandered over and asked, "And who do we have here?" I introduced Michael. I no sooner had I said his name when he repeated his invitation. It sounded like a great night out; I was keen, and so was Ronan.

The jewellery sold well, by four pm we began to pack away the jewellery. Ronan arrived to help carry and store it in the jeep, we dropped Petra off at the van, Ronan and I went to the Blue Goose pub for a night of Poetry, Michael was there greeting us both with a cup of mulled apple cider. As Michael read his work, I was lulled into the pattern; the poetry reminded me of a musical score, sliced and spliced, held together by words, a living book of rhyme connecting the ear to the heart. He had also produced a book that was for sale, beautifully put together with stunning artwork, each and every page imprinted with the essence of Michael's personality.

I purchased two copies one for Petra the other for me. The poem that brought a smile to my face was called "The Glass Ships," Poetry is one of my passions; I loved how the words melded into a scene before my eyes.

Morning had arrived, once again I had slept well, my friends had left for the markets. Sorting out my day, first breakfast porridge with yoghurt, a hot cup of tea, take a shower, tidy up the van, and read until they got back. As I began to journal, an idea I had once casually considered really took root. Write my own book, I reached for my laptop, the title written before I could even think about it *The what & where of Tara*. Better yet, I could design a blog page, write my stories for all to read. I had to stop and take a deep breath; excitement coursed through my chest as the possibilities seemed endless.

I knew I was right where I was meant to be, Russ had guided me till now, I no longer felt that deep ache of loneliness inside. I was happy and enjoying myself. I also had Petra and Ronan to thank; they had nurtured a part of me that had been stale with old beliefs and customs. I sensed the change in my thinking, I felt it in my heart, and I felt it in my body. I was growing, and it was exhilarating. Life was exciting and I had to start somewhere, so why not today, right here and now? Checking my phone, I had time to call Rae and quickly email Jo. Jess answered the phone; "Nana, guess what? we're living at your house. I'm back at my old school and I've got a fish tank with four goldfish. "When are you coming back? It's weird here without you."

It dawned on me that I was part of a much bigger picture than I ever thought possible. All the people you meet, whether it be with love, despair, agree or disagree, including family, are all part of a vast mesh of crossroads in your life. It's a challenging road if you stay closed off; once you open yourself to learning, it becomes easier.

Rae, once on the phone, sounded puffed, but, like Jess, there was a contentment to her voice. 'Hi honey, how's it all going? All moved in and settled yet? I could hear the angst in her voice "Mum, I'm so big and bloated that I waddle. I can't wait until this little one is born. What are you up to Mum? I told her about my plans to tour some of the South Island with Petra. "you sure, Mum? You seem to meet up with a lot of weirdos from what Jo has told me." "They're not weirdo, Rae, just very different from what you are used to, however, the good news is that book I swore I would write one day? Remember how you and your Dad teased me about, well I have finally begun to put it together."

I expected Wow! That's so cool, instead she said 'Mum, you do know that Tim once worked for a Perth publishing company, he was hired to publish eBooks. His job was making deals with people who knew nothing about what they were getting into, the authors he signed up were then reached out to by his boss, a slimy con man if I ever met one. Sadly, what was signed was water tight; all they ended up with is a badly edited book on a cheap looking website. The authors were made a laughingstock of; many of these folk had spent thousands, they all ended up with nothing. Please Mum, be careful, they are an elusive lot, very smarmy, pretending to what they're not, the answer to your dreams with promises of best seller and or fame and glory, but once they have your money, it's see you later." I promised I would consider her advice; nothing was going to happen until I was home, maybe a web page and some stories on a blog page, that seemed to mollify her.

Petra didn't turn up until midday, warning me "It's really slow at the stall and its really cold; you're better off here in the warmth." Looking outside at the grey, drizzly day, I had to agree. I made her a hot cranberry juice, along with thick, buttery toast and my homemade jam. It brought back fond memories of Bridie. She saw the look on my face. "I see a story here; come on, spill." So, as it rained and blew outside, the two of us sat inside, warm and comfy, while I told her about my friend Bridie. When I finished, there was only silent, no comments, no advice.
My two friends decided to cuddle up in their small tent for the afternoon, which also served as the storage room for all our gear. I knew this was not about me; it was more about them. I offered to put a meal together at dinnertime; we had booked the camp site for four days, so there was plenty of time. So far, my job involved checking products, orders and banking. Next it was check on my lawyer's statements and my income from my assets

and what they were doing with the money from the will. It all seemed to be good. I gave up a prayer of thanks that Russ insisted we do all of the above, to put it plainly, I was quite well off.

Now it was time to make dinner, big pot of veggie soup, all prepared before we left and stored in the freezer. "Come and get it, it's on the table" I called, they both looked like a couple of bear cubs rolling out of the tent, pink in the face, laughing at each other, Ronan trying to stand up complaining of pins and needles in his feet, the van door opening, cold air rushing in, they gulped down soap and bread like there was not tomorrow, then decided it was time for a drive, they invited me but there are times when I just like to sit in the dark on my own, feeling my chest rise and fall with my breath, my heart quietening down, while I reflect on the day. I hadn't done much getting out and about so far, but it felt good to sit still for a day.

Tomorrow, Ronan would be busy, so would Petra, for the selling part they were the informed ones, I decided to do something I had never done before, *trout fishing*. I rang and booked a trout fishing day with a picnic lunch and a tour of this pretty town. Neil, the tour guide, would pick me up at seven a.m. to show me the ropes. The air was damp and clean; my two friends had gone, as their jeep was missing.

At the entrance was the minibus waiting, a puff of smoke from the muffler letting me know I could board immediately. "Kia Ora Tara, welcome to Trout fishing Taihape" Neil gave me the spiel about this city known as the gumboot capital of New Zealand. Why? They had a gumboot throwing competition that was taken very seriously by the locals and was almost internationally known, which explained the huge, corrugated gumboot statue I saw as we drove through the city.

Soon, we were at the river, trout rods out, hot coffees from a thermos. I wondered why does a hot drink in the cold open air taste so much nicer than from a cup in your own kitchen. Neil asked me if I wanted him to attach my fly tackle on, I wanted to this on my own, I chose a pretty fly with orange wings it was so light, Neil Giving me advice on flicking and trailing the line towards me, I worked off the grassy shore, I would have liked to waded into the water as he did, they did not provide waders due to a personal hygiene law that had been passed, and I was not going to wade in as I was the water was close to freezing. We fished for an hour or so than we sat down to a breakfast of smoked salmon on bread rolls, one bite and mouthwatering deliciousness invaded my taste buds.

The small cove where we were fishing was scenery to die for, Weeping Willow trees gracefully trailed long slender branches in the water, the water swirled deep green mid-stream the deepness in its sound as it swept past, its powerful strength not to be played with, around the riverbank, deep pools had formed, each one a haven for our quarry, that's if we caught anything thing today. If you looked up there was Mt Ruapehu capped with snow, totally magnificent in every way. This country was inspiring to say the least, I wondered just how many paintings and photos had been taken of this grand old dame, its crown wispy in smoke from the boiling lake this mountain contained deep inside it.

Oh, how I wish I had taken notice of the warning about midges a small biting flying insect, by the time we left the river, I was one very itchy camper. Petra advised lots of Calamine lotion, we were leaving tomorrow, and I would be doing most of the driving. I woke again in the late afternoon feeling much better, but still insanely itchy. The shower I had was wonderful, hot water and soft home-made soap streamed over my body, I did notice I was quite skinny, I could feel my ribs, my hair uncut, curled down past my shoulder blades. I found a photo on my phone of me that Margi had taken on the Marai, was that really me standing there, I looked frumpy and very unsure, the difference between now and then was noticeable.

When Petra arrived back asking if I wanted fish and chips for dinner-I almost drooled. This shop had the best fish and chips I have ever tasted in my life. Hurrying back to the van, I kept the chips wrapped in newspaper, tucked inside my coat, keeping my chest and hands toasty warm. Sitting outside on camp stools, we doused our food in tomato sauce, enjoying every delicious morsel we ate. She made two mugs of tea holding her mug in the air, she toasted "To clean air and good living," I raised my mug to her toast. "Amen to that," I added. 'How come everything feels lighter, clearer, brighter, today?" I asked. "Well, maybe because you're finally feeling comfortable with growing into the real Tara, no longer needing to build up physically, mentally, or spiritually. Your perfect the way you are."

She was right; I didn't need the weight of protection, either in body or emotion. "I'm proud of you, Tara. Some people carry their baggage from the past, never free of whatever drives them to be here in the first place. "Petra clinked her mug against mine. "Here's to fun, honesty, and life. That night as I lay in my single bed the other two snuggled up in their bed on the other side. I gave up silent thanks for all I had received and where I was at this moment, safe, loved, family and friends. Tomorrow we are moving on to Wanganui another riverside township, we had booked into the camp there for three weeks, as all around there were little towns having fetes, fairs and the CWA had invited

Petra to be the guest speaker for the annual dinner. From past history this is where she made her biggest sales of jewelry, and where I came into it, as she networked, I took care of sales. I was looking forward to this so much, once the alarm went on my phone, I was up, showered and started putting breakfast on the table, Petra and Ronan both had been up and used the camp facilities, not wanting to wake me. While Ronan made some porridge for breakfast, Petra and I packed away what we thought necessary. It went like clockwork we worked as a team. He threw me the keys, "Bring the jeep around, I'll hitch up the van," it was all done within ten minutes.

CHAPTER FORTY-NINE

Their tent and sleeping bags already stored in the boot. Wanganui here we come, I let out the clutch, the van tugging reluctantly for a second or two, I was busy looking at the rear vision mirrors, checking side mirrors, we very slowly started to gain speed, when Ronan said "Stop, can you hear that? My ears seemed to perk up and focus on that sound; it was my name being called. I scrambled out of the driver's seat to be enveloped in a bear hug "Tara, I thought it was you."

Once his arms had released me I recognised the face; Jeri from Waipu, how? What are you doing here?' So, few people knew me in New Zealand. "Touring, the same as you," he replied. I looked up at my two friends, both looking surprised that I actually knew someone here. "Guys, this is an old friend." Jeri walked over to the jeep and shook their hands. "Hi there, sorry if I scared you." Ronan's gruff "Mate, you have no idea, now, can we all go somewhere else, as we are in the way here?" That was becoming obvious; the camp was waking up; voices and motors were being started, and we were in the middle of the road.

"Why not stop outside the camp? Petra suggested. "You can quickly catch up, then we should be on our way." We all got back in the vehicle, following Jeri down the camp road, parking around the corner in the camp's parking bay. My arms open to this man who had befriended me on my 1st week in New Zealand. Our arms wrapped around each other he whispered, "I've thought of you often since we last met." I had explained in more detail to my two friends about Jeri, trying not to elaborate too much on his story, as it was his to tell. If he wanted to share, he would. It was getting late; time for us to move on. Ronan asked Jeri, "Where are you heading off too?' "Well, I thought I might meander down to Wellington," was his reply. That's a shame Ronan said, "We are stopping off elsewhere for a while then Wellington." I heard an edge to Ronan's voice, what was going on?

I sat behind the wheel, Jeri in the lead astride his bike, I had this sudden desire to be astride his bike with him, freedom with no attachments, sounded brilliant to me. Ronan's voice breaking my day dream, to double clutch, Jeri gave me a wave and drove away. Petra was now sitting beside me in the passenger's seat, giving directions. This road proved to be like the rest, winding through mountainous scenery or along steep hillsides. I was still unsure by all the gear changing and double clutching but seemed to manage well. Stopping at a truck park for a hot drink, the scenery was inspiring; many photos later and we were on the road again. This was my very first hill start with the caravan in tow.

Ronan offered to take over for me, but something stubborn made me think I could do it. My enthusiasm was my mistake, as I just couldn't get it right. I tried and tried until he yelled, "Enough! If you inch back again, we'll go over the side." They both wore severe expressions, I was relegated to the back seat feeling like a scolded child, as they expressed their displeasure at my actions.

I could have claimed he was "Unfair! I'm not experienced enough. You forced me to drive." The truth was, through being stubborn I had nearly caused a major accident, I was not proud of myself.

At last Wanganui, Ronan pulled into the camp and found our spot for the next three weeks, he and Petra both ignoring me while they talked between themselves, erecting the tent and placing their sleeping bags inside. Petra parked the jeep beside the van and set up the canvas annex. I made dinner since it was five-thirty in the afternoon, yet they still didn't stop to communicate. They chose to ignore my looks or any words I uttered, engaging only in conversation with each other. As I served up steamed rice and vegetables, I received the usual "Thank you" I was not invited to join in their dinner blessing, we ate in silence.

These two were carrying it a bit too far I thought, time to say something, "I've apologised twice now." Ronan looked at me, his dark eyes unreadable, 'Tara, Petra and I have discussed your obsession with following your own set of rules, it was a dangerous situation that you had us in completely ignoring my instruction's, we are prepared to give you another chance, then if you do not do as we ask of you then we have no use for you." it took a minute to seep in what he had said, I repeated it back "You'll have no use for me? You thankless barsted, who do you think you are? You're not exactly sunshine and roses' either mate, in fact away from your kingdom you just a bag of hot air." Muttering to myself about male stupidity I walked away.

Who are you talking to? A male voice queried, a shadow stepped towards me, 'Jeri' I gasped, how did you? His arms went around me, the kiss was long; passionate leaving my heart thumping, I was breathless. "I've wanted to do that since we met in Waipu." I nestled inside the circle of his arms, my head on his shoulder, when we ended up in his pup tent making love there was nothing to be sorry or embarrassed about.

It had been nearly two years since I had been with a man, my body was hungry for an intimate physical touch I crept into the van in the early morning, pulling blankets in a cocoon around me, the smell of Jeri still clinging to my body, I had enjoyed my night immensely, now time to sleep and dream of tomorrow. It arrived sooner than I expected. I was still groggy from a very late night. Petra made hot tea and toast inside the van, and I croaked, "Good morning." She took one look at me and said, "You're glowing." I sat up, so happy she was talking to me again. I tucked the blankets up around my shoulders. "Ronan can be a moody bugger at times" I shook my head "Petra, I put our lives in danger."

"He's a different man when we travel. Paradise is where he's the man I adore; but when we travel I don't like him as much." "Now my friend who's the man." My smile gave it away "Jeri? She said" I nodded. "I noticed how he took every little bit of you in when he stopped us this morning. My Ronan has conspiracy ideas about you two." Our laughter woke the grump, Ronan. "Bloody women, give a man some peace, be quiet while a man sleeps." For three weeks, I worked with Petra, accompanying her to fetes, fairs, and ladies' meetings of all kinds, as well as clubs and society meetings. Anyone who needed a speaker, we put our hands up. We drove for miles, attended all sorts of craft fairs, and met people. I took extensive notes, marked sales, noted receipts, tracked pending sales and filled her journal for the day ahead.

I had become her number one secretary. I enjoyed it but had been made aware that Ronan was the master of this trio, if he objected to anything I did, I would be travelling on my own. So many places, each just as pretty to visit as the others, Bulls, Fielding, Woodville, Levin, Stratford, Eketahuna, Dannevirke, Waikanae, and last but not least, Pahiatua. Each little township had its own specialty, whether it was collecting shells or painting toilet seats.

Yes, there were quite a few of those stalls around the country! One stall had painted large paint tins that were then semi squashed, which created an amazing colour effect. I had the pleasure of a close-up view of all sorts of art before it went on sale. The piece that caught my eye was a triangular canvas depicting the before and after of an old village. In every place we visited Petra was welcomed with open arms. Sometimes she taught the basics of fossicking for jewelry; other times, she shared knowledge on Kiwi bush medicine or how to make homemade soaps and lotions. In some little townships, she'd simply give a talk showcasing her crafts. Petra was a beloved public figure that everyone looked forward to each year, and the best part was, within her warm welcome, I was included too.

Some days were long, especially her teaching days, so accommodation was always provided for us both; she would always ring Ronan and explain we were tired, it was now dark, we had been invited to stay over. These nights I particularly enjoyed as around the kitchen table more often than not- we would listen to a females tale of her life here; how she came to be here, her family and her life in New Zealand. Most of them descendants' of the English or Irish, how hard their lives had been then, until one eighty year old exclaimed "But look what we've got now I love this modern age, don't you" she settled like a chook settling on its nest, lots of clucking and humming, finally with a big sigh in her big comfy arm chair, she slipped her feet into woolly slippers she popped a pipe into her mouth sucking on the stem contentedly. I felt my eyebrows shoot up, her face showed nothing peace and why not.

If the talk ever turned maudlin, as it sometimes did with certain ladies, we would comment on the amazing meals we had been given; not a day went by without some kind lady bringing us lunch. If dinner was offered, it was a communal feast most nights, with everyone adding their special dish to the already groaning table. I discovered I wasn't fond of smoked eel pie, but we devoured everything else, both of us ready with compliments for these hardworking, wonderful country folk. A kind word and the touch of another human hand can work wonders. They shared stories of the family now grown up, coping with the empty nest, or their husbands who had passed on, so a hug and a compliment meant the world to them.

The mantles over the fireplaces that warmed us were full of sepias and faded photographs, each one a story. One poor soul, Ruth, an eighty-four-year-old woman with a faint Scots burr, had a photo of six young kiddies all sitting on a log. Expecting to hear what they had done with their lives, we were both shocked to find out they had all passed away, a logging accident in Northland took four of them immediately, followed by her husband and the remaining two children due to septicemia. I asked about hospitals. "What hospitals, dear? We had a bush dispensary and bush medicine with limited healthcare" she replied. The rest of her clan, as she called them, contacted blood sepsis and died within months of each other. How her crushed heart must have felt, I know mine did. "I'm getting old and silly," she announced. I stood and opened my arms to her. "You may forget, Ruth, but they have not forgotten you." I hugged her tight.

Some homes were so old that I often worried about their safety. One in particular stayed with me, we had received a handwritten order for 20 blocks lavender soap, to be delivered to Hinemoa-an invite to stay for lunch had been included. When we informed the group of ladies Petra was speaking to where we were lunching, there was a silence, then a concern was voiced for our well-being. I saw Petra's eyes change from happiness to simmering anger.

We drove to the address on the outside of town, stopping at a wooden shack, the paint peeling off, a few plants struggling amidst the weeds. Inside, I would say was poverty, dirt floors, furniture made from fruit boxes, and old sacking or faded gingham covering the doorways and cupboards. The toilet was outside; the kitchen featured a plastic basin on a rickety old bench and one cold water tap.

Petra and I were both uncomfortable, reluctantly sitting on these old, stained cushions on wood boxes. However, as I looked around everything was polished, scrubbed, and swept. This tiny bird like lady smelt of lavender. Her pure white hair, pulled back into a severe bun, the wrinkles on her weathered face spoke of many hardships. Not once did she complain; on the contrary, after a dinner of macaroni and cheese cooked over the fireplace, she entertained us by played her ukulele, the old time tunes rippling out. I knew some of them, memories of my own folks came flooding back.

This was one lady I will never forget, Hinemoa, a true daughter of the Waikato country. As we left to go to another's home for the night, I asked if there was anything we could do for her. She looked up at me and said, 'I have everything I need, right here,' and she did. Petra and I put on our coats; the air was now chilly, with river mist covering the ground. I asked if I could contact anyone for her, she pointed to the sepia photograph, I understood these were her whanau, they had passed, Hinemoa was alone. "I hope that when my day comes, I'm as graceful and accepting as her," I said. Petra squeezed my arm, agreeing. Ronan? I hardly saw him, to be honest I was a tad miffed at his attitude of 'I'm the boss, obey or else.' When I was in the damp I was spending my nights being swept up in a warm embrace of an affair. It wasn't just intimacy; we talked about another world where we both came from.

We discussed my family and his, including his brothers and sister, an interest in visiting the USA had been ignited. We slowly got to know each other, our likes and dislikes. We went out on dates to the movies and to coffee clubs where jazz bands played, often just for a ride on his Harley around the countryside.

CHAPTER FIFTY

Once back at the camp, we cuddled up together, content just to be together. I didn't even think about asking him into the van; it wasn't mine to offer, and even if I had, it was obvious that Ronan would object. Jeri and I clicked, acknowledging the significant ten-year age gap. I reveled in the newfound Tara. Was I in love? No, I had given my heart once; I simply wanted to enjoy friendship and if passion cane wrapped up with it, yes by all means; a formal commitment to another? No.

The four weeks were up; Ronan announcing it was time to move on "Time to pull your socks up Tara, it's time to leave your man friend," myself and Petra aware of the sarcastic edge in Ronan's voice. "Tomorrow, we arrive in Wellington, that is, if we ever get there with Tara driving." Petra and I exchanged glances. This man had once advised me to speak my truth, so I did. "Ronan, I've endured your constant reminders about my mistake, you referring to it as near-death experience. It's unnecessary and insulting. I'm asking that you either be civil and polite to me or we can go no further than this." This was the longest conversation we'd had over the four weeks. The silence hung like a water balloon, ready to burst. I expected him to say, "Piss off," instead he admitted "I haven't enjoyed this trip like I usually do, with you showing off to blokes and Petra cheering you on.

I'm disappointed in you both. Where's your decorum, both of you?" Petra's face blazed with anger, she pointed her finger at him "You nasty old man, I've put up with you and your tantrums long enough; go back to Paradise and learn some manners. I sat there, horrified by the argument I had initiated. "No, no, both of you, this is all my fault that this has happened. I will leave; please stop, please don't do this to each other." Ronan and Petra looked at me, both simmering with deep anger. 'You were the fuse, Tara,' Petra said. "This keg has been waiting to blow for a while." Ronan stepped out of the van, It was still drizzling; he stood there, raindrops landing on his lashes and face, looking at her. 'I love you, Petra.' 'I love you too,' she replied. 'See you in Paradise.' With that, she closed the door, and it was over.

"What just happened here? You've kicked him out because I told him off," I said. "It's not just that, Tara; his moods had become intolerable, swinging from one end to the other. He's become opinionated-dare I say, a bully. He's not happy away from our home and never has been, although this is the worst I have seen him in a long while." With feelings of grief for this wonderful couple, I went for an evening walk. I felt hurt and guilty. I wandered down to the Jeri's tent, a soft glow welcoming me. Scratching at the nylon flap, "It's me." We hadn't arranged to meet tonight, but I wanted to talk to someone to sort out what was going on. Jeri opened the zip on the tent, only his face popping out. "Tara! I was asleep, I'm buggered, lovely, can we chat tomorrow? I turned away disappointed that I couldn't cuddle up and unload my worries. However, as I turned away, I heard him chuckle then whisper to someone to "Stop it." He had another person with him.

'What's wrong, Tara?' Her voice brimmed with concern. I sat beside her, "The fairy tale is over, Jeri has another interest." Her answer made me laugh, "Want me to go over and bash him? I knew she was kidding, and I loved her for being protective of me.

My time with Jeri had proved to me I wasn't emotionally dead. The morning broke with Petra saying, "Ronan will be in Wellington by now," her fingers punching in his number. "Hi, my darling, how are you?" We ate a quick breakfast, Petra helping me to hitch the caravan onto the jeep, it went well, we were becoming experts at this. We were all stowed away, hitched up, the motor running, while Petra dashed off to the toilet block.

I waited behind the wheel of the jeep, its motor quietly purring. Then beside me, I heard, "Tara, I'm really sorry." I looked up into troubled eyes. "Hello, Jeri," I smiled. "I was just about to text you to say goodbye." His eyes widened "You were?" he looked surprised. I quickly unbuckled, stepped out and hugged him tight, whispering, "You're one sexy man; have a great life." The look of shock on his face was priceless. Once Petra was back in the jeep it was Wellington, here we come! We both chorused, "Bye, Jeri." I glanced in the rearview mirror, Jeri looked stunned. Wellington, we are on our way. Along the way, we stopped off at Carterton, Masterton, Featherston, Paraparaumu, Cape Palliser, Upper Hutt, Lower Hutt, Petone, NaeNae and Lake Ferry, where there were drop off points for the orders. Each drop off point was at someone's home, and of course each drop off there were always cakes and hot drinks provided. Refusal was considered rude so by the time we arrived in Wellington we both felt like stuffed turkeys.

Petra was on the phone most of the time, so I relied heavily on the GPS. We pulled over on the main highway to lower Hutt so she could find her address and order book. My mind wandered about Jeri, thanks to him I had toured around Taihape, met many people from different motorbike groups. They had been a mixed lot, some bikers looked ancient, some seemed very young. The pillion riders had been mainly women, age was not limited, senior and youth were combined.

I had met a granny and her grandson-an Asian couple, married couples and couples having a romance. For the majority of them, it made no difference they were all one people within the different clubs. So why ruin it with negative thoughts? Bye, Jeri, be safe wherever you travel.

Lower Hutt city was a nightmare, the roads were a mishmash of turning circles, loops, plus new roads that had been built since the GPS had been programmed. Finding the Lower Hutt camping grounds was a miracle in itself; we soon sorted ourselves out, Petra guiding me onto our camp site, her order book bulging, under the single bunk in the van was a small cupboard that had been packed full of soaps, herbal remedies, and some of Ronan's miniature carving's, all had been bought over the internet via their web site. I read Petra the list of deliveries while she pulled them out and stacked them on the floor. She messaged the Evans family the drop off point for this city. "Yes they were home, see you tomorrow."

Tonight, it was Petra's turn to cook tea. I was tired from all the driving; I needed to stretch my legs and torso. A brisk walk followed by some yoga stretches was just what I needed, and that's exactly what I did. As I walked back to the van, the smell of cooking wafted through the air. I hoped it was coming from our van. Delicious! A huge meal of grilled lamb chops steamed veggies, and mashed spuds, it tasted like heaven. By the time we had cleaned up, showered, and crawled into bed, I really don't remember the lights being turned out. I was asleep. New Zealand birdlife isn't the raucous sound of Aussie birdlife, but it's just as welcoming. These birds sing, they don't squawk; they tweet, not burst into laughter like our Kookaburra. However, Magpies around the world warble the same tune.

This morning was wet and windy, no sound anywhere, just damp, wet, and miserable. I didn't want to move a muscle; I wanted to stay all wrapped up in my bed. Instead, I heard a cheery "Good morning" from the other side of the van. "Ready for today?" No! I just wanted to lie there. "I'll put the jug on, and you can have an extra ten minutes,' Petra offered. I agreed by nodding and snuggling back down into my blankets. "Are you not well?" she asked, looking at me intently. "I'm fine, thanks, just really tired today." I knew I was to drive her to deliver her parcels; it was part of our agreement. Still, I wanted a day or two off to tour, have a nana nap, and do some writing, reading, ring family, and check my emails. My personal life still needed attention. And I would kill for a massage, my lumbar complaining I was sitting for too long.

Petra was very intuitive most times but when focused on her work, she could be a workaholic. 'Are you sure you want to carry on doing this, you do look tired' once she had said that it was like someone had pricked my balloon, I admitted to needing some time out on my own, but I wanted to continue travelling with her as I had agreed to. "Tara just say the word, I can call on Ronan's help, you can go back to Paradise." I knew this was not fair on them, they had made plans, "I'm sure, I just need a day or two off. Although her gaze was still intense, she agreed, "Fair enough, then that's what you shall have. I'll do the driving until we get to the South Island, you can navigate" Is that okay? She then dropped a bombshell, "You're not getting any younger, Tara, Ronan, and I still have youth on our side." What the Hell did that mean? Did she just call me old? Disappointment surged through me and that niggling voice that had once said sell up and go home, became louder. Maybe it was time to call it quits, I had kept my promise, Petra was where she was supposed to be.

The feeling of homesickness for the Mermaid almost overwhelming, I shrugged it off as silly, mentally telling myself to get up and get on with it, my legs slowly obeying. I wanted to switch off the small talk my brain was having with me, the hot shower did not work as it normally did, the starting off a new day did not switch it on as it normally did, instead my brain constant chattered "You don't want to be here, it's cold, damp windy, its travelling nonstop, no stopping to tour or sight see, you don't want to do this Tara you're in your sixties woman, take some time out, you don't need to do this."

Every day we delivered their products, being told by a mechanical voice this way or that way. I began feel unhappy with my journey. I asked for two days on my own, Petra could have the jeep and go, do whatever she wanted the majority of deliveries had been done. The ever smiling Petra willingly agreed to this, she took off to meet and greet other clients. I stayed in the van tucked up against the cold southerly wind that froze you once you stepped outside, the mist and damp I kept at bay by tucking up inside, reading, ringing home, talking to my family and friends, and talking to Jo about do I go on or go back? telling someone my own age, how I felt, hearing sound advice from a much loved friend, encouraging me to follow what I had started. "You do know I live my adventures through your stories? As for romance? well Sweetpea, we've both had that and more."

She was right. Rae, was now into her second semester, telling me all of her baby shopping days with Jo and Jess's school activities, he was so happy to be runner up in the sprints competitions, an award he had won as *Ozzie of the Month* at his school, and fast becoming a netball fanatic, it all sounded settled and happy. I wanted to be there with them, I confided in Margi how I was feeling; she put it into a nutshell, "Are you being paid for this work you're doing?" Margi "It's not about money, I was offered an opportunity to travel in safety, but I really miss travelling on my own."

Margi was never backwards in saying what she thought. "Perhaps you are becoming too old for all the travel, they both have twenty years on you at least. I love them dearly. I'm also aware that Ronan can be a grumpy arsehole, and Petra? She can be friend or foe in one breath. I had to agree, as friends they were both great, watching them as business entrepreneurs? Hmm not so much, from what I had seen from their bookkeeping. Her advice was to be truthful with myself; it's you whose asking the questions Tara."

I guess to bring it all into focus for me I had been there done that, I had done the hard slog to be where I am today, I did not want to rush all over the place on a time schedule, or as Ronan had once put it "We are time poor, so we need to be totally focused on the job." I hated to say, "I don't this want a job," this was my time, I was here to here was to see more of New Zealand, not dash off here there and everywhere to make a sale or contact.

CHAPTER FIFTY-ONE

Had I made a mistake? No, I had enjoyed myself all the way, Ronan was not one to hold back on critiques, but then again I had also learnt being meek and mild gets you nowhere. I made it my intention to break the new to Petra tonight. The opportunity to make a definite decision never came my way; I was busy sorting out the last of the deliveries for the North Island, cataloguing what Petra needed for the South Island, when Petra bolted into the caravan, she was white and shaking, tears streaming down her face, in dismay I asked 'Petra what on earth' as I held out my arms, I had never seen her like this before ever, she looked like ten thousand demons where after her.

'It's Ronan she sobbed; he has been badly hurt." One cold flannel and many tissues later she had calmed down to tell me, she had been buying some goods, had intended to buy me some lunch and bring it home, when she got a phone call from their local hospital, Ronan had been admitted, his legs crushed by a log falling off a trailer, he was being transferred to Wellington hospital by helicopter that would be here by this afternoon. After a hot cup of tea with honey in it for us both, Petra- her shaking almost stopped, the tears now intermittent, we talked about what we should do, our first urgency was to get to the hospital, Petra packed up any of his personal bathroom gear he had left behind, placing my hand on her knee, "It's going to be okay; he's in the right place to heal," there was only a nod from her.

The GPS announced, 'You have reached your destination,' as we turned into the hospital car park. Petra bolted out the door, running for the main entrance. I parked and followed. Ronan was unconscious, the medical staff had induced a coma. A huge sheet draped over a cage covered both his legs, and pain flickered across his face as Petra kissed him, holding him close while whispering her love for him. I turned and sat just outside the curtain, feeling there was nothing I could do for them, but I was there for them, nonetheless. The surgeon arrived and examined Ronan's legs. We need scans before my team can explore how to fix this problem. I'm concerned about the left knee, though; it's a bit of a mess. Scans were ordered; Petra, Ronan and the medical team disappeared in the lift. I felt utterly helpless; there was nothing I could do or say to make things better for either of them.

In the end, this was a journey they would have to make together, but I would stay to help for as long as I was needed. I stayed with them all that day; Petra called it their *Black Friday*, and to them, it must have been, nothing hurts more than a loved one who is injured or not well. I silently sent up a thank you for my health and my family's health. Petra just sat there like a stone, not moving in the visitor's waiting room, refusing any form of food or drink; I had to force water into her by saying "He is going to need you to be well to look after him," she sipped a cup of cold water. Five hours later, the surgeon suddenly appeared, his work done, and he gave us the thumbs-up sign. "We've done what we can for now, he's in the recovery unit. At the moment we can allow only one of the family to be with him," Petra almost ran to the room he was in, and who could blame her, I remembered how that felt when I was in Petra's shoes. Driving back to the Lower Hutt campgrounds at dusk with the wind and rain hammering the Pajero was a nightmare, the traffic was so bad we crawled along just about the only thing visible, was bright red taillights winking on and off.

The Pacific Ocean pounding the shore not twenty meters away, the ocean spray cascading over us as well as the rain, the wiper groaning under the onslaught, the vision was so bad I was expecting at any time to rear end the car in front; finally, I drove into the campgrounds I was exhausted, a cup of tea and my bed was it for me, I was asleep before my head hit the pillow. Woken by my mobile ringing it was Rae and Jess, this was unusual I always rang them, "Mum, are you okay, I keep getting weird vibes about you, are you in trouble? I told her what had happened, "Oh Mum how awful, does that means you're coming home soon? Or are you going to stay and help them?" I knew what my answer was before I spoke it, "I'm coming home honey, but before you get too excited, I have to drive back to collect then sell the Metal Mermaid and the Suzuki. The relief in her voice was palpable. "Great, can't wait Mum, send me your arrival dates, I'll pick you up.

By the time I had finished the phone call, Petra had arrived; she had hired a taxi, her conversation was stilted, she undressed, drank two big glasses of water than crept into her bed. Her voice muffled in between sobs saying, "I was so scared Tara, I thought I was going to lose him."

We cuddled up together that night, our Doonas piled high as the wind and rain buffeted the van on the outside, but inside, we were safe and warm. She woke early, asking me to drive her into the hospital. Ronan was wide awake as we entered the ward, holding his arms out to his beloved partner. Petra stood up and beckoned me over to his beside; Ronan wants to ask you something. His voice barely a whisper, his hand squeezed mine, "Look after her will you? How do you say "No! I'm leaving as soon as possible" to a badly injured man; his wife is in shock, and they are both relying on you to be their support? You don't, you smile and nod.

Downstairs at the café, a hot cappuccino in my hand, I began flipping looking through an old newspaper, while my brain and heart argued. You want to leave; you want to be with your own family. Yet, you are needed right here, today and by the looks of it many tomorrows. I had agreed to support them, could I do this by phone? So many questions in my tired mind. And what do I do while I'm here in Wellington? Petra would be with Ronan, the newspaper in my hand offered me a clue. Why not see Wellington city? it seemed to have a lot to do and see; I was particularly interested in the cable car ride that went from Lambton Quay in the city all the way up into the mountains. Once back down, there was a mini tour bus around the city. Also, Te Papa, the new museum, sounded great, and the Zoo, the oldest in New Zealand, had a guided tour that sounded like fun.

My days consisted of delivering Petra to the hospital, where she stayed with Ronan for the day; occasionally, I would go up to the wards to say hello to him. From what I saw and heard, he was healing well. I toured this windy, cold city, loved travelling on the cable car and then visited TePapa the museum. It was magnificent, and as promised, the guided tour was so full of information.

The rose gardens heaven, the perfume from all the open flowers you could not describe. Then the Zoo? I stayed till late afternoon, enjoying the feeling of life not loneliness or grief. Amongst the grounds was an old Victorian glasshouse which sheltered a range of orchids, from tiny, dainty Singapore orchids to massive Brazilian jungle ones that clung tenaciously to their tree trunk hosts. Ferns also thrived in this space from tiniest miniature maidenhair ferns to the robust, dramatic varieties that flourished in African jungles. I even spotted an Australian pig fern standing triumphantly among its African peers, butterflies flitted about, enjoying the humid environment of the glasshouse. This tour I was sad to leave as everywhere you looked, life grew in abundance.

As I waited for Petra to meet me in the hospital café I lightly skimmed the newspaper for tours in Wellington when an advert stood out, almost yelling at me to read it. My heart skipped a beat, and if all aligned I could possibly do something I'd dreamed of for a long time. I was looking at an advert for a cruise on the Northern Princes cruise ship, leaving from Auckland to Fremantle, Perth. It sounded like the perfect way to go home; it was a ten day cruise to Perth, Australia. That saying "You know when you know" well I knew. It was time for this traveller to wander back to her home. First things first, I thought; let's find out the what, ifs and buts about Ronan; the one thing I did not want to happen was for them to feel I had abandoned them while they needed support.

Looking at these two very much-in-love friends holding hands, quietly talking to each other and making plans on how to get him home once he was discharged. The surgeon had visited and discussed another operation to replace the left kneecap, the right kneecap they were hoping would heal by itself, although the cartilage would be removed. First and foremost, they wanted Ronan to heal from the first surgery.

Following that, there would be physiotherapy; once improvement occurred without setbacks, there would be daily physiotherapy, back at paradise, where the real healing would take place. They were told it could take up to a year or even longer, considering his age, medication, and other factors. There was a lengthy list of what might happen and what may not. The log carving would have to wait, as he would be in a wheelchair for as long as necessary.

Petra's healing was being done with good sleep and good food, I was there for her whenever she wanted to talk. Her need for a woman's support reinforced when driving home one night she reached over to grab my hand. "Tara, I don't want to lose you, You've been like a mum to me. But I need to be close to Ronan, which means I'll be here as long as he is. I would love it if you could stay, but I feel deep down it is time for you to return to your home and family." I had to agree; I was missing my homeland. I also wanted to be part of Rae's life, play a significant role in Jess's life, and hold my new grandchild in my arms from the day it was born.

I still felt responsible; I had caused the argument that led to Petra chucking him out. Again, I told her how I felt, she shook my arm. "Don't be so daft, Tara. We have always had this problem, and we always will. Ronan, when away from Paradise, suddenly becomes Sir Ronan, and along with this so called title and pride, he grows immense balls." Her of beat humour was priceless. So, I told her of my plans, returning to Paradise, selling up the Metal Mermaid and the Jeep, then catching the cruise ship home. Her mouth agape, spluttering "What? When? Petra took a big breath, I feel you should book your passage immediately; you certainly don't need our permission.

I knew exactly what I have to do, first I booked and paid for the cruise, the receipt and booking immediately confirmed by email. I then arranged for a hire car to drive back to paradise. I placed an advert in the Auckland and Wellington newspapers to sell my Jeep and Mermaid. A tiny wiggle of joy began in my breastbone; I was going home.

CHAPTER FIFTY-TWO

The day arrived that I was to pick up my hire car, visiting Ronan, on my last day in Wellington. The two of them had encouraged my spiritual growth to truly know who I was. And I got it, it was not the land or the people, it was understanding your own heart, that sometimes we have to leave behind what we call ours and who we think we are, to become who we were meant to be. In my travels around Australia and New Zealand, I had dug deep, to find my very core of who Tara was. Ronan gave me one more piece of advice "Never look back Tara, you're not going that way." Now it was time to head back to the van and pack my gear into the hire car, as tomorrow marked the start of my journey back to paradise.

What an incredible place New Zealand is, however I for one would be genuinely relieved to escape this frigid, icy weather. Petra had sat there watching me pack; a tear escaped, "I'm just struggling to let go, that's all." Her arms engulfed me, "You're part of our family now." We held each other tight; family is not always blood and bone sometimes it's a heart connection. I was glad to be going home, no regrets, no sorrow. I had met some wonderful people, experienced some weird and fantastic moments, and been a guest in an amazing land. Believe me when I say there was nothing small about New Zealand.

I had been made aware while I had been here that there's a huge rivalry between our two countries, for the life of me, I could not understand why? We had fought side by side in both the First and Second World Wars, gaining a reputation as the Anzac's. Our two nations had intermarried over the centuries, both countries has become vital to one another, hopefully our future generations would claim the success, not the rivalry. My phone alarm buzzed, it was 6 am, I'm sure I made enough noise to wake the camp, but Petra still slept on. After a while, impatience set in, and I was eager to leave. The hire car puffing out small clouds of white exhaust into the damp, rainy air. "Petra, wake up, it's time for me to leave" giving her a gentle shake. Her voice was muffled "Tara, just go, I can't say goodbye," I knew how she felt, as we both loathed farewell's. I switched out the lights, clicked the van door shut, giving it a light rap with my knuckles, got in the car, and drove away.

Looking back, I saw her face pressed against the window, her eyes following me out of the park, I knew she, like me would be crying, I merged into the hectic traffic of a Wellington workday. My tears causing rainbows in the oncoming headlights. Levin was my next port of call. Glancing at the GPS map it revealed there was a three hour drive ahead. It rained and blew, the little hire car shaking when the wind gave it a hefty push. The Levin road sign read twenty kilometers to go, I could not wait, I had pre booked a motel for tonight, a slight headache was creeping in behind my eyes; it was time for me to stop driving and have a cup of tea and a lie down.

I found the motel, my room key was handed over, parking in front of my room, I went in and lay down, bursting into tears. How confusing is the heart? I was chomping at the bit to get going, yet I felt devasted at leaving. Dining at the motel café that night, indulging myself with a small glass of sherry, I slept well. Breakfast was served in the dining room, hot porridge with honey; I indulged myself with a cocoa.

Next stop, Palmerston North-another three hour drive, once there, I pulled into a garage, they were most accommodating checking for oil and water, topped up the petrol, and checked the tyres. I waited at the café across the road, ringing Petra, she sounded happy, friends had rung and suggested they move in with them, a problem shared is halved or so they say. It sounded like she had what she needed for now. Palmerston North, or Palmy as they call it, is quite a big township. I love how the Kiwis blend all the old and new; it's seamless, as the older homes and streets give way to new development. It's very easy to drive around, or was it because that bloody awful rain had finally stopped?

Whatever it was, I was happy to be here, going onto Google I found a B& B close by. Being winter, booking a room was not a problem and it was half price. My room was what I would call olde world, dainty, pretty and spotless in every way. A large white fluffy towel and face cloth rested on the bed, a cane table and chair against a window. Apart from the white towel and face cloth, everything else was in different shades of pink, from ceiling to floor, including the light shades. Relaxing on the bed I read up on what to do and or see in Palmerston North.

Winter had closed this place down except for a movie theater Hidalgo was showing all about an early 19th century cowboy, I enjoyed every swashbuckling minute of it and of course the hero got the sexy lady. Purchasing a Subway sandwich for dinner I headed back to my pink room, made myself a cup of tea, making myself comfy, packing all the pink pillows up behind me, began adding my thoughts to my diary.

The shower was communal, like my room decorated in pink, it looked like there was no one else staying here as I seemed to have the place to myself. I just stood there and let the water run down my body. Toweling off then dressing in the fluffy bathrobe that was supplied, as I wandered back to my room that feeling of being alone snuck in; I took a big breath- this was what Ronan had called sub-conscious, the hidden emotions, they sneak up when you're not looking, reminding myself to breath; it's perfectly okay to be alone. Sleep took a long while to steal me away that night. Waking up refreshed and ready to tackle the road to Wanganui. I was so close to Opunake, where Paradise and the Mermaid was waiting for me.

As I drove, I wondered just how far it was to Opunake, maybe I did not have to stay another night in a motel in Wanganui. The reception on my phone was poor, I pulled over, got out, held my phone up hoping to improve the one bar showing, when a massive truck whooshed past. A wave I swear as big as the car itself launched itself from under the truck and rushed straight towards me. "Shit", I burbled, spitting out muddy water. I was soaked, water steaming from head to toe. Inside the car was one muddy puddle. I went from shock to rage in two seconds. "What the" I spluttered. The taillights of this offending vehicle winked ahead, then seemed to stop. Right, this time I was not letting go as everyone advised me to, "Oh, just let I go Tara" not this bloody time. I followed the giveaway red lights. My anger boiling, ready to rip into the driver who was sitting nice and dry in his warm cabin pouring himself a hot drink.

This was how I met Brandon, standing outside the cab door yelling abuse at him in the pouring rain. At first he did not look down at me, he looked like he was asleep, I began to bang on the cab door. He still ignored me? the cheeky bugger. Maybe a rock through his window would get his attention. I was armed and ready to hurl one large rock when his eyes focused on me. He was up and out of the cab in an instant. "What the fuck" he yelled, grabbing the rock out of my hand. "Where the hell did you spring from?" By now, I was almost incoherent with rage. "You dam near drowned me and my car." He looked at my car then at me, "Were you in that parked car?

He looked shocked when I screeched; "No, I was standing outside the car, when you drove past." Suddenly I was spent, I could feel my blood pressure drop, I was becoming hypothermic. Brandon also saw my distress, bundled me up, pushing me into the sleeper of his cabin, I have no idea how he stripped me from my wet clothes, I came to with him rubbing me down with a rough towel. Once I was capable of putting two words together, he poured me a hot very sweet coffee.

"So, what am I going to do with you?" he asked, my brain refused to work properly, "Can you fine a motel and drop me off, please. I'm expected in Opunake in two days. Brandon had a drawl when he spoke "Opunake huh" I nodded. 'Well ma'am; what say I try starting your car for you, I'm sure we can sort something out. He left me in the cab, ten minutes later he was back, "Sorry ma'am, it's not possible, everything is fried. That number on your screen the hire car one? Is that who I ring? Once more he disappeared, I heard him speaking then he was back in the cab. "Not a lot we can do tonight, they advised me to lock your car up, they send a Towie out tomorrow or once the weather has settled. "What do you need?" I asked for "My suitcase and handbag."

As I had learnt many times before, you are exactly where you should be, no matter how tough it was. I was warm, safe and being dropped off in Opunake, no need to stress, well; not yet.
 It took hours of slow travelling, through such heavy weather, little conversation, a lot of snoozing on my part, to reach Opunake. Then. there it was -Paradise. Brandon turned into the driveway, "This is as far as I can go Tara, the truck carries to much weight I can't chance it being stuck. I don't have much to offer you except this," he pulled out an old umbrella. The rain continued to pelt down, the wind was merciless as it screamed, pushed and blew its mighty force around us. The poor man did not know quite what to do.

Opening the cab door, I stepped down into one of the worst storms I had yet experienced. The power of the wind carrying the foam tops off the crashing waves, slapping them into my hair and face, branches big and small being ripped off trees, whipping around my body, it was terrifying, I could not stand upright so I crawled to the door, I have never felt such relief when I knocked on the door of Paradise. Kingsly answered the door staring in amazement; David alongside him reaching out to pull me inside. They led me to the warm fire, I was offered a hot shower and hot food, then offered a warm bed, I accepted all of it in that order, waking up the next day to the sound of someone knocking on the front door, David shook me fully awake, softly saying "You have visitors." Brandon and an older women stood in the doorway, he introduced us "Tara, this is my mum; Titch."

From that moment and the look in her eye I knew no matter what happened I would not miss my ride home to Australia. This was one lady who knew exactly what to do, quietly and efficiently, by late that afternoon I was ensconced in their cabin, perhaps an hour from Opunake. I soon released that Titch stood for no nonsense and no back chat, she had dealt with the hire car company, and the insurance company.

She had found my journal, ringing the one Auckland phone number I had in there, Margi's, telling her of my whereabouts. I was safe in the spare room, her eyes followed me, if Brandon and I were together talking, she suddenly appeared asking her son to do an errand. Titch was my senior by at least ten years; her son Brandon was younger than me. He looked like her, large, hooded hazel eyes, strong jaw line, and lean long body, greying curly hair.

Listening to their conversations I learnt that he had inherited his father's cattle trucking business, his father passing over two years ago, patches of conversation flowed over and around me as they chatted; I was not included. In a way I thought it a bit rude but in a weird way relieved. Brandon had dried out my paperwork, Titch had washed and dried my clothes, my phone was replaced with an old one of theirs, Brandon had transferred my sim card, I copied phone numbers into the old phone. Four days of being looked after was enough, I was feeling eighty percent better, time to get some energy flowing into my body, I asked if I could use their shower, an abrupt nod of her head was my answer, Titch did not believe in wasting words with a stranger.

I felt warmed in and out by the hot water, while drying myself, Titch knocked on the door, walked in, "Excuse me", I squeaked; she looked me up and down, then gave me a pile of my own freshly laundered clothes, "Here", was all she said. I knew it had nothing to do with me, this was Titch, not rude or nasty, she was in control of her life and her sons life. However, things were about to change considerably, and I unintentionally was the instigator. Funny how life works out, if Brandon had not drowned me in that roadside puddle that night or if I had not stopped to ring Petra, or if Ronan had not been injured, none of what was about to unfold would have happened. Time to ring those I loved, first Petra, Ronan they asked so many questions they were tripping over each other's sentences; I smiled as they sounded happy and together that was the main thing.

Rae and Jess were next, both concerned they had heard nothing, no emails or text's, I told them why, both concerned, but happy I was now up and about, both pea green with envy on my cruise from Auckland to Fremantle. Jo calling me a "Lucky cow, how did you score that cruise?" My last call was to Margi who was concerned, I would not make the cruise but was there to help if and when she could, "Let me know if I can help I any way."

The same afternoon the hire car firm rang, wanting written confirmation of exactly what had happened from Brandon, they had never had this happen before, the car was a write off, the water damage was considerable, "Tell me about it" I said, "I was a recipient of the water" the woman on the phone chuckled "What a thing to happen, that's a story for the grandchildren." Grandchildren how that word made my heart sing, and soon I would be holding another baby that had my blood in its veins. All I had to, was find a ride back to Paradise to pick up the Suzuki and the Mermaid. The for sale adverts I had placed in the paper had attracted no one.

I got excited thinking about it, time for action. Titch watched me from the kitchen window I could feel her eyes on my back as I sought Brandon out. He was in the shed in their back yard, this was obviously Brandon's private quarters, there were curtains at the windows, geraniums grew in terracotta pots around a small porch, it all said private property. I decided my needs were a tad more important than Brandon's privacy. I knocked and my world as I knew it turned once again. Brandon called out 'come in Mum' ' It's not Mum it's me Tara' I answered, the door was opened and there stood the saddest man have ever seen, the eyes said it all, empty sadness, it was tangible, palpable, it hit me in the chest I put my hand on his arm "What on earth is wrong, are you unwell?"

I led him to the seat beside the fireplace. "What's up?"

I saw raw loneliness and a hurt so deep it wrenched me at my core. It took all afternoon for him to get his story out, buried deep in the fear of hurting his mum, Titch, and "Letting the old girl down," as he put it. We spoke of the choices he had. Much later, I went to bed in the main house for my afternoon nap, pondering Brandons dilemma. Titch had made scones and left one on a saucer with butter and peach jam spread on it; the cup and tea bag sat beside it for me to help myself. Titch sat in front of the fire with her back to me, her knitting needles working furiously, her shoulders stiff and unyielding.

I wanted to put my hand on her shoulder; her body language screaming *go away*. What Brandon had confided in me was how unhappy he was, he wanted something different in his life, now stuck with cattle delivery which he loathed, he was simply there to look after Titch till she died, in unpaid servitude as he put it, no love was shown between them, he was an investment that was paying off family debt.

CHAPTER FIFTY-THREE

I had said very little, offering him an ear was all I could do, letting Brandon spill his thoughts into the room, getting it all out. He wanted an escape-he wanted to work on his passion, which I could see displayed around me. Brandon loved to weave, a small loom sat in one corner, his work hung on the wall he loved to spin wool, card it, dyeing it in different colours then spinning it and knitting it into creations that he designed, he had sold his work many times, offered commissions, which meant travel, his father ignoring his creative talent, Titch too scared of being left alone to encourage her son, both telling him from any early age it was a sissies occupation, leave it to the women they had both said, how sad. When he stopped talking, I explained my intrusion "Would he give me a ride back to Opunake tomorrow?" It took a minute or two of silence then he agreed.

Titch was making breakfast when I woke up, I could hear her and Brandon talking in the kitchen. "Good morning to you both" I chirped "What a lovely day." it was greeted with a silence then Titch spoke, "Your things are packed and in the car, your leaving for Opunake in half an hour. Your breakfast is on the table and so is the bill." I heard breakfast then the word bill. On the table was a handwritten invoice for $450.00. "I have not charged for petrol to bring you here, only the meals and home care you have received" I was speechless. Brandon grabbed the note, exclaiming, "Mum, enough!" and he screwed it up and threw it in the fire. I grabbed my bag, noting I had all the documents and my passport inside, Titch grabbed her car keys "Actually Titch, Brandon and I discussed this yesterday I would prefer he drove. I walked out into a bright blue new day, Opunake and my Mermaid here I come. I was really upset at the whole situation; I had not expected extortion from Titch.

Kingsly and David were very enthusiastic at my return to Paradise, hot tea was made, Brandon was invited to join us. I was asked where to next said Home to Australia I was going on a cruise ship. I looked up to see Brandon's face, he looked horrified at me wanting to travel on my own, all the way back to Perth and on a cruise ship. When Kingsly asked him, "Have you ever travelled to Brandon? Even I was surprised when he answered, "Oh yes Auckland and back delivering cattle" I asked "So, you don't just take off for a weekend with your mates? "No, Mum won't allow it." Good lord I wanted to shake him. I had learnt very early on in my life that *Blaming keeps us helpless*. Sometimes lessons are truly learned the hard way, but if your unhappy, or your situation is proving difficult then you have the right to speak up. Brandon's situation with Titch was none of my business.

I just about ran to where my gear was stored, the storm had eased off, I hauled open the barn door and there they both were the Suzuki and the Metal Mermaid, waiting patiently for me; if I could have had a homecoming party with all the bells and whistles right there and then I would have. Brandon walked around me running his hands over the Mermaid's body; there was a look of longing as sit inside my Mermaid in his eyes. I wished Brandon a good night, thanking him for helping out of a difficult situation, and for caring for me as he and Titch had done.

He had decided to drive back to his home, he had no sooner left when I quickly unlocked my van door stepped in and I was home, all my trinkets and photos around me, making the bed, opening windows and skylight to get rid of the closed-up smell, I undressed and wrapped myself in my blankets for the night, setting the phone alarm for five am. Closing my eyes I settled down to sleep on my bed in my home for the first time in eight weeks. Tomorrow was my last day here; I slept soundly, while once again the storm raged outside.

The alarm rang, I was up and out, while I showered in the house David had hitched the Mermaid up for me, the Suzuki was on the driveway, my time here had come to an end, these two great men had made me a picnic hamper, with a thermos of hot tea, there was nothing more to do but hug them both goodbye. I was on my way. When Petra rang, "Everything alright? A lump formed in my throat "I'm about to take off, love you both" I clicked the off button. Today no storm brewed in the sky, I waved goodbye to Kingsley and David. My heart sang all the way to Stratford then onto the highway to Taupo, then the desert road. Stopping at the last petrol pump before the desert road. I was in the middle of the North island, mountains, volcanic rocks and sparse bush, not an ocean in sight. Time to stop and have a cup of tea and a sandwich, as I got out to have a stretch, my legs not used to driving for so long felt a little wobbly, I found the silence was at first unnerving then as my nervous system calmed down it became enjoyable.

I walked to the front of the Suzuki, leaning against the hood of this vehicle that had seen me through thick and thin and not missed one beat. The tears crept up on me, I knew this was the last I would be seeing of the North Island, I felt like I was saying goodbye to a friend, I tried to shake the feeling off, but it persisted, so I let it go and let the tears fall. I was in my own world thinking of the up and coming cruise, when I heard the faint sound of a horn honking of a horn, looking into my rear vision I could see a lights coming up behind me at a fast rate of knots, the honking became louder, I panicked and put my foot down, the gauge leapt to the 100 mark then 120 kilometers, the Mermaid having difficulty in keeping up, she started to sway. The truck was now even closer, its horn now screaming for me to give way or pullover as it came closer, the Mermaid now began to sway, I was going much too fast for the Suzuki to tow safely.

My heart was in my mouth as the truck overtook me, the air horn and lights blinding and deafening me, my one thought was this maniac is going to kill us both, tears spilt down my face as the threat of death took over. The truck roared past me, then swerved right in front of me, what the? I was speechless as he slowed down to a crawl, then the air brakes hissing as it stopped. What's with this manic idiot redneck, my words were mumbled and hysterical; he had nearly killed me, I sat behind the wheel shaking and crying at the same time, he got out the truck and slowly walked over to the Jeep. I was now expecting a bullet or an axe through the window, my head beaten in, robbed, raped all these awful thoughts rushed through my terrified brain. His face was not recognisable under the Stenson hat he wore, the last of sun's bright yellow rays were behind him making it hard to look at him, his large fist banged on the window, I sat motionless, finding it hard to breathe.

"Tara" the shadow said, "It's me Brandon," I wound down my window and gawped at him, "Brandon? What the hell? Then my fear poured out, "You bloody maniac, you idiot, stupid, unholy, nutter till I ran out of breath. "Brandon you stupid bloody fool what on god's name do you want? you could have killed us both! How old are you?" I burbled.

'Tara, you wouldn't stop or answer your phone. I had to chase you. You can certainly drive though; I'll give you that. I was stunned, "What the hell do you want?' I snarled; I was in no mood to play games. I just wanted to go home, so he needed to get out of my way. "Tara, I need to speak with you, there's a servo down the road a bit what say we meet there." I nearly refused, I did not have the answers for him he needed to grow up and face his own demons. 'First, I'm sorry I scared you, second, I want to buy the Mermaid.' Again, I was stunned. 'You what? Buy my Mermaid? What? You can't, can you? Why?' I blurted out. "Because I want to see what you've seen, go where you've gone." I wanted to ask, what about Titch? But it was none of my business. A voice in my heart said, "It's time to say goodbye, time to take that leap and trust," taking a big breath, I agreed.

We met at the servo, Bandon had already ordered a takeaway tea for me and a coffee for himself, we sat outside, the wind on the desert road was freezing, wrapping my hands around the paper cup, grateful for the warmth. "Okay Brandon, what's this all about? You want to buy the Mermaid, yes?" Before I could finish my sentence he reached into his overalls and pulled out a ratty pile of grubby money held together by an old, worn hair band, placing it on the picnic table. He gestured at it "It's all there," fifteen thousand dollars sat between us. How on earth did he know my asking price?

I looked at him and then at the money. "Are you sure?" Again, I asked "How did he know the amount I was asking for?" "You put an advert in the paper; I read it, thought about it, then put two and two together once you came to stay with us, "Tara; your Mermaid is my escape." I shut my mouth; it was none of my business. Brandon smiled. "I can see you're having a hard time; Don't stress, it's all mine I've earnt every penny, this is from my weaving and knitting. I kept saving it, wishing for a rainy day. I want to travel down South and visit the folk who have hired me in the past to weave and spin. I want to pick up new ideas from them. I want to expand." Wow, that was a huge sentence for this quiet bloke. How does one refuse? "Let me get the paperwork for you" I said softly.

All the questions again were building up, the where's, what's, if's, and why's. but I bit my lip, if the Universe had planned this, then who was I to say No? We both signed, I put the money into my handbag, passing over the keys. All I wanted was the photos of my kids and a few personal items." Brandon again patted her rear. "Hello Mermaid," he said, while I whispered my goodbyes. Collecting my gear, I stowed it in the Suzuki, Brandon now owned a fully functioning caravan. He held out his arms to me, I stepped into the circle, knowing I was safe with this bloke. He kissed my cheek. I asked one thing from him. "Brandon, be who you want to be, Darl. Do what makes you happy; the answer is not in the dollar; it's in your heart."
We hugged, then I pulled away. It was time for me to go and for Brandon to begin a new life. I pondered on Titch for a moment, she would find this hard, no matter who or why Bandon was her boy, and she loved him. What or how he was going to get the Mermaid home was no business of mine. Brandon looked like a kid who had just discovered Christmas. In fact, his actions were like mine when I first bought the mermaid, excited and unsure,

but unbelievably happy. As I drove off, I took one last look at the Mermaid. Brandon stood beside her, waving goodbye to me as I pushed forward. Auckland, here I come.

I have twenty-four to sell the Suzuki, spend some time with Margi, then catch the ship home. It all seemed to be flowing, the money that was in my bag now locked away in the glove box I seemed to go faster now, the radio pumping out the music of a New Zealand artist, Bic Runga. On the first township I would find a bank to deposit the money, I saw the parking sign and pulled over. It was much easier now without the Mermaid attached. However, to deposit this amount of money I could not use the ATM, I had to go into the bank and make the transaction, all time consuming as my goal was to reach Auckland by late tonight. Another stop at a gas station, I checked the oil and water all perfect. Auckland and Margi, I'm on my way. Once at the junction to Auckland, there are so many signs calling me to pop over and visit Morrinsville, Ngāruawāhia, Huntly, Raglan, all with stories to tell and people to meet. Sadly, I knew I wouldn't be back this way again.

The journey home had already begun for me; if I could advise any one it would be that *your Journey takes place in the heart, strength and character are you vehicle,* and I felt this had my lesson. If I had been lacking endurance and or strength of character before I had been part of this adventure; I knew I had certainly topped that gap up. I could remember Russ with love and not feel the crushing grief. I would cherish my time here in New Zealand without needing to revisit. I had journeyed in my heart and my life, with many friends showing me the way. I considered myself blessed. Now, it was time to return to my home and my family. New Zealand is truly a beautiful country; her people are hospitable and welcoming; I will add, I was more than over the continuous cold and damp.

I rang my friend, saying, 'I'm on the roundabout now, Margi, about half an hour away." Her voice was music to my ears. 'Welcome back, Tara!' As I found her street, I did not need "You have reached your destination." From the GPS as Margi and the whole family were standing there, smiling, and welcoming. Turning off the key and opening the door, I was enveloped in so many arms, legs, and faces, what a wonderful welcome! Margi was shouting instructions, 'Stand back, get out of my way, coming through!' Flicking them away with the ever-present tea towel over her shoulder, she huffed her way towards me. "Tara, Kia Ora, welcome back."

Once inside, the questions started. The first one was, 'Aunty, where's the Mermaid?' They all leaned forward, waiting for my explanation. "I sold her because I'm going home to Australia tomorrow." 'How can you sell a mermaid?' one child I hadn't seen before asked, and Margi explained that it was the name of my caravan. "Where are all the presents?" Margi's youngest asked, the smile on her face so wide, it lit the room. I'd played this game with Jess, so I shrugged and winked at Margi, saying, "What presents? Oh, you mean the bag of lollies in the Suzuki No, I don't know where they are." A second's hesitation followed as they realised that Aunty Tara was joking. Soon, all seven children were munching on a massive bag of lollies, slurping, and sucking noises coming from all around me. The kids were sent into the TV room under the strict supervision of the older kids. "No blinkin' noise," Margi warned. "We adults are talking." The three of us sat down in the now-quiet kitchen, and I told them about Ronan and Petra. They were very concerned and thought they might pay them a visit soon when they had returned to Paradise. I asked how they all knew each other since they were on opposite ends of the pole, so to speak.

Their story was that Tom was a woodcarver who took classes years ago. He advertised for students, and Ronan enquired. As they talked, Tom discovered that Ronan was as passionate about wood as he was, especially swamp kauri gum. They both ended up visiting each other and became friends. I mentioned Hinemoa and the poverty I had seen then I told them the story about Brandon and Titch, with Margi exclaiming, "She did what?" They both thought my story about Brandon chasing me with his truck was funny; Margi wiping the tears of laugher off her face with the tea towel. "Tara, you should write a book." Funny that she should say that? Tom stood up, scratching his large tummy. "I'm off to bed, and you have to work tomorrow, Ma," his name for Margi. She looked back at me "You've certainly grown, from the scared little wimp I first met. Well, I'm off to bed, night sleep tight.

CHAPTER FIFTY-FOUR

Russ was in my thought's as I also drifted towards my dreams. The morning arrived, and in Margi's house, it was like a Chinese market. The noise could wake the dead, with kids and Margi yelling directions and orders while Tom moaned about his breakfast. I stayed in bed until I heard the kids rush out the door for school. Margi yelled at me, 'I'm on the roster till three pm, then I'll drive you to the ship, okay? "Okay," I yelled back, 'see you then." Then Tom popped his head in the room, "I'm going out, see you later, Tara." As I heard the front door slam shut, excitement grabbed me.

I leapt off the little bed and yelled, 'whoop I'm cruising back to Perth!' What to do first? My hands were shaking as I made a list of what to do, what to pack, who to ring, and who to see. My main concern was selling the Suzuki or finding someone to sell it on my behalf. I rang the car salespeople from whom I'd bought the Jeep. He was delighted to hear from me but said they had no interest in a second-hand Jeep. They wanted to know how it ran and if there were any problems; I was honest, saying, "She drives like a dream" it was still a firm No! not interested.

Disappointed, I showered, dressed, then cleaned the Suzuki out. Everything was piled onto the front lawn, it was obvious that people were enjoying the side show, as one neighbour had stopped her curtain twitching and was now peering at my efforts full-time. Some came out and stood by their letterbox's to watch me. All my clothing was now in Margi's washing machine, which chugged relentlessly. During the morning, I had rung quite a few 2nd hand car dealers, no one showed any interest. I toyed with the idea of asking Margi and Tom to sell it for me, but I didn't want to be pushy. Finding a comfy seat, I rang Rae. "Mum, how are you going, excited yet?" 'you don't know the half of it." When Petra rang I invited them to come to Perth anytime. 'I can't replicate paradise, but I'll do my best,' I promised.

Brandon rang to say farewell, Titch had had a huge meltdown when he got home, and I was definitely off her Christmas card list. He was now in Palmerston North staying with a friend. I was pleased that this grown man had finally taken the step to explore his world. However, I felt sad to hear that Titch had lost it; it couldn't be easy to be in her position.

In the back of my mind was the saying, '*blaming keeps you helpless.*' And Titch would have blamed me for her problems in life. He was still touring in the Mermaid and wasn't changing her name; 'she's magic,' he said. He did not have to tell me that; as the Mermaid would always have a place in my heart. Margi arrived home at three pm, right behind her were the family off the school bus, and Tom came in a few minutes later. It was one big, bustling, yelling, scrambling family, oozing love, support, and care for each other. Margie's voice came over the top of the noise, "Hey Tara, I'm as dry as a wooden Tiki, I'll have a cuppa first ten help you pack the cab Tom looked at me then at the Suzuki, "No takers." I shook my head 'Leave it there Tara, it'll sell in time. Okay, that was the best I could do, time had run out.

Finally, we arrived at the cruise ship depot, the ship looked enormous, my stomach was in knots. Once my passport and papers scrutinised by guards and machines, a tiny silver disc on a lanyard was placed around my neck. This was now my passport on and around the ship. I was informed if you wanted to purchase, order or attend an event on board, you simply produced the silver disc, a wee bit scary to think it recorded your everywhere abouts. A lump like a brick formed in my throat as I looked at these dear people who had been such a driving force in my travels through New Zealand. Their faith in me had never wavered; they always offered a welcome and a hug , along with advice on what to see and whom to meet. I owed them a lot.

They began to sing 'Pokarikariana,' a song I had loved since they sang it at the Marae up North in Awanui. My face puckered up, my eyes stung, and a huge sob erupted from my gut. Their voices weaving in beautiful harmony. It felt ancient, leaving a tattooed Moko on my heart forever. Margi hugged me gently and said, 'Harerai Tara, Godspeed.' We touched noses. 'Love you and thank you always.' As I walked away I could still hear them singing. When I looked back, Margi stood there alone, our eyes locked. We waved just once. She was my Māori sister in New Zealand; we had formed a spiritual connection that was forever. Bye Margi, and goodbye to all my wonderful friends, hopefully, one day, we'll see each other again.

CHAPTER FIFTY-FIVE

I was shown to my cabin on Dolphin Deck, room 223, it was a creamy coloured safe haven, exactly what I wanted-spotlessly clean, with a large wardrobe, bathroom, and a double bed. A small wooden stool was tucked under a large dresser, topped with a sizable mirror. I was now on another Metal Mermaid, for the next 10 days, except this one taking me home. The ship's horn let out a shrieking blast, the ship shuddering with delight as we cast off. I watched it all: the pilot now leading us out to sea. My journey home had begun. Rod Stuarts song 'Sailing Away' swelled from the ship's speakers.

From the moment you stepped into the Horizon breakfast bar, which groaned under the weight of every food imaginable, planning your day was a true pleasure. Every day, classes on board ranged from card making and knitting circles to belly dancing, art exhibitions and guided tours discussing our next port of call, movies, or a massage and pedicure—they had it all, and if you went on any tour, once the boat was docked everything was managed seamlessly for you.

When Sydney loomed in the misty morning; the excitement I felt at being back in my own country bubbled in my tummy. We visited the famous coat hanger bridge, Sydney Opera House, and Luna Park by coach. It was a fun-filled day, then back on board for a huge afternoon tea. Afterwards often having a nana nap before dinner. Some days, I would choose to catch an afternoon movie or take a quick walk around the deck. Brisbane was warm and sunny, so I chose to go on a boutique brewery tour. It was interesting enough, but not being a big drinker, I was a bit disappointed as it was not what the description detailed; instead, we were driven to a local pub where we were expected to guzzle huge pints of five different beers that were produced.

It was my choice whether to tour or not. I could have stayed on board and participated in many of the classes advertised in the Princess Patter, this small newsletter produced every night for our convenience. It was filled with classes, talks, movies, and the nighttime entertainment was amazing again: cabarets, dining and dancing, comedians, and impersonators of Dolly Parton and Rod Stewart. Mike Harris, the comedian, was so funny that I was in stitches every time I attended one of his shows.

Then, at the Wheelhouse Bar after the cabaret, if I chose to, I could sit and listen to a Spanish songbird whose voice could melt honey, or at times a young English songstress belting out all the old rock and roll tunes. If I felt like a quiet supper, I could order room service or make my way to the top deck 14 and join a small crowd having a light supper before bed.

Airlie Beach was a blast! We hit the afternoon markets, which had everything from massages and Tarot readings to fresh veggies and mango drinks made on the spot, along with trinkets from Indonesia and pretty batik clothing. Buying gifts for Rae was a not a problem-she loved sarongs. I grabbed a couple of pretty frocks and a necklace or two for myself, and one for Jo that I knew she would love. I bought Jess T-shirts emblazoned with carton caricatures and Robin a set of cocoanut serving napkins.

Once back on board at four pm, I stowed all my purchases in my cabin. As always, the attendant had tidied up after I left, and my cabin was spotless, complete with fresh towels and a sparkling clean bathroom. I then met up with Mary, a new friend at a small coffee bar behind the casino discussing our day and our purchases, she admitted being envious that I was buying for the baby soon to be expected.

When I first came on board, I was allocated a dinner time and seated at one of the two silver service restaurants. The meals were superb, and the atmosphere at my table was delightful. I was joined by four others, both married couples, and we all got on famously discussing the day's events. One couple was around my age, while the other was about ten years older; both were wonderful to chat with. As a single person, I could observe the contented togetherness of the older couple and the restless younger couple.

She spent her days at the casino, while he attended shipboard talks and watched movies. That night, my thoughts drifted to my Russ. I wondered if I would always miss him; a small nagging thought crept in about what we might have been doing if he were with me then, a question that would never be answered. I guess that's what folks mean when they say, *'grief becomes a pinhole in the heart, it never leaves entirely.'*

CHAPTER FIFTY-SIX

After dinner that night, I found the super screen on main deck, about 40 deck chairs had been arranged in a semi-circle with tartan blankets draped over them, a few people were watching the film about Winston Churchill, all snuggled in their blankets. So, I picked a deck chair, wrapped myself in a blanket, soon a young attendant approached, offering a hot drink, popcorn, or a chocolate biscuit. I couldn't help but chuckle; this is definitely the way to travel, I thought, munching through it all, 'bugger the diet.'

The next day, we found ourselves at sea. I headed up for breakfast, and while savoring fresh pancakes and crispy British bacon on a sun-kissed deck, I mapped out what I wanted to do for the day. First on the agenda was a towel-folding demonstration-what the Asian porters could create with a hand towel was astounding! From a simple, plain towel emerged an octopus, a turtle, a dove, a parrot, monkeys, and dolphins. It continued on and on, with the grand finale being a parrot perched on a wooden hanger, just like a real bird. The crowd went wild, with cheers echoing around the Atrium.

Next, I attended a two-hour wine tasting that was incredibly informative. Who knew that so much effort went into making wine, I was impressed. Then decided to treat myself to a dreamy pedicure called the Fire and Ice treatment—it was divine! I floated out of the spa, made my way to my cabin, and had a snooze for an hour. That night, I had the option of dining at a restaurant or the famous pizza place. I opted for a pizza and a light beer; relaxation was the name of the game on this cruise. Or, as Tim, the cruise director, would often yell over the intercom, 'Enjoy yourselves, you're on a holiday.' How right he was.

Port Douglas was our next stop, where I had organised a tour with a bloke named Grubs, who owned a motor trike tour company. He was very informative, fun, and a wee bit mad, just what the doctor ordered to chase away any lingering blues. We zipped through the bush and waterfalls, met the locals, he knew them all; we rushed through the mountain air to the peak of the ranges before heading back down to the heat of Port Douglas. In just two hours, I covered so much of this charming little place that I felt mentally winded, but it was exhilarating and wonderful another unforgettable tour.

Another day at sea awaited us before we docked in Darwin, first a discovery talk on Darwin's immigration history, a light salad for lunch, then a walk around the deck. As I approached the ship's main floor, the Atrium, there was a jazz band playing, and they were fabulous. If you thought you could belt out a tune in time, you got up and gave it a go. The atmosphere was so happy and relaxed. I watched, clapped, and cheered on the singers as did the other onlookers. As I climbed into bed that night, the thought of being home very soon stirred that little excited worm in my gut.

Life on board continued; every day, something new and exciting happened. I met so many people from all walks of life, all eager to tell me about themselves. I heard stories of heartbreak, lovesick souls, seasick passengers, widowers, couples, and places I had never seen and likely never will. I encountered others who could hardly stand to be together, and yet others who adored each other. The world is a vast sea of experiences, and on this cruise, there were many stories to be heard; I loved it. Every morning, you sat with someone different and engaged in so many varied activities, or you could simply sit still in the sun and relax.

We sailed past the Kimberley Coastline, the land of red, gold, and bronze that had stolen my Russ's heart. This desert land glowed in the sun as the sunset transformed into deep scarlet and brown. The sunsets, yes, everything the magazines and newspapers write about were magnificent in every way. Photographers snapped away until the light faded, and night approached; even that was amazing. The Southern Star shone as bright as ever in the clear night air.

Broome soon arrived. I booked a tour to the Willy Creek Pearl Farm. Boarding the coach was simple; however, the coach ride to the pearl farm was horrendous. We bucked, jolted, and shuddered over disgusting, unkempt roads that made my back ache. The woman sitting behind me was in agony; she was white and in tears as she explained that she had recently had surgery. We both agreed that the condition of the road should have been advertised as unfit for folks with back problems. Once we reached our destination, half the coach were complaining about the travel we asked if it was possible to take another form of transport back to the cruise ship. She was very understanding. "I have the perfect thing," she announced, "a helicopter ride."

Now that sounded like fun and much better than the crashing, bashing coach ride we had just come off, so we asked how much it would cost. Her answer was $180 per person; the other folks were in couples, to pay out a hundred dollars for the Pearl farm tour, then on top of that an extra $180.00 for a quick comfy ride? It seemed very unfair to me. I opted to stay with the coach tour, and thankfully the ride back was handled very smoothly. A big thank you to our driver, who I might add, was not the one who drove us to the destination.

In fact, our driver back to the cruise ship was excellent, giving us all the snippets of information about Broome and taking a little detour so we could drive through the neighbourhood township. Two more days at sea, again it was up to you and what you made of it, laid back sitting on deck soaking up the sun or a swim in the massive pools or have a Jacuzzi. Eating, drinking, hobby, or dance classes plus meeting other people.

We reached Lombok, I again took a tour, opting for the tribal Batik and pottery tour, we were greeted by a hill-pony and cart, they carried three of us together and no more, and I can't blame them as some of us had certainly enjoyed the food while on board -including myself.

Off we went with a sprightly little trot the sound of tinkling bells all around us as the ponies all set to take us to the villages. I was greeted so warmly by the people there, the pottery, I fell in love with it but had nowhere to put it to take home. At the Batik village market, I was greeted with drums, song and dance a display of Lombok sword fighting and a pretty batlike scarf put around my shoulders in greeting. By four pm we were back aboard. A crisp white envelope was in my bed; it was a formal invitation to dine at the Captain's table that night. That meant I was to dress up and put on the bling, I considered this fun, as how many chances do you get to play dress-ups as an adult.

Another day passed at sea again, and any class you wanted to take was at my fingertips, I chose to have a cup of tea in the small café in the casino, here, you could quietly watch so many people with so many different expressions on their faces. One couple caught my eye; they were my age, I guess, although both had a glimmer of youth still on their faces. They had walked in holding hands, stopped at a blackjack table, talked to the croupier and walked away, she was slim, tall, with silver hair and hazel eyes that seemed to hold a touch of a sceptic and was looking very doubtful; he was a little shorter, slim and trim, greying hair, with bright blue eyes, he seemed to be talking to her enthusiastically about placing a bet.

I saw her shake her head and stand up to walk away, he followed and whispered something to her; she smiled while he pulled out some loose change, and her smile got even bigger as he slapped it onto the table. I have no idea how much he put down on the table, but with one fell swoop, he had doubled his money. Now the excitement of a win showed, I could see it on his face. Hers was still doubtful, but trusting in him entirely together, they placed it back on the Blackjack table again, the rattle of the ball inside the wheel and poof, money was gone, they had lost it all. She covered her mouth with one hand and then started to laugh.

I heard her say, "Told you so," and off they walked hand in hand out of the casino, now that's how it should be, I thought to myself, "Have a go, if you fall, get up and walk away. To me these two were in total sync with each other.

That night a comedian was telling jokes in the Wheelhouse bar, some of them so close to being rude but he seemed to slip around them very well, I was sitting with a group of people and enjoying their comments as well as his very quick repartee back at them, when suddenly one woman took serious offence at his sarcasm, she was quite drunk and what was supposed to be a fun time turned into an nasty insulting match between her and the comedian who very quietly said "Dear God, your mother should have kept the afterbirth, not you" the problem was he forgot he had the microphone in his hand, or did he? the place erupted in screech of dismay from her and laughter from the audience, as this particular silly soul sashayed out of the room.

The huge sigh of relief that went up from all of us, the audience settled in to have some laughs before supper and bedtime. The exploding applause was his reward as he expressed his regret for the commotion. And at supper that night there she was again picking on other people's conversations and acting so insulted at their angry reactions, I guess there is one on every cruise.

Geraldton was our next port; I did not want to go ashore I did what a lot of others were doing staying on board, reclining on deck chairs, going up for an iced snow cone, soaking up the sun, walking briskly around the deck, walking off that extra nibble we had just enjoyed, and relaxing, Tim the Cruise Director was on and off the ships intercom egging us on to this or that, join in and have some fun, repeating his mantra "You're on holiday" it must of been his voice as you could actually see people stop and smile as he spoke. I rang Rae 'I'm 24 hours away honey', her voice as excited as mine, then Jess spoke his voice was changing I guess at twelve that's when it all happens for a young man.

Then my cell phone cut out as they do on board a cruise ship. I walked down to the internet room and library, logging on to email Jo and Fred I would be arriving in 24 hours, I noticed I had twelve emails waiting, so I answered them six were 'Do ya wanna buy' and five from New Zealand, all my friends there had all wished me the very best for my travels and to keep in touch please, the sixth one was a photo of the Metal Mermaid, my heart lurched and ached as I enlarged the photo on the screen, on her little doorstep sat Brandon. Holding a beer in one hand and a meat pie in the other, hanging from around his neck was a cardboard sign saying Home Sweet Home, the biggest silliest grin on his face, I also noticed the road sign next to the van announcing you have entered Kaikoura South Island, so he had done it, made the break and travelling his dream, I wrote back, 'enjoy and live your life.'

The next twenty-four hours, I felt like my body was wired to an electrical socket, I was so excited I was coming home. I knew I was a different person. I certainly looked different. I also knew I ached to see and hold my daughter and my grandson; I wanted to go home to where Russ and I once lived, and now I was sharing it with our family. I slept very lightly that night and was woken the next day by the rattling of chains; we had arrived in Freemantle.

CHAPTER FIFTY-SEVEN

I showered dressed in jeans and T-shirt my hair up in a ponytail then went up for breakfast and to say goodbye to all my new acquaintances, some were carrying on with the cruise as from here it sailed around the world. I had been offered this deal as well, but I was ready and only too willing to go home to my family and beautiful Rockingham by the sea.

As I packed the last of the clothes, applied a touch of makeup, and stowed away all the things you take on a holiday, my heart knew I was making the right choice for myself. Finally, I stepped out of my cabin, my bags had been taken ashore, there was just customs to clear. Then I was over the line, finally standing in Perth once again. And even though it's been suggested that I'm biased, I still think Perth is the prettiest city I've ever been to.
I heard Jess before I saw any of them. "There's my Nana!" A tall young man rushed up to wind his arms around me. My arms naturally opened to embrace him, hugging him back. We stood there for a moment, my face buried in his auburn hair, tears stung my eyes as my grandson said, "Nana, you're home."

The End

ABOUT THE AUTHOR

Kez Wickham St George

Kez Wickham St George is a 5-Star Gold Award-Winning Best-Selling Author whose influence in the literary world is profound and far-reaching. Acclaimed as a highly gifted speaker, global writer's consultant, and leader in her profession, Kez's wisdom and passion have touched countless lives. Her dedication to championing people from diverse backgrounds to tell their stories and write with passion is at the core of her work.

With multiple best-selling books and two prestigious Gold Titan Awards to her name, Kez is recognised as a literary force to be reckoned with. Her storytelling prowess and commitment to creative writing have earned her numerous accolades, including the People's Choice ABLE Book Award, where her latest release, *Tapestry*, is a contender.

A true global citizen, Kez has spoken nationally and internationally, sharing her knowledge about the process of writing, editing, and producing all forms of written communication. She is widely travelled, and her experiences have shaped her expansive authorship, encouraging others to think outside the box and redefine what authors can achieve in the digital age.

Kez's work has been celebrated by two royal families in the UK and Sweden, and she has coordinated and compiled several anthologies, including one on the lives of eighteen international women and another with Michiko Sato, featuring authors and artists from Ako, Japan. With fourteen books to her name, including two celebrated trilogies, a book of poems and quotes, plus a recent anthology with an international publishing house Kez continues to captivate readers with her diverse and compelling narratives.

In her Western Australian community, Kez is known for her efforts to empower others to write, creating writers' workshops, and giving back through her volunteer work with Global Book Reviews. She has co-produced and co-hosted a weekly international show that highlights the work of authors and artists from around the world. Her creative energies and refreshing idealism are reflected in her consistent dedication to her craft, culminating in a short film adaptation of the prologue from her novel *Scribe*, which was shown in theatres across Australia.

Beyond her literary achievements, Kez is a prominent figure in the media, contributing to numerous magazines and co-hosting TV and radio shows where she shares her passion for personal development and women's global access to resources. Her books are not only designed to captivate readers but also to encourage women of all ethnicities to speak up, live their lives fully, and turn their dreams into words that will inspire future generations.

Kez believes in the power of education for all women globally, seeing it as the key to achieving equality. She encourages everyone to express themselves through art, no matter the genre, and her favorite quote, "Be seen, be heard, be known," embodies her approach to life and work.

Ready to elevate your writing career? Contact Kez for expert mentoring, book promotion, or to gain visibility through her renowned book reviews. With her extensive experience and passion for storytelling, Kez Wickham St George is here to help you gain the recognition you deserve.

kezwickhamstgeorge.com

BOOK AWARDS AND REVIEWS

The Story Tellers Series

Jigsaw

Book 1 in the Storytellers Series 2023

Literary Titan Review

Kez Wickham St George is an engrossing and emotionally charged narrative that delves into the Deeply concealed world of Parental childhood Trauma. At the heart of this tale is Cassie, the protagonist who endures a life riddled with abuse and neglect within the confines of her family home, desperately yearning. For love and acceptance. Compelled into a marriage with a narcissistic alcoholic as a result of her families Cult like obligations. Cassie is faced with the bleak choice of either succumbing to despair or embarking. On a courage journey to discover her true self. Throughout the narrative the author skilfully Weaves themes of escape, love, resilience, and the Patriarchal systems cruel oppression while exploring the enigmatic paranormal aspects that entwine themselves in Cassie's life. Jigsaw is a poignant, gripping Masterpiece, adeptly unwavering the profound story of a child growing through the profound abuse into the success story we have before us today.

Tapestry

Book 2 in the Storytellers Series 2024

Literary Titan Review

Tapestry is an intricate, multi-generational tale that weaves together the stories of women who have been marginalised and oppressed but are fiercely resilient. Set against the backdrop of historical periods where patriarchy, sexism, and injustice reigned supreme, the book tells the stories of women like Aida and Rosalie, whose lives were marked by pain but also by fortitude and wisdom. At its core, the book is a tribute to the strength of ancestral female wisdom and the persistence of the human spirit. What struck me immediately was the rawness of the storytelling. There's something visceral in how the author portrays Aida's life in the 1700s. The imagery of her as a child left to survive in a pigpen, later abused, and sold, but ultimately rising to become a healer, was both heartbreaking and triumphant. The writing captures not just the brutality of her circumstances, but also her inner strength and resilience, particularly when she delivers babies and saves lives with her herbal knowledge.

While the stories are compelling, the pacing in some sections, like Petra's story in the convent, was slower and more introspective, while other parts, such as the vivid descriptions of Rosalie's journey on the convict ship, were packed with action and emotion. The lengthy descriptions and heavy use of historical context sometimes pulled me out of the emotional depth of the characters' journeys. I would've loved more balance between the historical backdrop and the intimate personal moments that define these women's lives.

Another standout element is how the book dives into themes of female solidarity. The interactions between Aida, Ursula, and the group of women they eventually join in the woods felt empowering. These women, despite being rejected by society, form their own community, sharing knowledge and supporting one another. That part of the book, to me, was a beautiful ode to the strength of women when they come together. The detailed descriptions of the forest life, the food they gather, and the herbal remedies they concocted made these scenes feel rich and alive.

Tapestry is a bold and sweeping story that showcases the harsh realities faced by women throughout history but also their incredible resilience and ability to thrive despite it all. I would recommend this book to readers who enjoy historical fiction with deep emotional depth and a strong focus on female empowerment.

Review by Annie Gibbins Women's Biz Global

"A Masterpiece of Resilience and Ancestral Legacy"

Kez Wickham St George has crafted a remarkable and evocative novel in Tapestry: The Book of Lost Worlds. This book is a profound exploration of the courageous women who defied societal norms, battled against the injustices of their times, and left an indelible mark on history. Wickham St George's storytelling prowess shines as she weaves together the lives of these women, creating a rich tapestry of narratives that are both heart-wrenching and inspiring.

Through the lens of these brave female ancestors, the novel delves into themes of resilience, strength, and the enduring impact of ancestral legacies. The author masterfully captures the emotional depth and complexities of each character, allowing readers to connect with their struggles and triumphs on a deep personal level. The vivid descriptions and historical contexts enrich the narrative, bringing to life the harsh realities faced by women who fought against the constraints of religion, sexism, and societal expectations.

The prose is lyrical and haunting, with each chapter serving as a testament to the fortitude of these women. Wickham St George's ability to intertwine these stories with a sense of reverence for the past makes Tapestry a compelling and unforgettable read. This book not only honors the memory of those who came before but also serves as a powerful reminder of the strength and resilience that lies within all of us.

Tapestry: The Book of Lost Worlds is more than just a historical novel; it is a celebration of the human spirit and the enduring power of storytelling. It is a must-read for anyone who appreciates rich, character-driven narratives that explore the complexities of history and the legacy of those who dared to stand against the tide. Kez Wickham St George has created a literary gem that will resonate with readers long after the final page is turned.

Review by Geoff Bailey USA book reviews

Tapestry book 2 of the Storyteller Trilogy by Kez St. George is a beautifully told series of stories from her family ancestral record. Each chapter and character captured beautifully with a caring authority that has shown compassion for the hard life of her ancestors. Being a huge genealogy fan and consider collections like Tapestry to be so important for us to understand who we are and where we come from. Reading Tapestry made me appreciate New Zealand where the Author originated from and now resides in Australia. I consider stories and memoirs like those in Tapestry such an important capture of a people, their cultures their lives, and their histories. I would go as far to say I found Tapestry a true national treasure, and no doubt a bestseller. Thank you for an entertaining and enlightening read Kez Wickham St. George.

The People's Choice Award

Able Book Awards

2024

The Campfire Trilogy

Metal Mermaid - *Book 1 of the series*

No #1 Amazon Best Seller in 5 categories and 6 countries

Titan Gold & Silver awards medallions
mmhpress Gold award
WA Literati recommendations award.

Literary Titan Review ☆☆☆☆☆

Metal Mermaid 5-star Review by Titan by Kez Wickham St George is a beautifully written memoir that takes readers on a spiritual and physical adventure. Tara and her husband Russ set off on a journey to explore Western Australia, but unexpected events quickly change their plans. Tara's journey of self-discovery takes her on a new path, one that challenges her both physically and emotionally. She meets fellow travelers and experiences the joys of the caravanning world, making her way from Australia's upper coast to New Zealand's northern island.

In this thought-provoking book, Wickham St George skillfully weaves a tale of courage, resilience, and determination that is both inspiring and captivating. The author's descriptive writing style transports readers to the various locations Tara visits, allowing them to feel the change of seasons and experience the heat and cold of the land. The side characters in the book are equally intriguing, with rich backstories and tales of their own. Metal Mermaid is an immersive memoir that provides readers with clear insight into the caravanning world and introduces them to various cultures.

Wickham St George's straightforward writing style makes the book an easy and engaging read. The book is infused with culture and worldly sights, and readers will feel like they are part of Tara's journey. Metal Mermaid is an outstanding book that I highly recommend to readers looking for inspirational that showcases the beauty of life's Journey. The authors ability to tell such a captivating story that takes its readers on a spiritual journey is nothing short of Impressive. Metal Mermaid is an outstanding book that I highly recommend to readers looking for an inspirational book that highlights the beauty of life's journey. The author's ability to tell a captivating story that takes readers on a spiritual adventure is nothing short of an impressive literature experience.

The Cuppa Tree - Book 2 of the series

A story of a woman who lived loved and learned caravaning in the outback. Sit around the metaphorical campfire with author Kez Wickham St George as she brings you on an unexpected journey throughout the pages of The Cuppa Tree. This natural-born storyteller will share tales from experiences and stories shared on her travels around Australia.

Scribe

Book 3 of the series

When Tara the lead character finds herself battling illness and snowstorms in the far South Island if New Zealand. When she is called a catalyst for what she is being asked to do, that is die. "The world is in state of great change" she is told "We the greater good ask you to Scribe for the deceased, those who have not told their stories before they passed over.

Co-authored Anthology's

Memoirs of Successful Women

Memoirs of Successful Women is a collection of stories from women who have lived, breathed, and elevated their brand.

Women's Biz Publishing. 2023

The Colors of Me

The Colors of Me is a multinational contribution of 18 authors, each one sharing her empowering and inspirational story.

Inspired Connections

Unleashing the Magic of Deeper Relationships

No #1 Amazon in 37 categories – 2021/ 2023

There will be many roadblocks and many dysfunctions along the way. Your job in life is to sort out the noise and nonsense, to trust your intuition and acknowledge your own truth.

Hille House Publishing. 2021

Build Your Success

Leadership Tips from the World's Best CEO's and Leaders

A co-authored book that sheds light on leadership and many success tips from the world's best leaders and Mentors. Critical thinkers and role models who have proven success, built on ideology plus uncovering the essential tools for risk-taking, goal setting, and most of all purpose.

Translation of Māori words used in Metal Mermaid.

Pōwhiri – Welcome ceremony
Whare – House
Marae – Meeting house/land
Moko – Traditional facial or chin tattoo
Waka – Canoe or boat
Tiki – Māori symbol or figure (often considered a deity or good luck charm)
Wahine – Woman
Toa – Warrior (traditionally male, though modern usage can apply to all genders)
Kia ora – Hello / Welcome
Haere mai – Welcome / Come here
Haere rā – Goodbye
Kai – Food
Puku – Stomach / Tummy
Mokopuna – Grandchild
Whānau – Extended family
Taniwha – Mythical guardian or shape-shifting spirit

www.ingramcontent.com/pod-product-compliance
Lightning Source LLC
Chambersburg PA
CBHW051242210726

48287CB00002B/353